SOME COUPLINGS ARE IRRESISTIBLE.
CHAMPAGNE AND CAVIAR, FOR INSTANCE.
MOONLIGHT AND ROSES.
AND OF COURSE—
SEX AND HORROR.

Let horror master Robert Bloch take you on the cruise of a lifetime with a seductive model who gives new meaning to the term drop-dead gorgeous.

Put yourself in the justly celebrated hands of Ray Bradbury as he peels back the daylight to reveal the nightmare face of an all-American dreamboat.

Brace yourself for shock as Ramsey Campbell lures you to an elderly woman's bizarre home and unlocks the door to a history of deadly desire.

These are just three chilling morsels of the macabre—from Michele Slung's unforgettable collection of 22 seductive spellbinders.

SHUDDER AGAIN

SHUDDER AGAIN

22 TALES OF SEX AND HORROR

EDITED BY

MICHELE SLUNG

A ROC BOOK

ROC
Published by the Penguin Group
Penguin Books USA Inc., 375 Hudson Street,
New York, New York 10014, U.S.A.
Penguin Books Ltd, 27 Wrights Lane, London W8 5TZ, England
Penguin Books Australia Ltd, Ringwood, Victoria, Australia
Penguin Books Canada Ltd, 10 Alcorn Avenue, Toronto, Ontario,
Canada M4V 3B2
Penguin Books (N.Z.) Ltd, 182–190 Wairau Road, Auckland 10,
New Zealand

Penguin Books Ltd, Registered Offices:
Harmondsworth, Middlesex, England

Published by Roc, an imprint of Dutton Signet,
a division of Penguin Books USA Inc. Previously published in a
Roc hardcover edition.

First Mass Market Printing, January, 1995
10 9 8 7 6 5 4 3 2 1

ROC REGISTERED TRADEMARK—MARCA REGISTRADA

Printed in the United States of America

Cover art by Mel Odom

PUBLISHER'S NOTE
These are works of fiction. Names, characters, places, and incidents either are the product of the authors' imagination or are used fictitiously, and any resemblance to actual persons, living or dead, events, or locales is entirely coincidental.

for Stephen King

It is here that I would like to acknowledge my debt—in some cases a bit overdue—to the following:

Mike Ashley, Neil Barron, Ev Bleiler, Mike Dirda, The Fantasy Centre, Charles L. Grant, Peter Haining, Steve Jones, T.E.D. Klein, Hugh Lamb, Kay McCauley, Linda Marotta, Otto Penzler, David Pringle, Stuart H. Schiff, David Streitfeld, Jack Sullivan, Doug Winter, and Bob Wyatt. Also, John Silbersack and Chris Schelling, as well as Lorraine Shanley and her indispensable Market Partners.

CONTENTS

PREFACE

It simply never occurred to me when I was putting together the precursor* of this volume that it would appear to some readers I was promoting the notion that the literature of fright is in and of itself erotic. While I don't argue that there are people out there who might themselves feel this is so, I not only don't agree with them but I'd really much rather stay home with a good vampire novel than chance running into any of these worrisome types after dark.

Yet it seems awfully obvious to me (and this was my perhaps too-simple point) that repeatedly, and using its every formidable weapon, horror fiction seeks to invade our psyches where those highly sensitive but clinically unfindable "organs" are most vulnerable. (Only in the crudest way can a surgeon probe our fears or provoke our shudders. But just give a horror writer the same task ...) And, given that intention, one recognizes, with little need for guesswork, the most likely target area.

So whether taking the most basic situations (see, for example, David Kuehls's "The First Time") or ones of more confounding complexity ("Ravissante" by Robert Aickman), such tales serve to unsettle us (or worse) be-

*I Shudder at Your Touch (1991; now available in a ROC paperback)

cause it is our sexual selves that we—or the stories' pro-
tagonists standing in for us—despair of protecting, try as
we (and they) will. Moreover, identifying this material
as "erotic horror" merely means that it is horror *about*
sexual feelings (a legitimate usage, after all) and not horror meant to arouse them.

Naturally, the possibilities for discovering the places—
those all-too-assailable spots—where this coupling of
seemingly magnetized elements meet up are many. They
range from the more ordinary potential for risk in the
travails of courtship, betrothal, sexual initiation, childbirth, adultery, or sexual preference to the dark intricac-
ies of aberration and perversion. In the same way, the
rarely welcome, frequently destructive emotion of sexual
jealousy may provide the necessary opening for an act
of horror; or consider instead incest, that paralyzingly
powerful taboo, and the deep shadows that trail in its
wake.

At the same time, however, I must note, in case you
hadn't thought of it, the human body's lack of a better,
bipartite system for registering gooseflesh. The truth is
that the shivers we experience in a situation of reactive
revulsion and the ones we feel when all positive sensual
systems are starting to fire just happen to turn up on the
same skin. And they certainly do resemble each other,
even when the conscious mind does its duty and makes
the appropriate distinctions between pleasure and fear.
In this regard, the connection between sex and horror
may be seen as a "simple" physical one. But of course
it really can never be only that, and this is because it
also draws force from that link, always acknowledged,
between sex and death. (T. H. White skillfully interplays,
and powerfully underscores, the interrelation of these
very elements in his story "Kin to Love," forgoing any
ambiguity at all.)

Plus, what further confuses the issue is the delight horror's many frequent readers, and even its occasional
ones, obtain from the sensation of feeling scared.
Though I myself refuse, absolutely, ever to get on a
roller coaster, still, as a lover of weird fiction I'm able
to empathize with the plunge junkies who want "that

feeling" all over again. Even if I can't say for sure that it's Danger I'm after, I know I welcome the jolts of oddness, the messing about with reality (whatever *that* is), and the cautious relaxing into unease, all of the special effects that creepy writing at its best brings with it. And there's no question but that these add up to an addictive form of entertainment once you've allowed yourself to just say "yes" for a change: after all, horror is a mood-altering high that's still perfectly legal, completely affordable, and should haunt only your dreams, not your waking hours ... if you're lucky, that is.

Twenty-two very different imaginations lie in wait for you now. Each one has taken on the task of revealing that extremely protean beast, sexual dread, the general shape of which I've been attempting myself to delineate. You'll see that in some of the stories it will be sprawled in full view, flaunting its menace, while in others it will be lurking, concealed, under the bed, intending to reach out and grab your ankle. The only thing for sure is that it knows you better than you know it, so the trick is to be careful.

But not *too* careful, or as I've been trying to tell you, you'll miss a good deal of the fun.

APHRA

NANCY A. COLLINS

"Since her eyes were without lids, Aphra's gaze
was so intense it felt as if she were looking into
the bottom of my soul."

*Nancy A. Collins is a risk-taker, and it's very clear that
in her refusal ever to play it safe—or soft—her first prior-
ity when she's writing is simply to please herself. But, as
is so often the case with born storytellers, Collins's enjoy-
ment of her own powers—especially when she's pushed
past "daring" to arrive at "dangerous"—just adds to the
reader's pleasure. A thoroughly contemporary writer,
whose fans look to her for the high-intensity thrills and
visceral jolts characteristic of late-twentieth-century horror
fiction, she nonetheless displays frequent unmistakable appreciation of older genre traditions. And in "Aphra" this
translates into a slowly building tale of sexual obsession
that, with its effects cut so close to the bone, has the feel
of the instant classic.*

It all started with X-Ray Specs.

I can still remember the ad, even after thirty years. It
was lying in wait for me between the covers of *Lucky*

Ducky #66. I was eight years old at the time and would have preferred the adventures of Batman or The Flash to those of a talking duck, but my mother forbade such strong, potentially warping stuff.

Sandwiched between the antics of Lucky Ducky and his half-wit antagonist, Bully Dog, was a full-page advertisement trumpeting the glories of Olson's Laff-N-Magic Novelties, Inc. of Newark, New Jersey. The page was divided into smaller boxes, each illustrating a "surefire gag."

The X-Ray Specs were listed between the Red Hot Gum ("Gets Lots of Laffs!") and the ever-popular Joy Buzzer ("Watch 'Em Jump!"). The crude drawing depicted an underfed young man wearing the spiral-patterned glasses, beads of sweat leaping from his forehead as he stared in terrified awe at his right hand, now rendered fleshless. This captured my imagination in ways a talking duck never could.

What really grabbed me, however, was the smaller illustration placed in an insert in the left-hand corner of the box. It showed the same agitated bespectacled man gaping at a woman dressed in a calf-length skirt. The artist had turned the dress transparent from the knees down, so the readers could see what the perspiring man was looking at. The look on his face was the exact same grimace of shock and revulsion he'd worn when his hand was stripped to the bone.

I knew what the sweating man was *really* looking at. He was looking at what Coach Fisher had lectured us about in gym class. Coach Fisher had told us it was nasty to stand under the monkey bars and look up the girls' dresses. Up until Coach told us not to, I had never wanted to look up a girl's skirt.

Now the idea of being able to look at a girl and see her Thing intrigued me. I knew I would not be able to live my life until I had my own pair of X-Ray Specs.

I saved my allowance for three weeks and sent away for them. While awaiting their arrival, I imagined myself lounging nonchalantly around the jungle gym during recess while wearing my miraculous X-Ray Specs. No one would ever suspect me of looking at the girls' Things. It was the Perfect Crime.

During the proscribed six to eight weeks necessary for delivery, I spent a lot of time trying to picture what a girl's Thing looked like. I knew it wasn't like a boy's, but that was about it.

Coach Fisher taught Health & Hygiene when it wasn't football season. We got to watch a lot of films. One of the films showed what people looked like without their skin. It wasn't too gross, since there were lots of little cartoon characters in it. But there was some footage shot with a special X-ray camera of an actual skeleton walking up stairs, eating, and talking. I thought about it the rest of the day.

When I got home, I snuck my father's old college anatomy textbook into my bedroom, determined to look at the naked women displayed between the covers. What I found was disappointing and more than a little gross.

There were plenty of pictures showing flayed women, their faces peeled and organs coiled. But their exposed muscles and yellow layers of subcutaneous fat were far too "gooshy." I much preferred the hard, sharp angles hidden at the core of the human machine. There was something about the perfection of bone that made my palms sweat and my head hurt. I studied the eternally smiling female while imagining how great life would be once I had my X-Ray Specs.

Nothing would be secret anymore! I could see what was going on inside the people around me! I was especially looking forward to discovering the secret girls kept locked inside their Things. I knew enough from eavesdropping on my older brother that whatever it was the girls had inside them, it was very, very important. Just thinking about it made me hard. I'd overheard my older brother and his friends discussing "jerking off," but I didn't know why someone would want to do it. Staring at the nameless, fleshless woman, her secrets exposed to my hungry eyes, I attained a sudden understanding.

In my youthful inexperience, I got some of it on the book. Terrified of being found out, I tore out the stained page and returned the textbook to my father's bookshelf.

If he ever discovered the vandalism, he never mentioned it.

Finally the day dawned when my X-Ray Specs arrived in the mail. They were hardly what I'd expected. The rims were made from hard plastic and the lenses were pieces of cardboard stamped with a garish "pop-art" design. When I put them on I found myself staring through a pair of small holes covered in red cellophane. All it did, besides eliminate my peripheral vision and turn my surroundings the color of cherry Kool-Aid, was give me an intense headache.

It's funny, but I thought I'd forgotten all that. Now it's coming back to me, with all its rawboned excitement and embarrassing sharp edges intact.

I grew up normal, I guess. As normal as any other American male born during the Baby Boom. My home life was stable. My parents looked after me. I had friends at school. I was well liked. I dated girls.

Most of my friends in high school went for the cheerleader types. You know, the ones with huge tits and good skin. I preferred the tall, willowy ones. The ones who wanted to be models.

When I went away to college I started getting involved sexually with various women. During my sophomore year I was engaged to this girl who was anorexic. She'd put on some weight since high school, but she was still thin. My friends thought I was nuts. A couple of months before we were to get married, she had a cardiac arrest and died in her apartment. The doctors said it was because of the anorexia; it had weakened her heart. I was really broken up over her for some time. I even dropped out of college for a semester.

I dated off and on for several years after that, but never seriously. Then I met the woman I would eventually marry.

She was really beautiful back then. She looked just like a model. Up until she got pregnant, people were always telling her she should quit her job and be a model. She could have done it, too. I discovered after we were engaged that she had an "eating disorder"; she was bulimic. She would eat huge amounts of food—more than you'd imagine a woman her size could possibly hold—then excuse herself from the table and force herself to vomit. Our marriage was a happy one, I guess. Until the pregnancy.

My wife was very excited about it, once the doctor confirmed what she'd suspected. She never bothered to ask me if *I* wanted a child. The topic of what I did or didn't want never came up when she rattled on about baby names and the proper color scheme for the nursery. I didn't say anything and she didn't notice.

It didn't seem to bother her that she was getting fat. It bothered me, though.

I was relieved when she miscarried. Saved us both a lot of bother. My wife didn't see it that way, however. She was devastated, as her doctor was quick to point out to me. He hinted that the reason she'd lost the baby had something to do with the bulimia. He insisted I take her on a vacation, so we could be together and Come To Grips With The Tragedy. So we went to Florida for two weeks.

While we were in Florida, I found a piece of coral washed up on the beach near our hotel. It was as white as bone. That's what I thought it was, at first. That's why I picked it up. It was delicate and resembled, in size and shape, a woman's finger bone. The little one. I held it in my hand for a long time. Up close it didn't look like real bone. It was much too porous and knobby, like an arthritic grandmother's amputated digit. Still, I found myself getting excited. When I got back to the room I masturbated in the shower. I did not tell my wife.

By the time we got back from Florida the distance between us yawned even wider. Every day my interest in her dwindled further. Whenever I think about her— on those rare occasions I *do* think of my wife—I see her as a tiny, ill-defined figure; as if I'd spent seven years looking at her through the wrong end of a pair of binoculars.

The extra pounds she'd put on during the pregnancy stayed after the miscarriage. She became sullen and wore dark clothes and ate a lot of chocolate. I spent most of my time trying to avoid her.

One of my hobbies is garage sales. I enjoy sitting behind the wheel of a car and plotting my route with the help of a city map and the classified ads. Sometimes I discovered neighborhoods I never knew existed. It was like having an adventure in my own backyard.

One Saturday afternoon, while I was out avoiding my wife, I happened across the yard sale that changed my life. You may think I'm being facetious, but I'm *very* serious.

It wasn't listed in the paper and it didn't have any homemade signs tacked to nearby trees or telephone poles. It was just a jumble of old odds and ends lumped on the yard fronting an old two-story house. A bored young man sat in a folding chair next to the driveway.

The neighborhood wasn't one I normally visited, but my interest was piqued by a pair of stuffed owls atop a pile of discarded clothes. The old house, like most of those on the block, had once been home to a well-to-do family at the start of the century. Now it was in need of extensive repairs.

"Uh—this your stuff?" I asked the bored young man.

He looked up from his dog-eared Stephen King paperback and shrugged indifferently. "Guess you could say that. Actually, all this shit used to belong to my uncle. He died a couple of months ago."

"Sorry to hear that."

The young man shrugged again. "I didn't even know he was alive until he died and willed me this dump!"

"Oh."

"I'm only here for the weekend to sell off this crap before I turn the property over to a real estate agent. They think they can sell it to some developer who'll turn it into apartments."

I grunted and began pawing through the piles of moldering cardboard boxes and mildewed steamer trunks. I found several leather-bound books, most of them Latin, scattered among the stripped copies of *Fate* and *Cat Fancy*. If dust is any measure of antiquity, they had to have been at least a hundred years old.

I also found a trunk full of sealed jars containing pickled baby sharks, adult vipers, various species of squid, and some deformed dog fetuses. I located a group of bullfrogs playing scaled-down mariachi instruments and wearing doll-sized sombreros. There was a rusty astrolabe, a cracked pestle, and several boxes filled with strangely shaped glass tubing, similar to the equipment found in the mad scientist's laboratory on the late-late show. The heir's uncle had obviously boasted eclectic taste.

"What was your uncle's last name?" I asked, hefting a stuffed baby alligator outfitted in tiny bathing trunks and fixed to a miniature surfboard.

"Drayden," the young man replied without looking up from his book.

I remembered reading an article in the paper about a man called Drayden. He'd been a recluse who lived with several dozen cats in a dreary old house. When he finally dropped dead it took the police a couple of weeks to find out about it. When they forced open the front door, the old man's cats spilled across the threshold and into the surrounding neighborhood. The old man's carcass had been badly chewed.

I glanced up just in time to see a scruffy, thin-flanked calico cat creep along the roof of the nearby garage. Its eyes were yellow-green and untamed. Unnerved, I returned to sorting through the late Mr. Drayden's possessions.

She was in an old wooden produce box, wrapped in faded yellow tissue paper, like the fragile glass Christmas ornaments my mother brought from Germany when I was a child.

I knew she was female from the very first. I'm not exactly sure *how* I knew, but I did. I reached into the box and ran my trembling fingers across the ivory smoothness of her cranium. Empty sockets stared back at me, offering an unobstructed view of the interior of her skull. This exquisite glimpse of mystery reminded me of the wafer-thin sections of chambered nautilus sold as key chains in Florida tourist traps.

Except for the seam where they'd opened it to extract the brain, the skull was in perfect condition. There was a small stainless-steel eye riveted through the top of her head that, once hung from a hook, permitted the fully jointed skeleton to stand upright. A quick survey of the crate's contents proved that the skeleton was intact, although the arms, legs, torso, and skull had been detached and wrapped separately. I felt like a child finding a toy train set under the tree on Christmas morning.

"How much you want for this?" I tried to hide my excitement, but my voice quavered. Old Man Drayden's nephew squinted at the disassembled skeleton and scratched his head.

"Oh, that thing! Umm ... thirty bucks? There's a stand that goes with it, I think. It's in the garage." I handed the nephew three crisp ten-dollar bills, trying to hide my delight. "It's just inside the door. You can't miss it. Go ahead, it's unlocked."

I headed up the cracked drive to the detached garage squatting in the shadow of the old house. The double doors squealed when I opened them. Something small, furry, and low to the ground scuttled deeper into the shadows. The smell of cat piss made me gag. Breathing through my mouth didn't help much, but it did reduce the stench enough for me to navigate in the gloom.

I saw the skeleton's metal stand and dragged it clear of the garage doors. It was heavier than I'd first thought and nearly as tall as I was. It would take some doing, but I could fit it in the back of my car.

I stashed my treasure in the trunk and drove away. The nephew watched me leave with bored, piggy eyes. Funny how I hadn't noticed how heavyset he was before.

My study isn't really a study; it's a half-finished basement. The real estate agent, when he showed my wife and me the house, insisted on calling it a "rumpus room," whatever that means. When my wife and I moved in, she decided it would be my study. I have a desk, a couple of chairs, and an old hide-a-bed sofa down there. There's also a tiny bathroom and a separate entrance that leads to the garage. Whenever my wife was depressed or upset, I stayed here.

It took me several hours to put the skeleton together. It's not as easy as it looks. There were little pins and wing nuts holding the bones together and it took some time before I understood exactly how things were supposed to go together. That I was so excited my hands shook didn't help much, either.

After working for over three hours straight, I became so frustrated I burst into tears. I must have been crying pretty hard because my wife came down to see what was wrong. When I heard her coming down the stairs I jumped up and hurried to meet her before she had a chance to see what I was doing. I don't know why I didn't want her to see; I just didn't.

When my wife realized I'd been crying, she threw her arms around me and began crying, too. She kept telling me how it was all right for me to show my feelings and how we were both still young enough to try again. I agreed with everything she said in order to get her back upstairs. She kept insisting we have sex. She dragged me into the bedroom and spent an hour trying to get me hard. Nothing worked. She ended up crying herself to sleep. I put my clothes back on and returned downstairs.

Like I said, I knew she was female from the start. Most people can't tell the difference between male and female bones. How strange. Imagine not being able to tell naked men from naked women! And believe me, you can't get any nuder!

I cleaned the stand before hanging up my prize. That's when I learned her name. It was inscribed on a small copper plate affixed to the base. At first I thought it was the manufacturer's mark or the name of the medical supply house she'd come from, but after a few ounces of Brass-O, I saw it was an elaborately engraved inscription. All it said was *Aphra*.

I assumed it was her name. I liked it; it sounded exotic and mysterious. I wonder who or what Aphra had been, back when she wore a skin. Was she a derelict or a priestess? A pauper or a prostitute? I knew that most human skeletons used in modern anatomy classes were imported from somewhere overseas like Bangladesh, but Aphra was larger than the average Third Worlder. She was very old, yet at the same time eternally young. Maybe she had been an unfortunate female criminal back during Queen Victoria's reign whose unclaimed

body had been stripped of its flesh and sold into postmortem white slavery to recoup the money spent on her
when she was alive.

The sound of my wife on the stairs shook me from
my fanciful reverie. When she saw Aphra she cried out
in disgust.

"My God, Reg—what the hell is *that*?"

"It's, um, a skeleton, dear."

"I can *see* that! But what is it doing *here*?"

"I bought it at a garage sale today ..."

My wife stared at me, her arms wrapped around herself as if she were cold. "Are you *crazy*?"

"Honey, I can explain—"

"I don't want to know about it! I want that horrible
thing out of this house, do you hear me?"

"But, dear, it's just a skeleton. It's completely harmless ..."

"I don't care, Reg! It's unhealthy, you buying a thing
like that. It's *morbid*!"

"Honey—"

"I *said* I don't want it in the house, is that clear?"
She turned and left. Discussion closed. I knew better
than to argue.

I cast a guilty glance over my shoulder at Aphra.

She was grinning at me. *What she doesn't know won't
hurt her, Reg.*

After that I kept Aphra in the closet until I was certain my wife was asleep. Every family has a skeleton in
the closet.

I liked to put Aphra in the corner behind my desk,
so she could watch over me while I worked. It was comforting, knowing she was there. I could look at her whenever I liked; she never complained. Soon I began idly
caressing the curve of her pelvic girdle. She never re-
proached me for my boldness, even when I fingered the
curl of her coccyx.

What is mere surface beauty compared to the poetry
of bone, the sublime ballet of socket and joint, the perfection of a carpal?

I started bringing more and more work home. It was

a good excuse to stay up late, waiting for my wife to go to bed.

Confronted with Aphra's sleek perfection, I became more and more dissatisfied with my wife. The natural beauty that had first attracted me to her was now concealed in layers of muffling fat. The sight of her naked body was enough to make me ill. I began sleeping on the sofa bed in the study.

I was celibate during this time, my mind consumed by erotic fancies. Although my libido seemed stuck in overdrive, I couldn't help but notice how horribly *thick* all the women at work had become. Even the ones I had previously flirted with at the water cooler looked immense, swaddled in acres of jiggling blubber.

I stopped eating at the cafeteria during my lunch hour. The sight of gargantuan secretaries shoveling cottage cheese into their vast maws ruined my appetite. I could hardly wait for the day to end, so I could return to the comfort of my study and the silent balm of Aphra's eternal smile.

Still, I am a man. And a man has needs. Needs that must be met if he is to live something resembling a productive life.

Near where I work is one of the city's seamier districts. It doesn't look it during the day, but come twilight the sidewalks swarm with the flotsam of inner-city life; pimps, whores, junkies, dealers, winos, and lunatics of every age, race, and sexual proclivity can be found. You look at their eyes and you can see that all they are is meat. Meat to be shunned or used.

She was standing on a street corner looking bored, just like the cliché. The moment I saw her I had to have her. She was under five feet six, but her extreme thinness made her look taller. She was a junkie, her arms and legs long and gangly with absurdly large elbows and knees. Her face was horsey, the cheekbones straining against the drawn skin. Her hair, damaged by malnutrition, was frizzy with split ends. She wore the mandatory hooker costume of hot pants and halter top, exposing skinny flanks and matchstick ribs. My erection was immediate and intense.

She leaned into the open passenger window, eyeing me with the same indifference as an order clerk at the corner McDonald's. Over one billion served.

The bargaining was quick and efficient. She got in the car and I drove her to my house. Outside of our brief price negotiation, she did not speak to me.

It was late. My wife was asleep. We wouldn't be disturbed.

The only time anything resembling human expression registered on the whore's face was when I dragged Aphra from her hiding place in the closet and stationed her at the foot of the bed.

Once naked, the whore's addiction was painfully obvious. The veins in her arms had collapsed and there were red pinpricks between her toes from self-administered injections. Her breasts were small and lay flat against her bony chest. The only thing about her that looked alive was the dark tangle of pubic hair between her bird-like legs. Its vitality was obscene compared to how wasted the rest of her was.

She was dry when I entered her. She lay under me, moving feebly in response to my violent thrusts. She was so frail that every push of my hips made her flop like a huge rag doll. I pumped against her frantically, bruising myself on the sharp angles of her hips.

In the split second before orgasm, it seemed as if her skin grew suddenly translucent and I stared, transfixed, at the papery flutter of lungs and rhythmic fisting of cardiac muscle. Then my thirty-dollar climax disrupted the vision and I withdrew, shivering, from her depths.

My lust spent, I was repulsed by the sight of the whore. How could I have yearned to empty myself inside a woman so obese? She looked like one of those hideously bloated fertility goddesses in the museums; all quivering buttock and pendulous tit. I was unable to understand how I could have deluded myself into accepting her as a substitute for Aphra's pared-down sensuality. I hurried the whore back to the city and left her on a busy street corner.

I stopped by a late-night liquor joint and bought a bottle of cheap whiskey, determined to burn the memory of being clasped between her heavy thighs from my brain.

I'd swallowed most of the fifth by the time I got home. My brief liaison had relieved the sexual tensions stored in me, but something still ached for completion. It was a hunger that went beyond mere physical need, raging in my heart like a trapped beast.

Aphra was still standing where I'd left her, empty sockets staring at the sofa bed's soiled sheets. I was overwhelmed by guilt and sorrow. I began to cry. I was still crying when I entered the shower and allowed my tears to be sluiced down the drain.

Before I went to bed I returned Aphra to her place in the closet. As I prepared to close the door on her, I leaned forward and pressed my lips to the hard plane of her right cheek. I never kissed her good night before. I don't know why. It was such a perfectly natural thing to do.

The sound of something bumping woke me a couple of hours later. I lay very still, my senses still fogged by the liquor I'd consumed earlier, and tried to figure out what was making the noise and where it was coming from. My heart froze when I realized it was coming from the closet.

I sat up, clutching the bedclothes between white knuckles, and stared at the slowly turning doorknob. The rattling inside the closet grew even more agitated, then fell silent. The doorknob ceased its movement. I wondered if the hook atop her skull had frustrated her attempt at freedom. Before I had a chance to decide if I was awake or dreaming, the closet door opened and Aphra stepped into the room.

The pale moonlight filtering through the curtains limned her snow-white clavicle and cast the spaces between her ribs in deep shadow. I was surprised to see suspended above the empty triangle of her nasal cavity a pair of luminous yellow-green eyes. Since her eyes were without lids, Aphra's gaze was so intense it felt as if she were looking into the bottom of my soul.

She moved toward me, every step made with slow, studied grace. Her bones clacked in gentle counterpoint to her actions. She was smiling, of course, her beautifully sculptured hands held before her in supplication.

I knew what I was seeing was impossible; that it had to be a crazy dream. But I wanted it to be real. Even more, I *needed* it to be real. I did not move when Aphra sat on the foot of the bed for fear I would break the spell and wake up. If this was a dream, I wanted it to last as long as possible before being faced with reality.

I wanted to tell her that the whore had meant nothing to me; that no one, not even my wife, commanded my love and loyalty like she did. I opened my mouth but she lay her twiglike fingers on my lips. She knew. I could see it in the serene way she held her skull, the lidless eyes alert and omniscient. There would be no recriminations.

My pulse quickened as she leaned forward, pulling aside the sheet that hid my nakedness. Her pale, fleshless face brushed against mine, the hard ivory of her teeth pressing against my lips. I caressed the curve of her pelvis. As I ran my trembling hands down the smooth hard length of her femur, she shivered in response. The sound reminded me of the bead curtain I'd owned in college.

I gasped as Aphra's articulated phalanges wrapped themselves around my erect penis, the knucklebones rattling like dice with every stroke. The pleasure was so intense my vision was obliterated by pulsating blobs of darkness.

I must have blacked out, because the next thing I knew it was daylight and my wife was standing over me, shrieking obscenities and sobbing hysterically. She slapped me a couple of times before I could figure out what was going on. Then I realized Aphra was still in bed with me.

My wife left me that same day. I have not seen her since, although I keep finding letters from her lawyer in the mail. I never open them.

With my wife gone, there was no longer any need for me to keep Aphra hidden in the closet. I proudly carried her upstairs to the master bedroom—her rightful place. Although she didn't say so, she was thrilled.

At first I kept up pretenses at work, although I knew

it was only a matter of time before the intercompany gossip spread the news of my wife leaving me. My superior began commenting on my appearance. He kept asking me if I was eating right. I couldn't figure out what he was driving at.

Once my wife's desertion became common knowledge I was bombarded with female attention. Some of the secretaries even went so far as to sit on the corner of my desk, flashing vast expanses of cellulite-engorged thigh. It was the best I could do to keep from being ill. After a couple of weeks they got the hint and stopped bothering me. Some voiced the same concern about my eating habits. I simply smiled and assured them I was perfectly healthy and nothing was wrong with my appetite. I knew that if I told them the truth, that I was no longer interested in food, they would not understand.

A month after my wife left me, my fat slob of a superior called me into his office. He was Worried About Me. He thought I Needed A Rest. Some time to Think Things Over. To Decide What To Do. He ordered me to take a sabbatical. I didn't argue. Being away from my Aphra for more than a few minutes was unspeakable torment.

That was—what? two? three? months ago. I'm afraid I'm having more and more trouble remembering exact dates. Time, when I'm with my precious immortal, holds little meaning for me.

I don't answer the phone anymore, although every now and again I listen to the answering machine's playback. My boss hasn't called in a long time. I don't care. I'm not going back to work. I knew that when I left, but I wouldn't admit it to myself.

Aphra's a lot more active now than when I first got her. In the beginning she would only move around on her own after dark. Now she walks around the house all day long. I make sure to keep the drapes closed. The neighbors give me enough grief about how the yard looks without Aphra traipsing around undressed in front of the windows.

I don't go out much anymore. I don't miss the outside, really. The last time I left the house the streets were full of gigantic, swollen grubs stuffed into suits and slit skirts. I ended up puking in a hedge and coming home before I got to wherever it was I was going.

The time before that I stopped by the old house where I'd found Aphra to find out what had happened to Drayden's other belongings. All I found was a charred husk with sheets of plywood nailed over the windows and doors.

Sometimes Aphra likes to dress up in the clothes my wife left behind. (Not that any of them fit her. My wife was absolutely elephantine!) Aphra likes my wife's old negligees—the ones from before the pregnancy. She's wearing one now as I write this; the Paris original in mauve chiffon with lace at the throat. It was always one of my favorites.

Aphra's sitting in front of the vanity table, playing with the silver-plated brush my wife gave me for my thirty-sixth birthday. I can see myself reflected in the mirror as she gives her phantom hair one hundred strokes.

My skin is pale, except for the angry red that marks my thighs, shoulders, and groin. The infection's at its worst on my foreskin, although the bite on my shoulder is pretty bad. My Aphra is a passionate woman. Far more than my wife ever was; or any other woman could be.

I was walking down the stairs this morning and became so weak I nearly fainted. I had to cling to the banister with both hands to keep from falling. When I got downstairs I found a shut-off notice from the power company in the mail. I think it's December outside. It might even be next year.

Aphra's finished her evening toilet. She turns from her place in front of the mirror and smiles at me. Although she has never spoken, we have shared an intimacy that goes far deeper than mere words ever could.

I feel as if I'm poised on the edge of a great mystery, the solution finally within my grasp. As I grow weaker, I understand more and more of the answer. It won't be long before I'll be able to see everything. No more secrets. The giddiness that accompanies true love has turned me into a philosopher.

It's taken me three days to write this. I won't be adding any more after this. It's too much of an effort to pick up the pen. I'm too tired to even read it from the beginning to see if I got it right. Not that it matters.

She comes to me, the negligee swirling about her like colored mist, her teeth clacking in anticipation of our lovemaking. My skin burns, awaiting her sharp caress. She promises me perfection; unchanging and eternal.

Soon. Let it be soon.

EYE OF THE LYNX

THOMAS LIGOTTI

"Behind still another door, which had no distinguishing marks, a single candle glowed through red
glass, just barely keeping the room out of total
blackness. It was hard to tell how many were in
there, more than a couple, less than a horde."

*In each new generation of horror writers, a few figures
are quickly awarded cult status—but, even so, the admiration Tom Ligotti has elicited from his peers is rather extraordinary. One theme, however, central to all of the
praise he has gathered, is that, somehow, what he's doing
is truly* different. *Ligotti himself will cite the influence of
Lovecraft and Poe, as well as Beckett, Borges, Nabokov,
and others, yet Ramsey Campbell has correctly noted:
"Despite faint echoes of writers he admires . . . Ligotti's
vision is wholly personal."*

*And with equally idiosyncratic flair, he's also given to
revealing in odd hybrid creations (works that are part
story, part pedagogy, and always irresistibly quotable) his
own guiding beliefs and metaphysical speculations on
weird literature. For example, here's an idea from "Professor Nobody's Little Lectures" (Songs of a Dead
Dreamer): "Supernatural horror, in all its bizarre con-*

structions, enables a reader to taste a selection of treats at odds with his well-being."

Certainly, the curious noir-gothic narrative that follows—one of Ligotti's most unsettling "dreams for sleepwalkers"—superbly illustrates the way we willingly, even eagerly, allow the altered consciousness of a stranger's shifting nightmare to become our own.

No architectural go-betweens divided the doorway—a side entrance off a block of diverse but connected buildings—from the sidewalk. The sidewalk itself was conjugally flush with the curb that bordered a street which in turn radiated off a boulevard of routine clamor, and all of this was enveloped by December's musty darkness. Sidewalk doorway, doorway sidewalk. I don't want to make too much of the matter, except to say that this peculiarity, if it was one, made an impression on me: there was no physical introduction to the doorway, surely not in the form of a little elevated slab of cement, certainly not even a single stair of stone. No structure of any kind prefaced the door. And it was recessed into the building itself with such deliberate shallowness that it almost looked painted directly onto the wall. I looked over at the traffic light above the intersection; it was amber going on red. I looked back at the door. The sidewalk seemed to slip right under it, urging one to step inside. So I did, after noting that the wall around the doorway was done up, somewhat ineptly, like a castle tower flanked by toothy merlons.

Inside I was immediately greeted by a reception committee of girls very professionally lounging in what looked like old church pews along an old wall. The narrow vestibule in which I found myself scintillated with a reddish haze that seemed not so much light as electric vapor. In the far upper corner of this entranceway a closed circuit camera was bearing down on us all, and I wondered how the camera's eye would translate that redly dyed room into the bluish hues of a security monitor. Not that it was any of my business. We might all be electronically meshed into a crazy purpurean tapestry, and that would have been just fine.

A fair-haired girl in denim slacks and leather jacket stood up and approached me. In the present light her blondness was actually more a murky tomato soup or greasy ketchup than fresh strawberry. She delivered a mechanical statement that began "Welcome to the House of Chains," and went on and on, spelling out various services and specific terms and finally concluding with a legal disclaimer of some carefully phrased sort. "Yes, yes," I said. "I've read the ads, the ones set in that spiky Gothic type, the ones that look like a page out of an old German Bible. I've come to the right place, haven't I?"

"Sure you have," I thought to myself. "Sure you have," echoed the blonde with blood-dyed hair. "What will it be tonight?" I inwardly asked me. "What will it be tonight?" she asked aloud. "Do you see anything you like?" we both asked me at the same time. From my expression and casual glances somewhere beyond the claustrophobic space of that tiny foyer, she could see right away that I didn't see anything, or at least that I wanted her to think I didn't. We were on the same infrared wavelength.

We stood there for a moment while she took a long delicious sip from a can of iced tea, pretending with half-closed eyes that it was the best thing she'd ever washed her insides with. Then she pushed a button next to an intercom on the wall behind her and turned her head to whisper some words, though still keeping those violent eyes hooked on mine.

And what did those eyes tell me? They told me of her life as she lived it in fantasy: a Gothic tale of a baroness deprived of her title and inheritance by a big man with bushy eyebrows, which he sometimes sprinkles with glitter. (She once dreamed that he did.) And now this high-born lady spends much of her time haunting secondhand shops, trying to reclaim her aristocratic accoutrements and various articles of her wardrobe which were dispersed at auction by the glitter-browed man who came out of the forest one spring when she was away visiting a Carmelite nunnery. So far she's done pretty well for herself, managing to assemble many items that for her are charged with sentiment. Her collection includes several dresses in her favorite shade of monastic black. Each of them tapers in severely under the bustline, while belling out below the waist. A biblike bodice buttons in her ribs, ascending to her neck where a strip of dark velvet is seized by a pearl brooch. At her wrist: a frail chain from which dangles a heart-shaped locket, a whirlpooling lock of golden hair inside. She wears gloves, of course, long and powdery pale. And tortuous hats from a mad milliner, with dependent veils like the fine cloth screen in a confessional, delicate flags of mourning repentance. But she prefers her enveloping hoods, the ones that gather with innumerable folds at the shoulders of heavy capes lined in satin that shines like a black sun. Capes with deep pockets and generous inner pouches for secreting precious souvenirs, capes with silk strings that tie about her neck, capes with weighted hems which nonetheless flutter weightlessly in midnight gusts. She loves them dearly.

Just so is she attired when the glitter-browed villain peers in her apartment window, accursing the casement and her dreams. What can she do but shrink with terror? Soon she is only doll-size in dark doll's costume. Nevertheless, quivering bones and feverish blood are the stuffings of this doll, its entrails tickled by fear's funereal plume. It flies to a corner of the room and cringes within enormous shadows, sometimes dreaming there throughout the night—of carriage wheels rioting in a lavender mist or a pearly fog, of nacreous fires twitching beyond the margins of country roads, of cliffs and stars. Then she awakes and pops a mint into her mouth from an unraveled roll on the nightstand, afterward smoking half a cigarette before crawling out of bed and grimacing in the light of late afternoon.

"C'mon," she said after releasing the button of the intercom. "I think I can help you."

"But I thought you couldn't leave the reception area," I explained, almost apologetically. "Of course, if I'd known . . ."

"C'mon," she repeated with both hands in her jacket pockets. And her loud heels led me out of that room where every face wore a fake blush.

We walked through a pair of swinging doors which met in the middle and were bound like books, imitation leather tightly stretched across their broad boards and thick spines. Title page:

House of Chains, A Romance in Red
Decorated with
Divers Woodcuts

Page one: Deep into December, as the winds of winter howled beyond the walls, two children, one blond and the other dark, found themselves in the heart of a great castle in the heart of a gloomy forest. The central chamber of the castle, as is a heart's wont, glowed with a warm red light, though the surrounding masonry was of damp gray stone. A great many people of the court capered about, traveling aloft or below by means of sundry stairways, ingressing and egressing through the queerly shaped portals of shadowed corridors (which seemed everywhere), and thronging here and there as in the curious bazaars of oriental scenes. Uncouth voices and harsh music fell upon the children's ears.

Decoration opposite opening page: Two children, one blond and the other not; passing through a tunnel of tangled forest which looks as if it's about to descend and devour them both. The girl, open mouthed, is pointing with her left hand while holding onto her brother with the right; the boy, all eyes, seems to be gazing in every direction at once, amazed at the pair's wondrous incarceration.

"Can I get the ninety-eight cent tour," I asked my hostess. "I'm from out of town. We don't have anything like this where I come from. I'm paying for this, right?"

Half of her mouth found it possible to smirk. "Sure," she said, drawing out the word well past its normal duration. She moved in a couple of false directions before guiding me toward some metal steps which clanged as we descended into a blur of crimson shadows. The vicious vapor followed us downstairs, of course, tagging along like an insanely devoted familiar.

Surprisingly enough, there was a window in the vaguely institutional basement of the House of Chains (I was beginning to enjoy that name), but it was composed of empty panes looking out upon a phony landscape. Pictured were vast regions of volcanic desolation towered over by prehistoric mountains which poked into a dead-end darkness. The scene was illuminated by a low-watt bulb. I felt a bit like a child peeking into a department store model of Santa's workshop, but I can't say it didn't create a mood.

"Nice painting," I said to my companion. "Kind of spooky, don't you think?" I looked at her for a reply to my patter, but no counter-patter was forthcoming. She simply stared at me as if I'd just told a joke she didn't get.

"There's not much down here," she finally said. "Just a couple of hallways that don't go anywhere and a bunch of rooms, most of them locked. If you want to see something spooky, go to the end of that hall and open the door on the right."

I faithfully followed her instructions. On the door handle hung a rather large animal collar at the end of a chain leash. The chain jingled a little when I pushed open the door. The red light in the hallway barely allowed me to see inside, but there was little to see anyway except a small, empty room. Its floor was bare cement and there was straw laid down upon it. The smell was terrific.

"Well?" she asked when I returned down the hallway.

"It's a start," I answered, winking the subtlest possible wink. We just stood for a moment gazing at each other in a light the color of fresh meat. Then she led me back upstairs.

"Where did you say you're from?" she asked as that noisy stairway amplified our footsteps into reverberant dungeon-like echoes.

"It's a real small place," I replied. "About a hundred miles outstate. It's not even on the maps."

"And you've never been to a place like this before?"

"Uh-uh, never."

She stopped at the top of the stairs. "Then before we go any further," she said, "I want to give you some advice and tell you to go back where you came from."

I just looked at her, shaking my head slowly and insolently.

"Okay, then. Let's go."

We went.

And there was much to see on the way—a Punch and Judy panorama which was staged between the chasmical folds of a playhouse curtain of rich inky red, and getting redder every passing second. Each scene flipped by like a page in a storybook: that frozen stage where the players are stiffened with immortality and around which the only thing that stirs is the reader's roving eye.

Locked doors were no obstacle.

Behind one, where every wall of the room was painted with heavy black bars from floor to ceiling, the Queen of the Singing Kingdom—riding crop raised high—sat atop her magic flying leopard, which unfortunately had been recently transformed into a human. And, sadly, the animal had lost one of its paws. What good fortune that it could still fly! But did it want to? Or did it prefer to lumber lamely around its cage, with the Queen herself growing out of its back like a Siamese twin, her royal blood and his beast's now flowing together, tributaries from distant worlds mingling in a hybrid harmony. The animal was so pleased that it yowled a tune as the Queen beat time upon its flanks with her stinging crop. Sing, leopard, sing!

Behind another door, one with a swastika splashed negligently on its front in such a way that the paint had dripped from every appendage of the spidery symbol, was a scene similar to the previous. Inside, some colored lights were angled down upon the floor, where a very small man, his hunchback possibly artificial, knelt with head bowed low. His hands were lost in a pair of enormous gloves with shapeless fingers which lolled around like ten drunken jacks-in-the-box. One of the numb fingers was trapped beneath the pointy toe at the base of a lofty boot. See the funny clown! Or rather *jester* in a jingly cap. His ringed eyes patiently gazed upward into the darkness, attentive to the hollow voice hurling anger from on high. The voice was playing up the moral disparity between its proudly booted self and that humiliated freak upon the floor, contrasting its warrior's leaping delights with the fool's dragging sack of amusements. *But couldn't the stooping hunchback's fun be beautiful too?* his eyes whispered with their elliptical mouths. *But couldn't—* Silence! Now the little monkey was going to get it.

Behind still another door, which had no distinguishing marks, a single candle glowed through red glass, just barely keeping the room out of total blackness. It was hard to tell how many were in there, more than a couple, less than a horde. They were all wearing the same gear, little zippers and big zippers like silver stitches scarring their outfits. One very little one had an eyelash caught in it, I could tell that much. For the rest of it, they might as well have been human shadows that merged softly with one another, proclaiming threats of ultimate mayhem and wielding oversized straight razors. But although these gleaming blades were always potently poised, they never came down. It was only make-believe, just like everything else I had seen.

The next door, and for me the last, was at the end of an exhausting climb in what must have been a tower.

"Here's where you get your money's worth, mister," said my date, blind to the signs of apprehension—clutching my coat, lightly pawing my cheek—I was beginning to exhibit like an insecure artist about to reveal his unseen canvases.

"Show me the worst," I said, eyeing the undersized door before us.

The situation here was as transparent as the others. Only this time it wasn't pet leopards, pathetic clowns, or paranoid shadows. It was, in fact, two new characters: a wicked witch and her assistant in the form of an enchanted puppet. The clumsy little creature, due to an incorrigibly mischievous temperament, had behaved badly. Now the witch was in the process, which she had down to perfection, of putting him back in line. She swept across the room, her dark dress swirling like a maelstrom, her hideous face sunken into an abundant hood. Behind her a stained-glass window shone with all the excommunicated tints of corruption. By the light of this infernal rainbow of wrinkled cellophane, she collared her naughty assistant and chained him hands and feet to a formidable-looking stone wall, which buckled aluminumlike when he collapsed against it. She angled down her hooded face and whispered into his wooden ear.

"Do you know what I do with little puppets who've been bad?" she inquired. "Do you?"

The puppet trembled a bit and would have beamed bright with perspiration had he been made of flesh and not wood.

"I'll tell you what I do," the witch continued half-sweetly. "I make them touch the fire. I burn them from the legs up."

Then, surprisingly, the puppet smiled.

"And what will you do," the puppet asked, "with all those old dresses, gloves, veils, and capes when I'm gone? What will you do in your low-rent castle with no one to stare, his brow of glittering silver, into the windows of your dreams?"

Perhaps the puppet was perspiring after all, for his brow was now glistening with tiny flecks of starlight.

The witch stepped back and whipped off her black hood, exposing blond hair beneath it. She wanted to know how I knew about all that stuff, which she had never revealed to anyone. She accused me of peeping-tomism, of breaking and entering, and of illicit curiosity in general.

"Let me out of these chains and I'll tell you all about myself," I shouted.

"Forget it," she answered. "I'm going to get someone to throw you out of here."

"Then I'll just have to release myself," I said more calmly.

The manacles opened around my ankles, my wrists, and the chains fell away.

"You can't pretend," I continued as I approached her, "that there isn't something familiar about me. After all we've meant to each other, after all we've done together, over and over and over. You're not bored, are you? I hate to think what that would mean ... for both of us. You've been cooped up here in this silly place too long. For someone like you, that can be deadly. You've always known you were special, haven't you? That someday— and it was always just around the corner, wasn't it?— great things were going to happen, great things that didn't quite have a name yet. But they were there, as real as the velvet embrace of your favorite cape, the one with the silver chain that draws its curtainy wings together at your bosom. As real as the tall candles you love to light during storms, and which you drunkenly knocked over once, burning your right hand. No, don't cover up the scar, I'm sure no one's noticed it before now. You love those storms, don't you, with their chains of raindrops whipping against your windows. All that craving for noise and persecution. All that beautiful craziness! The storms: your eyes stared into their eyes, and into mine.

"But now you're in danger of losing all that, which is why I showed up tonight. You've got to get out of this tinsellated sideshow. This is for hicks, this is small time. You can do better than this. I can take you places where the stories of tortuous romance and the storms never end. I'll take you there. Please, don't back away from me. There's nowhere to go and your eyes tell me you want the same things I do. If you're worried about the hardships of traveling to strange faraway places, don't! You're almost there now. Just fall into my arms, into my heart, into— There, that was easy, wasn't it?"

Afterward I retraced my steps down stairways and through corridors of scarlet darkness. "Good night, everybody!" I said to the girls in the reception room. Back out on the street, I paused and looked at that peculiar door again. I could now see the logic of doing away with gratuitous barriers between one place and another, between those on the outside and those within. Bring down the walls! But watch out for escapees.

Actually she made only a single attempt. It wasn't serious, though. A drunk I passed on the sidewalk saw an arm shoot out at him from underneath my shirt, projecting chest-high at a perfect right angle to the rest of me. He staggered over, shook the hand with a jolly vigor, and then proceeded on his way. And I proceeded on mine, once I'd got her safely back inside her fabulous prison, a happy captive of my heart. We fled down the sidewalk. We breathed the cold of that winter night. We were one forever.

At the corner the amber traffic light had finally burst into a glorious red as my old flame and I approached the ultimate intersection of our flesh ... as well as our dreams.

HEAVY SET

RAY BRADBURY

"She could not see him. But she felt the bed shake
as if he were laughing. She could hear no sound
coming from him, so she could not be sure."

*This is a little-seen story from a master spinner of tales
whose enduring popularity has caused him to be called
the "most anthologized writer in America." Ray Bradbury, more a national treasure than merely a much beloved writer, might also be described as a one-man
amusement park, where all the rides and sideshows are
guaranteed to keep you coming back blissfully for repeat visits.*

*"Heavy Set" takes familiar Bradbury themes—endless
boyhood, children's rituals, the comfy-creepy pleasures of
Halloween, a mother's devotions—and turns them around
in that insidious manner he has long since perfected, sub-
verting the normal, funhouse-fashion. As for its sexual com-
ponents, I can only suggest that they are most felt in their
absence and are rendered the more grotesque by the way
they lurk so elusively along the edges of what we understand. Just try driving down any street in any quiet neighborhood after you read this, in the hopes of regaining your
innocence . . . you'll find, I fear, that it won't be so easy.*

The woman stepped to the kitchen window and looked out. There in the twilight yard a man stood surrounded by barbells and dumbbells and dark iron weights of all kinds and slung jump ropes and elastic and coiled-spring exercisers. He wore a sweat suit and tennis shoes and said nothing to anyone as he simply stood in the darkening world and did not know she watched.

This was her son, and people called him Heavy Set.

Heavy Set squeezed the little bunched, coiled springs in his big fists. They were lost in his fingers, like magic tricks; then they reappeared. He crushed them. They vanished. He let them go. They came back.

He did this for ten minutes, otherwise motionless.

Then he bent down and hoisted up the one-hundred-pound barbell, noiselessly, not breathing. He motioned it a number of times over his head, then abandoned it and went into the open garage among the various surfboards he had cut out and glued together and sanded and painted and waxed, and there he punched a punching bag easily, swiftly, steadily, until his curly golden hair got moist. Then he stopped and filled his lungs until his chest measured 50 inches, and stood, eyes closed, seeing himself in an invisible mirror poised and tremendous, 220 muscled pounds, tanned by the sun, salted by the sea wind and his own sweat.

He exhaled. He opened his eyes.

He walked into the house, into the kitchen and did not look at his mother, this woman, and opened the refrigerator and let the arctic cold steam him while he drank a quart of milk straight out of the carton, never putting it down, just gulping and swallowing. Then he sat down at the kitchen table to examine the Halloween pumpkins.

He had gone out earlier in the day and bought the pumpkins and carved most of them and did a fine job: they were beauties and he was proud of them. Now, looking childlike in the kitchen, he started carving the last of them. You would never suspect he was thirty years old, he still moved so swiftly, so quietly, for a large action like hitting a wave with an uptilted and outthrust board, or here with the small action of a knife, giving sight to a Halloween eye. The electric light bulb filled the summer wildness of his hair, but revealed no emotion, except this one intent purpose of carving, on his face. There was all muscle in him, and no fat, and that muscle waited behind every move of the knife.

His mother came and went on personal errands around the house and then came to stand and look at him and the pumpkins and smile. She was used to him. She heard him every night drubbing the punching bag outside, or squeezing the little metal springs in his hands, or grunting as he lifted his world of weights and held them in balance on his strangely quiet shoulders. She was used to all these sounds even as she knew the ocean coming in on the shore beyond the cottage and laying itself out flat and shining on the sand. Even as she was used, by now, to hearing Heavy Set each night on the phone saying he was tired to girls and saying no, no he had to wax the car tonight or do his exercises to the eighteen-year-old boys who called.

She cleared her throat. "Was the dinner good tonight?"

"Sure," he said.

"I had to get special steak. I bought the asparagus fresh."

"It was good," he said.

"I'm glad you liked it, I always like to have you like it."

"Sure," he said, working.

"What time is the party?"

"Seven-thirty." He finished the last of the smile on the pumpkin and sat back. "If they all show up—they might not show up—I bought two jugs of cider."

He got up and moved into his bedroom, quietly massive, his shoulders filling the door and beyond. In the room, in the half dark, he made the strange pantomime of a man seriously and silently wrestling an invisible opponent as he got into his costume. He came to the door of the living room a minute later licking a gigantic peppermint-striped lollipop. He wore a pair of short black pants, a little boy's shirt with ruff collar, and an Eton cap. He licked the lollipop and said, "I'm the mean little kid!" and the woman who had been watching him laughed. He walked with an exaggerated little child's walk, licking the huge lollipop, all around the room while she laughed at him and he said things and pretended to be leading a big dog on a rope. "You'll be the life of the party!" the woman cried, pink-faced and exhausted. He was laughing now, also.

The phone rang.

He toddled out to answer it in the bedroom. He talked for a long time and his mother heard him say Oh For Gosh Sakes several times and finally he came slowly and massively into the living room looking stubborn. "What's wrong?" she wanted to know.

"Aw," he said, "half the guys aren't showing up at the party. They got other dates. That was Tommy calling. He's got a date with a girl from somewhere. Good grief."

"There'll be enough," said his mother.

"I don't know," he said.

"There'll be enough for a party," she said. "You go on."

"I ought to throw the pumpkins in the garbage," he said, scowling.

"Well you just go on and have a good time," she said. "You haven't been out in weeks."

Silence.

He stood there twisting the huge lollipop as big as his head, turning it in his large muscular fingers. He looked as if at any moment now he would do what he did other nights. Some nights he pressed himself up and down on the ground with his arms and some nights he played a game of basketball with himself and scored himself, team against team, black against white, in the backyard. Some nights he stood around like this and then suddenly vanished and you saw him way out in the ocean swimming long and strong and quiet as a seal under the full moon or you could not see him those nights the moon was gone and only the stars lay over the water but you heard him there, on occasion, a faint splash as he went under

and stayed under a long time and came up, or he went
out sometimes with his surfboard as smooth as a girl's
cheeks, sandpapered to a softness, and came riding in,
huge and alone on a white and ghastly wave that
creamed along the shore and touched the sands with the
surfboard as he stepped off like a visitor from another
world and stood for a long while holding the soft smooth
surfboard in the moonlight, a quiet man and a vast
tombstone-shaped thing held there with no writing on it.
In all the nights like that in the past years, he had taken
a girl out three times one week and she ate a lot and
every time he saw her she said Let's Eat and so one
night he drove her up to a restaurant and opened the
car door and helped her out and got back in and said
There's the Restaurant. Solong. And drove off. And
went back to swimming way out, alone. Much later, a
girl was half an hour late getting ready and he never
spoke to her again.

Thinking all this, remembering all this, his mother
looked at him now.

"Don't stand there," she said. "You make me
nervous."

"Well," he said, resentfully.

"Go on!" she cried. But she didn't cry it strong
enough. Even to herself her voice sounded faint. And
she did not know if her voice was just naturally faint or
if she made it that way. She might as well have been
talking about winter coming; everything she said had a
lonely sound. And she heard the words again from her
own mouth, with no force: "Go on!"

He went into the kitchen. "I guess there'll be enough
guys there," he said.

"Sure, there will," she said, smiling again. She always
smiled again. Sometimes when she talked to him, night
after night, she looked as if she were lifting weights, too.
When he walked through the rooms she looked like she
was doing the walking for him. And when he sat brooding, as he often did, she looked around for something
to do which might be burn the toast or overfire the
steak. She made a short barking faint and stifled laugh
now, "Get out, have a good time." But the echoes of it

moved around in the house as if it were already empty
and cold and he should come back in the door. Her lips
moved: "Fly away."

He snatched up the cider and the pumpkins and hurried them out to his car. It was a new car and had been
new and unused for almost a year. He polished it and
jiggered with the motor or lay underneath it for hours
messing with all the junk there, or just sat in the front
seat glancing over the strength and health magazines,
but rarely drove it. He put the cider and the cut pumpkins proudly in on the front seat, and by this time he
was thinking of the possible good time tonight, so he did
a little child's stagger as if he might drop everything,
and his mother laughed. He licked his lollipop again,
jumped into the car, backed it out of the gravel driveway, swerved it around down by the ocean, not looking
out at this woman, and drove off along the shore road.
She stood in the yard watching the car go away. William,
my son, she thought.

It was seven-fifteen and very dark now; already the
children were fluttering along the sidewalks in white
ghost sheets and zinc-oxide masks, ringing bells, screaming, lumpy paper sacks banging their knees as they ran.

William, she thought.

They didn't call him William, they called him Heavy
Set and Sammy which was short for Samson. They called
him Butch and they called him Atlas and Hercules. At
the beach you always saw the high school boys around
him feeling his biceps as if he were a new sports car,
testing him, admiring him. He walked golden among
them. Each year it was that way. And then the eighteen-
year-old ones got to be nineteen and didn't come around
so often and then twenty and very rarely and then
twenty-one and never again, just gone, and suddenly
there were new eighteen-year-olds to replace them, yes,
always the new ones to stand where the others had stood
in the sun, while the older ones went on somewhere to
something and somebody else.

William, my good boy, she thought. We go to shows
on Saturday nights. He works on the high-power lines
all day, up in the sky, alone, and sleeps alone in his

room at night, and never reads a book or a paper or listens to a radio or plays a record, and this year he'll be thirty-one. And just where, in all the years, did the thing happen that put him up that pole alone and working out alone every night? Certainly there had been enough women, here and there, now and then, through his life. Little scrubby ones, of course, fools, yes, by the look of them, but women, or girls, rather, and none worth glancing at a second time. Still, when a boy gets past thirty ... ? She sighed. Why, even as recently as last night the phone had rung. Heavy Set had answered it, and she could fill in the unheard half of the conversation; she had heard thousands like it in a dozen years:

"Sammy, this is Christine." A woman's voice. "What you doing?"

His little golden eyelashes flickered and his brow furrowed, alert and wary. "Why?"

"Tom, Lu, and I are going to a show, want to come along?"

"It better be good!" he cried, indignantly.

She named it.

"That!" he snorted.

"It's a good film," she said.

"Not that one," he said. "Besides, I haven't shaved yet today."

"You can shave in five minutes."

"I need a bath, and it'd take a long time."

A long time, thought his mother, he was in the bathroom two hours today. He combs his hair two dozen times, musses it, combs it again, talking to himself.

"OK for you." The woman's voice on the phone. "You going to the beach this week?"

"Saturday," he said, before he thought.

"See you there, then," she said.

"I meant Sunday," he said, quickly.

"I could change it to Sunday," she replied.

"If I can make it," he said, even more quickly. "Things go wrong with my car."

"Sure," she said. "Samson. Solong."

And he had stood there for a long time, turning the silent phone in his hand.

Well, his mother thought, he's having a good time now. A good Halloween party, with all the apples he took along, tied on strings, and the apples, untied, to bob for in a tub of water, and the boxes of candy, the sweet corn kernels that really taste like autumn. He's running around looking like the bad little boy, she thought, licking his lollipop, everyone shouting, blowing horns, laughing, dancing.

At eight, and again at eight-thirty and nine she went to the screen door and looked out and could almost hear the party a long way off at the dark beach, the sounds of it blowing on the wind crisp and furious and wild, and wished she could be there at the little shack out over the waves on the pier, everyone whirling about in costumes, and all the pumpkins cut, each a different way, and a contest for the best homemade mask or makeup job, and too much popcorn to eat and—

She held to the screen doorknob, her face pink and excited, and suddenly realized the children had stopped coming to beg at the door. Halloween, for the neighborhood kids anyway, was over.

She went to look out into the backyard.

The house and yard were too quiet. It was strange not hearing the basketball volley on the gravel or the steady bumble of the punching bag taking a beating. Or the little tweezing sound of the hand squeezers.

What if, she thought, he found someone tonight, found someone down there, and just never came back, never came home. No telephone call. No letter, that was the way it could be. No word. Just go off away and never come back again. What if? What if?

No! she thought, there's no one, no one there, no one anywhere. There's just this place. This is the only place.

But her heart was beating fast and she had to sit down.

The wind blew softly from the shore.

She turned on the radio but could not hear it.

Now, she thought, they're not doing anything except playing blindman's buff, yes, that's it, blind tag, and after that they'll just be—

She gasped and jumped.

The windows had exploded with raw light.

The gravel spurted in a machine-gun spray as the car jolted in, braked and stopped, motor gunning. The lights went off in the yard. But the motor still gunned up, idled, gunned up, idled.

She could see the dark figure in the front seat of the car, not moving, staring straight ahead.

"You—" she started to say, and opened the back screen door. She found a smile on her mouth. She stopped it. Her heart was slowing now. She made herself frown.

He shut off the motor. She waited. He climbed out of the car and threw the pumpkins in the garbage can and slammed the lid.

"What happened?" she asked. "Why are you home so early—?"

"Nothing." He brushed by her with the two gallons of cider intact. He set them on the kitchen sink.

"But it's not ten yet—"

"That's right." He went into the bedroom and sat down in the dark.

She waited five minutes. She always waited five minutes. He wanted her to come ask, he'd be mad if she didn't, so finally she went and looked into the dark bedroom.

"Tell me," she said.

"Oh, they all stood around," he said. "They just stood around like a bunch of fools and didn't do anything."

"What a shame."

"They just stood around like dumb fools."

"Oh, that's a shame."

"I tried to get them to do something, but they just stood around. Only eight of them showed up, eight out of twenty, eight, and me the only one in costume. I tell you. The only one. What a bunch of fools."

"After all your trouble, too."

"They had their girls and they just stood around with them and wouldn't do anything, no games, nothing. Some of them went off with the girls," he said, in the dark, seated, not looking at her. "They went off up the beach and didn't come back. Honest to gosh." He stood

now, huge, and leaned against the wall, looking all dis-
proportioned in the short trousers. He had forgotten the
child's hat was on his head. He suddenly remembered it
and took it off and threw it on the floor. "I tried to kid
them. I played with a toy dog and did some other stuff,
but nobody did anything. I felt like a fool, the only one
there dressed like this, and them all different, and only
eight out of twenty there, and most of them gone in half
an hour. Vi was there. She tried to get me to walk up
the beach, too. I was mad by then. I was really mad. I
said no thanks. And here I am. You can have the lollipop. Where did I put it? Pour the cider down the sink,
drink it, I don't care."

She had not moved so much as an inch in all the time
he talked. She opened her mouth.

The telephone rang.

"If that's them, I'm not home."

"You'd better answer it," she said.

He grabbed the phone and whipped off the receiver.

"Sammy?" said a loud high clear voice. He was holding the receiver out on the air, glaring at it in the dark.
"That you?" He grunted. "This is Bob." The eighteen-
year-old voice rushed on. "Glad you're home. In a big
rush, but—what about that game tomorrow?"

"What game?"

"What game? For cri-yi, you're kidding. Notre Dame
and SC!"

"Oh, football."

"Don't say Oh Football like that, you talked it, you
played it up, *you* said—"

"That's no game," he said, not looking at the telephone, the receiver, the woman, the wall, nothing.

"You mean you're not going? Heavy Set, it won't be
a *game* without you!"

"I got to water the lawn, polish the car—"

"You can do that Sunday!"

"Besides, I think my uncle's coming over to see me.
Solong."

He hung up and walked out past his mother into the
yard. She heard the sounds of him out there as she got
ready for bed.

He must have drubbed the punching bag until three in the morning. Three, she thought, wide awake, listening to the concussions. He's always stopped at twelve, before.

At three-thirty he came into the house.

She heard him standing just outside her door.

He did nothing else except stand there in the dark, breathing.

She had a feeling he still had the little-boy suit on. But she didn't want to know if this were true.

After a long while the door swung slowly open.

He came into her dark room and lay down on the bed, next to her, not touching her. She pretended to be asleep.

He lay face up and rigid.

She could not see him. But she felt the bed shake as if he were laughing. She could hear no sound coming from him, so she could not be sure.

And then she heard the squeaking sounds of the little steel springs being crushed and uncrushed, crushed and uncrushed in his fists.

She wanted to sit up and scream for him to throw those awful noisy things away. She wanted to slap them out of his fingers.

But then, she thought, what would he do with his hands? What could he put in them? What would he, yes, what would he do with his hands?

So she did the only thing she could do—she held her breath, shut her eyes, listened, and prayed, Oh God, let it go on, let him keep squeezing those things, let him keep squeezing those things, let him, let him, oh let, let him, let him keep squeezing ... let ... let ...

It was like lying in bed with a great dark cricket.

And a long time before dawn.

MR. WRONG

ELIZABETH JANE HOWARD

"If any spasm about what had recently happened attempted to invade her essential blankness, she concentrated upon seeing her mother's face, smelling the dinner in the kitchen, and hearing her father call out who was there."

It is the quiet accumulation of horrific effect in this story by English writer Elizabeth Jane Howard that makes it extremely hard to forget once the last page is turned. However, as a literary figure, she is better known for her elegantly ironic novels than for tales of sinister fate like the one you're about to read. Yet, in fact, she first published in the field of horror back in 1951, when she and a friend, Robert Aickman, then at the beginning of his own career in the genre, joined forces to produce the collection We Are for the Dark.

Meg, the virginal protagonist of "Mr. Wrong," is struggling to do what everyone, particularly her parents, expects of her. But in ways she can never quite manage to control, her eagerness to please continually works against her. Unfortunately, by the time she has learned even a little how better to assert herself, it is too late. As a study in automotive awfulness, "Mr. Wrong," by the way, predates Stephen King's Christine *by a decade.*

Everybody—that is to say the two or three people she knew in London—told Meg that she had been very lucky indeed to find a car barely three years old, in such good condition and at such a price. She believed them gladly, because actually buying the car had been the most nerve-racking experience. Of course she had been told—and many times by her father—that all car dealers were liars and thieves. Indeed, to listen to old Dr. Crosbie, you would think that nobody could *ever* buy a second-hand car, possibly even any *new* car, without its brakes or steering giving way the moment you were out of sight of the garage. But her father had always been of a nervous disposition: and as he intensely disliked going anywhere, and had now reached an age where he could fully indulge this disapprobation, it was not necessary to take much notice of him. For at least fifteen of her twenty-seven years Meg silently put up with his saying that there was no place like home, until, certain that she had exhausted all the possibilities of the small market town near where they lived, she had exclaimed, "That's just it, Father! That's why I want to see somewhere else— *not* like it."

Her mother, who had all the prosaic anxiety about her only child finding "a really nice young man, Mr. Right" that kind, anxious mothers tend to have—especially if their daughter can be admitted in the small hours to be "not exactly a beauty"—smiled encouragingly at Meg and said, "But, Humphrey, dear, she will always be coming back to stay. She *knows* this is her home, but all young girls need a change." (The young part of this had become emphasized as Meg plodded steadily through her twenties with not a romance in sight.)

So Meg had come to London, got a job in an antique shop in the New King's Road, and shared a two-room flat with two other girls in Fulham. One of them was a secretary, and the other a model: both were younger than Meg and ten times as self-assured; kind to her in an offhand manner, but never becoming friends, nothing more than people she knew—like Mr. Whitehorn, who ran the shop that she worked in. It was her mother who had given Meg three hundred pounds toward a car, as the train fares and subsequent taxis were proving beyond her means. She spent very little in London: she had bought one dress at Laura Ashley, but had no parties to go to in it, and lacked the insouciance to wear it to work. She lived off eggs done in various ways, and quantities of instant coffee—in the shop and in the flat. Her rent was comfortingly modest by present-day standards, she walked to work, smoked very occasionally, and set her own hair. Her father had given her a hundred pounds when she was twenty-one: all of this had been invested, and to it she now added savings from her meager salary and finally went off to one of London's northern suburbs to answer an advertisement about a secondhand MG.

The car dealer, whom she had imagined as some kind of tiger in a loud checked suit with whiskey on his breath, had proved to be more of a wolf in a sheepskin car coat—particularly when he smiled, which displayed a frightening number of teeth that seemed to stretch back in his raspberry mouth and down his throat with vulpine largesse. He smiled often, and Meg took to not looking at him whenever he began to do it. He took her out on a test drive: at first he drove, explaining all the advantages of the car while he did so, and then he suggested that she take over. This she did, driving very badly, with clashing of gears and stalling the engine in the most embarrassing places. "I can see you've got the hang of it," Mr. Taunton said. "It's always difficult driving a completely new car. But you'll find that she's most reliable: will start in all weather, economical on fuel, and needs the minimum of servicing."

When Meg asked whether the car had ever had an accident, he began to smile, so she did not see his face when he replied that it hadn't been an accident, just a slight brush. "The respray, which I expect you've noticed, was largely because the panel work involved, and mind you, it *was* only panel work, made us feel that it could do with a more cheerful color. I always think aqua-blue is a nice color for a ladies' car. And this is definitely a ladies' car."

She felt his smile receding when she asked how many previous owners the car had had. He replied that it had been for a short time the property of some small firm that had since gone out of business. "Only driven by one of the directors and his secretary."

That sounded all right, thought Meg: but she was also thinking that for the price this was easily the best car she could hope for, and somehow, she felt, he knew that she knew she was going to buy it. His last words were "I hope you have many miles of motoring before you, madam." The elongated grin began, and as it was for the last time, she watched him—trying to smile back— as the pointed teeth became steadily more exposed down his cavernous throat. She noticed then that his pale gray eyes very nearly met, but were narrowly saved from this by the bridge of his nose, which was long and thrusting, and almost made up for his having a mouth that had clearly been eaten away by his awful quantity of teeth. They had nothing going for each other beyond her buying and his selling a car.

Back in the showroom office, he sank into his huge moquette chair and said, "Bring us a coffee, duck. I've earned it." And a moony-faced blonde in a miniskirt with huge legs that seemed tortured by her tights smiled and went.

Meg drove the MG—her *car*—back to London in the first state of elation she had ever known since she had won the bending competition in a local gymkhana. She had a car! Neither Samantha nor Val were in such a position. She really drove quite well, as she had had a temporary job working for a doctor near home who had lost his license for two years. Away from Mr. Taunton (*Clive* Taunton he had repeatedly said), she felt able and assured. The car was easy to drive, and responded, as MGs do, with a kind of husky excitement to speed.

When she reached the flat, Samantha and Val were so impressed that they actually took her out to a Chinese meal with their two boyfriends. Meg got into her Laura Ashley dress and enjoyed every sweet and sour moment of it. Everybody was impressed by her, and this made her prettier. She got slightly drunk on rice wine and lager and went to work the next day, in her car, feeling much more like the sort of person she had expected to feel like in London. Her head ached, but she had something to show for it: one of the men had talked to her several times—asking where she lived and what her job was, and so forth.

Her first drive north was the following Friday. It was cold, a wet and dark night—in January she never finished at the shop in time even to start the journey in the light—and by the time she was out of the rush, through London and on Hendon Way, it was raining hard. She found the turn off to the M1 with no difficulty: only three hours of driving on that and then about twenty minutes home. It was nothing, really; it just seemed rather a long way at this point. She had drunk a cup of strong black instant at Mr. Whitehorn's, who had kindly admired the car and also showed her the perfect place to park it every day, and she knew that her mother would be keeping something hot and home-made for her whatever time she got home. (Her father never ate anything after eight o'clock in the evening for fear of indigestion, something from which he had never in his life suffered and attributed entirely to this precaution.)

Traffic was fairly heavy, but it seemed to be more lorries than anything else, and Meg kept on the whole to the middle lane. She soon found, as motorists new to a motorway do, that the lanes, the headlights coming toward her, and the road glistening with rain had a hypnotic effect, as though she and the car had become minute, and she were being spun down some enormous, endless striped ribbon. "I mustn't go to sleep," she thought. Ordinary roads had too much going on in them for one to feel like that. About half her time up the motorway, she felt so tired with trying not to feel sleepy that she decided to stop in the next park, open the windows, and have a cigarette. It was too wet to get out, but even stopping the windscreen wipers for a few minutes would make a change. She stopped the engine, opened her window, and before she had time to think about smoking again, fell asleep.

She awoke very suddenly with a feeling of extreme fear. It was not from a dream; she was sitting in the driver's seat, cramped, and with rain blowing in through the open window, but something else was very wrong. A sound—or noises, alarming in themselves, but, in her circumstances, frighteningly out of place. She shut her window except for an inch at the top. This made things worse. What sounded like heavy, labored, stertorous, even painful breathing was coming, she quickly realized, from the *back* of the car. The moment she switched on the car light and turned round, there was utter silence, as sudden as the noise stopping in the middle of a breath. There was nobody in the back of the car, but the doors were not locked, and her large carrier bag— her luggage—had fallen to the floor. She locked both doors, switched off the car light, and the sounds began again, exactly where they had left off—in the middle of a breath. She put both the car light and her headlights on, and looked again in the back. Silence, and it was still empty. She considered making sure that there was nobody parked behind her, but somehow she didn't want to do that. She switched on the engine and started it. Her main feeling was to get away from the place as quickly as possible. But even when she had started to do this and found herself trying to turn the sounds she had heard into something else and accountable, they wouldn't. They remained in her mind, and she could all too clearly recall them, as the heavy breaths of someone either mortally ill, or in pain, or both, coming quite distinctly from the back of the car. She drove home as fast as she could, counting the minutes and the miles to keep her mind quiet.

She reached home—a stone and slate-roofed cottage—at a quarter past nine, and her mother's first exclamation when she saw her daughter was that she looked dreadfully tired. Instantly, Meg began to feel better; it was what her mother had always said if Meg ever did anything for very long away from home. Her father had gone to bed: so she sat eating her supper with surprising hunger, in the kitchen, and telling her mother the week's news about her job and the two girls she shared with and the Chinese-meal party. "And is the car nice, darling?" her mother asked at length. Meg started to speak, checked herself, and began again. "Very nice. It was so kind of you to give me all that money for it," she said.

The weekend passed with almost comforting dullness, and Meg did not begin to dread returning until after lunch on Sunday. She began to say that she ought to pack; her mother said she must have tea before she left, and her father said that he didn't think that *anyone* should drive in the dark. Or, indeed, at all, he overrode them as they both started saying that it was dark by four anyway. Meg eventually decided to have a short sleep after lunch, drink a cup of tea, and then start the journey. "If I eat one of Mummy's teas, I'll pass out in the car," she said, and as she said "pass out," she felt an instant, very small ripple of fear.

Her mother woke her from a dreamless, refreshing sleep at four with a cup of dark, strong Indian tea and two Bourbon biscuits.

"I'm going to pack for you," she said firmly. She had also unpacked, while Meg was finishing her supper on Friday night. "I've never known such a hopeless packer. All your clothes were cramped up and crushed together as though someone had been stamping on them. Carrier bags," she scolded, enjoying every minute; "I'm lending you this nice little case that Auntie Phil left me."

Meg lay warmly under the eiderdown in her own room watching her mother, who quite quickly switched from packing to why didn't Meg drink her tea while it was hot. "I know your father won't drink anything until it's lukewarm, but thank goodness, you don't take after him. In that respect," she ended loyally, but Meg knew that her mother missed her, and got tired and bored dealing with her father's ever-increasing regime of what was good or bad for him.

"Can I come next weekend?" she asked. Her mother rushed across the room and enfolded her.

"I should be most upset if you didn't," she said, trying to make it sound like a joke.

When Meg left, and not until she was out of sight of home, she began to worry about what had happened on the journey up. Perhaps it could have been some kind of freak wind, with the car window open, she thought. Being able even to think that encouraged her. It was only raining in fits and starts on the way back, and the journey passed without incident of any kind. By the time Meg had parked, and slipped quietly into the flat that turned out to be empty—both girls were out—she really began to imagine that she had imagined it. She ate a boiled egg, watched a short feature on Samantha's television about Martinique, and went to bed.

The following weekend was also wet, but foggy as well. At one moment during a tedious day in the shop (where there was either absolutely nothing to do, or an endless chore, like packing china and glass to go abroad), Meg thought of putting off going to her parents but they were not on the telephone, and that meant that they would have to endure a telegram. She thought of her father, and decided against that. He would talk about it for six months, stressing it as an instance of youthful extravagance, reiterating the war that it had made upon his nerves, and the proof it was that she should never have gone to London at all. No—telegrams were out, except in an emergency. She would just have to go—whatever the weather, or anything else.

Friday passed tediously: her job was that of packing up the separate pieces of a pair of giant chandeliers in pieces of old newspaper and listing what she packed. Sometimes she got so bored by this that she even read bits from the old, yellowing newsprint. There were pages in one paper of pictures of a Miss World competition: every girl was in a bathing dress and high-heeled shoes, smiling that extraordinary smile of glazed triumph. They must have an awfully difficult time, Meg thought, fighting off admirers. She wondered just how difficult that would turn out to be. It would probably get easier with practice.

At half past four, Mr. Whitehorn let her go early: he was the kind of man who operated in bursts of absent-minded kindness, and he said that in view of her journey, the sooner she started the better. Meg drank her last cup of instant coffee, and set off.

Her progress through London was slow, but eventually she reached Hendon Way. Here, too, there were long holdups as cars queued at signal lights. There were also straggling lines of people trying to get lifts. She drove past a good many of these, feeling her familiar feelings about them, so mixed that they canceled one another out, and she never, in fact, did anything about the hitchers. Meg was naturally a kind person: this part of her made her feel sorry for the wretched creatures, cold, wet, and probably tired; wondering whether they would *ever* get to where they wanted to be. But her father had always told her never to give lifts, hinting darkly at the gothic horrors that lay in wait for anyone who ever did that. It was not that Meg ever consciously agreed with her father; rather that in all the years of varying warnings, some of his anxiety had brushed off on her—making her shy, unsure of what to do about things, and feeling ashamed of feeling like that. No, she was certainly not going to give anyone a lift.

She drove steadily on through the driving sleet, pretending that the back of her car was full of pieces of priceless chandeliers, and this served her very well until she came to the inevitable hold-up before she reached Hendon, when a strange thing happened.

After moving a few yards forward between each set of green lights, she finally found herself just having missed yet another lot, but head of the queue in the right-hand lane. There, standing under one of the tall, yellow lights, on an island in the steaming rain, was a girl. There was nothing in the least remarkable about her appearance at first glance: she was short, rather dumpy, wearing what looked like a very thin mackintosh and unsuitable shoes; her head was bare; she wore glasses. She looked wet through, cold and exhausted, but above all there was an air of extreme desolation about her, as though she was hopelessly lost and solitary. Meg found, without having thought at all about it, that she was opening her window and beckoning the girl toward the car. The girl responded—she was only a few yards away—

and as she came nearer, Meg noticed two other things about her. The first was that she was astonishingly pale—despite the fact that she had dark, reddish hair and was obviously frozen: her face was actually livid, and when she extended a tentative hand in a gesture that was either seeking reassurance about help, or anticipating the opening of the car door, the collar of her mackintosh moved, and Meg saw that, at the bottom of her white throat, the girl had what looked like the most unfortunate purple birthmark.

"Please get in," Meg said, and leaned over to open the seat beside her. Then two things happened at once. The girl simply got into the back of the car—Meg heard her open the door and shut it gently, and a man, wearing a large, check overcoat, tinted glasses, and a soft black hat tilted over his forehead slid into the seat beside her.

"How kind," he said, in a reedy, pedagogic voice (almost as though he was practicing to be someone else, Meg thought); "we were wondering whether anyone at all would come to our aid, and it proves that charming young women like yourself behave as they appear. The good Samaritan is invariably feminine these days."

Meg, who had taken the most instant dislike to him of anyone she had ever met in life, said nothing at all. Then, beginning to feel bad about this, at least from the silent girl's point of view, she asked, "How far are you going?"

"Ah, now that will surprise you. My secretary and I broke down this morning on our way up, or down to Town," he sniggered, "and it is imperative that we present ourselves in the right place at the right time this evening. I only wish to go so far as to pick up our car, which should now be ready." His breath smelled horribly of stale smoke and peppermints.

"At a garage?" The whole thing sounded to Meg like the most preposterous story.

"Between Northampton and Leicester. I shall easily be able to point the turning out to you."

Again, Meg said nothing, hoping that this would put a stop to his irritating voice. "What a bore," she thought: "I *would* be lumbered with this lot." She began to consider the social hazards of giving people lifts. Either they sat in total silence—like the girl in the back—or they talked. At this point he began again.

"It is most courageous of you to have stopped. There are so many hooligans about, that I always say it is most unjust to the older and more respectable people. But it is true that an old friend of mine once gave a lift to a *young man,* and the next thing she knew, the poor dear was in a ditch; no car, a dreadful headache, and no idea where she was. It's perfectly ghastly what some people will do to some people. Have you noticed it? But I imagine you are too young: you are probably in search of *adventure—romance*—or whatever lies behind those euphemisms. Am I right?"

Meg, feeling desperately that *anything* would be better than this talking all the time, said over her shoulder to her obstinately silent passenger in the back: "Are you warm enough?"

But before anyone else could have said anything, the horrible man said at once, "Perfectly, thank you. Physically speaking, I am not subject to great sensitivity about temperature." When he turned to her, as he always seemed to do, at the end of any passage or remark, the smell of his breath seemed to fill the car. It was not simply smoke and peppermints—underneath that was a smell like rotting mushrooms. "She must be asleep," Meg thought, almost resentfully—after all there was no escape for *her*—she could not sleep, was forced to drive and drive and listen to this revolting front-seat passenger.

"Plastic," he continued, ruminatively (as though she had even *mentioned* the stuff), "the only real use that plastic has been to society was when the remains, but unmistakable—unlike the unfortunate lady—when the remains of Mrs. Durand Deacon's red plastic handbag were discovered in the tank full of acid. Poor Haigh must have thought he was perfectly safe with acid, but of course, he had not reckoned on the durable properties of some plastics. That was the end of *him.* Are you familiar with the case at all?"

"I'm not very interested in murder, I'm afraid."

"Ah—but fear and murder go hand in hand," he said at once, and, she felt, deliberately misunderstanding her. She had made the mistake of apologizing for her lack of interest—

". . . in fact, it would be difficult to think of any murder where there had not been a modicum, and sometimes, let's face it, a very great deal of fear." Glancing at him, she saw that his face, an unhealthy color, or perhaps that was the headlights of oncoming cars, was sweating. It could not still be rain: the car heater was on: it was sweat.

She stuck it out until they were well on the way up the M1. His conversation was both nasty and repetitive, or rather, given that he was determined to talk about fear and murder, he displayed a startling knowledge of different and horrible cases. Eventually, he asked suddenly whether she would stop for him, "a need of nature," he was sure she would understand what he meant. Just there a lorry was parked on the shoulder, and he protested that he would rather go on—he was easily embarrassed and preferred complete privacy. Grimly, Meg parked.

"That will do perfectly well," she said as firmly as she could, but her voice came out trembling with strain.

The man slid out of the car with the same reptilian action she had noticed when he got in. He did not reply. The moment that he was out, Meg said to the girl: "Look here, if he's hitching lifts with you, I do think you might help a bit with the conversation."

There was no reply. Meg, turning to the back, began almost angrily: "I don't care if you are asleep—" but then she had to stop because a small scream seemed to have risen in her throat to check her.

The back seat was empty.

Meg immediately looked to see whether the girl could have fallen off the back seat onto the floor. She hadn't. Meg switched on the car light; the empty black mock-leather seat glistened with emptiness. For a split second, Meg thought she might be going mad. Her first sight of the girl, standing under a lamp on the island at Hendon, recurred sharply. The pale, thin mac, the pallor, the feeling that she was so desolate that Meg had *had* to stop for her. But she had *got into* the car—of course she had! Then she must have got out, when the man got out. But he hadn't shut his door, and there had been no noise from the back. She looked at the back doors. They were both unlocked. She put out her hand to touch the seat: it was perfectly dry, and that poor girl had been so soaked when she had got in—*had got in*—she was certain of it, that if she had *just* got out, the seat would have been at least damp. Meg could hear her heart thudding now, and for a moment, until he returned, she was almost glad that even that man was some sort of company in this situation.

He seemed to take his time about getting back into the car: she saw him—as she put it—slithering out of the dark toward her, but then he seemed to hesitate; he disappeared from sight, and it was only when she saw him by the light of her right-hand side light that she realized he had been walking round the car. *Strolling* about, as though she were simply a chauffeur to him! She called through the window to him to hurry up, and almost before he had got into the car, she said, "What on earth's become of your secretary?"

There was a slight pause, then he turned to her: "My secretary?" His face was impassive to the point of offensiveness, but she noticed that he was sweating again.

"You know," she said impatiently; she had started the engine and was pulling away from the shoulder: "The girl you said you'd had a breakdown with on your way to London."

"Ah yes: poor little Muriel. I had quite forgotten her. I imagine her stuffing herself with family high tea and, I don't doubt, boyfriend—some provincial hairdresser who looks like a pop star, or perhaps some footballer who looks like a hairdresser."

"What *do* you mean?"

He sniggered. "I am not given to oversight into the affairs of any employee I may indulge in. I do not like prolonged relationships of any kind. I like them sudden—short—and sweet. In fact, I—"

"No—*listen*! You know perfectly well what I'm talking about."

She felt him stiffen, become still with wariness. Then, quite unexpectedly, he asked, "How long have you had this car?"

"Oh—a week or so. Don't make things up about your secretary. It was her I really stopped for. I didn't even see you."

It must be his sweat that was making the car smell so much worse. "Of course. I noticed at once that it was an MG," he said.

"The girl in the back," Meg said desperately: he seemed to be deliberately stupid as well as nasty. "She was standing on the island, under a lamp. She wore a mac, but she was obviously soaked to the skin, I beckoned to her, and she came up and got into the back without a word. At the same time as you. So come off it, inventing nasty, sneering lies about your secretary. Don't pretend *you* didn't know she was there. You probably used her as a decoy—to get a lift at all."

There was a short, very unpleasant silence. Meg was just beginning to be frightened, when he said, "What did your friend look like?"

It was no use quibbling with him about not being the girl's friend. Meg said, "I told you ..." and instantly realized that she had done nothing of the kind. Perhaps the girl really hadn't been his secretary ...

"All you have done is allege that you picked up my secretary with me."

"All right. Well, she was short—she wore a pale mac—I told you that—and, and glasses—her hair was a dark reddish color—I suppose darker because she was wet through, and she had some silly shoes on and she looked *ill*, she was so white—a sort of livid white, and when she—"

"Never heard of her—never heard of anyone like her."

"No, but you *saw* her, didn't you? I'm sorry if I thought she was your secretary—the point is you saw her, didn't you? *Didn't* you?"

He began fumbling in his overcoat pocket, from which

he eventually drew out a battered packet of sweets, the kind where each sweet is separately wrapped. He was so long getting a sweet out of the packet and then starting to peel off the sticky paper that she couldn't wait.

"Another thing. When she put out her arm to open the door, I saw her throat—"

His fingers stopped unwrapping the paper. She glanced at them: he had huge, ugly hands that looked the wrong scale beside the small sweet—

"She had a large sort of birthmark at the bottom of her throat, poor thing."

He dropped the sweet: bent forward in the car to find it. When, at last, he had done so, he put it straight into his mouth without attempting to get any more paper off. Briefly, the smell of peppermint dominated the other, less pleasant odors. Meg said, "Of course, I don't suppose for a moment you could have seen *that.*"

Finally, he said, "I cannot imagine who, or what, you are talking about. I didn't see any *girl* in the back of *your* car."

"But there couldn't be someone in the back of my car without my knowing!"

There seemed to Meg to be something wrong about his behavior. Not just that it was unpleasant; wrong in a different way; she felt that he knew perfectly well about the girl, but wouldn't admit it—to frighten her, she supposed.

"Do you mind if I smoke?"

He seemed to be very bad at lighting it. Two matches wavered out in his shaky hands before he got an evil-smelling fag going.

Meg, because she still felt a mixture of terror and confusion about what had or had not happened, decided to try being very reasonable with him.

"When you got into the car," she began carefully, "you kept saying 'we' and talking about your secretary. *That's* why I thought she must be."

"Must be what?"

A mechanical response; sort of playing-for-time stuff, Meg thought.

"You must excuse me, but I really don't know what you are talking about."

"Well, I think you *do*. And before you can say 'do what?' I mean *do* know what you are talking about."

She felt rather than saw him glance sharply at her, but she kept her eyes on the road.

Then he seemed to make up his mind. "I have a suggestion to make. Supposing we stop at the next service area and you tell me all about everything? You have clearly got a great deal on your mind; in fact, you show distinct symptoms of being upset. Perhaps if we—"

"No thank you." The idea of his being the slightest use to talk to was both nauseating and absurd. She heard him suck in his breath through his teeth with a small hissing sound: once more she found him reminding her of a snake. Meg hated snakes.

Then he began to fumble about again, to produce a torch and to ask for a map. After some ruminating aloud as to where they were, and indeed where his garage was likely to be, he suggested stopping again "to give my, I fear, sadly weakened eyes an opportunity to discover my garage."

Something woke up in Meg, an early warning or premonition of more, and different, trouble. Garages were not marked on her map. She increased their speed, stayed in the middle lane until a service station that she had noticed marked earlier at half a mile away loomed and glittered in the wet darkness. She drove straight in and said:

"I don't like you very much. I'd rather you got out now." Again she heard him suck his breath in through his teeth. The attendant had seen the car, and was slowly getting into his anorak to come out to them.

"How cruel!" he said, but she sensed his anger. "What a pity! What a chance lost!"

"Please get out at once, or I'll get the man to turn you out."

With his usual agility, he opened the door at once, and slithered out.

"I'm sorry," Meg said weakly, "I'm sure you did know about the girl. I just don't trust you."

He poked his head in through the window. "I'm far from sure that *I* trust *you*." There were little bits of scum at the ends of his mouth. "I really feel that you oughtn't to drive alone if you are subject to such extreme hallucinations."

There was no mistaking the malice in his voice, and just as Meg was going to have one last go at his admitting that he *had* seen the girl, the petrol attendant finally reached her and began unscrewing her petrol cap. He went, then. Simply withdrew his head, as though there were not more of him than that, and disappeared.

"How many?"

"Just two, please."

When the man went off slowly to get change, Meg wanted to cry. Instead, she locked all the doors and wound up the passenger window. She had an unreasonable fear that he would come back and that the attendant might not help her to oust him. She even forgot the change, and wound up her own window, so that nobody could get into the car. This made the attendant tap on her window; she started violently, which set her shivering.

"Did you—did you see where the man who was in the front of my car went? He got out just now."

"I didn't see anyone. Anyone at all."

"Oh, thank you."

"Night." He went thankfully back to his brightly lit and doubtless scorching booth.

Before she drove off, Meg looked once more at the back seat. There was no one there. The whole experience had been so prolonged, as well as unnerving, that apart from feeling frightened she felt confused. She wanted badly to get away as fast as possible, and she wanted to keep quite still and try to sort things out. He *had* known that the girl had been in the car. He had enjoyed—her fear. Why else would he have said "we" so much? This made her more frightened, and her mind suddenly changed sides.

The girl *could not* have got out of the back without opening and shutting—however quietly—the door. There had been no sound or sounds like that. In fact, from the moment the girl had got into the car she had made no sound at all. Perhaps she, too, had been frightened by the horrible man. Perhaps she had *pretended* to get in, and at the last moment slipped out again.

She opened her window wide to get rid of the smells in the car. As she did so, a possible implication of what the petrol attendant had said occurred. He hadn't seen *anyone;* he hadn't emphasized it like that, but he had repeated "anyone at all." Had he just meant that he hadn't looked? Or had he looked, and seen nobody? Ghosts don't talk, she reminded herself, and at once was back to the utterly silent girl.

Her first journey north in the car, and the awful breathing sounds coming from its back, could no longer be pushed out of her mind. The moment that she realized this, both journeys pounced forward into incomprehensible close-ups of disconnected pictures and sounds, recurring more and more rapidly, but in different sequences, as though, through their speed and volume, they were trying to force her to understand them. In the end, she actually cried out, "All *right*! The car is haunted. Of course, I see that!"

A sudden calm descended upon her, and in order to further it, or at least stop it as suddenly stopping, she added: "I'll think about it when I get home," and drove mindlessly the rest of the way. If any spasm about what had recently happened attempted to invade her essential blankness, she concentrated upon seeing her mother's face, smelling the dinner in the kitchen, and hearing her father call out who was there.

". . . thought he might be getting a severe cold, so he's off to bed. He's had his arrowroot with a spot of whiskey in it and asked us to be extra quiet in *case* he gets a wink of sleep."

Meg hugged her without replying: it was no good trying to be conspiratorial with her mother about her father; there could never be a wink or a smile. Her mother's loyalty had stiffened over the years, until now she could relate the most absurd details of her father's imaginary fears and ailments with a good-natured but completely impassive air. "Have we got anything to drink?" she asked.

"Darling—I'm sure we have somewhere. But it's so unlike you to want a drink that I didn't put it out. It'll be in the corner cupboard in the sitting room."

Meg knew this, knew also that she could find the untouched half bottles of gin and Bristol Milk that were kept in case anyone "popped in." But the very few people who did always came for cups of tea or coffee at the appropriate times of day. Her parents could not really afford drink—except for her father's medicinal whiskey.

When she brought the bottles into the kitchen, she said, "You have one too. I shall feel depraved drinking all by myself."

"Well, dear, then I'll be depraved with you. Just a drop of sherry. We needn't tell Father. It might start him worrying about your London life. Been meeting anyone interesting lately?"

Meg had offered her mother a cigarette with her sherry, and her mother, delighted, had nearly burned her wispy fringe bending over the match to light it, and was now blowing out frantic streams of smoke from her nose before it got too far. It was all right to smoke if you didn't inhale. On a social occasion, that was. Like it being all right to drink a glass of sherry at those times.

"This *is* nice," her mother said, and then added, "Have you been *meeting* anyone nice, dear? At all your parties and things?"

It was then that Meg realized that she could not possibly—ever—pour out all her anxieties to her mother. Her mother simply would not be able to understand them. "Not this week," she said. Her mother sighed, but Meg was not meant to hear, and said that she supposed it took time in a place like London to know people.

Meg had a second, strong gin, and then said that she would pay her mother back, but she was tired, and needed a couple of drinks. She also smoked four cigarettes before dinner, and felt so revived that she was able to eat the delicious steak-and-kidney pie followed by baked apples with raisins in them. Her mother had been making Meg Viyella nightgowns with white lace ruffles, and wanted to show them to her. They were brought into the kitchen, which was used for almost everything in winter as it saved fuel. "I've been quite excited about them," her mother said, when she laid out the nightgowns. "Not quite finished, but such fun doing each one in a different color."

She listened avidly when Meg told her things about Mr. Whitehorn and the shop: she even liked being told about the *things* in the shop. She laughed at Meg's descriptions when they were meant to be in the least amusing, and looked extremely earnest and anxious when Meg told her about the fragility and value of the chandeliers. When it was time to go to bed, and she had filled their two hot-water bottles, she accompanied Meg to the door of her bedroom. They kissed, and her mother said, "Bless you, dearie. I don't know what I'd do without you. Although, of course, one of these days I shall have to when Mr. Right comes along."

Meg cleaned her teeth in the ferociously cold bathroom and went back to her—nearly as cold—bedroom. Hot-water bottles were essential: Viyella nightdresses would be an extra comfort. From years of practice, she undressed fast and ingeniously, so that at no time was she ever naked. Whenever her mother mentioned Mr. Right she had a vision of a man with mustaches and wearing a bowler hat mowing a lawn. She said her prayers kneeling beside her high, rather uncomfortable bed, and the hot-water bottle was like a reward.

In the night she awoke once, her body tense and crowded with fears. "I could *sell* the car, and get another," she said, and almost at once relaxed, the fears receded until they fell through some blank slot at the back of her mind and she was again asleep.

This decision, combined with a weekend of comfortingly the same ordered, dull events made her able to set aside, almost to shut up, the things—as she called them—that had happened, or seemed to have happened, in the car. On Sunday morning she found her mother packing the back with some everlasting flowers "for your flat," a huge, dark old tartan car rug "in case you haven't enough on your bed," and a pottery jar full of homemade marmalade "to share with your friends at breakfast."

"There's plenty of room for the things on the floor, as you're so small, really, that you have your driving seat pushed right forward."

When she said good-bye and set off, it was with the expectation of the journey to London being uneventful, and it was.

The trouble, she discovered, after trying in her spare time for a week, was that she *could not* sell the car. She had started with the original dealer who had sold it to her, but he had said, with a bland lack of regret, that he was extremely sorry, but this was not the time of year to sell secondhand cars and that the best he could offer was to take it back for a hundred pounds less than she had paid for it. As this would completely rule out having any other car excepting a smashed-up or clapped-out Mini that would land her with all kinds of garage bills (and, like most car owners, Meg was not mechanically minded), she had to give up that idea from the start.

She advertised in her local newspaper shop (cheap, and it would be easy for people to try out the car) but this only got her one reply: a middle-aged lady with a middle-aged poodle who came round one evening. At first it seemed hopeful; the lady said it was a nice color and looked in good condition, but when she got into the driver's seat with Meg beside her to drive round the block, her dog absolutely refused to get into the back as he was told to do. His owner tried coaxing, and he whimpered and scrabbled out of the still-open door; she tried a very unconvincing authority: "Cherry! Do as you are told at once," and his whimpering turned to a series of squealing yelps. "He *loves* going in cars. I don't know what's come over him!"

Out in the street again, all three of them, he growled and tried to snap at Meg. "I'm sorry, dear, but I can't possibly buy a car that Cherry won't go in. He's all I've got. Naughty Cherry. He's usually such a mild, sweet dog. Don't you dare bite at Mummy's friends."

And that was that. She asked Mr. Whitehorn and her

flatmates, and finally their friends, but nobody seemed to want to buy her car, or even wanted to help her get rid of it. By Friday, Meg was in a panic at the prospect of driving north again in it. She had promised herself that she wasn't going to, and as long as the promise had seemed to hold (surely she could find *someone* who would want it) she had been able not to think about the alternative. By Friday morning she was so terrified that she did actually send a telegram to her mother, saying that she had flu and couldn't drive home.

After she had sent it, she felt guilty and relieved in about equal proportions. The only way she could justify such behavior was to make sure of selling the car that weekend. Samantha told her to put an ad in the *Standard* for the next day. "You're bound to make the last edition anyway," she said. So Meg rang them, having spent an arduous half hour trying to phrase the advertisement. "Pale blue MG—" was how it finally began.

Then she had to go to work. Mr. Whitehorn was in one of his states. It was not rude to think this, since he frequently referred to them. There was a huge order to be sent to New York that would require, he thought, at least a week's packing. He had got hold of tea chests, only to be told that he had to have proper packing cases. There was plenty of newspaper and straw in the basement. He was afraid that that was where Meg would have to spend her day.

The basement was whitewashed and usually contained only inferior pieces, or things that needed repair. While working, Meg was allowed to have an oil stove, but it was considered too dangerous to leave it on by itself. Her first job was a huge breakfast, lunch, tea and coffee service bought by Mr. Whitehorn in a particularly successful summer sale in Suffolk. It had to be packed and listed, all two hundred and thirty-six pieces of it. It was lying on an old billiard table with a cut cloth, and Meg found that the most comfortable way to pack it was to bring each piece to a chaise longue whose stuffing was bristling out at every point, and put the heap of newspapers on the floor beside her. Thus she could sit and pack, and after each section of the set she could put things back on the table in separate clutches with their appropriate labels. She was feeling much better than when she had woken up. Not having to face the drive; having put an advertisement into a serious paper almost made her feel that she had sold the car already; Val had said that she might go to a film with her on Sunday afternoon if her friend didn't turn up and she didn't think he would, so that was something to look forward to; and packing china wasn't really too bad if you took it methodically and didn't expect ever to finish.

In the middle of the morning, Mr. Whitehorn went out in his van to fetch the packing cases. He would be back in about an hour, he said. Meg, who had run up to the shop to hear what he said—the basement was incredibly muffled and quiet—made herself a mug of coffee and went back to work. There was a bell under the door rug, so that she could hear it if customers came.

She was just finishing the breakfast cups when she saw it. The newspaper had gone yellow at the edges, but inside, where all the print and pictures were, it was almost as good as new. For a second, she did not pick up the page, simply stared at a large photograph of head and shoulders, and M1 MYSTERY in bold type above it.

The picture was of the girl she had picked up in Hendon. She knew that it was, before she picked it up, but she still had to do that. She *might* be wrong, but she knew she wasn't. The glasses, the hair, the rather high forehead . . . but she was smiling faintly in the picture . . .

". . . petite, auburn-haired Mary Carmichael was found wrapped in her raincoat in a ditch in a lane not one hundred yards from the M1 north of Towcester. She had been assaulted and strangled with a lime-green silk scarf that she was seen wearing when she left her office . . . Mr. Turner was discovered in the boot of the car—a black MG that police found abandoned in a car park. The car belonged to Mr. Turner, who had been stabbed a number of times and is thought to have died earlier than Miss Carmichael . . ."

She realized then that she was reading a story continued from page one. Page one of the newspaper was missing. She would never know what Mr. Turner looked like.

She looked again at the picture of the girl. "Taken on holiday the previous year." Even though she was smiling, or trying to smile, Mary Carmichael looked timid and vulnerable.

"... Mr. Turner, a traveling salesman and owner of the car, is thought to have given a lift or lifts to Mary Carmichael and some other person, probably a man, not yet identified. The police are making extensive inquiries along the entire length of the route that Mr. Turner regularly traveled. Mr. Turner was married, with three children. Miss Carmichael's parents, Mr. and Mrs. Gerald Carmichael of Manchester, described their only daughter as very quiet and shy and without a boyfriend."

The paper was dated March of the previous spring.

Meg found that her eyes were full of tears. Poor, poor Mary. Last year she had been an ordinary, timid, not very attractive girl who had been given a lift, and then been horribly murdered. How frightened she must have been before she died—with being—assaulted—and all that. And now, she was simply a desolate ghost, bound to go on trying to get lifts, or to be helped, or perhaps even to *warn* people ... "I'll pray for you," she said to the picture, which now was so blurred through her tears that the smile, or attempt at one, seemed to have vanished.

She did not know how long it was before the implications, both practical and sinister, crept into her mind. But they did, and she realized that they had, because she began to shiver violently—in spite of feeling quite warm—and fright was prickling her spine up to the back of her neck.

Mystery Murders. If Mr. Turner was not the murderer of Mary, then only one other person could be responsible. The horrible man. The way he had talked of almost nothing but awful murders ... She must go to the police immediately. She could describe him down to the last detail: his clothes, his voice, his tinted spectacles, his frightful smell ... He had been furious with her when she had put him down at the service station ... but, one minute before that, before *then,* when she had let him out on the shoulder where the lorry was, he had taken ages to come back into the car—had walked right round it, and then, when he got in, and she had questioned him about the girl, and described her, he had become all sweaty, and taken ages to reply to anything she said. He must have *recognized* the car! She was beginning to feel confused: there was too much to think about at once. This was where being clever would be such a help, she thought.

She began to try to think quietly, logically: absolutely nothing but lurid fragments came to mind: "a modicum, and sometimes, let's face it, a very great deal of fear"; the girl's face as she stood under the light on the island. Meg looked back at the paper, but there was really no doubt at all. The girl in the paper *was* the same girl. So—at last she had begun to sort things out—the girl *was* a ghost: the car, therefore, must be haunted. He certainly knew, or realized, something about all this: his final words—"I'm far from sure that *I* trust *you*"—that was because she had said that she didn't trust him. So—perhaps he thought she *knew* what had happened. Perhaps he had thought she was trying to trap him, or something like that. If he *really* thought that, and he was actually guilty, he surely wouldn't leave it at that, would he? He'd be afraid of her going to the police, of what, in fact, she was shortly going to do. He couldn't *know* that she hadn't seen the girl before, in the newspaper. But if he couldn't know, how could the police?

At this point, the doorbell rang sharply, and Meg jumped. Before she could do more than leap to her feet, Mr. Whitehorn's faded, kindly voice called down. "I'm back, my dear girl. Any customers while I've been away?"

"No." Meg ran up the stairs with relief that it was he. "Would you like some coffee?"

"Splendid notion." He was taking off his teddy-bear overcoat and rubbing his dry, white hands before the fan heater.

Later, when they were both nursing steaming mugs, she asked, "Mr. Whitehorn, do you remember a mystery murder case on the M1 last spring? Well, two murders, really? The man was found in the boot of the car, and the girl—"

"In a ditch somewhere? Yes, indeed. All over the papers. The real trouble is that, although I adore reading detective stories, *real* detective stories, I mean, I always find real-life crime just dull. Nasty, and dull."

"I expect you're right."

"They caught the chap though, didn't they? I expect he's sitting in some tremendously kind prison for about eighteen months. Be out next year, I shouldn't wonder. The law seems to regard property as far more important than murder, in my opinion."

"Who did they catch?"

"The murderer, dear, the murderer. Can't remember his name. Something like Arkwright or James. Something like that. But there's no doubt at all that they caught him. The trial was all over the papers, as well. How have you been getting on with your marathon?"

Meg found herself blushing: she explained that she had been rather idle for the last half hour or so, and suggested that she make up the time by staying later. No, no, said Mr. Whitehorn, such honesty should be rewarded. But, he added, before she had time to thank him, if she *did* have an hour to spend tomorrow, Saturday morning, he would be most grateful. Meg had to agree to this, but arranged to come early and leave early, because of her advertisement.

The worst of having had that apparently comforting talk with Mr. Whitehorn was that if they *had* already caught the man, then there couldn't be any point in going to the police. She had no proof that she hadn't seen a picture of poor Mary Carmichael; in fact, she realized that she might easily have done so, and simply not remembered because she didn't read murder cases. Going to the police and saying that you had seen a ghost, given a ghost a *lift* in your car, and *then* seen a picture in a newspaper that identified them, would just sound hysterical or mad. And there would be no point in describing the horrible man, if, in fact, he was just horrible but not a murderer. But at least she didn't have to worry about him: his behavior had simply seemed odd and then sinister, *before* Mr. Whitehorn had said that they had caught the murderer. There was nothing she needed to do about any of it. Except get rid of a haunted car.

After her scrambled eggs and Mars bar, she did some washing, including her hair and her hairbrush, and went to bed early. Just before she went to sleep, the thought occurred to her that her mother always thought that people—all people—were really better than they seemed, and her father was certain that they were worse. Possibly, they were just *what* they seemed—no more and no less.

In the morning, second post, she got a letter from her mother full of anxiety and advice. The letter, after many kind and impractical admonitions, ended: "and you are not to think of getting up or trying to drive all this way unless you are feeling completely recovered. I do wish I could come down and look after you, but your father thinks he may be getting this wretched bug. He has read in the paper that it is all over the place, and is usually the first to get anything, as you know. Much love, darling, and take *care* of yourself."

This made Meg feel awful about going to Mr. Whitehorn's but she had promised him, and letting down one person gave one no excuse whatsoever for letting down another. Samantha had promised to sit on the telephone while Meg was out, as she was waiting for one of her friends to call.

When she got back to the flat, Samantha was on the telephone, and Val was obviously cross with her. "She's been *ages* talking to Bruce and she is going out with him in a minute, and I said I'd do the shopping, but she won't even say what she wants. She's a drag."

Samantha said, "Hold on a minute—six grapefruit and two rump steaks—that's all," and went on listening, laughing, and talking to Bruce. Meg gazed at her in dismay. How on earth were people who had read her advertisement and were *longing* to ring her up about it to get through? The trouble about Samantha was that she was so *very* marvelous to look at that it was awfully difficult to get her to do anything she didn't want to do.

Val turned kindly to Meg and said loudly, "And your ad's in, isn't it? Samantha—you really are the limit. Meg, what would you like me to shop for you?"

Meg felt that this was terribly kind of Val, who was also pretty stunning, but in a less romantic way. Neither of the girls had ever shopped for her before; perhaps Val was going to become her friend. When she had made her list of cheese, apples, milk, eggs, and Nescaff, Val said, "Look, why don't we share a small chicken? I'll buy most of it, if you'll do the cooking. For Sunday," she added, and Meg felt that Val was almost her friend already.

Val went, and at once, Samantha said to the telephone: "All *right:* meet you in half an hour. Bye." In one graceful movement she was off the battered sofa and stood running her hands through her long, black hair and saying: "I haven't got a *thing* to wear!"

"Did anyone ring for me?"

"What? Oh—yes, one person—no, two, as a matter of fact. I told them you'd be in by lunchtime."

"Did they sound interested in the car?"

"One did. Kept asking awful technical questions I couldn't answer. The other one just wanted to know if the car could be seen at this address and the name of the owner." She was pulling off a threadbare kimono, looking at her face in a small, magnifying mirror she seemed always to have with her. "Another one ...! They keep bobbing up like corks! I've gone on to this diet not a moment too soon."

An hour went slowly by: nobody rang up about the car. Samantha finally appeared in fantastically expensive-looking clothes as though she were about to be photographed. She borrowed 50p off Meg for a taxi and went, leaving an aura of chestnut bath stuff all over the flat.

The weekend was a fearful anticlimax. On Saturday, three people rang up—none of them people who had called before; one said that he thought it was a drop-head, seemed, indeed, almost to accuse her of it not being, although she had distinctly said saloon in her ad. Two said they would come and look at the car: one of these actually arrived, but he only offered her a hundred pounds less than she was asking, and that was that. On Sunday morning Meg cooked for ages, the chicken and all the bits, like bread sauce and gravy, that were to live up to it. At twelve-thirty Val got a call from one of her friends, and said she was frightfully sorry, but that she had to be out to lunch after all.

"Oh, dear! Shall I keep it till the evening? The chicken will be cold, but the other—"

Val interrupted her by saying with slight embarrassment that she wouldn't be back to dinner, either. "*You* eat it," she ended, with guilty generosity.

When she had gone, the flat seemed very empty. Meg tried to comfort herself with the thought that anyway, she *couldn't* have gone to the cinema with Val, as she would have to stay in the flat in case the telephone rang. But she had been looking forward to lunch. If a person sat down to a table with you and had a meal, you stood a much better chance of getting to know them. Sundays only seemed quieter in London than they were in the country, because of the contrast of London during the week. As she sat down to her leg of chicken with bread sauce, gravy, and potatoes done as her mother did them at home, she wondered whether coming to London was really much good after all. She did not seem to be making much headway: it wasn't turning out at all how she had imagined it might, and at this moment she felt rather homesick. Whatever happened, she'd go home next weekend, and talk to her mother about the whole thing. Not—the car—thing, but Careers and Life.

Two more people rang during the afternoon. One was for Samantha, but the other was about the car. They asked her whether she would drive it to Richmond for them to see it, but when she explained why she couldn't they lost interest. She kept telling herself that it was too long a chance to risk losing other possible buyers by going out for such a long time, but as the gray afternoon settled drearily to the darker gray evening, she wondered whether she had been wrong.

She wrote a long letter to her mother, describing Samantha's clothes and Val's kindness, and saying that she was already feeling better (another lie, but how could

she help it?); then she read last month's *Vogue* magazine
and wondered what all the people in it, who wore rich
car coats and gave fabulous, unsimple dinner parties and
shooting lunches and seemed to know at least eight ways
of doing their hair, were doing now. On the whole, they
all seemed in her mind to be lying on velvet or leather
sofas with one of their children in a party dress sitting
quietly reading, and pots of azaleas and cyclamen round
them in a room where you could only see one corner of
a family portrait and a large white or honey-colored dog
at their feet on an old French carpet. She read her horoscope: it said, you will encounter some interesting people, but do not go more than halfway to meet them, and
watch finances—last month's horoscope anyway, so that
somehow whether it had been right or not hardly
counted. When she thought it must be too late for any
more people to ring up, she had a long, hot bath, and
tried to do her hair at least one other way. But her hair
was too short, too fine, and altogether too unused to any
outlandish intention, and obstinately slipped or fell back
into its ordinary state. It was also the kind of uninterest-
ing color that people never even bothered to describe in
books. She yawned, a tear came out of one eye, and she
decided that she had better get on with improving her
mind, to which end she settled down to a vast and heavy
book on Morocco that Val said people were talking
about . . .

All week she packed and packed: china, glass, silver,
and bits of lamps and chandeliers. On Wednesday, someone rang up for her at the shop while she was out buying
sausage rolls and apples for Mr. Whitehorn's and her
lunches. Mr. Whitehorn seemed very vague about them:
it hadn't seemed to be about the car, but something
about her weekend plans, he thought. He *thought,* he
reiterated, as though this made the whole thing more
doubtful. Meg could not think who it could be—unless
it was the very shy young man with red hair and a stam-
mer who had once come in to buy a painting on glass
about Nelson's death. He had been very nice, she
thought, and he had stayed for quite a long time after

he had bought the picture and told her about his collection of what she had learned to call Nelsoniana. That was about the only person it could be, and she hoped he'd ring again, but he didn't.

By Wednesday, she had long given up hope of anyone buying the car as a result of the advertisement. Val and Samantha told her that Bruce and Alan both said it was the wrong time of the year to sell secondhand cars, and she decided that she had better try to sell it in the north, nearer home.

On Wednesday evening she had a sudden, irrational attack of fear. However much she reasoned with herself, she simply did not *want* to drive up the M1 alone in the car that she was now certain was haunted. She couldn't stand the thought of hearing the sounds she had heard, of seeing the girl again in the same place (possibly, why not?—ghosts were well known for repeating themselves); and when Samantha and Val came in earlier than usual and together, she had a—possibly not hopeless—idea. Would either or both of them like to come home for the weekend with her?

Their faces turned at once to each other; it was easy to see the identical appalled blankness with which they received the proposal. Before they could *say* that they wouldn't come, Meg intercepted them. "It's lovely country, and my mother's a marvelous cook. We could go for drives in the car—" but she knew it was no good. They couldn't possibly come, they both said almost at once: they had dates, plans, it was awfully kind of her, and perhaps in the summer they might—yes, in the summer, it might be marvelous *if* there was a free weekend . . .

Afterward, Meg sat on her bed in the very small room that she had to herself, and cried. They weren't enough her friends for her to plead with them, and if she told them why she was frightened, they would be more put off than ever.

Next morning she asked Mr. Whitehorn if he had ever been up north to sales and auctions and things like that.

Yes, he went from time to time.

"I suppose you wouldn't like to come up this weekend

to stay? I could drive you to any places you wanted to go."

Mr. Whitehorn looked at her with his usual tired face, but also with what she could see was utter amazement.

"My dear child," he said, when he had had time to think of it, "I couldn't possibly do anything, *anything* at all like that at such short notice. It would throw out all my plans, you see. I always make plans for the weekend. Perhaps you have not realized it," he went on, "but I am a homosexual, you see. I thought you would know; running this shop and the states I get into. But I *always* plan my free time. I am lunching with a very dear friend in Ascot, and sometimes, not always, I stay the night there." The confidence turned him pink. "I had absolutely no intention of *misleading* you."

Meg said of course not, and then they both apologized to each other and said it didn't matter in the least.

On Thursday evening both girls were out, and Meg, who had not slept at all well for the last two nights, decided that she was too tired to go on her own to the cinema, although it was *A Man for All Seasons* that she had missed and always wanted to see. She ate a poached egg and half a grapefruit that Samantha said was left over from her diet, and suddenly she had a brain wave. What she was frightened of, she told herself, was the idea that the poor girl would be waiting for her again at Hendon. If, therefore, she *avoided* Hendon, and got on to the M1 farther north, she would be free of this anxiety. There might still be those awful sounds again, like she had heard the first time, but she would just have to face that, drive steadily home, and when she got there, she decided, she would jolly well tell her mother about the whole thing. The idea, and the decision to tell her mother, cheered her so much that she felt less tired, and went down to the car to fetch the map. There, the car rug that her mother had given her in case she did not have enough on her bed pricked her conscience. She had managed to toil up the stairs with the flowers and marmalade and her case, but she had completely forgotten the rug; this was probably because her mother had put it in the car herself, and it now lay on the floor in the back. She would take it home, as she really didn't need it, and usually her father used it to protect his legs from drafts when he sat in or out-of-doors.

She found a good way on the map. She simply did not go left on to Hendon Way, but used the A1000 through Barnet and turned left on to the St. Albans road. She could get on to the M1 on the way to Watford. It was easy. That evening she packed her party dress so that her mother could see it. She always packed the night before, so that she didn't rush too much in the mornings, got to work on time, and parked her car, as usual, round the corner from the shop. Mr. Whitehorn had simply chalked "No Parking" on the brick wall, and so far it had always worked.

On Friday morning, she and Mr. Whitehorn met each other elaborately, as though far more had occurred between them than had actually happened: the first half hour was heavy with offhanded goodwill, and they seemed to get in each other's way far more often than usual. They used the weather as a kind of demilitarized zone of conversation. Mr. Whitehorn said that he heard on the wireless that there was going to be fog again, and Meg, who had heard it too, said oh dear and thanked him for telling her. Later in the morning, when things had eased between them, Mr. Whitehorn asked her whether she had been successful in selling her car. Trains were so much easier in this weather, he added. They were, indeed. But she could hardly tell him that as she lived seventeen miles from the station, and her parents didn't drive, and the last bus had left by the time the train she would be able to catch had arrived, and her salary certainly couldn't afford a taxi ... she couldn't tell him any of that: it would look like asking, begging for more money—she would never do it ...

But the train became a recurrent temptation throughout the long cold and, by the afternoon, foggy day. She banished the idea in the end by reminding herself that, with the cost of the advertisement, she simply did not have the money for the train fare: the train was out of the question.

Mr. Whitehorn, who had spent the morning typing

lists for the Customs (he typed with three fingers in erratic, irritable bursts), said that he would buy their lunch, as he needed the exercise.

When he had gone, Meg, who had been addressing labels to be stuck on to the packing cases, felt so cold that she fetched the other paraffin heater from the basement and lit it upstairs. She did not like to get another cardigan from her case in the car, as in spite of its being so near, it was out of sight from the shop, and Mr. Whitehorn hated the shop to be left empty for a moment. This made her worry, stupidly, whether she had locked the car. It was the kind of worry that one had like wondering if she had actually posted a letter *into* the letter box: of course, one would have, but once any idea to the contrary sets in, it would not go. So the moment he came back with hot sausages and Smith's crisps from the pub, she rushed out to the car. She had, in fact, left one back door open; she could have sworn that she hadn't, but there it was. She got herself another cardigan out of her case in the boot, and returned to her lunch. It was horrible out; almost dark, or at any rate opaque, with the fog, and the bitter, acrid air that seemed to accompany fogs in towns. At home, it would be a thick white mist—well, nearly white, but certainly not smelling as this fog smelled. The shop, in contrast, seemed quite cozy. One or two people came to "look around" while they ate; but there was never very much to see. Mr. Whitehorn put all the rubbish that got included in lots he had bid for on to trays with a mark saying that anything on the tray cost 50p or £1. Their serious stuff nearly always seemed to go abroad, or to another dealer. Mr. Whitehorn always made weak but kindly little jokes about his rubbish collectors, as he called the ones who bought old photograph albums, molded glass vases, or haircombs made of tortoiseshell and bits of broken paste.

While she was making their coffee, Meg wondered whether perhaps Mr. Whitehorn would be a good person to talk about the haunted car to. Obviously, asking him to stay had been a silly mistake. But he might be just the person to understand what was worrying her; to be-

lieve her and to let her talk about it. That was what she
most wanted, she realized. Someone, almost anyone, to
talk to her about it: to sort out what was honestly frightening, and what she had imagined or invented as fright.

But immediately after lunch, he set about his typing
again, and got more and more peevish, crumpling up bits
of paper and throwing them just outside the wastepaper
basket, until she hardly liked to ask him, at five, whether
she might go.

However, she did ask, and he said it would be all right.

He could not know how difficult she found it to leave:
she said good night to him twice by mistake, started to
put her old tweed coat on, and then decided that with
the second cardigan she wouldn't need it, took ages tying
on her blue silk head square, and nearly forgot her bag.
She took out her car keys while she could find them
easily in the light, shut the shop door behind her, and
after one more look at him, angrily crouched over his
typewriter, went to the car.

Once she got into the car, her courage and common
sense returned. It was only, at the worst, a four-hour
journey: she would be home then, and everything would
be all right. She flung her overcoat into the back—it was
far easier to drive without it hanging round the gear
lever—had one final look at her map before she shut
the car door, and set off.

It was more interesting going a different way out of
London, even though it seemed to be slower, but the
traffic, the fog, and making sure all the time that she
was on the right road occupied her mind, almost to the
exclusion of anything else. She found her way on to the
M1 quite easily; the signs posting it were more frequent
and bigger than any other sign.

She drove for over an hour on the motorway, and
there was no sound in the car, no agonized, labored
breathing—nothing. It was getting rather hot, but the
heater cleared the windscreen and she couldn't do without it for long. The fog was better, too, although patchy,
and in the clearer bits she could see the fine misty rain
that was falling all the time. She was sticking to the left-
hand lane, because although it meant that lorries passed

her from time to time, she felt safer in the fog than if she had been in the middle, and possibly unable to see either side of the road. She opened a crack of window because the car seemed to be getting impossibly hot and full of stale air. Another two hours, she thought, and decided that she might as well stop to take off her thick cardigan—she could use the hard shoulder just for that— and perhaps she had made far too much of her nerves and anxiety about the whole journey. She drew up carefully, and then saw a service area ahead—safer in one of those. "At least I didn't give in," she thought, and thought also how ashamed of herself she would have been if she had.

As she drew up in the car park, she was just about to get out of her cardigan, when a huge hand reached out in front of her and twitched the driving mirror so that she could see him. He was smiling, his eyes full of triumph and malice. His breath reeked over her shoulder as she gave a convulsive gasp of pure shock. "You must be a ghost!" She heard herself repeating this in a high voice utterly unlike her own. "You must be a ghost: you *must* be!"

"Only had to pick the car lock twice. You shouldn't have locked it *again* in the middle of the day."

She knew she should start the car and drive back out on to the road, but she couldn't see behind her, and nearly lost all control when she felt something hard and pointed sticking into the back of her neck.

"They caught Mr. Wrong, you see. But you seemed to know *so much,* and as you were driving the same car, I simply had to catch up with you somehow. Two birds with one stone, as it were."

She made an attempt to get the brake off, but a hand clamped over her wrist with such sudden force that she cried out.

"Ever since you turned me out in that unkind manner, I have been trying to track you down. That is all I have done, but your advertisement was a great help." She saw him watching her face in the mirror and licking the scum off his lips. She made a last effort.

"I shall turn you out again—any minute—I shall!"

He sucked in his breath, but he was still smiling.

"Oh no, you won't. This time, it will all be done my way."

She thought she screamed once, in that single second of astonished disbelief and denial before she felt the knife jab smoothly through the skin on her neck when speechless terror overwhelmed her and she became nothing but fear—heart thudding, risen in her throat as though it would burst from her: she put one hand to the wound and felt no knife—only her own blood—there, as he said:

"Don't worry *too* much: just stick to fear. The fate worse than death tends to occur after it. I've always liked them warm."

THE RUNAWAY LOVERS

RAY RUSSELL

"A dank draft of air tinkled the bones of an old
skeleton that hung by dry wrists from rusted ceiling
chains. It drew their eyes and their unvoiced wonderings: who had it been and how long ago and
was it a man or a woman?"

*Ray Russell has enjoyed considerable success as both an
editor and a writer. In the former role, while employed
at* Playboy *during its early years, he was instrumental in
advancing the careers of numerous important contributors
to the genres of sf, horror, and fantasy, including that of
Charles Beaumont [see "The Crooked Man," p. 210].
Russell's own best-known story is probably the rictus-
themed "Sardonicus," filmed with the addition of a polite
"Mr." to the title by the irrepressibly gimmick-prone B-
director William Castle. (For this 1961 costume feature
Castle lured audiences into theaters with "Punishment
Cards," offering them a chance to vote on the villain's
fate. Naturally, mass bloodthirstiness prevailed each time.)*
    "The Runaway Lovers," though set in an even earlier

epoch than "Sardonicus," one in which handsome trou-
badours wooed fair ladies despite the presence of inconve-
nient husbands, is a similarly mock-gothic homage.
Always sophisticated—but having a slapstick urge to keep
one hand on the rug beneath our feet—Russell, as you'll
see, most loves to tease readers with variations on the old
bait-and-switch.

The runaway lovers were captured just before they
reached the border of the duchy.

They were dragged immediately before His Grace, the
Duke, whose noble mien and halo of snowy curls lent
him the aspect of a painted angel; and his face was sad
as he looked reproachfully at his errant young wife, then
at her troubadour lover, and then, with a great sigh and
tears brimming in his soft old eyes, paid their captors in
gold and turned the two prisoners over to his warder.

The Duke's curt instructions to the warder were surprising, for he enjoyed a reputation far and wide as a
clement and a pious lord.

The lovers were to be taken to the dungeons and severely punished for a total of seven days—one day for
each of the cardinal sins—finally to be irrevocably demised upon the seventh. During this time, they were to
be prohibited, by the most direct of means, from looking
upon or speaking to each other, from proffering solace
by either words of courage or glances of love.

"The most direct of means," chattered the genial
warder as, keys jangling, he led the unhappy pair down
into the subterranean dungeons. "Aye, that would be to
remove your eyes and tongues." They howled in out-
raged protest, but he laughed merrily and assured them
it was a simple operation, done with pincers and hot
irons in a few seconds.

Still, all the world loves lovers, and the warder was a
merciful man. He chose to postpone removing their eyes
and tongues until the morrow, allowing them the night
in which to see and speak to each other. See and speak,
but not touch or fondle, for after stripping them he
stuffed them into separate cages, tiny cages designed for

minimum ease. Leaving one smoky torch flickering in a wall sconce, the warder took his leave of them. The lovers, squatting on bare haunches, their toes gripping the hard iron of the cages' floors, were free to console each other as best they could with words and looks.

The woman was the first to speak. "See to what a sorry state we have come," she said through tears. "And all because of you."

"Of *me*?" the youth replied. "It was I who insisted you remain with your husband the Duke, for we could easily take our pleasure of each other under his sanctimonious old nose and he be none the wiser. But no—you had to run away."

"Any other course would have been ignoble. Running away was the only decent thing to do."

"You speak of decency? *You*?" he cried. "All hot and hungry mouth you were from head to foot, burning with thirst, parched from an old husband's neglect, bold, unquenchable, depraved—"

"Shut your vile lips! *You* are to blame for our foul fortune. I would not be crouching here naked, like a plucked peacock in a parrot cage, awaiting seven days of torture, if you had not made advances to me in the first place."

"Your memory is as tarnished as your virtue! It was *you* made the first sign toward me!"

"You are a liar!"

"You are a trollop!"

She wept. Repenting a little of his words, he grumbled, "It well may be it is no fault of ours but of your hoary hymn singer of a husband ..."

"Whorey? No, that is the very rub, he did not—"

"You misrender me. His fault, I mean, to wed a wife whose years are but a third his threescore span. His fault to let her languish unslaked. His fault to throw the two of us so much together, telling me how much you loved my songs, telling you how much I loved your singing of them. His fault for living in such purblind holiness, such ignorance of fleshly wants, such idiot innocence that he could not foresee the natural outcome of it all. Yes, *his* the fault! All his! Ah, damn him for a prating prig!"

She murmured tonelessly, "It was of latter days the Duke eschewed my bed. When first we wed, my youthful flesh so kindled him that his silver locks and holy ways were quite forgot, and he was less like monk and more like a monkey, or, as one might say, like goat or bull or stallion, what you will. Then, for reasons never understood but which I took for sad depletion of his aged energies, he grew mild and no more than a brother to me ..."

"Brother?" the troubadour scoffed. "Grandsire!"

A dank draft of air tinkled the bones of an old skeleton that hung by dry wrists from rusted ceiling chains. It drew their eyes and their unvoiced wonderings: who had it been and how long ago and was it a man or a woman? For what had it died and how had it died—strung up with grim simplicity to starve, or had there been other things, less simple? The man shuddered and the woman wept afresh and both were silent for a while.

Then he said, "Let us think clearly. In all his long life, has the Duke ever been feared for harshness? Has he condemned to torture even the most black-hearted malefactors? Has he so much as flogged the lowest churl? Is he not laughed at by lackeys for his softness? Sneered at as a weak and womanish wight? Is not his meekness the mock and marvel of the land? Is he not praised by priests and prelates for his piety, his charity, his unending orisons, his saintliness? Well? Do I speak true?"

A stifled "Yes" escaped the crouched woman in the neighboring cage.

He resumed: "How, then, can it be that such a man could visit hideous torments upon two human creatures, and one of them his comely wife?"

She sniffled, her head crammed between her knees, her tears running in rivulets down her bare legs to glisten on her toenails. "You grasp at straws," she moaned. "You heard him. Seven days of torture—"

"Of *punishment*!" he crowed. "And what, pray, does *he* deem punishment, that lily-livered nun of a man? Fasting and kneeling and praying and mortifying the flesh? Hair shirts for seven days? Stern sermons, righteous rhetoric?" He laughed. "A little discomfort, a humble show of repentance, and a deal of yawning bore-dom! *That* is the 'torture' you fear!" He laughed again, rocking back on his heels as far as the cage would permit.

The woman delivered herself of a despondent sigh. "You are a fool," she said without rancor, as a plain statement of fact. "On the seventh day, we die. That was his command."

"Demised!" he said. "We are to be *demised* upon the seventh day!"

"The selfsame thing . . ."

"Not so! A word of many meanings! Chief among them: to be *released*!" He laughed louder. "Released! Can corpses be released? Can cold cadavers be granted freedom? No! We will but genuflect and beg forgiveness for seven short days—one day for each of the cardinal sins, you heard the pious dotard—and then we will be set free. Free! 'Irrevocably demised'—released without revoke! Our worries are for naught!"

Her eyelids, puffed and pink from weeping, opened slowly and her eyes sought his, scornfully, piteously. "Do you so soon forget? Is that thing within your skull of no more substance than a fishnet? Has fear so much un-manned you that your mind does not recall what else was said? A thing about our *eyes and tongues*?"

He opened his mouth to speak, but closed it. Sick horror shadowed his face once more.

She sneered, "Equivocate your way out of that!"

Soon, he smiled. "For your unkindness and unpleasant words, I should allow you to continue thinking we will lose those necessary and delightful organs. Why should I comfort you, when for my pains I reap but snide re-bukes?" He chuckled. "And so I will be mum."

A long silent moment passed. At length, she cried out, "Speak, wretch!"

He laughed triumphantly. "Because I love you, sweet-meat, I will speak. And you will hearken. Call back to mind those dreadful words about our eyes and tongues. Recall who spoke them. Was it your saintly husband? Or was it a somewhat lesser lord, a slavering menial, none other than our lackwit turnkey?"

She gave it thought. "My husband said ..."

"Your husband said we must not look upon or speak to one another. This is to be done, said he, by the most direct of means. Well, then. Gags and blindfolds! Are they not more direct than pincers and hot irons? Our stupid jailer was but wool-gathering, unlawfully elaborating upon your husband's orders. Those orders, when they are carried out, will be no more stringent than the rapping of a child's knuckles. Believe this, my saucy chuck—fear is a phantasm born out of air; it has not dam nor sire. Fret no further, dry your tears. A week of sackcloth and ashes, and we will be absolved, forgiven, and most magnanimously *demised*."

His words contained a certain logic. She began to be assured. "I pray you are right," she said.

"Trust in me," he replied. "Your husband would not allow us to be either tortured or slain."

A little later, the warder, that kindly man, returned and greeted them with a cheery smile and sat down near them to eat a bowl of gruel, his meager supper. Between slurpings and smackings, he spoke:

"His Grace, the Duke, he says as how 'twould be unjust for you to dwell in ignorance of what is soon to come. Fair's fair, he says, being no cruel man, no tyrant like some I've served, no fiend who would allow poor gentles like yourselves to fear that worst of all bad fates—that is to say, things unknown. Far better, says he, for them to know what lies in store for them, and certain it is there's truth and wisdom in that, by bloody Christ's own hooks, if my lady will forgive the language. So go, good man, he says to me, go back to them and tell them both each single thing that will be done to them, the seven things in seven days, and be not chary of detail, he says, for it is good they know the most, that they may fear the least and in serenity consign their souls to Heaven. Aye, he's a fine man, a godly man, is His Grace."

Wiping his lips and setting aside his empty bowl, the jolly fellow said, "Well, now, tomorrow is the first day of the seven, is it not, so at the brink of dawn, after the good night's sleep I hope you'll have, this is what will be done upon the pair of you ..."

When he told them of the First Day, they paled. When he told them of the Second Day, they groaned. When he told them of the Third Day, they cursed. When he told them of the Fourth Day, they wept. When he told them of the Fifth Day, they screamed. When he told them of the Sixth Day, they retched. When he told them of the Seventh and Final Day, a day that took almost a score of minutes in the telling, they fainted in the middle of it and he had to douse them into wakefulness with cold water, in order to finish it out. "And that be the whole of it," he smiled, "after which there will be no vile heathen disrespect for the remains but decent burial and Christian obsequies for both. So said His Grace. Good night to you, then, my lady, young sir. Sleep well." Humming a tune, he left the dungeon, closing the metal door with a dismal clang.

The youth, maddened by despair, rattled the bars of his cage, beat his fists against them, clawed at the lock until his fingers bled. At length, he collapsed into a lump of quivering, whimpering flesh.

She, her eyes blank with shock, mouthed disjointed words in a voice no stronger than a whisper. "Obscene ... disgusting ... more loathsome than I could ever dream ... more horrible than all the agonies of Hell! *Seven days!* Each day unending! Oh, God! To suffer thus? To undergo such foul abominations for a few moments of pleasure? No! No! ..."

Her lover looked up at her with a slackened face. He blubbered: "You must beg him, plead with him, entreat him! Tell him it was *you* who tempted me, and I, poor human clay, was sucked inexorably to the lodestone of your lust. Tell him that! Why should we *both* die so horribly? Why should I suffer for your unfaithfulness?"

She shrieked at him: "Coward! Serpent! You would see me ripped and broken, to save your own skin? *You* must seek his mercy, tell him you snared my soul with devilish tricks and necromantic arts, rendering me a helpless slave to your cravings!"

"I? Scream my throat to shreds for seven unthinkable

days and nights—all for a wench? A pair of lips, and eyes, and—and—and—"

His stammering tongue was impaled by something he saw outside his cage. He blinked. He licked dry lips. "Look," he said, pointing with an unsteady hand.

She looked. There on the stone floor, near the empty bowl, not far from the cages in which they were bent double, lay a heart-lifting circle of hope: the warder's key ring.

"*The k—*" she began to shout, but "Shhh!" her lover cautioned, his finger to his lips. He whispered hoarsely: "Not a word. Not a sound. This is the Hand of Providence itself."

Also in a whisper, she said, "Stop prating holy hogwash like my husband and *get it.*"

He stretched his arm out between the bars of his cage, but his reach fell far too short. He squeezed his naked shoulder painfully between the bars, extending his reach, but still his fingertips raked empty air, inches away from the ring of keys. Finally, exhausted, he went limp.

Now she, from her cage, reached between the cold black iron of the bars, her tapering slim fingers writhing like little snakes in the attempt to grasp the key ring. Grunting indelicately, cursing vulgarly, she stretched her pretty arm still farther, one round ripe fruit of a breast crushed cruelly against the bars. A sheen of sweat covered her whole body, despite the dungeon's chill. But still her fingers did not touch the taunting keys.

He, watching her efforts, whined, "No use ... no use ..."

She was loath to give up so easily. Hissing an unladylike oath, she now unbent her shapely long legs, and wincing at the pins of pain that shot through them after the hours of squatting restraint, she forced them between the bars, toward the metal circle of keys that lay between them and escape. Her toes flexed and curled, reaching for the keys. Her legs stretched still farther, as her full thighs now were scraped and squashed by the cage bars. Biting her lip, she gripped the bars with her hands and pressed her belly and loins relentlessly against the unyielding iron, almost splitting herself in two on the bar that separated her thighs, gasping in pain, her toes clenching and unclenching, the sweat streaming from her flesh, until, at length, with a moan of thanksgiving, her efforts were rewarded, her feet closed upon the ring, she felt the welcome cold shafts of the keys between her toes, and slowly, carefully, she drew her feet back toward the cage, reached out and seized the key ring in her hand, then fell back, slimed with sweat and the blood of scraped skin, panting, sobbing, victorious.

Her lover in the other cage, eyeing the keys almost lasciviously, croaked, "The locks! Open the locks!"

She inserted one of the dozen keys into the lock of her cage door. It did not fit. She tried the next. And the next. Both lovers cursed, despair flooding them again and filling the great space hope had excavated in their hearts, as she tried key after key.

The tenth key worked. She swung open the creaking door of her cage and crawled out upon the stone floor of the dungeon. Slowly, agonizingly, she pulled herself to her feet and stood at her full height, magnificently, nudely beautiful.

Then, walking past his cage, she went straight to the dungeon door.

"Wait!" he cried. "Would you leave me here?"

"Who travels light travels best," she said, and unlocked the dungeon door.

"Strumpet! Open this cage!"

She laughed softly and blew him a mocking kiss.

"You need me!" he screamed. "You need me to overpower the guards, to steal horses, food, clothing. If you leave without me, I will bellow my lungs out, awaken the entire castle, the warder and the guards will apprehend you before you reach the first wall!"

She looked at him thoughtfully. Then, smiling, she walked back to his cage. "I was but teasing you," she said, and released him.

"I choose to believe you," he growled, "bitch!"

The two of them swung open the heavy dungeon door. Quiet and swift, hardly daring to breathe, they padded on bare feet up a narrow corkscrew of stone stairs to the armory.

There, serried ranks of soldiers stood in wait!

No: thus they appeared to be at first glimpse, but were soon revealed to be no more than empty suits of armor, the eyeslits as devoid of life as the sockets in the grinning skull below.

Up more stairs they climbed, and skittered spiderishly along a pitch-black, airless corridor so constructed that it seemed to grow narrower as they penetrated it, the ceiling built gradually lower and lower until they were obliged to crouch, the walls themselves so close together at one point they had to go in single file and then to crawl on their bellies through the foul air and impenetrable dark.

It seemed upward of an hour before they felt cool air and, shortly after, crawled out and stood upright in a place no less dark but which felt to be a specie of tunnel. They ran blindly through what proved to be a vexing, labyrinthine network of such tunnels, often colliding painfully with hard stone walls, until they heard a liquid sound and knew the maze to be a system of drains or conduits or somewhat, for soon they were splashing in filthy, stinking water up to their ankles, then to their knees, then feeling panic seize them as the icy wetness lapped their naked backsides.

An eternity of headlong splashing flight they suffered, hearing the chattering of rats and seeing their red eyes in the dark, before a pinpoint of light in the far distance brought harsh sobs of triumph from their throats and they ran toward it pell-mell, splashing, sliding, falling, scrambling to their feet again, and plunging on toward the blessed beckoning spot of light, out of the noisome water that now fell to below their knees, then to their ankles, until they were running in dryness again, the light growing brighter and bigger until, with aching limbs and flaming lungs, they burst out of the tunnel and into—

The dungeon. The selfsame dungeon whence they had escaped. For there were the cages, with the doors standing open, and there was the dangling skeleton, and there was their amiable warder, a truncheon in his hand, greeting them with a gap-toothed smile.

"A trick," the troubadour groaned, collapsing to his knees.

"Aye, lad," the warder nodded. "A trick to pass the time and take your minds off your troubles."

The woman shrieked, "A fiendish trick! A trick to raise our hopes and dash them down again! A gloating demon's trick!"

"Now, now," the warder chided, "into your little cages, the pair of you, and quick about it or I'll be obliged to break a bone or two with this ..." He raised the truncheon meaningfully. Taking the key ring from her hand, he locked them in the cages again.

"All wet, are you, all wet and bare and blue with cold?" the warder said, solicitously. "Take heart, there will be heat enough at dawn." And, significantly, with broad winks, he opened a cabinet and took down a pair of branding irons which he placed upon a bench. "Aye, fire enough and heat enough," he grinned. From the cabinet he also took two long sharp blades, like gigantic paring knives. "Fire and heat and other things as well," he added, placing the awful knives next to the branding irons. He then closed the cabinet, squinted at the hideous equipment on the bench, and said, "That be enough. For the First Day, at least, it be enough." Then, deliberately shaking the key ring and filling the air with its sour jangle, he walked toward the dungeon door, saying, "This time I'll not be forgetting my keys, like a naughty knave. Good night, my lady, young sir, or rather good morning, for dawn will break in less than an hour."

The door clanged shut.

The Duke's face wore an expression of shock. "Dead, you say? Both of them?"

"Aye, that they be, Your Grace," replied the warder, "and by their own hands. Behind my back, they reached out from their cages and took the blades Your Grace bade me put upon the bench for them to look at. The Lord have mercy on their souls."

The Duke crossed himself, dismissed the warder, and turned to the tonsured clergyman at his side. "You heard, Monsignor? Smitten by remorse, consumed by guilt, they took their own lives."

"And, as suicides," solemnly said the priest, "plummeted straight to the fires of Perdition—there to suffer chastisement infinitely more severe than if they had died by your command."

"True, true, poor burning souls," said the Duke. "I never, as you know, intended bodily harm to come to them."

"Of course not. Such cruelty would have marred the good repute you bear among all men."

"Those grisly tales I bade the warder tell them, those skeletons and other things, were but to harrow and humble their spirits for a night. Oh, I do repent me—"

"Of those harmless tales and bones?"

"Not they so much, Monsignor, as I repent my overtrusting nature that placed those two young people in temptation's path. Is mine the blame? Is mine the hand that led them to depravity, discovery, and death?"

The priest spoke firmly. "No! Your Grace's guileless goodness cannot bear the blame for the sins of others!"

"It is good of you to say it."

"You never could foresee or wish the death of your young wife!"

"Oh, no."

"You never could desire to yet *again* become a widower!"

"Heaven forbid."

"And dwell in mournful loneliness once more!"

"O doleful day!"

"No man in all the realm can blame you."

"I pray not."

"The hearts of all your friends, your faithful courtiers, the meanest churls, the highest lords, His Majesty, the Church itself—all these mourn with you in this heavy hour!"

"Thank you, Reverend Father."

"But if I may, without offense, speak of your sudden sad unmarried state, I would remind Your Grace that a certain advantageous alliance is now possible with a family whose name is so illustrious I need not give it breath . . ."

"At such a time as this," the Duke replied, "one cannot think of marriage. But when I have composed myself, then we may have some words anent that prince to whom you have alluded, and whose sister is, I do believe, of fifteen summers now and therefore ripe for wedding. To you, Monsignor, I leave all small details of the nuptial ceremony, which must take place, I need not say, only after what is called a decent interval."

"A decent interval, of course," replied the priest.

THE FIRST TIME

DAVID KUEHLS

"Rod looked at the pamphlet over Scott's shoulder. **Don't You Wish You Knew Then What You Know Now?** the come-on teased in big, bold letters."

There are lots of unpleasant secrets in everyone's past, and obviously, some lurk nearer the surface of our consciousness than others. David Kuehls displays both considerable charm and surprising ruthlessness as he steers this mind-popping little fable to its inevitable denouement.

Rod Taylor slipped the plastic ID card into the slot and punched in his name on the keyboard. Then he looked into the monitor and let the machine scan through his corneas, pick his brains, and compare it to the card.

The card. His whole life was on that card. In particular, the one microchip that contained everything from his IQ to the fact that he was left-handed to memories of fourth-grade recess. Three seconds later there was a beep, his card popped out, the door unbolted, and Rod Taylor stepped into the cafeteria.

That's a lot of security just for a turkey sandwich, Rod

thought. He slid his tray along the metal tubing, and picked out a bowl of applesauce in addition to the sandwich. But first he raised it to his nose, sniffing for freshness. Rod hated day-old applesauce. It had an invisible film that you could smell and taste. It smelled like the metal dish it was in, and tasted like it, too. The first one he picked up contained day-old applesauce. Rod went to put it back down but Gary from accounting bumped his tray from behind and said hurry up. Rod slid his tray up to the cashier.

She was a human. Rod could tell by the dogeared romance novel draped across one thigh. Droids didn't read for pleasure. And even if they did, Rod supposed it wouldn't be a romance novel. Maybe a polymer schematic.

She smiled back at him and Rod felt his face turn hot. He wanted to say something back to her but his mouth wouldn't open. She lifted her finger and pointed to his face. "You've got applesauce on your glasses," she said.

Rod blushed, removed his glasses, and spied the blob of applesauce, about the size of a pencil eraser, clinging to the frame at the bottom of the left eyepiece. Rod wiped it off carefully with a napkin. Then he turned back to the girl.

She looked at the register. "Turkey on white, applesauce, and white milk. That'll be 4.3 credits."

Rod paid her and was about to say something to her when Gary from accounting bumped his tray from behind and said hurry up.

His name was Rod Taylor but he looked nothing like the old-time movie star, the actor who played in his uncle's favorite film, *The Birds*. Rod must have seen that movie a hundred times when he was a kid. Uncle Harry used to put it on in the den when Mom and Dad were out and Harry was stuck baby-sitting. Little Rodney would watch from his playpen, transfixed for hours, until the film ended and Rodney suddenly had to pee. Then he'd start to cry. And Harry would come in from the next room, smelling of beer and chuckling to himself.

Something about Hitchcock, bladders, and perfect timing.

Rod should've been named something like Caspar Milquetoast or Fielding Mellish, a name more suited to his bodily makeup: thin, short, bespectacled, and balding. But this was real life, not the movies, and as it was, Rod Taylor was the wimpiest-looking Rod Taylor around. To make matters worse, he was thirty-nine years old, unmarried, and his birthday was on Friday.

Rod set his tray down at his usual seat at table number sixteen. The gang was already present and discussing topic numero uno: sex.

There was Jim Collins, thirty-six. He'd had more dates than Rod had had fantasies. Jim was the leader of the pack when it came to women. Then there was Tim Black, thirty-eight, six feet four inches, married, but not above fooling around on the side. Rumor was—and that rumor came from Tim's mouth at lunchtime—that Tim was the only one to "snag" the new secretary in shipping. "She has this thing about tall men," Tim snickered. "She believes that everything is proportionally bigger. And who was I to let her down?" Finally, there was Scott Bolton, thirty-five, twice married, twice divorced. Scott had a thing for droids.

Scott moved his tray to make room for Rod.

"So there I was with Carla in the supply room," Tim was saying while chewing on a roll. "I *knew* she wanted me again after last week. She closed the door behind her, so we could be alone. I stepped back, feigning surprise. She came toward me and started unbuttoning her blouse."

"Right there in the supply room?" Scott's eyes were bulging out like some alien creature. "You did her right in the supply room?"

Tim waved a hand to quiet the crowd. "I'm not through yet." He paused. "Where was I? Oh, yes. She came toward me unbuttoning her blouse. She whispered something about wanting me again right here and now."

"So you did her? You did her?" Scott looked like a kid sitting on Santa's lap.

Tim frowned. "No I didn't. I told her that the first

time was a mistake, and I didn't want it to happen again. I told her I was a *married* man and didn't make it a practice of fooling around on my wife."

"You didn't," Scott said.

"I did," Tim said, and smiled a shit-eating grin.

Jim finally spoke up. "Good man. We can't have these women thinking that they can take advantage of us anytime they want to. Ain't that right?"

"Right," Scott said.

"Damn right," Tim said.

Then all three turned to Rod. Sometimes he didn't know why he kept them as his friends. All this macho bullshit about women as objects, conquering them and then kicking them aside. But then Rod reminded himself that Jim, Tim, and Scott were his only friends. "Sure," Rod said. "Sure." He took another bite of his turkey sandwich, started chewing it seventeen times. *One, two, three* . . .

"I'm glad we got that settled," Jim said, "because I've got something new for you guys, just tried it myself last night. It's from the good folks at Datadates."

Tim made a face. "Wait a second. Weren't they the ones with the defective droids?"

"Yeah, their feet would fall off during simulated orgasm," Scott added. "And you had to carry them back out to the truck for all the neighbors to see."

Tim looked at Scott. "I see you got stuck with a lemon once."

"Twice actually," Scott said. Then quickly added: "But that's only because they assured me that they'd gotten all the kinks worked out."

Jim began to chuckle. Tim joined in. And Rod faked it.

"Well," Jim said finally, "I can assure you that all the kinks are worked out this time—and they've added something extra special." He took a sip of ginger ale from a sweating glass. "I don't know why someone didn't think of it a long time ago, the concept seems so . . . so marketable."

"What?" Tim asked.

"Yeah what?" Scott looked anxious.

Even Rod's interest was piqued. He leaned in a bit closer to the group.

"Here," Jim said, "let me show you." He withdrew a brochure from his shirt pocket. "It's called *The First Time.*" He handed it to Tim, who unfolded it.

Rod looked at the pamphlet over Scott's shoulder.

Don't You Wish You Knew Then What You Know Now? the come-on teased in big, bold letters. And it continued: "Well, now you can with **The First Time** dating service." There was fine print below, the usual notice that a cranial card was required. But then Jim started talking.

"It was incredible. She came to the door and I could have sworn it was her."

"Who?" Scott asked.

Jim's eyes softened for just a second. "Becky Milton, head cheerleader at Quayle High in Indianapolis."

"Your old flame?" Tim tore off another piece of roll and popped it into his mouth.

"Sort of," Jim said. "I was a sophomore and she was a senior. Man, the legs on her. Becky Milton." He said the name slowly, savoring the memory like a glass of expensive wine. "I must've gone to every game that year just to watch her perform at halftime. The team was oh and twelve, but I didn't care. She was gorgeous."

"So?" said Scott.

Jim continued dreamily, "So, the night of their senior party me and some friends crashed it. We were drinking beers outside in the parking lot when Becky burst out the door in tears. She and Chip Thompson, the varsity quarterback, had gotten into a big fight. Becky was crying, and she asked us for a ride home. And being no dummy, I knew that that was my big chance, so I volunteered. I drove her to her home, but she didn't want to go in—just yet. She said she wanted to drive around for a while. So I drove around for a while, palms sweating, mouth dry, the whole bit. I was trying to keep my eyes on the road and not her skirt. Finally, she said stop. Then she asked me if I wanted to crawl in the back seat with her."

"You never told us this?" Scott said, a bit upset.

"I know," Jim said, and paused. "Because it was a disaster. I didn't have the foggiest notion of what to do. And it was obvious that she wanted someone who did. But I did it. It wasn't pretty, but I did it."

"That was your *first time*?" Tim asked.

Jim nodded and took a sip of ginger ale.

Scott coughed. "And so last night some droid who looked like Becky . . . ? Becky . . . ?"

"Milton."

"Some droid made up to look like Becky Milton comes to your place and you do it over again."

"That's right," Jim said. "Only it wasn't just some droid made up to look like her. It *was* her. Right down to the skirt and the tears and the lines about how she didn't want to see Chip Thompson ever again. Exactly as I remembered it."

"And then you laid her?" Tim asked. "You screwed her brains out in your apartment?"

"No," Jim said, grinning. "Becky Milton wanted to go for a ride."

Scott let it sink in and then gulped down hard.

Rod looked down at the brochure. So did Scott and Tim and Rod. Jim was smiling like a cat.

Don't You Wish You Knew Then What You Know Now?

Rod's apartment was as white as his cubicle at work. White walls, white furniture, even a white rug. The only thing to break the monotony was the bird pictures on the walls.

Jim had made copies of the brochure that afternoon and now one rested on Rod's white kitchen table. While he microwaved dinner, Rod flipped through the brochure again, and thought about his first time—with Tammy Wilson and what happened after the dance his senior year in college. For a moment he was back there, underneath the trees, smelling the pine needles and the lemon scent in her hair.

And they were laughing at him!

Then the microwave beeped. The chicken and potatoes were ready.

*   *   *

After dinner, Rod again looked at the brochure.

"This is stupid," he said to himself. "I don't know a whole lot more now than I knew then. There's been what? Three women since, one encounter each. That doesn't exactly make me a Don Juan." And besides, he didn't want to get started on the droids. If they were good, Rod knew they could be habit forming. Just ask Scott. And that's not what he wanted. Rod wanted a real woman, someone he could talk to—about books, perhaps.

Rod wanted the cashier in the cafeteria. But how to go about it?

Rod sighed, then crumpled the brochure into a little ball, sent it sailing into the wastebasket. "Two points," he said. "Two points."

Rod forced a smile. He was feeling better already. He'd made a decision and now it was up to him to stick to it.

And besides, he told himself, tonight was the first time he'd "scored" in quite a while.

And the laughter didn't return at all that night.

"I couldn't believe it," Scott said. "You were right."

Jim smiled and sucked ginger ale through his straw. Tim listened attentively. Rod took a bite of his turkey on white, chewed seventeen times. Before he sat down, Rod had managed to say "Hi" to the cashier, but that was all the conversation he could muster. His face was still flushed from the encounter, and he was mentally kicking himself in the butt for chickening out.

Jim withdrew the straw from his mouth and turned to Scott. "Of course I was right about the droids. I wouldn't lie to you guys."

"Tell us about it," Tim said. "What was she—I mean, it—like? Was she good?"

Scott said, "It felt like the real thing. I couldn't tell the difference."

Rod continued to chew. He wanted to tell Scott that he wasn't exactly an expert witness. But then he thought better of it. They'd only turn on him then, tease him about *all* his women. And Rod wasn't in the mood.

"Her name was Mrs. Watson," Scott began. "She was twenty-six, divorced, and built like a brick shithouse. I used to do handy work for her when I was in high school. Cut the grass, clean out the gutters, wash the car. That kind of stuff. Well, anyway, one summer's day I was trimming her hedges—"

"I'll bet you were," Jim grinned.

Scott winked. "I was trimming her hedges and she came out and asked me if I would like to take a break. She'd made a pitcher of lemonade and said if I wanted a glass I could come inside."

"I'll bet you did," grinned Tim.

"She was wearing a halter top and some white short shorts. And heels. Red high heels."

"No. I don't believe it," Jim said, feigning disbelief. "This sounds like one of those letters to *Penthouse*."

Scott raised three fingers and said, "Scout's honor."

"Okay, I believe you," Jim said quickly. "Go on."

"There's really not much more to tell. Before I knew it, she was sitting on my lap; her breasts were smashed up against my face. I had an instant boner. In no time we were rolling around on the floor." Scott stopped, popped a brownie into his mouth.

"So that's what happened last night?" Tim asked. "The same thing."

Scott swallowed. "Well yes and no."

"What do you mean *yes and no*?" Jim asked.

"It was the spitting image of Mrs. Watson," Scott said. "But this time we sixty-nined each other and then I rode her doggie style."

Tim slapped an open palm on the table, and the silverware jumped. "Tell me you didn't!"

"Scout's honor," Scott said, raising three fingers.

Everybody laughed. Rod forced a grin onto his face. Finally, Rod spoke up. "But your Mrs. Watson. Was it *really* her?"

Scott made a tent out of his fingers, exhaled dramatically. "Let me tell you this. She came to the door wearing the exact same outfit I remembered." He paused. "And she was carrying an ice-cold pitcher of lemonade."

Tim made a little sound in the back of his throat. Jim and Scott caught each other's eyes and smiled.

That night, halfway through his dinner of microwaved chicken and potatoes, Rod put down his fork and went over to the wastebasket. He rummaged around for a few seconds, then he found it.

He took the brochure and unfolded it. Rod smoothed out the creases with his hand, then placed it flat on the table, weighing down each end with an empty bowl. He sat back down and cut himself another small piece of chicken and proceeded to chew it seventeen times. Rod looked at the brochure, thought about Tammy Wilson, and masticated.

She was wearing a white dress that night, with frills. Rod remembered holding her hand. The pressure felt wonderful. They'd gone outside and the cool spring air was filled with moisture. The sky was a handful of winking diamonds on black velvet. Rod was a little drunk. Tammy even more so. Someone had spiked the punch. Sweat trickled down the back of Rod's neck as she led him to a spot out beyond the football field. There was a patch of pine trees and a soft carpet of dry needles. They sat down—

And the laughing began!

Just then the phone rang.

Rod swallowed the tiny piece of chicken. It felt like a pill going down. He punched in the phone and turned on the monitor. Mom and Dad were smiling from Seattle.

"Happy birthday to you. Happy Birthday to you. Happy Birthday, dear Rodney. Happy Birthday to you."

Mom held up a candle and Dad blew it out. They looked much older. But if they were that old, what about him?

"Happy Birthday, son," Dad said, smiling.

Rod put down his fork. "But it's not until tomorrow."

"We decided to call a day early," Mom said. "We wanted to be the first. And besides, tomorrow is Friday and you'll be out on a date." She paused. "Right?"

Rod answered quickly. "Yeah, that's right, mom. I'll be out on a date."

"Who is she?" Mom said.

Rod looked at the brochure. "Someone I used to . . . someone I work with."

"That's good," Mom said. "You'll have something in common."

Then they talked for ten minutes about the usual things: how his job was going, other dates, and how his job was going. As the conversation was drawing to a close, Dad suddenly became animated.

"Oh. I almost forgot," he said. "Quick. What's your PakFax number?"

Rod told him.

Dad pressed a few buttons in Seattle and five seconds later a light went off by Rod's phone. He reached over and opened the delivery chute. A CD of *The Birds* still wrapped in cellophane was sitting inside.

"It's from Uncle Harry," Dad said.

Rod stared at the credits and saw his own name next to Tippi Hedren's.

"Tell Uncle Harry thank you for me," Rod said.

"We will," Dad said. "Happy birthday again, son."

Then the screen blipped and went black.

Friday at lunch the cashier wasn't there, and Rod felt his heart sink like a ship. A droid, who looked like a sadistic schoolmarm from some nineteenth-century novel, had replaced her. She—it—didn't answer when Rod asked where the other cashier was. It only recited the price for his turkey on white and applesauce, then rang it up on the register.

At the lunch table, it was Tim's turn. And his was the best story, yet. Rod took a bite of his sandwich, chewed seventeen times, and listened.

"I was always kind of embarrassed to admit this, but the first time I ever got laid was with Linda."

Jim raised an eyebrow. "Your wife?"

"Nahhhh," Scott said. "Not that overweight cow. No way, José."

"It's true," Tim said. "But that overweight cow was

once the hottest number in high school. You should have seen her on the balance beam. Legs like a vise grip, breasts like full melons.''

"You're beginning to sound like some cheap poet." Jim sucked his straw and air bubbles gurgled in the bottom of his glass.

"But it *was* poetry," Tim said. "At least for the first few years. And that first time. Wow! It was after school. She was working out in the gym and I was coming back from the weight room, trying to build some muscles so I wouldn't get pushed around on the basketball court so much. It was late. No one else seemed to be around but the night janitor. And he was out in the hallway with the buffer.''

"While you were in the gym *buffing* Linda." Scott squealed like a pig at his joke.

"Well, yes." Tim almost blushed. "That was the gist of it. We'd been out casually once or twice. But nothing other than a good night kiss had come from it. She was dating other guys, but I'd heard that none of them had gotten any further with her either. So that day I sat down on the bleachers, towel around my neck, and watched her routine. She was good, very good. And afterward she came over and sat down next to me. We made small talk. And then, since we were both hot and sweaty, I made a joke about me taking a shower in the girls' locker room and she taking one in the boys'—since no one else was around. But then she said, 'Why don't we take one together?' "

"Nooo," Jim said. The straw fell out of his mouth.

Tim smiled. "She blushed as soon as she said it. And I could tell that the idea excited her as much as it did me. So I took her hand and led her to the locker room."

"Which one?" Rod asked. He wanted to be part of the conversation, too.

"Boys', of course. I didn't want any girls to see me naked."

"Funny," Jim said. "And last night? The same?"

"I rented a room on the East Side. Linda"—Tim made quotation marks in the air—"came to the door looking like she did eighteen years ago. She was wearing her gymnast's outfit. A thin sheen of sweat slicked her body. And she was holding a bar of soap."

"Oh, my," Scott said.

Rod looked at his watch. It read 12:23. He was born at 12:18.

Rod was now forty years old.

Rod's white apartment felt especially sterile tonight. No one at work had said anything about his birthday, and that left a pit in his stomach the size of a soup bowl. Rod stared at the bird pictures on the wall for a moment, then walked over to the refrigerator. Just one package of chicken and potatoes was left in the freezer. But tomorrow was Saturday, and he'd do his shopping at the market in the morning—just like last Saturday morning. And the Saturday morning before that. And the Saturday morning before that ...

Rod put the packet in the microwave, set the heat on low and the timer on long (he wasn't hungry just yet), and pressed the start button. Then he walked into the living area and put on *The Birds* for company. Rod watched until he spotted Hitchcock walking those ridiculous-looking dogs, then his attention wavered. He looked about the room.

And spotted the envelope.

It sat on the end table by the window. It was a plain white envelope and on the outside someone had written "Rod" in black ink. Rod wasted no time, but he opened it carefully, tearing a straight line through the crease with a fingernail. He pulled out the card. On it, a fat guy with a piece of pizza in his mouth and his arm around a buxom blonde was smiling. The caption said: *Happy 39th birthday!* Rod opened the card. The punchline said: *Again!* It was signed by the guys: Jim, Scott, and Tim.

That brought a smile to Rod's face. But underneath their signatures was a postscript: *Enjoy your "First Time." Compliments of lunch table #16.*

Rod put the empty envelope on the table, then saw that there was something else in it. He picked it up and turned it upside down. His cranial card popped out.

"How did ... ?" Rod reached for his wallet and

opened it. His cranial card was missing. The card in the envelope was his.

"How did . . . ?" Then Rod remembered his 2:30 lab experiment in the hyperclean room. He'd left his wallet and street clothes in the dressing room. And wasn't Scott hanging around there for no reason?

Of course.

Rod looked at the video screen. Rod Taylor, his namesake, was flirting with Tippi Hedren. And that brought up thoughts of Tammy Wilson. Would he have to flirt with her, too? In no time the doorbell would ring and she—or a *perfect* droid in the image of Tammy at twenty-one—would be standing at the door. Would she—it—be wearing that same white dress? Would she be a little tipsy on wine?

The microwave beeped. But Rod let the chicken and potatoes turn cold. Once again, he thought about that night.

They had run to the pine trees out by the athletic fields. There was a full moon that night and it cast a silvery glow on the trees and grass. "It looks like something out of a Walt Disney movie," Rod remembered saying. And Tammy added: "How romantic."

They sat on a bed of soft pine needles, the strong smell filling his head, numbing it, as though he'd smoked opium.

They kissed and her lips tasted like red wine. She giggled as she fumbled with the buttons on Rod's shirt. He felt himself getting hard as he reached behind her and attempted to undo her bra.

"Here," she said. "Let me help you with that." Her long black hair fell in front of her eyes as she looked down at her chest and unsnapped the bra. "It opens from the front." She smiled.

His shoes were next, then his pants; they landed in a heap near a pine root shaped like an S, on top of her panties. He took off his glasses.

It's all so perfect, he remembered thinking. As perfect as perfect can be. Her skin smelled of soap and her hair like lemon shampoo. He entered her and she moaned. He remembered thinking that he was going to come right there and so he tried to fight it off. He thought of baseball, lab tests. He wanted to please her too.

But then the laughter. The mocking laughter!

Rod felt their eyes on the back of his neck. He pictured their faces behind him, staring at his white ass glowing palely in the moonlight. Did one of them have a camera? Or, worse still, a camcorder?

And suddenly Rod didn't have to worry about being too quick. He went instantly limp inside her. He stopped thrusting, but Tammy continued to roll her hips.

Then she stopped. "Rod? What's the matter?"

The laughter continued.

"Rod? Are you okay?"

He looked down at her and his heart ached. He didn't want it to be like this. But what choice did he have.

"I can't *do it* . . . I can't make love with *them* here."

"Who?"

"They must have followed us down here from the dance. I'm sorry. *Real* funny, guys. *Real funny.*" Rod said the last words louder than the others.

Tammy brushed a strand of hair from her green eyes. "What are you talking about, Rod?"

He slipped out of her and started to roll over. "You mean you can't hear them, laughing at us?"

"Rod. No one's laughing at us. We're out here all alone."

Rod squinted in the darkness, then padded around in the pine needles until he found his glasses. Moonlight made the pines glow like silver statues. Off in the distance he could see the lights from the party. A couple of voices echoed from very far away.

Rod looked around him. Tammy was right: they were alone.

Tammy continued, "Why there's no one else here except us . . ."

Rod rechecked to his left, and right.

". . . except us and those birds."

Rod looked up. About a dozen blackbirds sat on a limb.

Then they started laughing.

*   *   *

The laughter was interrupted by the doorbell. Rod awoke as if from a dream. He walked to the door, dizzy and shaken. He had a headache and his mouth was dry. On the screen, a flock of blackbirds was amassing on a jungle gym.

Rod opened the door.

And in walked Uncle Harry.

He wore overalls with paint stains on the front. Thick black hair grew like fur on the backs of his hands. He looked just like he did thirty-five years ago.

Harry paused when he saw the movie playing. He coughed and his breath smelled like beer.

"Why, Rodney," Uncle Harry said. "How thoughtful. I see you're playing our song."

Harry laughed and the birds on screen took flight. Children screamed and ran pell-mell out of a schoolhouse.

Rodney took a step backward and opened his mouth to scream but nothing came out.

And there was nowhere to run.

THE CEREMONY

ARTHUR MACHEN

"Then she saw herself put down for a moment on the grass, and the red color stained the grim stone, and there was nothing else—except that one night she woke up and heard the nurse sobbing."

It is difficult for me to resist devoting somewhat greater space to an appreciation of Arthur Machen, since he was one of the writers whose unmistakable themes and strongly flavored style cemented my early fascination with the horror genre. His career, I've since learned, was an oddly patterned one: initially a private tutor for children, then a translator, he took to the stage as a traveling Shakespearean actor after the death of his first wife, eventually managing to support himself as a journalist and writer of popular magazine fiction. Yet only the kindness of strangers—in the form of a charitable subscription funded by admiring American and British readers—sustained him near the very end of his life. It was clear that many of his contemporaries never knew whether to regard him, to cite one of them, as "an actor who amuses his leisure by writing books or as an author who fills up his evenings by appearing on stage."

There is also no question but that Machen was a self-

consciously dramatic man of letters: it is said that once, wandering about London in his usual, anachronistic scholar's garb, he found himself mistaken by a street urchin for the very late Dr. Johnson. But his eccentricities also provided the wellspring for Machen's unique contributions to the literature of What Lies Beyond. Presenting glimpses into regions ruled by strange ecstacies co-joined there with even stranger horrors, he was guided by his belief (as stated in the supremely antisentimental fairy story "The Novel of the Black Seal") that "every branch of human knowledge if traced up to its source and final principle vanishes into mystery."

Readers unfamiliar with Machen's longer works should know that the deliciously over-the-top "The Great God Pan," a fin de siècle melodrama of unnatural science written back in an era when the word "decadent" still carried some serious weight, has recently been made available again in David Hartwell's anthology, Foundations of Fear. However, the seminal "The Novel of the White Powder," Machen's most important creation, possibly will prove less easily accessed. Here, though, in the very brief, tantalizingly perverse "The Ceremony," written in 1897, you'll discover a story amazingly modern in its ability to create hauntingly large effects with small, almost invisible touches.

From her childhood, from those early and misty days which began to seem unreal, she recollected the gray stone in the wood.

It was something between the pillar and the pyramid in shape, and its gray solemnity amid the leaves and the grass shone and shone from those early years, always with some hint of wonder. She remembered how, when she was quite a little girl, she had strayed one day, on a hot afternoon, from her nurse's side, and only a little way in the wood the gray stone rose from the grass, and she cried out and ran back in panic terror.

"What a silly little girl," the nurse had said. "It's only the ... stone." She had quite forgotten the name that the servant had given, and she was always ashamed to ask as she grew older.

But always that hot day, that burning afternoon of her childhood when she had first looked consciously on the gray image in the wood, remained not a memory but a sensation. The wide wood swelling like the sea, the tossing of the bright boughs in the sunshine, the sweet smell of the grass and flowers, the beating of the summer wind upon her cheek, the gloom of the underglade rich, indistinct, gorgeous, significant as old tapestry; she could feel it and see it all, and the scent of it was in her nostrils. And in the midst of the picture, where the strange plants grew gross in shadow, was the old gray shape of the stone.

But there were in her mind broken remnants of another and far earlier impression. It was all uncertain, the shadow of a shadow, so vague that it might well have been a dream that had mingled with the confused waking thoughts of a little child. She did not know that she remembered, she rather remembered the memory. But again it was a summer day, and a woman, perhaps the same nurse, held her in her arms, and went through the wood. The woman carried bright flowers in one hand; the dream had in it a glow of bright red, and the perfume of cottage roses. Then she saw herself put down for a moment on the grass, and the red color stained the grim stone, and there was nothing else—except that one night she woke up and heard the nurse sobbing.

She often used to think of the strangeness of very early life; one came, it seemed, from a dark cloud, there was a glow of light, but for a moment, and afterward the night. It was as if one gazed at a velvet curtain, heavy, mysterious, impenetrable blackness, and then, for the twinkling of an eye, one spied through a pinhole a storied town that flamed, with fire about its walls and pinnacles. And then again the folding darkness, so that sight became illusion, almost in the seeing. So to her was that earliest, doubtful vision of the gray stone, of the red color spilled upon it, with the incongruous episode of the nursemaid, who wept at night.

But the later memory was clear; she could feel, even now, the inconsequent terror that sent her away shrieking, running to the nurse's skirts. Afterward, through the days of girlhood, the stone had taken its place among the vast array of unintelligible things which haunt every child's imagination. It was part of life, to be accepted and not questioned; her elders spoke of many things which she could not understand, she opened books and was dimly amazed, and in the Bible there were many phrases which seemed strange. Indeed, she was often puzzled by her parents' conduct, by their looks at one another, by their half words, and among all these problems which she hardly recognized as problems, was the gray ancient figure rising from dark grass.

Some semiconscious impulse made her haunt the wood where shadow enshrined the stone. One thing was noticeable; that all through the summer months the passersby dropped flowers there. Withered blossoms were always on the ground, among the grass, and on the stone fresh blooms constantly appeared. From the daffodil to the Michaelmas daisy there was marked the calendar of the cottage gardens, and in the winter she had seen sprays of juniper and box, mistletoe and holly. Once she had been drawn through the bushes by a red glow, as if there had been a fire in the wood, and when she came to the place, all the stone shone and all the ground about it was bright with roses.

In her eighteenth year she went one day into the wood, carrying with her a book that she was reading. She hid herself in a nook of hazel, and her soul was full of poetry, when there was a rustling, the rapping of parted boughs returning to their place. Her concealment was but a little way from the stone, and she peered through the net of boughs, and saw a girl timidly approaching. She knew her quite well; it was Annie Dolben, the daughter of a laborer, lately a promising pupil at Sunday school. Annie was a nice-mannered girl, never failing in her curtsy, wonderful for her knowledge of the Jewish kings. Her face had taken an expression that whispered, that hinted strange things; there was a light and a glow behind the veil of flesh. And in her hand she bore lilies.

The lady hidden in hazels watched Annie come close to the gray image; for a moment her whole body palpitated with expectation, almost the sense of what was to happen dawned upon her. She watched Annie crown the stone with flowers, she watched the amazing ceremony that followed.

And yet, in spite of all her blushing shame, she herself bore blossoms to the wood a few months later. She laid white hothouse lilies upon the stone, and orchids of dying purple, and crimson exotic flowers. Having kissed the gray image with devout passion, she performed there all the antique immemorial rites.

THE NATURE OF THE EVIDENCE

MAY SINCLAIR

"She slipped off the loose sleeves of the chiffon thing and it fell to her feet. Marston says he heard a queer sound, something between a groan and a grunt, and was amazed to find that it came from himself."

"The Nature of the Evidence" unfolds in the classic form—as an extraordinary tale related secondhand by a narrator who at the start, anticipating our mistrust, throws up the usual (metaphorical) hand to still any impending chorus of protest. "So that, if you ask me whether I believe this tale," he assures us, "all I can say is, I believe the things happened, because he said they happened and because they happened to him. As for what they were— well, I don't pretend to explain it, neither would he."

The noted scholar E. F. Bleiler has called this story of an unfortunate second marriage "surprising" for the period. Myself, I find it more than that: in fact, it's truly amazing, really, for any era—and the consummations of the . . . flesh Sinclair conjures up are all the more explicit for being left, in their fullest details, to our gasping imaginations.

———————

This is the story Marston told me. He didn't want to tell it. I had to tear it from him bit by bit. I've pieced the bits together in their time order, and explained things here and there, but the facts are the facts he gave me. There's nothing that I didn't get out of him somehow.

Out of *him*—you'll admit my source is unimpeachable. Edward Marston, the great K.C., and the author of an admirable work on "The Logic of Evidence." You should have read the chapters on "What Evidence Is and What It Is Not." You may say he lied; but if you knew Marston you'd know he wouldn't lie, for the simple reason that he's incapable of inventing anything. So that, if you ask me whether I believe this tale, all I can say is, I believe the things happened, because he said they happened and because they happened to him. As for what they *were*—well, I don't pretend to explain it, neither would he.

You know he was married twice. He adored his first wife, Rosamund, and Rosamund adored him. I suppose they were completely happy. She was fifteen years younger than he, and beautiful. I wish I could make you see how beautiful. Her eyes and mouth had the same sort of bow, full and wide-sweeping, and they stared out of her face with the same grave, contemplative innocence. Her mouth was finished off at each corner with the loveliest little molding, rounded like the pistil of a flower. She wore her hair in a solid gold fringe over her forehead, like a child's, and a big coil at the back. When it was let down it hung in a heavy cable to her waist. Marston used to tease her about it. She had a trick of tossing back the rope in the night when it was hot under her, and it would fall smack across his face and hurt him.

There was a pathos about her that I can't describe— a curious, pure, sweet beauty, like a child's; perfect, and perfectly immature; so immature that you couldn't conceive its lasting—like that—any more than childhood lasts. Marston used to say it made him nervous. He was afraid of waking up in the morning and finding that it had changed in the night. And her beauty was so much a part of herself that you couldn't think of her without it. Somehow you felt that if it went she must go too.

Well, she went first.

For a year afterward Marston existed dangerously, always on the edge of a breakdown. If he didn't go over altogether it was because his work saved him. He had no consoling theories. He was one of those bigoted materialists of the nineteenth century type who believe that consciousness is a purely physiological function, and that when your body's dead, *you're* dead. He saw no reason to suppose the contrary. "When you consider," he used to say, "the nature of the evidence!"

It's as well to bear this in mind, so as to realize that he hadn't any bias or anticipation. Rosamund survived for him only in his memory. And in his memory he was still in love with her. At the same time he used to discuss quite cynically the chances of his marrying again.

It seems that in their honeymoon they had gone into that. Rosamund said she hated to think of his being lonely and miserable, supposing she died before he did. She would like him to marry again. If, she stipulated, he married the right woman.

He had put it to her: "And if I marry the wrong one?"

And she had said, That would be different. She couldn't bear that.

He remembered all this afterward; but there was nothing in it to make him suppose, at the time, that she would take action.

We talked it over, he and I, one night.

"I suppose," he said, "I shall have to marry again. It's a physical necessity. But it won't be anything more. I shan't marry the sort of woman who'll expect anything more. I won't put another woman in Rosamund's place. There'll be no unfaithfulness about it."

And there wasn't. Soon after that first year he married Pauline Silver.

She was a daughter of old Justice Parker, who was a friend of Marston's people. He hadn't seen the girl till she came home from India after her divorce.

Yes, there'd been a divorce. Silver had behaved very decently. He'd let her bring it against *him*, to save her. But there were some queer stories going about. They didn't get round to Marston, because he was so mixed up with her people; and if they had he wouldn't have believed them. He'd made up his mind he'd marry Pauline the first minute he'd seen her. She was handsome; the hard, black, white, and vermilion kind, with a little aristocratic nose and a lascivious mouth.

It was, as he had meant it to be, nothing but physical infatuation on both sides. No question of Pauline's taking Rosamund's place.

Marston had a big case on at the time.

They were in such a hurry that they couldn't wait till it was over; and as it kept him in London they agreed to put off their honeymoon till the autumn; and he took her straight to his own house in Curzon Street.

This, he admitted afterward, was the part he hated. The Curzon Street house was associated with Rosamund; especially their bedroom—Rosamund's bedroom—and his library. The library was the room Rosamund liked best, because it was his room. She had her place in the corner by the hearth, and they were always alone there together in the evenings when his work was done, and when it wasn't done she would still sit with him, keeping quiet in her corner with a book.

Luckily for Marston, at the first sight of the library Pauline took a dislike to it.

I can hear her. "Br-rr-rh! There's something beastly about this room, Edward. I can't think how you can sit in it."

And Edward, a little caustic: "*You* needn't, if you don't like it."

"I certainly shan't."

She stood there—I can see her—on the hearth rug by Rosamund's chair, looking uncommonly handsome and lascivious. He was going to take her in his arms and kiss her vermilion mouth, when, he said, something stopped him. Stopped him clean, as if it had risen up and stepped between them. He supposed it was the memory of Rosamund, vivid in the place that had been hers.

You see it was just that place, of silent, intimate communion, that Pauline would never take. And the rich, coarse, contented creature didn't even want to take it. He saw that he would be left alone there, all right, with his memory.

But the bedroom was another matter. That, Pauline had made it understood from the beginning, she would have to have. Indeed, there was no other he could well have offered her. The drawing room covered the whole of the first floor. The bedrooms above were cramped, and this one had been formed by throwing the two front rooms into one. It looked south, and the bathroom opened out of it at the back. Marston's small northern room had a door on the narrow landing at right angles to his wife's door. He could hardly expect her to sleep there, still less in any of the tight boxes on the top floor. He said he wished he had sold the Curzon Street house.

But Pauline was enchanted with the wide, three-windowed piece that was to be hers. It had been exquisitely furnished for poor little Rosamund; all seventeenth-century walnut wood, Bokhara rugs, thick silk curtains, deep blue with purple linings, and a big, rich bed covered with a purple counterpane embroidered in blue.

One thing Marston insisted on: that *he* should sleep on Rosamund's side of the bed, and Pauline in his own old place. He didn't want to see Pauline's body where Rosamund's had been. Of course he had to lie about it and pretend he had always slept on the side next to the window.

I can see Pauline going about in that room, looking at everything; looking at herself, her black, white, and vermilion, in the glass that had held Rosamund's pure rose and gold; opening the wardrobe where Rosamund's dresses used to hang, sniffing up the delicate flower scent of Rosamund, not caring, covering it with her own thick trail.

And Marston (who cared abominably)—I can see him getting more miserable and at the same time more excited as the wedding evening went on. He took her to the play to fill up the time, or perhaps to get her out of Rosamund's rooms; God knows. I can see them sitting in the stalls, bored and restless, starting up and going out before the thing was half over, and coming back to that house in Curzon Street before eleven o'clock.

It wasn't much past eleven when he went to her room.

I told you her door was at right angles to his, and the landing was narrow, so that anybody standing by Pauline's door must have been seen the minute he opened his. He hadn't even to cross the landing to get to her.

Well, Marston swears that there was nothing there when he opened his own door; but when he came to Pauline's he saw Rosamund standing up before it; and, he said, *"She wouldn't let me in."*

Her arms were stretched out, barring the passage. Oh, yes, he saw her face, Rosamund's face; I gathered that it was utterly sweet, and utterly inexorable. He couldn't pass her.

So he turned into his own room, backing, he says, so that he could keep looking at her. And when he stood on the threshold of his own door she wasn't there.

No, he wasn't frightened. He couldn't tell me what he felt; but he left his door open all night because he couldn't bear to shut it on her. And he made no other attempt to go in to Pauline; he was so convinced that the phantasm of Rosamund would come again and stop him.

I don't know what sort of excuse he made to Pauline the next morning. He said she was very stiff and sulky all day; and no wonder. He was still infatuated with her, and I don't think that the phantasm of Rosamund had put him off Pauline in the least. In fact, he persuaded himself that the thing was nothing but a hallucination, due, no doubt, to his excitement.

Anyhow, he didn't expect to see it at the door again the next night.

Yes. It was there. Only, this time, he said, it drew aside to let him pass. It smiled at him, as if it were saying, "Go in, if you must; you'll see what'll happen."

He had no sense that it had followed him into the room; he felt certain that, this time, it would let him be.

It was when he approached Pauline's bed, which had been Rosamund's bed, that she appeared again, standing between it and him, and stretching out her arms to keep him back.

All that Pauline could see was her bridegroom backing and backing, then standing there, fixed, and the look on his face. That in itself was enough to frighten her.

She said, "What's the matter with you, Edward?"

He didn't move.

"What are you standing there for? Why don't you come to bed?"

Then Marston seems to have lost his head and blurted it out: "I can't. I can't."

"Can't what?" said Pauline from the bed.

"Can't sleep with you. She won't let me."

"She?"

"Rosamund. My wife. She's there."

"What on earth are you talking about?"

"She's there, I tell you. She won't let me. She's pushing me back."

He says Pauline must have thought he was drunk or something. Remember, she *saw* nothing but Edward, his face, and his mysterious attitude. He must have looked very drunk.

She sat up in bed, with her hard, black eyes blazing away at him, and told him to leave the room that minute. Which he did.

The next day she had it out with him. I gathered that she kept on talking about the "state" he was in.

"You came to my room, Edward, in a *disgraceful* state."

I suppose Marston said he was sorry; but he couldn't help it; he wasn't drunk. He stuck to it that Rosamund was there. He had seen her. And Pauline said, if he wasn't drunk then he must be mad, and he said meekly, "Perhaps I *am* mad."

That set her off, and she broke out in a fury. He was no more mad than she was; but he didn't care for her; he was making ridiculous excuses; shamming, to put her off. There was some other woman.

Marston asked her what on earth she supposed he'd married her for. Then she burst out crying and said she didn't know.

Then he seems to have made it up with Pauline. He managed to make her believe he wasn't lying, that he really had seen something, and between them they arrived at a rational explanation of the appearance. He had been overworking. Rosamund's phantasm was nothing but a hallucination of his exhausted brain.

This theory carried him on till bedtime. Then, he says, he began to wonder what would happen, what Rosamund's phantasm would do next. Each morning his passion for Pauline had come back again, increased by frustration, and it worked itself up to a crescendo, toward night. Supposing he *had* seen Rosamund. He might see her again. He had become suddenly subject to hallucinations. But as long as you *knew* you were hallucinating you were all right.

So what they agreed to do that night was by way of precaution, in case the thing came again. It might even be sufficient in itself to prevent his seeing anything.

Instead of going in to Pauline he was to get into the room before she did, and she was to come to him there. That, they said, would break the spell. To make him feel even safer he meant to be in bed before Pauline came.

Well, he got into the room all right.

It was when he tried to get into bed that—he saw her (I mean Rosamund).

She was lying there, in his place next to the window, her own place, lying in her immature childlike beauty and sleeping, the firm full bow of her mouth softened by sleep. She was perfect in every detail, the lashes of her shut eyelids golden on her white cheeks, the solid gold of her square fringe shining, and the great braided golden rope of her hair flung back on the pillow.

He knelt down by the bed and pressed his forehead into the bedclothes, close to her side. He declared he could feel her breathe.

He stayed there for the twenty minutes Pauline took to undress and come to him. He says the minutes stretched out like hours. Pauline found him still kneeling with his face pressed into the bedclothes. When he got up he staggered.

She asked him what he was doing and why he wasn't in bed. And he said, "It's no use. I can't. I can't."

But somehow he couldn't tell her that Rosamund was there. Rosamund was too sacred; he couldn't talk about her. He only said, "You'd better sleep in my room tonight."

He was staring down at the place in the bed where he still saw Rosamund. Pauline couldn't have seen anything but the bedclothes, the sheet smoothed above an invisible breast, and the hollow in the pillow. She said she'd do nothing of the sort. She wasn't going to be frightened out of her own room. He could do as he liked.

He couldn't leave them there; he couldn't leave Pauline with Rosamund, and he couldn't leave Rosamund with Pauline. So he sat up in a chair with his back turned to the bed. No. He didn't make any attempt to go back. He says he knew she was still lying there, guarding his place, which was her place. The odd thing is that he wasn't in the least disturbed or frightened or surprised. He took the whole thing as a matter of course. And presently he dozed off into a sleep.

A scream woke him and the sound of a violent body leaping out of the bed and thudding on to its feet. He switched on the light and saw the bedclothes flung back and Pauline standing on the floor with her mouth open.

He went to her and held her. She was cold to the touch and shaking with terror, and her jaws dropped as if she were palsied.

She said, "Edward, there's something in the bed."

He glanced again at the bed. It was empty.

"There isn't," he said. "Look."

He stripped the bed to the foot-rail, so that she could see.

"There *was* something."

"Do you see it?"

"No. I felt it."

She told him. First something had come swinging, smack across her face. A thick, heavy rope of woman's hair. It had waked her. Then she had put out her hands and felt the body. A woman's body, soft and horrible;

her fingers had sunk in the shallow breasts. Then she had screamed and jumped.

And she couldn't stay in the room. The room, she said, was "beastly."

She slept in Marston's room, in his small single bed, and he sat up with her all night, on a chair.

She believed now that he had really seen something, and she remembered that the library was beastly, too. Haunted by something. She supposed that was what she had felt. Very well. Two rooms in the house were haunted; their bedroom and the library. They would just have to avoid those two rooms. She had made up her mind, you see, that it was nothing but a case of an ordinary haunted house; the sort of thing you're always hearing about and never believe in till it happens to yourself. Marston didn't like to point out to her that the house hadn't been haunted till she came into it.

The following night, the fourth night, she was to sleep in the spare room on the top floor, next to the servants, and Marston in his own room.

But Marston didn't sleep. He kept on wondering whether he would or would not go up to Pauline's room. That made him horribly restless, and instead of undressing and going to bed, he sat up on a chair with a book. He wasn't nervous, but he had a queer feeling that something was going to happen, and that he must be ready for it, and that he'd better be dressed.

It must have been soon after midnight when he heard the doorknob turning very slowly and softly.

The door opened behind him and Pauline came in, moving without a sound, and stood before him. It gave him a shock; for he had been thinking of Rosamund, and when he heard the doorknob turn it was the phantasm of Rosamund that he expected to see coming in. He says, for the first minute, it was this appearance of Pauline that struck him as the uncanny and unnatural thing.

She had nothing, absolutely nothing on but a transparent white chiffony sort of dressing gown. She was trying to undo it. He could see her hands shaking as her fingers fumbled with the fastenings.

He got up suddenly, and they just stood there before

each other, saying nothing, staring at each other. He was fascinated by her, by the sheer glamour of her body, gleaming white through the thin stuff, and by the movement of her fingers. I think I've said she was a beautiful woman, and her beauty at that moment was overpowering.

And still he stared at her without saying anything. It sounds as if their silence lasted quite a long time, but in reality it couldn't have been more than some fraction of a second.

Then she began. "Oh, Edward, for God's sake *say* something. Oughtn't I to have come?"

And she went on without waiting for an answer. "Are you thinking of *her*? Because, if—if you are, I'm not going to let her drive you away from me. . . . I'm not going to. . . . She'll keep on coming as long as we don't— Can't you see that this is the way to stop it . . . ? When you take me in your arms."

She slipped off the loose sleeves of the chiffon thing and it fell to her feet. Marston says he heard a queer sound, something between a groan and a grunt, and was amazed to find that it came from himself.

He hadn't touched her yet—mind you, it went quicker than it takes to tell, it was still an affair of the fraction of a second—they were holding out their arms to each other, when the door opened again without a sound, and without visible passage, the phantasm was there. It came incredibly fast, and thin at first, like a shaft of light sliding between them. It didn't do anything; there was no beating of hands, only, as it took on its full form, its perfect likeness of flesh and blood, it made its presence felt like a push, a force, driving them asunder.

Pauline hadn't seen it yet. She thought it was Marston who was beating her back. She cried out: "Oh, don't, don't push me away!" She stooped below the phantasm's guard and clung to his knees, writhing and crying. For a moment it was a struggle between her moving flesh and that still, supernatural being.

And in that moment Marston realized that he hated Pauline. She was fighting Rosamund with her gross flesh and blood, taking a mean advantage of her embodied state to beat down the heavenly, discarnate thing.

He called to her to let go.

"It's not I," he shouted. "Can't you *see* her?"

Then, suddenly, she saw, and let go, and dropped, crouching on the floor and trying to cover herself. This time she had given no cry.

The phantasm gave way; it moved slowly toward the door, and as it went it looked back over its shoulder at Marston; it trailed a hand, signaling to him to come.

He went out after it, hardly aware of Pauline's naked body that still writhed there, clutching at his feet as they passed, and drew itself after him, like a worm, like a beast, along the floor.

She must have got up at once and followed them out onto the landing; for, as he went down the stairs behind the phantasm, he could see Pauline's face, distorted with lust and terror, peering at them above the stairhead. She saw them descend the last flight, and cross the hall at the bottom and go into the library. The door shut behind them.

Something happened in there. Marston never told me precisely what it was, and I didn't ask him. Anyhow, that finished it.

The next day Pauline ran away to her own people. She couldn't stay in Marston's house because it was haunted by Rosamund, and he wouldn't leave it for the same reason.

And she never came back; for she was not only afraid of Rosamund, she was afraid of Marston. And if she *had* come it wouldn't have been any good. Marston was convinced that as often as he attempted to get to Pauline, something would stop him. Pauline certainly felt that if Rosamund were pushed to it, she might show herself in some still more sinister and terrifying form. She knew when she was beaten.

And there was more in it than that. I believe he tried to explain it to her; said he had married her on the assumption that Rosamund was dead, but that now he knew she was alive; she was, as he put it, "there." He tried to make her see that if he had Rosamund he couldn't have *her*. Rosamund's presence in the world annulled their contract.

You see I'm convinced that something *did* happen that night in the library. I say, he never told me precisely what it was, but he once let something out. We were discussing one of Pauline's love affairs (after the separation she gave him endless grounds for divorce).

"Poor Pauline," he said, "she thinks she's so passionate."

"Well," I said, "wasn't she?"

Then he burst out. "No. She doesn't know what passion is. None of you know. You haven't the faintest conception. You'd have to get rid of your bodies first. *I* didn't know until—"

He stopped himself. I think he was going to say, "until Rosamund came back and showed me." For he leaned forward and whispered: "It isn't a localized affair at all. . . . If you only knew—"

So I don't think it was just faithfulness to a revived memory. I take it there had been, behind that shut door, some experience, some terrible and exquisite contact. More penetrating than sight or touch. More—more extensive: passion at all points of being.

Perhaps the supreme moment of it, the ecstasy, only came when her phantasm had disappeared.

He couldn't go back to Pauline after *that*.

THE FACE OF HELENE BOURNOUW

HARLAN ELLISON

"And when his first time was over, and she was readying him for a second, he begged her to put on the little girl clothes he knew she had brought in the wide-mouthed model's handbag. The short pinafore, the white hose, the patent-leather buckled shoes, the soft ribbon for the hair, the childish charm bracelet. She promised she would."

More fun than the proverbial barrelful of lower primates, Harlan Ellison has, on occasion, been known to be just as much trouble. But who would say he isn't worth it, with his alert, restless navigator's mind always set to track the savage ironies in any situation and with his ambidextrous ability to switch genres—from sf to horror to fantasy, from confessional essays to screenplays to TV reviews, with a little restaurant criticism on the side—at will? His energy, commitment, and intelligence form the bulk of his stock in trade, along with the volatile additions of the two important Ellisonian "p's"—pugnaciousness and perversity. He is, in short, a much-honored writer deserving of all his fame.

Moreover, his take-no-prisoners philosophy, here muted a bit by the mood of smoky nostalgia for a pulp-era New York, also makes a wonderful contrast to the sensibility of May Sinclair, who precedes him. At least in theory. But, in fact, after reading their two very different stories, "The Nature of the Evidence" and "The Face of Helene Bournouw," it may not be such an easy matter to decide which of these two masters has created "the most memorable succubus." You decide.

These are the sounds in the night: First, the sound of darkness, lapping at the edges of a sea of movement, itself called silence. Then, second, the fingertip-sensed sound of the cyclical movement of the universe as it gnaws its way through the dust-film called Time. And last, the animal sounds of two people making love. The moist sounds of two bodies in concert. Always the same sound, and only set apart from itself by the meters and stop-pauses of generators phasing down, of equipment being hauled into new positions for use.

Weltered, foundering, going down in this cloggage of sound, Helene Bournouw's mouth opened to receive a charcoal-scented passion as brief as the life of a leaf. Wind rushed silently past, deafening as it sucked the breath from both Helene Bournouw and her lover.

In the perfect minds of Gods too perfect even to have been conjured by mortals, there never existed a love as drenched in empathy as the love between Helene Bournouw and the man she accepted gratefully. Under the sun that burned bright and blue-white there was never a passion such as this: straight as steel ties to an indecipherable horizon, gleaming rhodium silver-white in perfection, filled to the top and to its own surface tension with amiability and laughter and random turnings in the dark that signified two merging into one, being taken in completely, warm and forever.

This was the way she made love, Helene Bournouw, the most beautiful woman who had ever seen man through eyes of wonder.

Richard Strike, the only one of the cilia-wafting Broadway columnists with a valid claim to literacy, once referred to her as the most memorable succubus he had ever encountered. The Times Square sharpers, of course, equated the phrase with oral pornography and let it pass; *they* knew what Helene Bournouw was; she was too beautiful.

Yet there was truth in what Strike had said, and the label was a fair one. There was something about Helene Bournouw that drained those who came into her life, within her reach. Of beauty there was no doubt; she *was* almost too beautiful. Abington was the only photographer she would allow to pose her, and together their model-photographer relationship brought forth portraits of Helene Bournouw that became testimonies to her unearthly loveliness, hers alone. (Whether those portraits sold sanitary napkins or compact cars, the viewer saw first Helene Bournouw, and when her image finally released him ... *then* the product.)

From these two elements—beauty that could not be denied and a nature that left others spent and empty—elements met and altered subtly by the catalyst that was Helene Bournouw, the legend grew. Her private life was her own, something peculiar and rare for a mover in that circle where publicity has monetary value. Other than superficialities concerning what young executive or visiting film star she was dating, little was known of her.

As Abington once remarked to a curious article writer from one of the women's slicks, "When she leaves the studio, I don't know where she goes. She lives on Sutton Place, but she's seldom there; Helene could be making her home in the fog, and we wouldn't know it. All I care about is that she's the loveliest woman I've ever photographed."

And that, from the man who discovered Suzy Parker, who did the first adult portraits of Elizabeth Taylor, who was commissioned to photograph the fifty most beautiful women in the world for *Life,* is perhaps the most telling argument for those who swear there has never been born a more fascinating, gorgeous creature than Helene Bournouw.

Seated early in the day in a corner booth at Lindy's, Helene Bournouw turned a veritable Niagara among smiles on her companion. Her deep gray eyes, subtly changing and compelling, were half drawn closed in a glance both unsettling and intoxicating.

"Jimmy, we're finished," she said with unarguable simplicity.

The clean, strong lines of her companion's face eroded. His glance wavered from hers, and his tongue broke from the cover of his mouth to moisten his lips inarticulately. It had been a week such as he had never known, this James P. Knoll, head of a multibillion-dollar shipping and cartage chain. A week in which he had known danger, love, excitement, challenge—a range of emotions that had left him spent. He had spent a full week with Helene Bournouw.

Now she had ended it, with three words.

Without preamble, without provocation, after a night so diamond-perfect in its wholeness that he had decided to break away to buy the ring, she had shattered it all.

James P. Knoll rose from the booth in Lindy's and knowing without question by the tone she had used, a tone he had thought incapable of coming from her, that they were indeed finished, dropped a hundred-dollar bill on the table to pay for the lunch that had not yet been served, and walked out onto Broadway.

Later that day he would remove the little German .22-caliber short revolver from his wall safe and put a neat, almost bloodless hole in his right temple.

Helene Bournouw ate sparingly of the lunch when it was served. A model with her qualities could not risk overweight.

Later that day, due to the untimely death of its sole driving force, its president, Knoll Transit Incorporated suffered heavily on the market, causing a stock run that quickly spread like plague to the other rolling cartage firms, causing a major disruption in shipping and trucking throughout the country. All very sudden.

Helene Bournouw moved to her second appointment of the day ...

Quentin Dean was not his real name, but whatever unpronounceable Polish or Latvian origin it had been, it in no way detracted from the quality of his painting. Quentin Dean, though living off day-old bread and canned cream of tomato soup in a Fourteenth Street loft, was perhaps the finest new artist of his generation. He had not yet been discovered by the critics; that might come in a year, perhaps eight months if he could find the right sort of patron, the right sort of interested party who would keep him eating, keep him working, show his efforts around till the break and the recognition came.

The critics had not yet found Quentin Dean, but Helene Bournouw had.

She cabbed over from Lindy's and climbed the four flights to Quentin Dean's airy, very clean, very light studio. Though barren—save for the lumber leaning and stacked against the walls, preparatory to becoming easels and frames; save for the hundreds of paintings resting with their faces against the other walls; save for the huge mattress thrown carelessly into the center of the room—Dean's studio was quite cheery.

Helene Bournouw came into it and the sunlight, so cold and demanding on this too-cold-for-May afternoon, grew warm and golden. She stood behind him, watching him spread the glow of yellow ocher across a city scene.

She laughed lightly. Almost gaily.

Quentin Dean, lost in his work to the exclusion of all sound, spun, brush held like a sword. He smiled as he saw her. "Helene ... honey, why didn't you call the drugstore? ... They'd have told me you were coming ..."

She laughed again, a faint elfin tinkle in the empty studio. "What do you call *that*, Quentin dear?" She pointed one slim white-gloved hand at the painting.

He tried to match her smile with a boyish, uncertain smile of his own, but it would not come. He turned to look at the painting, fearing he might have done something he had not seen, standing so close. But no, it was just the way he had wanted to say it, in just the proper tone and with just the right amount of strength. It was his city, the city that had welcomed him, had let him work, that had sent him Helene Bournouw to lift and succor him.

"It's Third Avenue. I've tried to incorporate a dream image—magic realism, actually—of the el, before they tore it down, as it might be seen by someone who had lived under the el's shadow all those years and suddenly began to get the sunlight. You see, it's ..."

She interrupted, very friendly, very concerned. "It's ludicrous, Quentin, dear. I mean, surely you must be doing it for a lark. You aren't considering it for part of your sequence on Manhattan, are you?"

He could not speak.

Weak as he had found he was, his strength, his sustenance, came from his work, and there he was a whole man. No longer the emotional cripple who had fled Chillicothe, Ohio, to find a place for himself, he had grown strong and sure in front of his canvases. But, she was saying ...

"Quentin, if this is the sort of drivel you're contemplating, I'm afraid I'll have to put my foot down. You can't expect me to take this over to Alexei for exhibit. He would laugh me out of the gallery, darling. Now, I have faith in you ... even if you've fallen back again ..."

Helene Bournouw stayed a long while, talking to Quentin Dean. She reassured him, she directed him, she slept with him and gave him the strength he needed to:

Slash most of the paintings with a bread knife.

Ruin the remainder of them with turpentine.

Break his brushes and turn over his easel.

Pack his three shirts in the reinforced cardboard container he had used to mail home dirty laundry from college, and return to Chillicothe, Ohio, where a year later he had submerged himself sufficiently in his family's tile-and-linoleum business to forget any foolishness about art.

Helene Bournouw moved to her third appointment of the day ...

When his social secretary told him Miss Bournouw was waiting in the refectory, the Right Reverend Monsignor Della'Buono casually replied he would go in immediately he had signed the papers before him. As the social secretary moved to the door, the Monsignor added, almost as an afterthought, that Miss Bournouw had something of the utmost seriousness to discuss—a personal problem, as he understood it—and they were not to be disturbed in the refectory. The woman nodded her understanding, passing a vagrant thought that the good Monsignor could not much longer support the tremors and terrors of his confidants, that he was certainly due for a rest before his hegira to the Vatican in November.

But when the door had closed behind her, the priest signed the papers without reading them and shoved back his ornate chair so quickly it banged against the wall. He gathered his cassock and went out of his office through the connecting door that led onto a short hallway ending at the refectory. He opened the dining-room door and stepped inside.

Helene Bournouw was leaning against the long oak refectory table, her arms rigid behind her, supporting her angled weight. The trench coat was open at the knee, exposing one slim leg, bent slightly and exposed. The priest closed the door tightly, softly, and locked it.

"I told you never to come here again," he said.

His voice belonged to another man than the one who had spoken to the social secretary. *This* man had the voice of helplessness through hopelessness.

"Joseph ..." she whispered. The barest fluting of moisture gathering in the bell of a flower anxiously awaiting the bagman bee, rasping down out of the sun. "I know what you need ..."

He went back against the door, the door he had locked without realizing he was locking it, not to keep others out, but to keep himself in. She unbuckled the belt of the trench coat, threw it wide, and let it slide down off her naked arms.

Helene Bournouw was silk and fulfillment, waiting in her nakedness for his body.

He swallowed nothing and plunged into her, smothering his face between her breasts. She took him to her with an air of Christian charity, and *he* took her, there, openly, on the refectory table. And when his first time was over, and she was readying him for a second, he begged her to put on the little girl clothes he knew she had brought in the wide-mouthed model's handbag. The short pinafore, the white hose, the patent-leather buckled shoes, the soft ribbon for the hair, the childish charm bracelet. She promised she would. Helene Bournouw knew what he needed, what was beyond the realities but not the wildest fever-dreams of the Monsignor, who was not allowed to molest small children in the basement of the cathedral. Not even in the Cathedral of his Soul, and certainly not in the Cathedral of his God.

Later that day, he would write his paper, his long-awaited theological treatise. It would serve to sever the jugular of the Judeo-Christian ethic. His God would smirk at him, but not at Helene Bournouw.

Even God does not take lightly a creature of a kind called Helene Bournouw.

But that day was a busy day for Helene Bournouw, for possibly the most beautiful woman in New York, and she moved from appointment to appointment, being the delicious, scented unbelievable Helene Bournouw that she was. A busy day. But hardly over.

She stood before the mirror, admiring herself. It was trite, and she knew it, but the admiration of such a beautiful animal as herself could, by the nature of the narcissistic object, transcend the cliché. She studied her body. It was a beautifully constructed body, tapered that infinitely unnameable bit dividing mere perfection from beauty that burns out the eyes.

It had not quite burned out the eyes of that U.N. delegate from a great Eastern power (who had flashed like a silver fish in still waters when he had seen whom he had been fixed up with by his attaché), but it had unsettled and angered him sufficiently when her favors were not forthcoming so that there would be no mercy or reason in him during the conferences beginning the next day.

Yes, a fine and maddening body.

The apartment on Sutton Place was four-in-the-morning quiet, barely carrying the sound of Helene Bournouw hanging up her evening gown (its work on U.N. delegates done) and showering. The apartment took no notice as Helene Bournouw donned slacks and sweater, flats and trench coat. It made only a small sound as she closed the door.

In the lobby, the doorman created his own mental gossip concerning Helene Bournouw and her need for a cab this late in the day ... or early in the morning, depending on whether you were a famous model or a night-working doorman.

The cabbie raised an eyebrow when Helene Bournouw gave him their destination. What sort of woman was it who wanted to be let out on a street corner of the Bowery at five in the morning? What sort of woman, indeed, with a face that held him stunned, even in a rearview mirror.

And when the cab had disappeared into the darkness, its angry red taillight smaller, then gone, Helene Bournouw turned with purpose and direction, and strode off down the Bowery. What sort of woman, indeed.

Her flats made soft, shuffling noises in the still, moist, Manhattan night. She walked four blocks into a section of deserted warehouses, condemned loft buildings and wetbrain saucehounds sleeping halfway to death in their doorways. She turned down a sudden alley, a mouth open where there had been darkness a moment before.

Down the alley and she stopped before the fourth door; door perhaps, more boards and filth and bricked up than door, but door nevertheless.

Her knock was a strangely cadenced thing.

Her wait was a self-contained, restful thing.

When the door opened, she stood silently for a moment, staring at the man. He was perhaps four feet tall, his legs thick and truncated-looking. His body was a shapeless protoplasmic thing, erupting in two corded arms deeply tanned and powerful. His head rested without neck on his shoulders, matched as though with another head by the grotesque and obscene hump on his back. His face was a nightmare fancy. Two eyes, small and beaded and crimson, like those of a white rat, cornered and ferocious. The mouth was a gnome's gash without teeth, without lips. The skin a dark-bock-beer tan, even more wooden across the tight cheekbones and in the pitted hollows under the fanatic eyes.

A mass of black hair, unkempt, filthy, spreading down across the cheekbones like devouring fire ants. A rag of clothing, no shoes, long and black-rimmed fingernails. The magnificent, lovely face of Helene Bournouw stared at this man and found nothing peculiar, found nothing wanting.

Without a word she marched past him across the empty warehouse floor, up the winding staircase high into the deserted building. At the top of the staircase a door stood partially open.

Helene Bournouw pushed it wider and walked into the room. Amid empty packing crates and piles of rubbish, a table with nine chairs dominated the shadowy room. In eight of the nine chairs sat eight dwarfed creatures, uglier by comparison than the one who had opened the door far below.

The door behind Helene Bournouw closed as the grotesquerie who had followed her moved to his vacated seat. The woman stood silently, shifting from foot to foot as the little men talked. She seemed to pay them no heed and, in fact, seemed bored. From time to time she looked around, seeing nothing.

The little men talked:

"You've gone too far!" the one with warts on his eyelids rasped. "Too far! All this involvement. The old ways were good enough, I say. The expenditures, the outlay, and the results . . ."

"The results," interrupted another, with running sores on his cheeks and forehead, "have been fantastic. In a time of public relations, automation, advertising, the only way we can hope to carry on our work is to use the tools of the era."

"But . . ." the warty one tried to interrupt.

Extending a leprous-fleshed finger, a third man cut him off. "We can't afford to be backward. We must deal with matters on their own terms. You've seen how badly we did when we held to the old ways. People just will not accept ideas if they aren't couched in terms they are familiar with. Now, we've gone over this a thousand times; let's get on to planning the directions for the next quarter!"

The warty one subsided angrily, reluctantly.

Helene Bournouw, bored, began to hum. Too loud. The nine faces turned. One of them said snappishly, "Ba'al, turn her off."

The diseased and foul creature who had opened the door for Helene Bournouw rose and, dragging an empty packing crate behind him, stopped very close to her. He climbed up onto it, and his fingers left grease marks across her white flesh as they strayed toward her hairline.

Streaks of dirt on the white, lovely face of Helene Bournouw as the little man reached up under the hairline and massaged a soft spot on the front of the cranium. A sigh escaped Helene Bournouw's lips, and the face that could lead men astray, make them do evil, destroy their purposes, went very blank, very empty, very dead.

The little man climbed down and began to turn. A voice from the table stopped him. "Ba'al, wipe her off; you know we've got to keep the rolling stock in good condition."

As the little man pulled the strip of chamois from his shirt the conversation began anew, with the warty one taking this opportunity to reassert himself: "I still say the old ways are best."

The murmuring rose around the table, and the argument waxed anew while the incarnation of evil itself wiped filth stains off the too, too beautiful face of Helene Bournouw.

Later, when they wearied of formulating their new image, when they sighed with the responsibility of market trends and saturation levels and optimum penetration campaigns, they would suck on their long teeth and use her, all of them, at the same time.

A HOST OF FURIOUS FANCIES

J. G. BALLARD

"But who then was Prince Charming? As I arrived at the great mansion at the end of its drive it occurred to me that I might be unwittingly casting myself in the role, fulfilling a fantasy demanded by this unhappy girl."

In a famous playground of the rich, a limousine drives up and discharges its two passengers. We see them first at the casino and then at the café: one of them, it appears, is obsessed with the other, and so, curious, we settle down, agreeably, to hear what it's all about.

That's only our first mistake. . . .

When a story locks in on itself, as this tantalizing J. G. Ballard tale soon does, systematically closing off all escape routes, the result for the reader is a condition of powerlessness that resembles pleasure only by force of will. Yet at the same time, isn't that peculiar, ambivalent effect the one we (not so) secretly seek? What Tom Ligotti, in fact, means when he suggests the notion that some of us very much enjoy treating ourselves to (fictional) experience inimical to our well-being?

For those who welcome such sensations—yet cleverly are able to keep the attendants bearing straitjackets at bay—there exists only one obvious next move after finishing a story so inventively horrid, so intentionally disorienting as "A Host of Furious Fancies." And that's to go back and read it all over again.

Don't look now, but an unusual young woman and her elderly companion are sitting down behind us. Every Thursday afternoon they leave the Casino and come here to the café terrace of the Hotel de Paris, always choosing the same two tables near the magazine kiosk. If you lean forward you can see the girl in the restaurant mirror, the tall and elegant one with the too-level gaze and that characteristic walk of rich young women who have been brought up by nuns.

The man is behind her, the seedy-looking fellow with the once-handsome face, at least twenty years older, though you probably think thirty. He wears the same expensive but ill-fitting gray suit and silver tie, as if he has just been let out of some institution to attend a wedding. His eyes follow the secretaries returning from their lunches, plainly dreaming of escape. Observing his sad gaze, one not without a certain dignity, I can only conclude that Monte Carlo is a special kind of prison.

You've seen them now? Then you will agree it's hard to believe that these two are married, and have even achieved a stable union, though of a special kind, and governed by a set of complex rituals. Once a week she drives him from Vence to Monte Carlo in their limousine, that gold-tinted Cadillac parked across the square. After half an hour they emerge from the Casino, when he has played away at the roulette wheels the few francs he has been given. From the kiosk of this café terrace she buys him the same cheap magazine, one of those dreadful concierge rags about servant girls and their

Prince Charmings, and then sips at her citron pressé as they sit at separate tables. Meanwhile he devours the magazine like a child. Her cool manner is the epitome of a serene self-assurance, of the most robust mental health.

Yet only five years ago, as the physician in charge of her case, I saw her in a very different light. Indeed, it's almost inconceivable that this should be the same young woman whom I first came across at the Hospice of Our Lady of Lourdes, in a state of utter mental degeneration. That I was able to cure her after so many others had failed I put down to an extraordinary piece of psychiatric detection, of a kind that I usually despise. Unhappily, however, that success was bought at a price, paid a hundred times over by the sad old man, barely past his forty-fifth year, who drools over his trashy magazine a few tables behind us.

Before they leave, let me tell you about the case ...

By chance, it was only the illness of a colleague that brought me into contact with Christina Brossard. After ten years of practice in Monaco as a successful dermatologist I had taken up a part-time consultancy at the American Clinic in Nice. While looking through the out-patients' roster of an indisposed colleague I was told by his secretary that a seventeen-year-old patient, one Mlle Brossard, had not arrived for her appointment. At that moment one of the nursing sisters at the Our Lady of Lourdes Hospice at Vence—where the girl had been under care for three years—telephoned to cancel the consultation.

"The Mother Superior asks me to apologize to Prof. Derain but the child is simply too distraught again."

I thought nothing of it at the time, but for some reason—perhaps the girl's name, or the nun's use of "again"—I asked for the clinical notes. I noticed that this was the third appointment to be canceled during the previous year. An orphan, Christina Brossard had been admitted to the Hospice at the age of fourteen after the suicide of her father, who had been her only guardian since the death of her mother in an air crash.

At this point I remembered the entire tragedy. A former mayor of Lyon, Gaston Brossard was a highly successful building contractor and intimate of President Pompidou's, a millionaire many times over. At the peak of his success this fifty-five-year-old man had married for the third time. For his young bride, a beautiful ex-television actress in her early twenties, he had built a sumptuous mansion above Vence. Sadly, however, only two years after Christina's birth the young mother had died when the company aircraft taking her to join her husband in Paris had crashed in the Alpes Maritimes. Heartbroken, Gaston Brossard then devoted the remaining years of his life to the care of his infant daughter. All had gone well, but twelve years later, for no apparent reason, the old millionaire shot himself in his bedroom.

The effects on the daughter were immediate and disastrous—complete nervous collapse, catatonic withdrawal, and a slow but painful recovery in the nearby Hospice of Our Lady of Lourdes, which Gaston Brossard had generously endowed in memory of his young wife. The few clinical notes, jotted down by a junior colleague of Derain's who had conscientiously made the journey to Vence, described a recurrent dermatitis, complicated by chronic anemia and anorexia.

Sitting in my comfortable office, beyond a waiting room filled with wealthy middle-aged patients, I found myself thinking of this seventeen-year-old orphan lost high in the mountains above Nice. Perhaps my anticlerical upbringing—my father had been a left-wing newspaper cartoonist, my mother a crusading magistrate and early feminist—made me suspicious of the Hospice of Our Lady of Lourdes. The very name suggested a sinister combination of faith-healing and religious charlatanry, almost expressly designed to take advantage of a mentally unbalanced heiress. Lax executors and unconcerned guardians would leave the child ripe for exploitation, while her carefully preserved illness would guarantee the continued flow of whatever funds had been earmarked for the Hospice of Gaston Brossard's will. As I well knew, dermatitis, anorexia, and anemia were all too often convenient descriptions for a lack of hygiene, malnutrition, and neglect.

The following weekend, as I set off for Vence in my car—Prof. Derain had suffered a mild heart attack and would be absent for a month—I visualized this wounded child imprisoned above these brilliant hills by illiterate and scheming nuns who had deliberately starved the pining girl while crossing their palms with the dead man's gold dedicated to the memory of the child's mother.

Of course, as I soon discovered, I was totally in error. The Hospice of Our Lady of Lourdes turned out to be a brand-new, purpose-built sanatorium with well-lit rooms, sunny grounds, and a self-evident air of up-to-date medical practice and devotion to the well-being of the patients, many of whom I could see sitting out on the spacious lawns, talking to their friends and relatives.

The Mother Superior herself, like all her colleagues, was an educated and intelligent woman with a strong, open face and sympathetic manner, and hands—as I always immediately notice—that were not averse to hard work.

"It's good of you to come, Dr. Charcot. We've all been worried about Christina for some time. Without any disrespect to our own physicians, it's occurred to me more than once that a different approach may be called for."

"Presumably, you're referring to chemotherapy," I suggested. "Or a course of radiation treatment? One of the few Betatrons in Europe is about to be installed at the Clinic."

"Not exactly ..." The Mother Superior walked pensively around her desk, as if already reconsidering the usefulness of my visit. "I was thinking of a less physical approach, Dr. Charcot, one concerned to lay the ghosts of the child's spirit as well as those of her body. But you must see her for yourself."

It was now my turn to be skeptical. Since my earliest days as a medical student I had been hostile to all the claims made by psychotherapy, the happy hunting ground of pseudoscientific cranks of an especially dangerous kind.

Leaving the Hospice, we drove up into the mountains toward the Brossard mansion, where the young woman was allowed to spend a few hours each day.

"She's extremely active, and tends to unsettle the other patients," the Mother Superior explained as we turned into the long drive of the mansion, whose Palladian façade presided over a now silent fountain terrace. "She seems happier here, among the memories of her father and mother."

We were let into the imposing hall by one of the two young nuns who accompanied the orphaned heiress on these outings. As she and the Mother Superior discussed a patient to be released that afternoon I strolled across the hall and gazed up at the magnificent tapestries that hung from the marbled walls. Above the semicircular flights of the divided staircase was a huge Venetian clock with ornate hands and numerals like strange weapons, guardians of a fugitive time.

Beyond the shuttered library a colonnaded doorway led to the dining room. Dustcovers shrouded the chairs and table, and by the fireplace the second of the nuns supervised a servant girl who was cleaning out the grate. A visiting caretaker or auctioneer had recently lit a small fire of deeds and catalogues. The girl, wearing an old-fashioned leather apron, worked hard on her hands and knees, meticulously sweeping up the cinders before scrubbing the stained tiles.

"Dr. Charcot . . ." The Mother Superior beckoned me into the dining room. I followed her past the shrouded furniture to the fireplace.

"Sister Julia, I see we're very busy again. Dr. Charcot, I'm sure you'll be pleased by the sight of such industry."

"Of course . . ." I watched the girl working away, wondering why the Mother Superior should think me interested in the cleaning of a fireplace. The skivvy was little more than a child, but her long, thin arms worked with a will of their own. She had scraped the massive wrought-iron grate with obsessive care, decanting the cinders into a set of transparent plastic bags. Ignoring the three nuns, she dipped a coarse brush into the bucket of soapy water and began to scrub furiously at the tiles, determined to erase the last trace of dirt. The fireplace was already blanched by the soap, as if it had been scrubbed out a dozen times.

I assumed that the child was discharging some penance repeatedly imposed by the Mother Superior. Although not wishing to interfere, I noticed that the girl's hands and wrists showed the characteristic signs of an enzyme-sensitive eczema. In a tone of slight reproof, I remarked: "You might at least provide a pair of rubber gloves. Now, may I see Mlle Brossard?"

Neither the nuns nor the Mother Superior made any response, but the girl looked up from the soapy tiles. I took in immediately the determined mouth in a pale but once attractive face, the hair fastened fanatically behind a gaunt neck, a toneless facial musculature from which all expression had been deliberately drained. Her eyes stared back at mine with an almost unnerving intensity, as if she had swiftly identified me and was already debating what role I might play for her.

"Christina . . ." The Mother Superior spoke gently, urging the girl from her knees. "Dr. Charcot has come to help you."

The girl barely nodded and returned to her scrubbing, pausing only to move the cinder-filled plastic bags out of our reach. I watched her with a professional eye, recalling the diagnosis of dermatitis, anorexia, and anemia. Christina Brossard was thin but not undernourished, and her pallor was probably caused by all this compulsive activity within the gloomy mansion. As for her dermatitis, this was clearly of that special type caused by obsessive hand-washing.

"Christina—" Sister Louise, a pleasant, round-cheeked young woman, knelt on the damp tiles. "My dear, do rest for a moment."

"No! No! No!" The girl beat the tiles with her soapy brush. She began to wring out the floor cloth, angry hands like bundles of excited sticks. "There are three more grates to be done this afternoon! You told me to clean them, didn't you, Mother?"

"Yes, dear. It does seem to be what you most want to do." The Mother Superior stepped back with a defeated smile, giving way to me.

I watched Christina Brossard continue her apparently unending work. She was clearly unbalanced, but somehow self-dramatizing at the same time, as if totally gripped by her compulsion but well aware of its manipulative possibilities. I was struck both by her self-pity and by the hard glance which she now and then directed at the three nuns, as if she were deliberately demeaning herself before these pleasant and caring women in order to vent her hate for them.

Giving up for the time being, I left her mopping the tiles and returned to the hall with the Mother Superior.

"Well, Dr. Charcot, we're in your hands."

"I dare say—frankly, I'm not sure that this is a case for me. Tell me—she spends all her time cleaning out these grates?"

"Every day, for the past two years, at her own wish. We've tried to stop her, but she then relapses into her original stupor. We can only assume that it serves some important role for her. There are a dozen fireplaces in this house, each as immaculate as an operating theater."

"And the cinders? The bags filled with ash? Who is lighting these fires?"

"Christina herself, of course. She is burning her children's books, determined for some reason to destroy everything she read as a child."

She led me into the library. Almost the entire stock of books had been removed, and a line of stags' heads gazed down over the empty shelves. One cabinet alone contained a short row of books.

I opened the glass cabinet. There were a few schoolgirl stories, fairy tales, and several childhood classics.

The Mother Superior stared at them sadly. "There were several hundred originally, but each day Christina burns a few more—under close supervision, it goes without saying, I've no wish to see her burn down the mansion. Be careful not to touch it, but one story alone has remained immune."

She pointed to a large and shabby illustrated book which had been given a shelf to itself. "You may see, Dr. Charcot, that the choice is not inappropriate—the story of Cinderella."

As I drove back to Nice, leaving behind that strange mansion with its kindly nuns and obsessed heiress, I found myself revising my opinion of the Mother Superior. This sensible woman was right in believing that all the dermatologists in the world would be unable to free Christina Brossard from her obsession. Clearly the girl had cast herself as Cinderella, reducing herself to the level of the lowest menial. But what guilt was she trying to scrub away? Had she played a still unknown but vital role in the suicide of her father? Was the entire fantasy an unconscious attempt to free herself of her sense of guilt?

I thought of the transparent bags filled with cinders, each one the ashes of a childhood fairy tale. The correspondences were extraordinarily clear, conceived with the remorseless logic of madness. I remembered the hate in her eyes as she stared at the nuns, casting these patient and caring women in the role of the ugly sisters. There was even a wicked stepmother, the Mother Superior, whose Hospice had benefited from the deaths of this orphan's parents.

On the other hand, where were Prince Charming, the fairy godmother and her pumpkin, the ball to be fled from at the stroke of midnight, and above all the glass slipper?

As it happened, I was given no chance to test my hypothesis. Two days later, when I telephoned the Hospice to arrange a new appointment for Christina Brossard, the Mother Superior's secretary politely informed me that the services of the Clinic, of Prof. Derain and myself, would no longer be called upon.

"We're grateful to you, Doctor, but the Mother Superior has decided on a new course of treatment. The distinguished psychiatrist Dr. Valentina Gabor has agreed to take on the case—perhaps you know of her reputation. In fact, treatment has already begun and you will be happy to hear that Christina is making immediate progress."

As I replaced the receiver a powerful migraine attacked my left temple. Dr. Valentina Gabor—of course I knew of her, the most notorious of the new school of self-styled antipsychiatrists, who devoted whatever time was left over from their endless television appearances to the practice of an utterly bogus psychotherapy, a fashionable blend of post-psychoanalytic jargon, moral uplift, and Catholic mysticism. This last strain had presumably gained her the approval of the Mother Superior.

Whenever I saw Dr. Valentina my blood began to simmer. This glamorous blonde with her reassuring patter and the eyes of a cashier was forever appearing on television talk shows, putting forward the paradoxical notion that mental illness did not exist but nonetheless was the creation of the patient's family, friends, and even, unbelievably, his doctors. Irritatingly, Dr. Valentina had managed to score up a number of authenticated successes, no doubt facilitated by her recent well-publicized audience with the Pope. However, I was confident that she would receive her comeuppance. Already there had been calls within the medical profession for a discreet inquiry into her reported use of LSD and other hallucinogenic drugs.

Nonetheless, it appalled me that someone as deeply ill and as vulnerable as Christina Brossard should fall into the hands of this opportunist quack.

You can well understand, therefore, that I felt a certain satisfaction, not to say self-approval, when I received an urgent telephone call from the Mother Superior some three weeks later.

I had heard no more in the meantime of the Hospice or of Christina. Dr. Valentina Gabor, however, had appeared with remorseless frequency on Radio Monte Carlo and the local television channels, spreading her unique brand of psychoanalytic mysticism, and extolling all the virtues of being "reborn."

In fact, it was while watching on the late evening news an interview with Dr. Gabor recorded that afternoon at Nice Airport before she flew back to Paris that I was telephoned by the Mother Superior.

"Dr. Charcot! Thank heavens you're in! There's been a disaster here—Christina Brossard has vanished! We're afraid she may have taken an overdose. I've tried to reach Dr. Gabor but she has returned to Paris. Could you possibly come to the Hospice?"

I calmed her as best I could and set off. It was after midnight when I reached the sanatorium. Spotlights filled the drive with a harsh glare, the patients were unsettled, peering through their windows, nuns with torches were fruitlessly searching the grounds. A nervous Sister Louise escorted me to the Mother Superior, who seized my hands with relief. Her strong face was veined with strain.

"Dr. Charcot! I'm grateful to you—I only regret that it's so late . . ."

"No matter. Tell me what happened. Christina was under Dr. Gabor's care?"

"Yes. How I regret my decision. I hoped that Christina might have found herself through a spiritual journey, but I had no idea that drugs were involved. If I had known . . ."

She handed me an empty vial. Across the label was Dr. Gabor's florid signature.

"We found this in Christina's room an hour ago. She seems to have injected herself with the entire dosage and then driven off wildly into the night. We can only assume that she stole it from Dr. Gabor's valise."

I studied the label. "Psilocybin—a powerful hallucinogenic drug. Its use is still legal by qualified physicians, though disapproved of by almost the entire profession. This is more than a dangerous toy."

"Dr. Charcot, I know." The Mother Superior gestured with her worn hands. "Believe me, I fear for Christina's soul. She appears to have been completely deranged—when she drove off in our oldest laundry van she described it to one of the patients as 'her golden carriage.' "

"You've called the police?"

"Not yet, Doctor." A look of embarrassment crossed the Mother Superior's face. "When Christina left she told one of the orderlies that she was going to 'the ball.' I'm told that the only ball being held tonight is Prince Rainier's grand gala in Monaco in honor of President Giscard d'Estaing. I assume that she has gone there, perhaps confusing Prince Rainier with the Prince Charming of her fairy tale, and hoping that he will rescue her. It would be profoundly awkward for the Hospice if she were to create a scene, or even try to . . ."

"Kill the President? Or the Rainiers? I doubt it." Already an idea was forming in my mind. "However, to be on the safe side I'll leave for Monaco immediately. With luck I'll be there before she can cause any harm to herself."

Pursued by the Mother Superior's blessings, I returned to my car and set off into the night. Needless to say, I did not intend to make the journey to Monaco. I was quite certain that I knew where Christina Brossard had fled—to her father's mansion above Vence.

As I followed the mountain road I reflected on the evidence that had come together—the fantasy of being a skivvy, the all-promising woman psychiatrist, the hallucinogenic drug. The entire fairy tale of Cinderella was being enacted, perhaps unconsciously, by this deranged heiress. If she herself was Cinderella, Dr. Valentina Gabor was the fairy godmother, and her magic wand the hypodermic syringe she waved about so spectacularly. The role of the pumpkin was played by the "sacred mushroom," the hallucinogenic fungus from which psilocybin was extracted. Under its influence even an ancient laundry van would seem like a golden coach. And as for the "ball," this of course was the whole psychedelic trip.

But who then was Prince Charming? As I arrived at the great mansion at the end of its drive it occurred to me that I might be unwittingly casting myself in the role, fulfilling a fantasy demanded by this unhappy girl. Holding tight to my medical case, I walked across the dark gravel to the open entrance, where the laundry van had ended its journey in the center of a flower bed.

High above, in one of the great rooms facing the sea, a light flickered, as if something was being burned in a grate. I paused in the hall to let my eyes feel their way in the darkness, wondering how best to approach this distraught young woman. Then I saw that the massive Venetian clock above the staircase had been savagely mutilated. Several of the ornate numerals tilted on their mountings. The hands had stopped at midnight, and someone had tried to wrench them from the face.

For all my resistance to that pseudoscience, it occurred to me that once again a psychoanalytic explanation made complete sense of these bizarre events and the fable of Cinderella that underpinned them. I walked up the staircase past the dismembered clock. Despite the fear-crazed assault on them, the erect hands still stood upright on the midnight hour—that time when the ball ended, when the courtships and frivolities of the party were over and the serious business of a real sexual relationship began. Fearful of that male erection, Cinderella always fled at midnight.

But what had Christina Brossard fled from in this Palladian mansion? Suppose that the Prince Charming who courted her so dangerously but so appealingly were in fact her own father. Had some kind of incestuous act involved the widowed industrialist and his adolescent daughter, herself an uncanny image of his dead wife? His revulsion and self-disgust at having committed incest would explain his apparently motiveless suicide *and* his daughter's guilt—as I knew only too well from my court attendances as an expert medical witness, far from hating the fathers who forced them to commit incest, daughters were invariably plagued by powerful feelings of guilt at their responsibility for their parent's imprisonment. So after his death she would naturally return to the house, and try to expiate that guilt as a servant girl. And what better model for an heiress than Cinderella herself?

Drawn by the distant flames, I crossed the upstairs hallway and entered the great bedroom. It was filled with paintings of young nudes cavorting with centaurs, unmistakably Gaston Brossard's master bedroom, perhaps where the act of incest had taken place.

Flames lifted from the fireplace, illuminating the ash-streaked face of Christina. She knelt by the grate, crooning as she fed the last of the pages torn from a familiar book of fairy tales. Head to one side, she stared at the soft blaze with overlit eyes, stroking the rough seams of the hospital tunic she wore over her bare legs.

I guessed that she was in the middle of her hallucination and that she saw herself in a resplendent gown. Yet her drifting eyes looked up at me with an expression of almost knowing calm, as if she recognized me and was waiting for me to play my role in the fable and bring it to its proper conclusion. I thought of the mutilated hands of the clock above the staircase. All that remained was to restore the glass slipper to its rightful owner.

Had I now to play the part of her rescuer? Remembering the familiar sexual symbolism of the foot, I knew that the glass slipper was nothing more than a transparent and therefore guilt-free vagina. And as for the foot to be placed within it, of course this would not be her own but that of her true lover, the erect male sexual organ from which she fled.

Reaching forward, she added the cover of the fairy tales to the dying blaze, and then looked up at me with waiting eyes. For a moment I hesitated. High on psilocybin, she would be unable to distinguish truth from fantasy, so I could play out my role and bring this psychoanalytic drama to its conclusion without any fear of professional disapproval. My action would not take place in the real world, but within that imaginary realm where the fable of Cinderella was being enacted.

Knowing my role now, and the object which I myself had to place in that glass slipper, I took her hands and drew her from her knees toward her father's bed.

I murmured: "Cinderella . . ."

But wait—they're about to leave the terrace. You can look at them now, everyone else is staring frankly at this attractive young woman and her decrepit companion. Sitting here in the center of Monte Carlo on this magnificent spring day, it's hard to believe that these strange events ever occurred.

It's almost unnerving—she's looking straight at me. But does she recognize me, the dermatologist who freed her from her obsession and restored her to health?

Her companion, sadly, was the only casualty of this radical therapy. As he sits hunched at his table, fumbling with himself like an old man, I can tell you that he was once a fashionable physician whom she met just before her release from the Hospice. They were married three months later, but the marriage was hardly a success. By whatever means, presumably certain methods of her own, she transformed him into this old man.

But why? Simply, that in order to make the incest fantasy credible, any man she marries, however young and princely, however charming, must become old enough to be her father.

Wait! She is coming toward this table. Perhaps she needs my help? She stands in front of the restaurant mirror looking at herself and her elderly husband, and places a hand on his shoulder.

That elegant face with its knowing smile. Let me try to shake that composure, and whisper the title of this cheap magazine on my lap.

"CINDERELLA . . ."

Her hand pats my shoulder indulgently.

"Father, it's time to go back to the Hospice. I promised the Mother Superior that I wouldn't overtire you."

Knowing, elegant, and completely self-possessed.

"And do stop playing that game with yourself. You know it only excites you."

And very punitive.

WHEN THE RED STORM COMES

OR, THE HISTORY OF A YOUNG LADY'S AWAKENING TO HER NATURE

SARAH SMITH

"The blood, crusted at the base of his fingers, still welled from the slit he had made in his palm. It was bright, bright red. I bent down and touched my tongue to the wound. The blood was salty, intimate, strong, the taste of my own desire."

In the autumn of 1991 I stretched out one evening prepared to read, at the urging of a friend, the manuscript of a first novel called The Vanished Child. *Its official publication was still some months in the future, and as I started to dip into the fat bundle of pages I was rather resentful, for the simple reason that comfort and loose sheets of paper are natural enemies. But even as more and more of the wretched flimsy things slipped off my chest to begin their messy drift floorward, I actually found myself oblivious to anything but the astonishingly assured and incredibly thrilling story, with its central theme of lost and hidden identity, unfolding before me.*

I was hooked, utterly. And having slowed down in order to savor the absorbing tensions of the plot's last twists, it wasn't until somewhere in the predawn hours that I happily allowed the few remaining pages to slide away. Moreover, I knew then with pretty fair certainty that Sarah Smith, who'd created such an original and unexpected entertainment in this novel I was so loath to finish, was someone I wished to see have a story in Shudder Again.

Thankfully, Sarah was intrigued by my proposal and, rising to the challenge, produced "When the Red Storm Comes," which, for want of an expression more in keeping with its innate elegance, knocked my socks off. In it, she reminds us—who live in a world where vampires are a rather devalued subculture, as likely to turn up at shopping malls as at Carpathian castles—once again of the immense strength there can be in returning to the deepest roots of any tradition. And while Anne Rice, Dan Simmons, Nancy Collins, Whitley Strieber, and so many others have obviously already tapped into this same, um, vein, Sarah Smith somehow manages the very enviable trick of sounding only like herself.

"Do you believe in vampires?" he said.

I snapped *Dracula* closed and pushed it under the tapestry bag containing my neglected cutwork. "Mr. Stoker writes amusingly," I said. "I believe I don't know you, sir."

"What a shame," he said, putting his hand on the café chair across from me. I looked up—and up; he was tall, blond; his uniform blazed crimson, a splash of blood against the green trees and decent New Hampshire brick of Market Square. The uniform was Austro-Hungarian; his rank I did not know, but clearly he was an officer.

"You should be better acquainted with vampires." He clicked heels and bowed. "Count Ferenc Zohary." Without invitation he sat down, smiling at me.

In this August 1905, in Portsmouth where I was spending the summer before my debutante year, negotiations were being held that might finish the long Russo-Japanese War. Aboard his yacht *Mayflower* at the naval yard,

President Roosevelt had hosted the first meeting between the Russian and Japanese plenipotentiaries, Count Serge Witte and the Marquis Komura. Now the opponents met officially at the naval yard and schemed betweentimes at the Wentworth Hotel. My aunt Mildred did not encourage newspaper reading for unmarried women, so I was out-of-date, but knew the negotiations were supposed to be going badly. The town was crowded with foreign men; there was a storminess in the air, a feel of heavy male energy, of history and importance. Danger, blood, and cruelty, like Mr. Stoker's book: it made my heart beat more strongly than any woman's should. *Don't talk to any of them,* Aunt Mildred had said. But for once my aunt was out of sight.

"You are part of the negotiations? Pray tell me how they proceed."

"I am an observer only."

"Will they make peace?"

"I hope not, for my country's sake." He looked amused at my surprise. "If they continue the war, Russia and Japan will bleed, Russia will lose, turn west; they will make a little war and probably lose. But if they sign their treaty, Russia will fight us five years from now, when they are stronger; and then the Germans will come in, and the French to fight the Germans, and the English with the French. Very amusing. My country cannot survive."

"Is it not wearying, to have such things decided and to be able to do nothing?"

"I am never wearied." My companion stretched out his hand, gathered together my half-finished cutwork linen, and waved it in the air for a moment like a handkerchief before dropping it unceremoniously on the ground. "Your mother makes you do this," he said, "but you prefer diplomacy. Or vampires. Which?"

I flushed. "My aunt controls my sewing," I said. Cutwork had been my task for this summer, sitting hour after hour on Aunt Mildred's verandah, sewing hundreds of tiny stitches on the edges of yards of linen, then clipping out patterns with my sharp-pointed scissors. Linen for my trousseau, said Aunt Mildred, who would not say the word "sheets." In the fall I would go to New York, planning my strategies for marriage like a powerless general. The battle was already hopeless; without greater wealth than I commanded, I could not hope to be in the center of events. I would become what I was fit for by looks but not by soul, the showy useless wife of some businessman, whose interest in war extended only to the army's need for boots or toothbrushes.

But now, because Admiral Togo had won at Tsushima, I had my taste of war, however faraway and tantalizing; I was sitting with a soldier, here in the hot thick sunlight and green leaves of Market Square.

"Do you like war," my companion asked, "or simply blood?"

An interesting question. "I think they both concern power."

"Precisely." He leafed through the book while I watched him secretly. In the exquisitely tailored crimson uniform, he had a look of coarseness combined with power. Above the stiff gold-braided collar, his neck was thick with muscle. His hands were short and broad-nailed, his fingertips square against the yellow-and-red binding of *Dracula*. Perhaps feeling my eyes on him, he looked up and smiled at me. He had assurance, a way of looking at me as though I were already attracted to him, though he was not handsome: a thick-lipped mouth, a scar on his jaw, and a nick out of his ear. And he had thrown my cutwork on the ground. "My name is Susan Wentworth," I said.

"Wentworth, like the hotel. That is easy to remember." No sweet words about my face being too beautiful for my name to be forgotten. "Do you stay at the hotel?" he asked.

A gentleman never asked directly where a lady lived, to save her the embarrassment of appearing to desire his company.

"My aunt has a cottage at Kittery Point."

"That is not far. Do you come to the tea dances at the hotel?"

"Seldom, Count Zohary. My aunt thinks the diplomatic guests are not suitable company."

"Very true. But exciting, no? Do you find soldiers exciting, Miss Wentworth?"

"Soldiering, yes, and diplomacy; I admit that I do."

"A certain amount of blood ... that is nice with the tea dances." With his thumbnail he marked a passage in the book and showed it to me. *As she arched her neck she actually licked her lips like an animal,* I read. "Do you find that exciting?"

"I am not a vampire, Count Zohary," I said, uneasily amused.

"I know that." My companion smiled at me, showing regular even teeth. "I, for instance, I am a vampire, and I can assure you that you are not one yet."

"You, Count Zohary?"

"Of course, not as this man Stoker describes. I walk in the sun, I see my face in my shaving mirror; I assure you I sleep in sheets, not dirt." He reached out and touched the thin gold cross I wore around my neck. "A pretty thing. It does not repel me." His fingers hovered very close to my neck and bosom. "The vampire is very sensual, Miss Wentworth, especially when he is also a soldier. Very attractive. You should try."

I had let him go too far. "I think you dare overmuch, Count Zohary."

"Ah, why I dare, that is the vampire in me. But you don't hold up your cross and say, 'Begone, *necuratul*!' " he said. "And that is the vampire in you. Do you like what you read, Miss Susan Wentworth? You look as though you would like it very much. Are you curious? If you will come to the tea dance at the hotel, I will show you the handsome hotel sheets, and teach you that vampires are—almost—as civilized as diplomats."

He looked at me, gauging my response: and for a moment, horrified, I felt I would respond. I wanted the brutal crude power of the man. "Count Zohary, you have mistaken me, I am respectable." I snatched the book away from him and stuffed it deep into my tapestry bag. "I have—*certainly* no desire to see your—" I would not give him the satisfaction of finishing the sentence. "You're making me talk nonsense."

He brushed his mustache with his finger, then lifted

one corner of his lip. "What will convince you, dear respectable Miss Wentworth? My fangs? Shall I turn into a wolf for you? Come into your chamber like a red mist, or charge in like cavalry?" Over our head the leaves rattled and wind soughed through the square. Count Zohary looked up. "Shall I tell you the future in your blood? Shall I control the sea for you, or call a storm? That is my best parlor trick. Let us have a thunderstorm, Miss Wentworth, you and I."

The tide controlled the sea, and the Piscatequa River called thunderstorms once or twice a week in August, without help from Hungarian counts. "If you can tell the future, Count Zohary, you know that everything you say is useless."

"It is not my most reliable gift, Miss Wentworth," he said. "Unfortunately, or I would not be here watching Witte and Komura, but back in New York drinking better coffee at the embassy. It works best after I have had a woman, or drunk blood. Shall we find out together what Witte and Komura will do? No? You do not wish to know?" On the café table there was a ring of condensation from my glass of ice water. With mock solemnity he shook salt from the table shaker over it and stared at the water as if into a crystal ball, making passes like a fortune-teller. "Seawater is better to look into; blood best. Ice water—*ach,* Miss Wentworth, you make me work. But I see you will come to the tea dance. Today, Wednesday, or Thursday you will come."

"I will not," I said. "Of course I will not."

"Tomorrow?"

"Certainly not."

"Thursday, then." From the direction of the ocean, thunder muttered above the white tower of First Church. Count Zohary made a gesture upward and smiled at me. I began to gather up my things, and he bent down, stretching out his long arm to pick up my fallen linen. "This is almost done; you must come Thursday."

"Why Thursday?" I asked unwillingly.

"Because I have made a bet with myself. Before you have finished this *Quatsch,*" he said, "I will give you what you want. I shall have turned you into a vampire."

A sea-salt wave of breeze rolled over the square, hissing; the leaves were tossed pale side up like dead fish. I stared at him, the smell of the sea in my mouth, an acrid freshness. He smiled at me, slightly pursing his lips. Flushing, I pushed my chair away. Count Zohary rose, clicked his heels, raised my hand to his lips; and through the first drops of rain I saw him stride away, his uniform the color of fresh blood against the brick and white of the Athenaeum, darkening in the rain. A soldier, his aide-de-camp, came forward with a black cape for him. Unwillingly I thought of vampires.

That night the rain shook the little-paned windows of my white bedroom. *This monster has done much harm already,* I read. Moisture in the air made the book's binding sticky, so that both my palms were printed with fragments of the red name backward. *The howling of wolves.* There were no wolves around Portsmouth, nor vampires either. I could tell my own future without help from him: this fall in New York would decide it, whatever my strategies. Women of my sort all had the same future.

How much less alive could I be if I were a vampire's prey?

I pictured myself approaching young men of my acquaintance and sinking my teeth into their throat. This was fancy; I had no access even to the ordinary powers of men such as the count.

But he had told me one quite specific thing, and it intrigued me: he was with the embassy in New York.

The next day, though I was tired, I assiduously sewed at my cutwork and pricked at it with my scissors, and finishing this respectable task, I felt as though I were again in control of myself, triumphant over Count Zohary, and ready to face him.

At my instigation, Mrs. Lathrop, my aunt's friend, proposed that we visit the Wentworth, and Aunt Mildred was persuaded to agree.

On Thursday, Elizabeth Lathrop and her daughter Lucilla, Aunt Mildred and I, all fit ourselves into the Lathrop barouche, and at a gentle pace we were driven through the curving streets of Kittery and past the Federal mansions of Portsmouth. It was a perfect day, the breeze from the sea just enough to refresh us, late day lilies and heliotrope blooming behind old-fashioned wooden trellis fences; a day for a pleasant, thoughtless excursion; yet as we passed through Market Square, I looked for his glittering red figure, and as we pulled into the handsome gravel driveway of the Wentworth, I found myself excited, as if I were going to a meeting of some consequence.

Aunt Mildred and Mrs. Lathrop found us a table by the dance floor, which was not large but modern and well appointed. An orchestra was playing waltzes; a few couples practiced their steps on the floor, and many soldiers sat at tables under the potted palms, flirting with young women. Mrs. Lathrop and Lucilla intended a sight of Count Witte, whose manners were reported to be so uncouth that he must eat behind a screen. I saw no sign of Count Zohary. At one table, surrounded by a retinue of men, the notorious Mme. N. held court, a laughing, pretty woman who was rumored to have brought down three governments. While the orchestra played, Mrs. Lathrop and my aunt Mildred gossiped about her. Lucilla Lathrop and I discovered nothing in common. From under my eyelashes I watched clever Mme. N.

Three women from the Japanese legation entered the dining room, causing a sensation with their kimonos, wigs, and plastered faces. I wondered if there were Japanese vampires, and if the painted Japanese ladies felt the same male energy from all those soldiers. Were those Japanese women's lives as constrained as mine?

"The heat is making me uneasy, Aunt Mildred; I will go and stroll on the terrace." Under my parasol, I let the sea wind cool my cheeks; I stared over the sandy lawn, over the sea.

"Miss Wentworth. Have you come to see my sheets?"

"By no means, Count Zohary." He was sitting at one of the little café tables on the terrace. Today he was in undress uniform, a brownish-gray. In the sea light his blond hair had a foxy tint. Standing, he bowed elaborately, drawing out a chair. "I would not give you the satisfaction of refusing." I inclined my head and sat down.

"Then you will satisfy by accepting?"

"Indeed not. What satisfaction is that?" I looked out over the sea, the calm harbor. While yachts swayed at anchor, the Star Island ferry headed out toward the shoals, sun gleaming off its windows and rail. I had seen this view for years from Aunt Mildred's house; there was nothing new in it.

"Come now, turn you head, Miss Wentworth. You don't know what I offer. Look at me." On his table was a plate of peaches, ripe and soft; I smelled them on the warm air, looked at them but not at him. A fly buzzed over them; he waved it away, picked up a fruit, and took a bite out of it. I watched his heavy muscular hand. "You think you are weary of your life, but you have never tasted it. What is not tasted has no flavor. I offer everything you are missing—ah, now you look at me." His eyes were reddish-brown with flecks of light. He sucked at the juice, then offered the peach to me, the same he had tasted; he held it close to my lips. "Eat."

"I will have another, but not this."

"Eat with me; then you will have as many as you want." I took a tiny nip from the fruit's pink flesh. Soft, hairy skin; sweet flesh. He handed the plate of fruit to me; I took one and bit. My mouth was full of pulp and juice.

"I could have your body," he said in a soft voice. "By itself, like that peach; that is no trouble. But you can be one of us, I saw it in the square. I want to help you, to make you what you are."

"One of us? What do you mean?"

"One who wants power," he said with the same astonishing softness. "Who can have it. A vampire. Eat your peach, Miss Wentworth, and I will tell you about your Dracula. Vlad Drăculeşti, son of Vlad the Dragon. On Tîmpa Hill by Braşov, above the chapel of St. Jacob, he had his enemies' limbs lopped and their bodies impaled; and as they screamed, he ate his meal beside them, dipping his bread into the blood of the victims, because the taste of human blood is the taste of power. The essence

of the vampire is power." He reached out his booted
foot and, under the table, touched mine. "Power is not
money, or good looks, or rape or seduction. It is simple,
life and death; to kill; to drink the blood of the dying;
but oneself to survive, to beget, to make one's kind, to
flourish. Komura and Witte have such power, they are
making a great red storm, with many victims. I too have
power, and I will have blood on my bread. Will you eat
and drink with me?"

"Blood—?"

He looked at me with his light-flecked eyes. "Does
blood frighten you, do you faint at the sight of blood,
like a good little girl? I think not." He took a quick bite
from his peach. "Have you ever seen someone die? Did
they bleed? Did you look away? No, I see you did not;
you were fascinated, more than a woman should be. You
like the uniforms, the danger, the soldiers, but what you
truly like, Miss Wentworth, is red. When you read about
this war in the newspapers, will you pretend you are
shocked and say *Oh, how dreadful,* while you look twice
and then again at the pictures of blood, and hope you
do not know why your heart beats so strong? Will you
say, I can never be so much alive as to drink blood? Or
will you know yourself, and be glad when the red storm
comes?" He tapped my plate of peaches with his finger.
"To become what you are is simpler than eating one of
those, Miss Wentworth, and much more pleasant."

"I wish some degree of power—who does not—but to
do this—" He was right; I had been fascinated. The next
day I had come back to the scene, had been disappointed
that the blood was washed away. "This is ridiculous, you
must wish to make me laugh or to disgust me. You are
making terrible fun of me."

"Drink my blood," he said. "Let me drink yours. I
will not kill you. Have just a little courage, a little curiosity. Sleep with me; that last is not necessary, but is very
amusing. Then—a wide field, and great power, Miss
Wentworth."

I swallowed. "You simply mean to make me your
victim."

"If it seems to you so, then you will be my victim. I

want to give you life, because you might take it and amuse me. But you undervalue yourself. Are you my victim?" For a moment, across a wide oval in front of the hotel, wind flattened the water, and through some trick of light and wave, it gleamed red. "See, Miss Wentworth. My parlor trick again."

"No—I often see such light on the water."

"Not everyone does."

"Then I see nothing."

By his plate he had a little sharp fruit knife. He picked it up and drew a cut across his palm; as the blood began to well, he cupped his palm and offered it to me. "The blood is a little sea, a little red sea, the water I like best to control. I stir it up, Miss Wentworth; I drink it; I live." With one finger of his right hand he touched his blood, then the vein on my wrist. "I understand its taste; I can make it flow like tide, Miss Wentworth, I can make your heart beat, Miss Wentworth, until you would scream at me to stop. Do you want to understand blood, do you want to taste blood, do you want your mouth full of it, salty, sweet, foul blood? Do you want the power of the blood? Of course you do not, the respectable American girl. Of course you do; you do."

He took my hand, he pulled me close to him. He looked at me with his insistent animal eyes, waiting, his blood cupped in his hand. I knew that at that moment I could break away from his grip and return to Aunt Mildred and the Lathrops. They would not so much as notice I had gone or know what monstrous things had been said to me. I could sit down beside them, drink tea, and listen to the orchestra for the rest of my life. For me there would be no vampires.

The blood, crusted at the base of his fingers, still welled from the slit he had made in his palm. It was bright, bright red. I bent down and touched my tongue to the wound. The blood was salty, intimate, strong, the taste of my own desire.

The white yacht was luxuriously appointed, with several staterooms. We sailed far out to sea. Count Zohary had invited the Lathrops and my aunt to chaperone me.

On deck, Mr. Lathrop, a freckled man in a white suit, trolled for bluefish and talked with Count Zohary. I heard the words *Witte, Sakhalin, reparations;* this evening there was to be an important meeting between the pleni-potentiaries. Aunt Mildred and Mrs. Lathrop talked and played whist, while Lucilla Lathrop's crocheting needle flashed through yards of cream-white tatting. I began still another piece of cutwork, but abandoned it and stood in the bow of the boat, feeling the sea waves in my body, long and slow. In part I was convinced Count Zohary merely would seduce me; I did not care. I had swallowed his blood and now he would drink mine.

Under an awning, sailors served luncheon from the hotel. Oysters Rockefeller, cream of mushroom soup with Parker House rolls, salmon steaks, mousse of hare, pepper dumplings, matchsticked sugared carrots, corn on the cob, a salad of cucumbers and Boston lettuce, summer squash. For dessert, almond biscuits, a praline and mocha-buttercream glazed cake, and ice cream in several flavors. With the food came wine, brandy with dessert, and a black bottle of champagne. I picked at the spinach on my oysters, but drank the wine thirstily. In the post-luncheon quiet, the boat idled on calm water; the sailors went below.

Mr. Lathrop fell asleep first, a handkerchief spread over his red face; then Lucilla Lathrop began snoring gently in a deck chair under the awning, her tatting tangled in her lap. Mr. Lathrop's fishing rod trailed from his nerveless hand; I reeled it in and laid it on the deck, and in the silent noon the thrum of fishing line was as loud as the engine had been. Aunt Mildred's cards sank into her lap. She did not close her eyes, but when I stood in front of her, she seemed not to see me. Alone, Mrs. Lathrop continued to play her cards, slowly, one by one, onto the little baize-colored table between her and my aunt, as if she were telling fortunes.

"Mrs. Lathrop?" She looked up briefly, her eyes dull as raisins in her white face, nodded at me, and went back to her cards.

"They have eaten and drunk," Count Zohary said, "and they are tired." A wave passed under the boat;

Aunt Mildred's head jerked sideways and she fell across the arm of her chair, limply, rolling like a dead person. I almost cried out, almost fell; Count Zohary caught me and put his hand across my mouth.

"If you scream you will wake them."

Grasping my hand, he led me down the stairs, below decks, through a narrow corridor. On one side was the galley, and there, his head on his knees, sat the cook, asleep; near him a handsome sailor had fallen on the floor, sleeping too; I saw no others.

The principal stateroom was at the bow of the ship, white in the hot afternoon. The bed was opened, the sheets drawn back; the cabin had an odor of lemon oil, a faint musk of ocean. "Sheets," he said. "You see?" I sank down on the bed, my knees would not hold me. I had not known, at the last, how my body would fight me; I wanted to be not here, to know the future that was about to happen, to have had it happen, to have it happening now. I heard the snick of the bolt, and then he was beside me, unbuttoning the tiny buttons at my neck. So quiet it was, so quiet, I could not breathe. He bent down and touched the base of my neck with his tongue, and then I felt the tiny prick of his teeth, the lapping of his tongue and the sucking as he began to feed.

It was at first a horror to feel the blood drain, to sense my will struggle and fail; and then the pleasure rose, shudders and trembling so exquisite I could not bear them; the hot white cabin turned to shadows and cold and I fell across the bed. I am in my coffin, I thought, in my grave. He laid me back against the pillows, bent over me, pushed up my skirts and loosened the strings of my petticoats; I felt his hand on my skin. This was what I had feared, but now there was no retreat, I welcomed what was to come. I guided him forward; he lay full on me, his body was heavy on me, pressed against me, his uniform braid bruising my breasts. Our clothes were keeping us from each other. I slid the stiff fastenings open, fumbled out of my many-buttoned dress, struggled free of everything that kept me from him. *Now,* I whispered. *You must.*

We were skin to skin, and then, in one long agonizing push, he invaded me, he was *in me,* in my very body. Oh, the death pangs as I became a vampire, the convulsion of all my limbs! I gasped, bit his shoulder, made faces to keep from screaming. Yet still I moved with him, felt him moving inside me, and his power flowed into me. I laughed at the pain and pleasure unimaginable, as the sea waves pulsed through the cabin and pounded in my blood.

"Are you a vampire now, little respectable girl?" he gasped.

"Oh, yes, I have power, yes, I am a vampire."

He laughed.

When I dressed, I found blood on my bruised neck; my privates were bloody and sticky with juice, the signs of my change. I welcomed them. In the mirror, I had a fine color in my cheeks, and my white linen dress was certainly no more creased than might be justified by spending an afternoon on the water. My blood beat heavy and proud, a conquering drum.

I went on deck and ate a peach to still my thirst, but found it watery and insipid. It was late, toward sunset, the light failing, the sea red. In the shadows of the water I saw men silently screaming. I desired to drink the sea.

Mr. Lathrop opened his eyes and asked me, "Did you have a pleasant afternoon, Miss Wentworth?" His eyes were fixed, his color faded next to mine. Lucilla's face, as she blinked and yawned, was like yellow wax under her blond hair. Flies were buzzing around Mrs. Lathrop's cards, and Mrs. Lathrop gave off a scent of spoiled meat, feces, and blood. "Good afternoon, Aunt Mildred, how did you nap?" She did not answer me. Oh, they are weary, I thought, weary and dead.

Count Zohary came up the stairs, buttoning his uniform collar gingerly, as if his neck were bruised too. To amuse him, I pressed my sharp cutwork scissors against the vein of Aunt Mildred's neck, and held a Parker House roll underneath it; but he and I had no taste for such as Aunt Mildred. I threw my scissors into the blood-tinged sea: they fell, swallowed, corroded, gone.

Under a red and swollen sky, our ship sailed silent

back to the white hotel. Count Zohary and I were the first to be rowed to shore. Across the red lawn, lights blazed, and outside the hotel a great crowd had assembled. "In a moment we will see the future," he said.

"I saw men dying in the ocean," I answered.

We walked across the lawn together, my arm in his; under my feet, sea sand hissed.

"Count Zohary, perhaps you have friends who share those interests that you have taught me to value? I would delight to be introduced to them. Though I know not what I can do, I wish for wide horizons."

"I have friends who will appreciate you. You will find a place in the world."

As we entered the even more crowded foyer, Count Sergei Witte and the Marquis Komura stood revealed, shaking hands. From a thousand throats a shout went up. "Peace! It is peace!"

"It is the great storm," said Count Zohary. For a moment he looked pensive, as though even vampires could regret.

He and I gained the vantage point of the stairs, and I looked down upon the crowd as if I were their general. Many of the young men were dead, the Americans as well as the foreign observers. I looked at the victims with interest. Some had been shot in the eye, forehead, cheekbone; some were torn apart as if by bombs. Their blood gleamed fresh and red. The flesh of some was gray and dirt-abraded, the features crushed, as if great weights had fallen on them. Next to me stood a woman in a nurse's uniform; as she cheered, she coughed gouts of blood and blinked blind eyes. Outside, Roman candles began to stutter, and yellow-green light fell over the yellow and gray faces of the dead.

But among them, bright as stars above a storm, I saw us, the living. How we had gathered for this! Soldiers and civilians; many on the Russian and Japanese staff, and not a few of the observers; the eminent Mme. N., who bowed to me distantly but cordially across the room; by a window a nameless young man, still as obscure as I; and my bright, my blazing Count Zohary. The hotel staff moved among us, gray-faced, passing us glasses of champagne; but my glass was hot and salty, filled with the sea of blood to come. For the first time, drinking deep, I was a living person with a future.

That autumn I was in New York, but soon traveled to Europe; and wherever I went, I helped to call up the storm.

RAVISSANTE

ROBERT AICKMAN

"I am trying to set down events and feelings exactly as they were, or as nearly as possible, and I am not going to pretend that I did not sense something queer about Madame A. from the very start, because there is nothing in the whole story of which I am more certain than that."

Although you may not realize it, this is a rather famous story, and like the other of Aickman's waking nightmares (for example, "The Swords," featured in I Shudder at Your Touch, *the volume preceding this one), it depends for its horror quotient a great deal on the power of "not knowing." Aickman, the son of an architect, who himself had taken some training in that field, knew indeed how to erect a structure. His fictional edifices, however, might be said to differ from more conventional ones in that he delighted in leaving out foundations. So that while you can be sure that this oddity of framework is kept from us at the first, the ultimate—and marvelous—effect could be likened to standing and waving from a second-floor window and suddenly recognizing that the stairway just climbed not only has completely disappeared but was probably never there to begin with.*

And thus we are left, uncertain of the exact method of

*our arrival and very, very worried about what is likely to
happen next.*

*As so much of Aickman does, "Ravissante" carries
echoes of Henry James (whose own ghost tales still can
take the breath away), and one might even see it as a
sort of feverish, freakish cross between "The Romance of
Certain Old Clothes" and "The Aspern Papers." But its
ending in particular summons to memory that poignant
cry of despair uttered by the nameless governess in "The
Turn of the Screw." ". . . for if he were innocent," she
asks, suddenly sensing the certain absence of rescue,
"when then on earth was I?"*

I had an acquaintance who had begun, before I knew
him, as a painter but who took to "compiling and edit-
ing" those costly, glossy books about art which are said
to sell in surprising numbers but which no person one
knows ever buys and no person one sees ever opens.

I first met this man at a party. The very modern room
was illuminated only in patches by dazzling standard
lamps beneath metal frames. The man stood in one of
the dark corners, looking shy and out of it. He wore a
light blue suit, a darker blue shirt, and a tie that was
pretty well blue-black. He looked very malleable and
slender. I walked toward him. I saw that he had a high,
narrow head and smooth dark hair, cut off in a sharp,
horizontal line at the back. I saw also that with him was
a woman, previously invisible, though, as a matter of
fact, and, when she had come into focus, rather oddly
dressed. Nonetheless, I spoke.

It seemed that I was welcome after all. The man said
something customary about knowing almost none of the
guests and introduced the nearly invisible woman to me
as his wife. He proceeded to chat away eagerly but a
little anxiously, as if to extenuate his presence among so
many dark strangers. He told me then and there about
his abandonment of painting for editorship: "I soon realized I could not expect my pictures to sell," he said,
or words to that effect. "Too farfetched." About that
particular epithet of his I am certain. It stuck in my mind

immediately. He offered no particulars but talked about
the terms he got for his gaudy pictorial caravanserais. I
have, of course, written a little myself from time to time,
and the sums he named struck me as pretty good. I
avoided all comment to the effect that it is the unread
book which brings in the royalty (after all, modern trans-
lations of the *Iliad* and the *Odyssey* are said to sell by
the hundred thousand, and the Bible to be more deci-
sively the best-seller of all with every year that passes)
and observed instead that his life must be an interesting
one, with much travel and, after all, much beauty to
behold. He agreed warmly and, taking another martini
from a passing tray, described in some detail his latest
business excursion, which had been to somewhere in
Central America, where there were strange things
painted on walls, perfect for color photography. He said
he hoped he hadn't been boring me. "Oh, no," I said.
All the time, the man's wife had said nothing. I remark
on this simply as a fact. I do not imply that she *was*
bored. She might indeed have been enthralled. Silence
can, after all, mean either thing. In her case, I never
found out which it meant. She was even slenderer than
he was, with hair the color (as far as I could see) of old
wheat, collected into a bun low on the neck, a pale face,
long like her husband's, and these slightly odd, dark garments I've mentioned. I noticed now that the man had
a rather weak, undeveloped nose. In the end, the man
said, Would I visit their flat in Battersea and have dinner? and I gave my promise.

It will be noticed that I am being discreet with names.
I think it is best because the man himself was so discreet
in that way, as will be apparent later. Moreover, at no
time did I become a close friend of the pair. One thing,
however, must have had importance.

The Battersea flat (not quite overlooking the park)
did exhibit some of the man's paintings. I might compare
them, though a little distantly, with the once controver-
sial last works of the late Charles Sims: apparently confused on the surface, even demented, they made one
doubt while one continued to gaze, as upon Sims's pictures, whether the painter had not in truth broken

through to a deep and terrible order. Titles of the Sims species, "Behold I Am Graven on the Palm of Thy Hand" or "Am I Not the Light in the Abyss?" would have served with this man's pictures also. In fact, with him there was no question of titles, not, I thought, only out of compliance with the contemporary attitude, but more because the man did not appear to see his works as separate and possibly salable objets d'art. "I found that I couldn't paint what people might want to buy," he said, smiling beneath his weak nose. His wife, seated on a hard chair and again oddly dressed, said nothing. As a matter of fact, I could imagine quite well these strange pictures being gathered for a time by fashion's flapping feelers, though obviously for entirely wrong reasons. I remarked to the two of them that the pictures were among the most powerful and exciting I had ever seen, and what I said was sincere, despite a certain non-professionalism in the execution. I am not sure that I should have cared to live surrounded by such pictures, as they did, but that is another matter. Perhaps I exaggerate the number: there were, I think, three of these mystical works in the living room, all quite large; four in the matrimonial bedroom, into which I was conducted to look at them; and one each in the small bedroom for visitors and in the bathroom. They were framed very casually, because the painter did not take them seriously enough and mingled them on his walls with framed proofs from the art books, all perpetrated at the fullest stretch of modern reproductive processes.

I went there several times to dinner, perhaps six or seven times in all; and I reciprocated by entertaining the two of them at the Royal Automobile Club, which at that time I found convenient for such purposes, as I was living alone in Richmond. The Battersea dinners were very much of a pattern: my host did most of the talking; his wife, in her odd clothes, seemed to say less and less; the food, cooked by her, was perfectly good though a trifle earnest; I was treated very consciously as a guest. From this last, and from other things, I deduced that guests were infrequent. Perhaps the trouble was that the establishment lacked magic. The painter of those pictures should, one felt, have had something to say, but everything he brought out, much though there was of it, was faintly disappointing. He seemed eager to welcome me and reluctant to let me go, but entirely unable to make a hole in the wall that presumably enclosed him, however long he punched. Nor, as will be gathered, can his wife be said to have been much help. Or, at least, as far as one could see. Human relationships are so fantastically oblique that one can never be sure.

Anyway I fear that the acquaintanceship slowly died, or almost died. The near-death was slow because I made it so. I felt, almost at the beginning, that anything quicker would have meant a painfulness, conceivably even a dispute. Knowing what I was doing (within the inevitable—exceedingly narrow—limits), I fear that I very slowly strangled the connection. I was sad about it in a general sort of way, but neither the man nor his wife had truly touched anything about me or within me, and associations that are not alive are best amputated as skillfully as possible before the rot infects too much of one's total tissue and unnecessarily lowers the tone of life. If one goes to parties or meets many new people in any other way, one has to take protective action quite frequently, however much one hates oneself in the process; just as human beings are compelled to massacre animals unceasingly, because human beings are simply unable to survive, for the most part, on apples and nuts.

Total death of the connection, however, it never was. The next thing that happened was a letter from a firm of solicitors. It arrived more than four years after I had last seen the Battersea couple, as I discovered from looking through my old engagement books after I had read it; and two years, I believed, after the last Christmas card had passed between us. I had moved during that latter period from Richmond to Highgate. The letter told me that my Battersea acquaintance had died ("after a long illness," the solicitors added) and that he had appointed me joint executor of his will. The other executor was his wife. Needless to say, it was the first I had heard of it. There was a legacy which the testator "hoped I would accept": the amount was £100, which, I regret to

say, struck me at once as having been arrived at during
an earlier period of Britain's financial history. Finally,
the letter requested me to communicate as soon as possible with the writers or directly with their client's wife.

I groaned a little, but when I had reached the office
where I worked before my marriage, I composed a letter
of sympathy and in a postscript suggested, as tactfully as
I could, that an evening be named for a first meeting of
the executors. The reply came instantly. In the smallest
number of words possible, it thanked me for my sympathy and proposed the evening of the next day. I put off
an engagement to meet my fiancée and drove once more
to Battersea.

I noticed that my co-executor had abandoned the unusual style of costume she had previously favored and
wore an unremarkable, even commonplace, dress from
a multiple store. Perhaps it was her response to the inner
drive that until recently swept the bereaved into black.
In no other respect could I observe a change in her.

She did not seem broken, or even ruffled, with grief,
and she had little more to say than before. I did try to
discover the cause of death, but could get no clear answer, and took for granted that it had been one of the
usual bitter maladies. I was told that there was no need
for me to put myself to trouble. She would do all there
was to be done, and I could just come in at the end.

I did remark that as an executor I should have to see
a copy of the will. She at once handed the original to
me in silence: it had been lying about the room. It was
simple enough. The body was to be cremated, and the
entire estate was left to the testator's wife, except for
my £100, and except for the fact that all the testator's
pictures were to be offered to the National Gallery of
British Art; if refused, to a long list of other public gal-
leries, ten or twelve of them; and if still refused, to be
burnt. I saw at once why I had been brought into the
settlement of the estate. I had been apprehensive ever
since I had heard from the solicitors. Now I was terrified.

"Don't worry," said my co-executor, smiling faintly.
"I dealt with that part myself while he was still alive.

None of the places would touch the pictures with a barge pole."

"But," I said, "as an executor I can't just leave it at that."

"See their letters." She produced a heap of paper and passed it over to me. "Sit down and read them."

She herself drew back her normal hard chair and sat half watching me, half not, but without taking up any other occupation.

I thought that I might as well settle the matter, if it really were possible, there and then. I checked the letters against the list in the will. Every named gallery was accounted for. All the letters were negative: some courteously and apologetically negative; some not. The correspondence covered rather more than the previous twelve months. Many public servants are slow to make up their minds and slower to commit themselves.

"Did he know?" I asked.

That was another question to which I failed to get a clear answer, because she merely smiled and even that only slightly. It seemed difficult to persist.

"Don't worry," she said again. "I'll look after the bonfire."

"But don't *you* want to keep the pictures?" I cried. "Perhaps you've lived with them so long that they've become overfamiliar, but they really are rather remarkable."

"Surely as executors we have to obey the will?"

"I am certain you can keep the pictures, as far as the law is concerned."

"Would *you* like to take them? Bearing in mind," she added, "that there's about a hundred more of them stored in Kingston."

"I simply haven't room, much though I regret it."

"Nor, in the future, shall I."

"I'd like to take *one* of them, if I may."

"As many as you wish. Would you like the manuscripts also? They're all in that suitcase." It was a battered green object, standing against the wall. I think it was largely her rather unpleasant indifference that made me accept. It was quite apparent what would happen to the manuscripts if I did not take them, and one did not like to think of a man's life disappearing in a few flames, as his body.

"When's the funeral?" I asked.

"Tomorrow, but it will be quite private."

I wondered where the body *was*. In the matrimonial bedroom? In the small room for guests? In some mortuary?

"We neither of us believed in God." In my experience of her, it was the first time she had taken the initiative in making such a general pronouncement, negative though it had proved to be.

I looked at the pictures, including the one I had mentally selected for myself. She said nothing more. Of course, the pictures had been painted a number of years earlier: perhaps before the painter had first met her.

She offered me neither a cup of coffee nor a helping hand with the picture and the heavy suitcase down the many flights of stairs in a Battersea block of flats. Driving home, it occurred to me that for the amount of work involved, my executor's legacy was not so inadequate after all.

The picture has traveled round with me ever since. It is now in the room next to the one which used to be the nursery. I often go in and look at it for perhaps five or six minutes when the light is good.

The suitcase contained the tumbled typescripts of the art books, apparently composed straight on to the machine. They were heavily gashed with corrections in different-colored inks, but this did not matter to me because it had never been in my mind to read them. All the same, I have never thrown them away. They are in the attic now, still in the green suitcase, with labels stuck on it from Mussolini's Italy. To that small extent, my poor acquaintance lives still. He must presumably have felt that I, more than most, had something in common with him, or he would not have made me his executor.

But the suitcase contained something else: a shorter, more personal narrative, typed out on large sheets of undulating foreign paper and rolled up within a thick rubber band, now rotten. It is to introduce this narrative, so strange and so intimate, to explain how it came my way and how it comes to be published, that I have written the foregoing. The sheer oddity of life seems to me of more and more importance, because more and more the pretense is that life is charted, predictable, and controllable. And for oddity, of course, one could well write mystery.

Under the will, a publication fee belongs to the widow, who plainly holds the copyright. I give notice that she has but to apply. Remembering that last evening, on the day before the funeral, I am not sure that she will. But we shall see. The rest I leave to the words of my poor acquaintance.

Yesterday I returned from three weeks in Belgium. While there, I had an experience which made a great impression on me. I think it may even have changed my entire way of looking at things; troubled my soul, as people say. Anyway, I feel that I am unlikely ever to forget it. On the other hand, I have learned that what one remembers is always far from what took place. So I am taking this first opportunity of writing down as many of the details as I can remember and as seem important. Only six days have passed since it happened, but I am aware that already there are certain to be gaps bridged by imagination, and unconscious distortions in the interests of consistency and effect. It is possibly unfortunate that I could not make this record while I was still in Brussels, but I found it impossible. I lacked the time or, more probably, the application, as people always say of me. I also felt that I was under a spell. I felt that something terrible and alarming might happen as I sat by myself in my bedroom writing it all down. The English Channel proves to have loosened this spell considerably, though I can still feel all those textures on my hands and face, still see those queer creatures, and still hear Madame A.'s croaking voice. I find that, when I think about it, I am frightened still, but attracted overwhelmingly also, as at the time. This, I believe, is what is properly meant by the word fascination.

As others may read this, even if only in the distant

future, I set forth a few basic facts. I am a painter and twenty-six years old: the age when Bonnington died. I have about £300 a year of my own, so can paint what interests me; at least I can while I remain on my own. Until now I have been quite happy on my own, though this fact seems to upset almost everyone I know. So far I have had very little to do with women, mainly because I cannot see that I have anything to offer that is likely to appeal to them, and because I detest the competitive aspect of the relations between the sexes. I should hate it for a woman to pity me, and, on the other hand, I should hate to be involved with a woman whom I had to pity; a woman, in fact, who was not attractive enough to be in the full sex war and who might, therefore, be available for such as me. I should not care to be involved with a woman who was anything less than very beautiful. Perhaps that is the artist in me. I do not really know. I feel that I should want only the kind of woman who could not conceivably want me. I cannot say that the whole problem does not trouble me, but by the standard of what I have read and heard, I am surprised that it does not trouble me more.

I find also that I have no difficulty in writing these things down. On the contrary, I find that I like it. I fancy that I could produce a quite long narrative about my own inner feelings, though this is obviously not the occasion, for I think I have already said all that is necessary. I have to strike a balance between clearing my own mind and imparting facts to strangers. I conceive of this narrative, if I finish it, as being read only by myself and by strangers. I should not care for someone intimately in my life to read it—if there ever is such a person. I doubt whether there ever will be. Sometimes this frightens me, but sometimes it reassures me.

At this point I remember to mention, for the strangers who may read, that both my parents died seven years ago in an airplane accident. It was my mother who insisted on their going to Paris by air. I was present when my father argued with her. It was the usual situation between them. All the same, I loved my mother very much, even though she was as bossy toward me as she was toward my father. No doubt this has affected me too. I fear that a woman would steal my independence—perhaps even kill me. Nor, from what I have seen, do I think these particularly unreal fears.

On the whole, I do not like people. I seem incapable of approaching them, but I find that when they approach me, I am often quite successful with them—more so, indeed, than many of those who have no trouble with bustling in and making the first gesture. When once I am started, I can talk on fluently and even amusingly (though I believe inwardly that I have no sense of humor at all) and frequently, usually indeed, seem to make a strong impression. I suppose I must get some pleasure out of this, but I do not think I ever exert any real influence. It is almost as if someone else were talking through me—wound up by an outsider, my interlocutor. It is not I who talk, and certainly not I who please. I seriously suspect that I myself never speak, and I am certain that if I did, I should never please. This is, of course, another reason why I could not sensibly think of living with anyone.

Similarly with my art. My pictures are visionary and symbolical and, from first to last, have seemed to be painted by someone other than myself. Indeed, I have the greatest difficulty in painting anything to command. I am useless at portraits, incapable of painting at all in the open air, and quite indifferent to the various kinds of abstract painting that have followed the invention of the camera. Also I am weak on drawing, which, of course, should be a hopeless handicap. I have to be alone in a room in order to paint, though then I can sometimes paint day and night, twenty hours at a stretch. My father, who was quite sympathetic to my talent, arranged for me to attend a London school of art. It was quite pointless. I could achieve nothing and was unhappier than at any other period of my life. It was the only time when I felt really lonely—though worse may, of course, lie ahead. I am thus almost entirely self-taught, or taught by that other within me. I am aware that my pictures lack serious technique (if there is a technique that can be distinguished from inspiration and invention). I should have given up painting them some time ago were it not that a certain number of people have seemed to find something remarkable in them, and have thus identified me with them and made me feel mildly important. If I were to give up, I should have to give up altogether. I could not possibly paint, as so many do, just as a hobby or on Sundays only. I am sure that soon I *shall* give up—or be given up. When I read about the mediumship of Willi and Rudi Schneider, and of how the gift departed first from one brother and then from the other, and when both were quite young, I felt at once that something of the same kind will happen to me and that I shall settle down, like Willi Schneider, as a hairdresser or other tradesman. Not that I wish to suggest any kind of mediumistic element in my works. It is simply that they contain a glory which is assuredly not in the painter, as the few who know him will confirm. It is a commonplace that there is often more than one soul in a single body.

I must admit also to certain "influences." This sounds pretentious, but it has to be said because it explains what I have been doing in Belgium and how I came to visit Madame A. I find that certain works, or the works of certain painters, affect me strongly, almost agonizingly on occasion, but only *certain* pictures and *certain* painters, really very few. Art in general leaves me rather cold, I regret to say, especially when put on public display to crowds, most of them, inevitably, insensitive. I am sure that pictures should always belong to single individuals. I even believe that pictures suffer death when shared among too many. I also dislike books about art, with their dreadful "reproductions," repellent when in color, boring when not. On the other hand, in the painters who *do* affect me, I become almost completely absorbed: in their lives and thoughts, to the extent that I can find out about these things or divine them, as well as in their works. The look of a painter and the look of the places where he painted can, I think, be very important. I have no use for the theory that it is the picture only that matters and the way the paint has been stuck on it. That idea seems to me both lazy and soulless. Perhaps "my" painters are my true intimates, and them only. I cannot believe I shall ever be so close to any living person as I was to Magnasco when first I sought him out. But there again, I should emphasize that these "influences" seem to me far from direct. I can see little sign of other people's mannerisms in my own pictures. The influence is far deeper than that. The "only-the-picture" people would not understand at all.

It has been possible for me to travel a little in search of my particular pictures because at all times I live simply and spend hardly anything. It was to look at pictures that I have been to Belgium: not, needless to say, the Memlings and Rubenses, fine though I daresay they once were, but the works of the symbolists and their kind, painters such as William Degouve de Nuncques, Fernand Khnopff, Xavier Mellery, who said (and who else has ever said it?) that he painted "silence" and the "soul of things," above all, of course, James Ensor, the charming baron. I had worked for months before I left, to equip myself with a list of addresses, many of the finest paintings of the school being happily still in private hands. Almost everyone was kind to me, though I can speak very little French, and for the first fortnight I was totally lost and absolutely happy. Not all the owners gave signs of appreciating their various properties, but, naturally, I did not expect that. At least they were prepared, most of them, to leave me alone and in peace, which was something I had seldom found among the private owners who survive in Italy. Of them many seemed to think they might sell me something; most made a great noise; and all refused me privacy.

One of the Belgian authorities with whom I exchanged letters told me that the widow of a certain painter of the symbolist school still survived in Brussels. Not even to myself, in the light of what has happened, do I wish to write the name of this painter. I shall simply call him A., the late A. The informed may succeed in identifying him. Even if they do, it will not matter so much by the time they are likely to read this report. If strangers read sooner than I expect, it will only be because I am dead, so that the burden of discretion will be upon them and not upon me.

The Belgian authority, without comment, gave me an address in Brussels to which I wrote from England in my basic French, not seriously expecting any kind of reply. My habitual concern with the lives and personalities of "my" painters may, however, have made me write more urgently and persuasively than I supposed. It seemed a considerable opportunity for me. Despite my great interest, I had never met one of my particular painters nor even a widow or relative. Many of the painters, in any case, had lived too long ago for such a thing. If now I received no reply, I was quite prepared to stand about outside the house and consider in the light of what I observed how best to get in. That proved unnecessary. Within three days, I heard from Madame A.

She wrote in a loose, curving hand and confined herself to the center of a large sheet of dark blue paper. Her letter looked like the springs bursting out of a watch in a nineteenth-century comic drawing. It would have been difficult to read even if it had been in English, but in the end I deciphered most of it. Madame A. said she was extremely old, had not left the house for years or received any visitors, but was enchanted that anyone should go out of his way to see her and would receive me at six o'clock on an evening she named with exactitude. I had given her the dates of my proposed stay in Belgium, but nonetheless was surprised by her decisiveness because it was without precedent. People with pictures had always left to me the time of a visit, and an embarrassing responsibility I had often found it. Madame A. ended by asking how old *I* was?

When the time came, I spent the afternoon at the Musée Wiertz because it seemed to be in much the same part of the city as the abode of Madame A. "Wiertz's work is noted rather for the sensational character of his subjects than for artistic merit," states, in true Beckmesser fashion, the English guidebook I had borrowed from my public library. Possibly it is true in a way. It was not true for me. I was enthralled by Wiertz's living burials and imminent decapitations; by his livid, gory vision of the "real" world which surely is livid and gory, though boring and monotonous also, which Wiertz omits. Wiertz's way of painting reality seems to me most apt to the character of reality. I was delighted also by the silence and emptiness of Wiertz's enormous, exciting studio. His official lack of merit keeps out the conducted art lover.

All the same, anxiety was rising in me about my commitment with Madame A. I had remained fairly confident through most of my visits to picture owners, even in Italy, but these had been accepted as business transactions, and I had had no difficulty in concealing that for me they were stations on a spiritual ascent. With Madame A. I might have to disclose much more of myself and find words, even French words, for comments that were not purely conventional. She might be very infirm and intractable. It was probable that she was. It was September, and I sat on a bench before "The Fight for the Body of Patroclus," all alone in the high studio except for the attendant, who was mumbling to himself round the corner, while evening fell and the many clocks chimed and boomed me forward to my ambiguous assignation.

The power of solitude, not least in the Musée Wiertz, delayed me, in fact, too long. I found that I had underestimated the distance from the Rue Wiertz to the street in the direction of the Boulevard de Waterloo where Madame A. lived. They are beautiful streets through which I walked, though unostentatious; quiet, well proportioned, and warmly alive with the feel of history. I have seen no other part of Brussels that I like so much. I loved the big opening windows, filling so much of every façade, and so unlike England. I even thought that this would be a perfect district in which to spend my life. One never really doubts that one will feel always what one feels at any given moment, good or bad; or, when the moment is good, at least that one *could* always feel it if one might only preserve the attendant framework and circumstances. The activity of walking through these unobtrusively beautiful streets quieted me. Also I com-

monly notice that for the *very* last stretch, I cease to
be anxious.

Madame A. lived in just another such house: only two
stories high, white and elegant, with rococo twirls in the
fanlight above the handsome front door, a properly sized
front door for a house, wide enough for a crinoline, tall
enough for an admiral, not a mere vertical slit for little
men to steal through on the way to work. The houses
to left and right repeated the pattern with subtle minor
variations. I am glad to have been born soon enough to
see such houses before either demolition or preservation:
so far all was well.

There was a light in an upper window. It was of the
color known as old gold.

There was a bell and I heard it ring. I expected some
kind of retainer or relative, since I visualized Madame
A. as almost bedridden. But the door opened, and it was
obvious that this was Madame A. herself. She looked
very short and very square, almost gnomelike in shape;
but the outline of her was all I could see because it
was now almost dark, the street lighting was dim (thank
goodness), and there was no light at all in the hall.

"Entrez," said Madame A. in her distinctive croak.
"Entrez, monsieur. Fermez la porte, s'il vous plaît."
Though she croaked, she croaked as one accustomed, if
she spoke at all, to speak only in terms of command.
Nothing less, I felt at once, interested her in the context
of human discourse.

Up from the hall led a straight, uncarpeted staircase,
much wider than in an English house of that size, and
with a heavy wooden baluster, just visible by a light from
the landing above.

"Suivez, monsieur."

Madame A. went clambering upward. It is the only
word. She was perfectly agile, but curiously uncouth in
her movements. In the dim light, she went up those stairs
almost like an old man of the woods, but I believe that
age not infrequently has this effect on the gait of all but
the tallest. I should say that Madame A.'s height was
rather under than over five feet.

The light on the landing proved to hang by a thick

golden chain in an art nouveau lantern of lumpy old gold
glass speckled with irregular dabs of crimson. I followed
Madame A. into a room which traversed the whole
depth of the house, with one window on to the street
and, opposite it, another at the back of the building. The
door of the room was already open. Standing ahead of
me in the big doorway, Madame A. looked squatter
than ever.

The room was lighted by lanterns similar to that on
the landing. They were larger than the lantern outside,
but the old gold effulgence of the room remained distinctly dim, and the crimson dabs cast irregular red
splashes on the shiny, golden wallpaper. The furnishings
were art nouveau also. Everything, even the common
objects of use, tended to stop and start at unexpected
places; to spring upward in ecstasy, to sag in melancho-
lia, or simply to overhang and break away. One felt that
every object was in tension. The colors of the room coa-
lesced into strikingly individual harmony. Almost as
soon as I entered, it struck me that the general color-
ation had something in common with that of my own
works. It was most curious. The golden walls bore many
pictures, mostly in golden frames: mainly, I could see,
the work of the late A., as was to be expected, and about
which I must not further particularize; but also some
esoteric drawings manifestly by Felicien Rops, and
stranger than his strangest, I thought as I sat among
them. In the substantial art nouveau fireplace blazed a
fire, making the room considerably too hot, as so often
on the Continent. Nonetheless, I again shut the door.
As I did so, I saw that behind it was a life-size marble
figure of a woman in the moment of maternity. I identified it at once as the work of a symbolist sculptor well
known for figures of this type, but, again, I had better
not name him because about this particular figure was
something very odd—odd even to me who know about
childbirth only from works of art, not least the works of
this particular man.

"*Mais oui,*" said Madame A., as I could not withdraw
my gaze from the figure. "*C'est la naissance d'un
succube.*"

But at this point I think I had better stop trying to remember what was said in French by Madame A. In the first place, I cannot succeed in doing so, though her very first words, those that I have set down, remain clearly with me. In the second place, Madame A. soon disclosed that she could speak English perfectly well—or rather, perhaps, and as I oddly felt, as well as she could speak French. There was something about her which suggested, even to an unsophisticate like me, that she was no more a native of Belgium or France than she was of Britain. I am trying to set down events and my feelings exactly as they were, or as nearly as possible, and I am not going to pretend that I did not sense something queer about Madame A. from the very start, because there is nothing in the whole story of which I am more certain than of that.

And now there she was standing dumpily before the big, bright fire with her long bare arms extended, almost as if to embrace me.

Yes, despite the impending autumn, despite the blazing fire, her arms were bare; and not only her arms. Her hairy legs were bare also, and her dull red dress was cut startlingly low for a woman of her years, making her creased bosom all too visible. My absurd impression was that this plain red scrap of a garment was all she was wearing, apart from the golden slippers on her small, square feet.

And yet old she certainly was; very old, as she had said in her letter. Her face was deeply grooved and grained. Her neck had lost all shape. Her stance was hunched and bowed under the weight of time. Her voice, though masterful, was senile. I imagined that her black hair, somewhat scant, but wiry and upstanding, could only be dyed. Her head was like an old, brown egg.

She made me sit and sweat before the fire, constantly urging me nearer to it, and plied me with cognac and water. She herself remained on her feet, though, even so, her corrugated brown cheekbones and oddly vague black eyes were almost on a level with mine. The chair in which she had put me had wings at the level of the sitter's head, thus making me even hotter, and every now and then, as she spoke, she leaned forward, put a hand on each of these wings, and, for emphasis or to indicate a confidence, spoke right at my face, coming almost near enough to kiss me. She appeared to drink very little herself, but she made me drink far more than I wanted, praising the quality of the brandy and also (little did she know, I thought) the power and strength of my youth. Her very first question when we had settled ourselves was, How old had I said I was? And, she continued, born in Scorpio? Yes, I replied, impressed but not astonished, because many people have this particular divination, even though the materialists say otherwise. And how do you interpret that? I went on, because different people emphasize different aspects. Secrecy and sensuality, she croaked back. Only the first, I smiled. Then I must direct myself to awakening the second, she replied rather horribly.

And yet, I thought, how hard I am, how unsympathetic, after all; and, at the same time, how weak.

She did soon begin to talk about art and the painters she had known long, long before. Perhaps she thought that this was the topic which would awaken me. She tended to lose the way in her long, ancient chronicles and to fill or overfill my glass while she recovered direction.

It was noticeable that she seemed neither to admire nor to have liked any of the men she spoke of, many of whom were and are objects of my particular regard. At least I hope they still are: an object of admiration is impaired by hostile criticism of any kind, however ill-judged, and there is nothing the admirer can do to mend the wound, even though his full reason may tell him that the critic has no case. Madame A.'s comments were hardly reasoned at all and thus all the more upsetting. They were jeers and insinuations and flat rejections.

"X.," she would say, "was an absurd man, always very dapper and with a voice like a goat." "Y!" she exclaimed. "I had a very close friendship with Y.—as long as I could stand him." "Z.'s pictures are supposed to be philosophical but really they're not even successfully pornographic." All the time she implied that my own enthusiastic assessments were grotesquely immature, and when I argued back, sometimes with success because she was not much of a hand with logic and not too accurate with her facts either, she flattened me with personal reminisces of the comic or shady circumstances in which particular works had come to be painted, or with anecdotes which, as she claimed, showed the painter in his true colors.

"J.," she asserted, "was madly in love with me for years, but I wouldn't have used him as a pocket handkerchief when I had the grippe, and nor would any other woman." Madame A. had a fine turn of phrase, but as I knew (though we did not mention) that J., painter of the most exquisite oriental fantasies, had hanged himself in poverty and despair, her line of talk depressed and disconcerted me very much. I felt that in too many cases, even though, I was sure, not in all, her harsh comments were true, even though doubtless not the whole truth. I felt that, true or not by my standards, so many people (among the few interested at all) would agree with these comments as thereby to give them a kind of truth by majority vote. I felt, most sadly of all, that what I have called harshness in Madame A. was simply a blast of life's essential quality as it drags us all over the stones, artists—these selected divinities of mine among them—included.

As so often, it would have been better not to know.

"K.!" croaked Madame A. "K. worked for three years as a police spy and it was the happiest period of his life. He told me so himself. He was drunk at the time—or perhaps drugged—but it was the truth. And you can see it in his pictures if you only look. They are the pictures of a self-abuser. Do you know why K.'s wife left him? It was because he was impotent with a real woman and always had been. He knew it perfectly well when he married her. He did it because she had inherited a little money and he was on cocaine already and the good God knows what else. When I read about K.'s pictures being bought for the Musée Royal des Beaux-Arts, I laugh. I laugh and I spit." And Madame A. did both. She had a habit of snatching at the neckline of her red dress as she spoke and dragging it yet farther down. It seemed by now to have become an unconscious reflex with her, or tic.

"L.," she said, "started as a painter of enormous landscapes. That was what he really liked to paint. He liked to spend days and weeks entirely by himself in Norway or Scotland just painting exactly what lay before him, bigger all the time. The trouble was that no one would buy such pictures. They were competent enough but dull, dull. When you saw them lined up against the walls of his studio, you could do nothing but yawn. And that's the way people saw them when he hoped they might buy them. You couldn't imagine anyone ever buying one. You wanted only to get out of the studio and forget about such dull pictures. All those pictures of L. that you talk about, the 'Salomés' and 'Whores of Babylon,' weren't what he liked at all. He turned to them because two things happened at once: L.'s money ran out and at about the same time he met Maeterlinck. He met Maeterlinck only once, but it did something to him. Maeterlinck seemed fashionable and successful, and L. couldn't see why he shouldn't be too. But it really wasn't in the little man, and before long he gave it all up and became a *fonctionnaire,* as you know, though it was a bit late in the day for that."

"No, madame, I didn't know."

"Why, he's alive still! He's got the jumps, some kind of disease that gives you the jumps. The 'Whore of Babylon' might have given it to him, but he never got near enough to her to make it possible. L.'s alive all right—just. I used to go and see him when I still went out. He liked to borrow my old art papers. I've got hundreds of them, all from before the war. Ah, *les sales Boches,*" added Madame A. irrelevantly, but as many people do in Belgium and France from force of habit.

Despite everything, I suppose my eyes must have lighted up at the mention of the prewar art journals. In such publications there is often information not to be found anywhere else and information of just the sort that I find most valuable and absorbing.

"Ah," croaked Madame A. almost jubilantly. "That's

better. You are getting accustomed to me, *hein*?" She grasped my hands.

By now, she was flowing on in English. It was a relief. At one moment, she had spoken several sentences in a language I could not even identify. She had doubtless forgotten about me, or was confusing me with someone else.

"But you look hot," cried Madame A., releasing me. "Why do you not remove your jacket?"

"Perhaps," I replied, "I could walk round the room and look at the pictures."

"But certainly. If you wish." She spoke as if it were a remarkably ridiculous wish, and perhaps discourteous also.

I struggled away from her and proceeded from picture to picture. She said nothing while I promenaded, but remained standing with her back to the fire and her short legs well apart; gnomic in more than one sense. I cannot say that her eyes followed me with ironical glances because her eyes were too vague for such a thing. The light in the room, though picturesque, was quite unsuited to the inspection of pictures. I could see hardly anything. At the end of the room away from the street and away from the fire, it was almost dark. It was absurd for me to persist, though I was exceedingly disappointed.

"It is a pity my adopted daughter is not here," said Madame A. from the brightness. "She could entertain you better than I can. You would prefer her to me."

She spoke in a tone of dreadful coyness. I could think of no convincing reply. "Where *is* your adopted daughter?" I asked lamely and tamely.

"Away. Abroad. With some creature, of course. Who knows where?" She cackled. "Who knows with whom?"

"I am sorry to have missed her," I said, not very convincingly, I am sure. I was indignant that I had not been invited for some hour when I could see the pictures by daylight.

"Come back over here, monsieur," cried Madame A., pointing with her right forefinger to my hot armchair and then slapping her knee with the palm of her hand, all as if she were summoning a small, unruly dog. It was *exactly* like that, I thought. I have often seen it, though I have never owned a dog myself. I forebore from comment and returned reluctantly to the hot fire. Madame A., as I have said, was commanding as well as coy.

And then an extraordinary thing happened. A real dog was there in the room. At least, I suppose. I am now not sure how real it was. Let me just say a dog. It was like a small black poodle, clipped, glossy, and spry. It appeared from the shadowy corner to the right of the door as one entered. It pattered perkily up to the fire, then round several times in a circle in front of Madame A. and to my right as I sat, then off into the shadow to my left and where I had just been standing. It seemed to me, as I looked at it, to have very big eyes and very long legs, perhaps more like a spider than a poodle, but no doubt this was merely an effect of the firelight.

At that moment, there was much to take in fairly quickly, but one thing was that Madame A., as I clearly realized, seemed not to see the dog. She was staring ahead, her black eyes expressionless as ever. Even while I was watching the dog, I divined that she was still thinking of her adopted daughter and was entranced by her thoughts. It did not seem particularly remarkable that she had missed the dog because the dog had been quite silent, and she might well have been so accustomed to seeing it around the house that often she no longer noticed it. What puzzled me at that stage was where the dog had hidden itself all the time I had been in the room with the door shut.

"Nice poodle," I said to Madame A. because I had to break the silence and because Englishmen are supposed to be fond of dogs (though I am, comparatively, an exception).

"*Comment*, monsieur?" I can see and hear her still, exactly as she looked and spoke.

"Nicely kept poodle," I said, firmly sticking to English.

She turned and stared at me but came no nearer, as at such moments she usually did.

"So you have seen a poodle?"

"Yes," I said, and still not thinking there was anything

really wrong, "this moment. If it's not yours, it must have got in from the darkness outside." The darkness was still on my mind because of the pictures, but immediately I spoke, I felt a chill, despite the blazing fire. I wanted to get up and look for the dog, which, after all, must still have been in the room; but at the same time I feared to do any such thing. I feared to move at all.

"Animals often appear in here," said Madame A. huskily. "Dogs, cats, toads, monkeys. And occasionally less commonplace species. I expect it will have gone by now."

I think I only stared back at her.

"Sometimes my husband painted them." It was the only reference she had made to her husband, and it was one which I found difficult to follow up. She dragged down the front of her dress in her compulsive way.

"I will talk to you," said Madame A., "about Chrysothème, my adopted daughter. Do you know that Chrysothème is the most beautiful girl in Europe? Not like me. Oh, not at all."

"What a pity I cannot have the pleasure of meeting her!" I said, again trying to enter into the spirit of it, but wondering how I could escape, especially in view of what had just happened. On the instant, and for the second time, I regretted what I had said.

But Madame A. merely croaked dreamily, staring straight ahead. "She appears here. She stays quite often. For a quite long time, you understand. She cannot be expected to remain longer. After all, I am far from being her mother."

I nodded, though it was obscure to what I was assenting.

"Chrysothème!" cried Madame A., rapturously clasping her hands. "My Chrysothème!" She paused, her face illumined, though not her eyes. Then she turned back to me. "If you could see her naked, monsieur, you would understand everything."

I giggled, uneasily, as one does.

"I repeat, monsieur, that you would understand everything."

It dawned on me that in some way she meant more than one would at first have thought.

One trouble was that I most certainly did not *want* to understand everything. I had once even told a fortune-teller as much; a big-nosed but beautiful woman in a tent when I was a schoolboy.

"Would you like to see her clothes?" said Madame A., quite softly. "She keeps some of them here, to wear when she comes to stay."

"Yes," I said. "I should." I cannot fully analyze why I said it, but I said it. Madame A. being what she was, I could claim that I was given very little voice in the matter. Perhaps I wasn't. But that time it didn't arise. I undoubtedly chose.

Madame A. took me lightly by the wrist and drew me out of the chair. I opened the big door for her, and then another big door which she indicated. There were two on the opposite side of the landing, and she pointed to the one on the right.

"I myself sleep in the next room," said Madame A. on the threshold, making the very wall sound like an invitation. "When I can sleep at all."

The room within was darkly paneled, almost to the ceiling. The corner on the left behind the door was filled by a paneled bed with a coverlet of dark red brocade. It seemed to fill more space than a single bed, but not as much space as a double bed. From the foot of it, the plain, dark paneling of the wall continued undecorated to the end of the room. In the center of the far wall stood a red brocaded dressing table, looking very much like an altar, especially as no chair stood before it. On the right was a window, now covered by dark red curtains of the heavy kind which my mother used to say collected the dust. Against the wall on each side of this window stood a big dark chest. There were several of the usual art nouveau lanterns hanging high on the walls, but the glass in them was so heavily obscured that the room seemed scarcely brighter than the dim landing outside. The only picture hung over the head of the bed in the corner behind the door.

"What a beautiful room!" I exclaimed politely.

But I was looking over my shoulder to see if the black dog had emerged through the open door on the other side of the landing.

"That is because many people have died in it," said Madame A. "The two beautiful things are love and death."

I went right into the room.

"Shut the door," said Madame A.

I shut it. There was still no sign of the dog. I tried to postpone further thought on the subject.

"Most of her clothes are in here," said Madame A. She pulled at the paneling by the foot of the bed, and two doors opened; then another pair; then a third. All that part of the bedroom paneling fronted deep cupboards.

"Come and look," said Madame A.

Feeling foolish, I went over to her. All three cupboards were filled with dresses, hanging from a central rail, as in a shop. If they had been antiquarian rags or expectant shrouds, I should hardly have been surprised, but they were quite normal women's clothes of today; as far as I could tell, of very high quality. There were garments for all purposes: winter dresses, summer dresses, and a great number of those long evening dresses which one sees less and less frequently. All the dresses appeared to be carefully looked after, as if they were waiting to be sold. It struck me that in that direction might lie the truth: that the dresses might never have been worn. Certainly the room looked extremely unoccupied. Apart from the dresses, it looked more like a chapel than a bedroom. More than a mortuary chapel, it suddenly struck me; with a sequence of corpses at rest and beflowered on the bierlike bed behind the door, as Madame A. had so depressingly hinted.

"Touch the clothes," said Madame A., reading my mind. "Take them out and see the marks of Chrysothème's body."

I hesitated. Unless one is a tailor, one instinctively dislikes the touch of other people's clothes, whoever they may be, and of unknown strangers' clothes not least.

"Take them out," repeated Madame A. in her commanding way.

I gingerly detached a random dress on its hanger. It was a workaday, woolen garment. Even in the poor light, the signs of wear were evident.

That point made silently between us, Madame A. showed impatience with my timid choice. She herself drew out an evening gown in pale satin.

"Marvelous, exquisite, incomparable," she exclaimed stridently. I think that if she had been tall enough, she would have held the dress against her own body as the saleswomen so curiously do in shops; but, as it was, she could only hold it out at the end of her long arms, so that most of it flowed across the dark red carpet like a train. "Kneel down and examine it." I hesitated. "Kneel," cried Madame A. more peremptorily.

I knelt and picked up the bottom hem of the dress. Now I was down on the floor, I noticed a big dark patch which the dark carpet was not dark enough to hide.

"Lift the dress to your face," ordered Madame A. I did so. It was a wonderful sensation. I felt myself enveloped in a complex silky nebula. The owner, the wearer of that elegant garment, began, even though entirely without definition, to be much more present to me than Madame A.

Madame A. dropped the dress and on the instant was holding out another in the same way. It also was a long dress. It was made of what I believe is called georgette, and was in some kind of mottled orange and red.

The pale satin dress lay on the floor between us.

"Kneel on it. Tread on it," directed Madame A., seeing me about to circumvent it. "Chrysothème would approve."

I was unable to do such a thing and crawled round the edges of the satin dress to the georgette dress. Immediately I reached the georgette dress, Madame A. threw it adroitly over my head so that I had a ridiculous minute or two extricating myself. I could not but notice, and more than just notice, that the georgette retained a most enchanting scent. Her scent made the wearer of the dress more real to me than ever.

Away to my left, Madame A. now extended a third long dress, this time in dark blue taffeta, very slender and skimpy.

"You could almost wear it yourself," cackled Madame A. "You like wearing blue and you are thin enough." I had, of course, not told her that I liked wearing blue, but I suppose it was obvious.

Madame A. twisted round a chair with her foot and laid the dress on it, with the low top hanging abandonedly over the back of it.

"Why don't you kiss it?" asked Madame A., jeering slightly.

Kneeling at the foot of the chair, I realized that my lips were only slightly above the edge of the seat. To refuse would be more foolish than to comply. I lowered my face and pressed my lips against the dress. Madame A. might be ridiculing me, but I felt now that my true concern was with that other who wore the dresses.

When I looked up, Madame A. was actually standing on another chair (there were only two in the room, both originally in the corners, both heavy, dark, and elaborate). She was holding up a short dress in black velvet. She said nothing, and I admit that, without bidding, I darted toward her and pressed the wonderful fabric against my face.

"The moon," gurgled Madame A., pointing to the pale satin dress on the floor. "And the night." She flapped the black velvet up and down and from side to side. It too smelled adorably. I clutched at it to keep it still and found that it was quite limp, inert in my grasp.

Madame A. had leaped off the chair with one flop, like a leprechaun.

"Do you like my adopted daughter's clothes?"

"They are beautiful."

"Chrysothème has perfect taste." Madame A.'s tone was entirely conventional. I was still sniffing the velvet dress. "You must see the lingerie," Madame A. added, merely as if to confirm the claim she had just made.

She crossed to the chest at the left of the curtained window and lifted the unlocked lid. "Come," said Madame A.

The big chest was full of soft underclothes in various colors, not ordered like the dresses, but tangled and clinging apparently at random.

I suppose I just stood and stared. And the same scent was rising hypnotically from the chest.

"Take off your blue jacket," said Madame A., almost with solemnity. "Roll up your blue sleeves, and plunge in your white arms."

Without question, I did what she said.

"Sink your face in them."

I hardly needed to be instructed. The scent was intoxicating in itself.

"Love them, tear them, possess them," admonished Madame A.

All of which I daresay I did to the best of my ability. Certainly time passed.

I began to shiver. After all, I had left a very overheated room.

I found that all my muscles were stiff with kneeling, and I suppose with concentration too. I could hardly rise to my feet in order to rescue my jacket. As I rolled down my shirtsleeves, I became aware that the hairs on my forearms really were standing on end. They seemed quite barbed and sharp.

"Blue boy!" exclaimed Madame A., waiting for me to make the next move.

I made it. I shut the lid of the chest.

"The other chest contains souvenirs," said Madame A., dragging at the neckline of her dress.

I shook my head. I was still shaking all over and could no longer smell that wonderful scent. When one is very cold, the sense of smell departs.

And at that moment, for the first time, I really apprehended the one picture, which hung above the wide bed in the corner. Despite the bad light, it seemed familiar. I went over to it and, putting one knee on the bed, leaned toward it. Now I was certain. The picture was by me.

But there were two especially strange things. Though I was quite certain that the picture could only be mine (my talent may be circumscribed, but it is distinctive), I could not remember ever having painted it, and there were things about it which could at no time have been put there by me. Artists, in their later years, do sometimes forget their own works, but I was, and am, sure that this could never happen in my case. My pictures are not of a kind to be forgotten by the painter. Much worse was the fact that, for example, the central figure, which I might have painted as an angel, had somehow become more like a clown. It was hard to say why this was, but, as I looked at it, I felt it irresistibly.

My attack of shivering was turning to nausea, as one often finds. I felt that I was in danger of making a final fool of myself by being actually sick on the floor.

"Quite right," said Madame A., regarding the picture with her vague eyes and speaking as she had spoken in the other room. "Not a painter at all. Would have done better as a sweeper out of cabinets, wouldn't you agree, or as fetcher and carrier in a horse-meat market? It is kept in here because Chrysothème has no time for pictures, no time at all."

It would have been absurd and undignified to argue. Nor could I be sure that she was clear in her mind as to who I was.

"Thank you, madame," I said, "for receiving me. I must detain you no longer."

"A souvenir," she cried. "At least leave me a souvenir."

I saw that she held a quite large pair of silvery scissors.

I did not feel at all like leaving even a lock of my hair in Madame A.'s keeping.

I opened the bedroom door and began to retreat. I was trying to think of a phrase or two that would cover my precipitancy with a glaze of convention, but then I saw that squatted on the single golden light that hung by a golden chain from the golden ceiling of the landing was a tiny fluffy animal, so very small that it might almost have been a dark furry insect with unusually distinct pale eyes. Moreover, the door into the big, hot room on my left was, of course, still open. I was overcome. I merely took to my heels, clattering idiotically down the bare, slippery staircase. I was lucky not to slide headlong.

"*Mais,* monsieur!"

I was struggling in the dark with the many handles, chains, and catches of the front door. It seemed likely that I should be unable to open it.

"*Mais,* monsieur!" Madame A. was lumbering down after me. But suddenly the door was open. Now that I could be sure I was not trapped, a small concession to good manners was possible.

"Good night, madame," I said in English. "And thank you again."

She made a vague snatch in my direction with the big, silvery scissors. They positively flashed in the light from the street lamp outside. She was like a squat granny seeing off a child with a gesture of mock aggression. "Begone," she might have said; or, alternatively, "Come back at once": but I did not wait to hear Madame A. say anything more. Soon I found that I was walking down the populous Chausée d'Ixelles, still vibrating, and every now and then looking over one shoulder or the other.

Within twenty-four hours I perceived clearly enough that there could have been no dog, no little animal squatted on the lantern, no picture over the bed, and probably no adopted daughter. That hardly needed saying. The trouble was, and is, that this obvious truth only makes things worse. Indeed, it is precisely where the real trouble begins. What is to become of me? What will happen to me next? What can I do? What am I?

A BIRTHDAY

LISA TUTTLE

"He was sure he was blushing. He had blundered
in where he was not wanted, and he knew he
wouldn't be able to question Jean further."

*Lisa Tuttle is a writer of arrestingly creepy short stories,
who also has produced fantasy and science fiction and
horror novels, edited anthologies of her own, been a frequent genre reviewer and interviewer, and still found time
to publish an authoritative encyclopedia of feminism. In
"A Birthday," which is newly revised for* Shudder Again,
*she manages the feat of catching us completely off guard
by presenting a situation that is as familiar as any in our
lives—a birthday visit with a parent—and turning it skin-
side out.*

Although they both lived in London, Peter Squyres did
not see his mother very often. Once every few months,
moved by a feeling of duty, he would phone her and a
meeting would be arranged. Sometimes he took her out
to dinner, and sometimes he went to her house in Holland Park. He was twenty-three, lived in a shared flat in
Wood Green, had friends, hobbies, and a job in a bank.
His mother, in her mid-forties, had a mysterious, busy

life into which he did not enter. This seemed to suit them both.

One morning, unusually, she phoned him at work and invited him to come round that evening for a drink. While he hesitated, trying to think what to say, she went on, "I know it's short notice, but I've only just remembered that it's my birthday, and I thought it would be nice ..."

His eyes went to the calendar on the wall, and he felt guilty.

"Yes, of course," he said. "I'd love to. I was meaning to drop by, anyway, after work, to bring you a present."

"Lovely," she said. "Shall we say sixish? Just a drink. You've probably made plans for dinner, so I won't keep you long."

"Why don't you let me take you out to dinner?"

"No, Peter, I wasn't fishing for an invitation. Don't change your plans for me."

"It's no problem ..."

"Peter, don't fuss. I asked you for drinks. Just drinks," she said. "Sixish."

He had to phone his girlfriend, then, and tell her about the change in plans.

"I didn't know you *had* a mother," said Anna.

"What does that mean? Don't you believe me? It's her birthday; I really couldn't say no ..."

"Yes, of course I believe you; don't get in a state. It doesn't matter. I understand about parents, believe me. Let's make it another night."

"We can still have dinner tonight," he said. "I want to see you. How about the Malaysian place, at eight. I'll phone for a reservation, all right?"

"If you like." He couldn't tell if she was annoyed or indifferent. She might even be smiling, pleased by his persistence. Only part of his difficulty was due to the fact that he couldn't see her expression. Peter and Anna had known each other for about three months, and had started sleeping together two weeks ago. He had thought that would make a difference, that sex would make things clear and definite between them, but it hadn't worked like that. He still didn't know what she thought, or how she felt about him, and it seemed he was always worrying, trying to please or placate her, as once, long ago, with his mother.

"I'll see you at the restaurant at eight," he said. "I miss you."

On his lunch break he went out to buy a present for his mother. He bought red roses and then, at a loss, a bottle of Glenfiddich.

"Happy birthday, Liz," he said when he opened the door. He had stopped calling her "Mummy" when he was five. He thought she looked smaller. He supposed most adults thought that about their parents, and he must have made that observation before, but it struck him with particular force as he bent down to her now.

She accepted his gifts with a gracious smile and conventional expressions of pleasure, as if he were any guest, any man she knew. There were always men in her life, but which of them were her lovers, or if one had ever meant more to her than the others, Peter never knew.

"What can I get you to drink?" she asked. "G and T?"

"G and T, yes, please." He sat down and watched as she fixed the drinks, his elegant, beautiful mother. Her hair was dark, without a trace of gray, cut short, and sleekly styled. She wore black silk trousers and a quilted Chinese jacket. Her shirt, also silk, was white with an odd, abstract pattern in red.

As she handed him his drink he frowned, seeing dirty fingerprints on the glass.

"This glass," he said, rising, "it seems to be—I'll get another . . ."

She reached out to take it from him, and then he saw that her hand was bleeding.

The whole hand was covered in blood.

"What?" she asked at his exclamation.

"Your hand," he said, afraid to touch it, afraid of putting pressure on the wound and hurting her. "You're bleeding."

She looked down at her hand with a grimace of distaste, and put it behind her back. "It's nothing," she said. "I didn't realize ... I'll go wash it off."

"Do you want me to help? Let me look ... How did you hurt yourself?"

"It's nothing," she said again. "It happened earlier ... it looks terrible, I know, but it doesn't hurt at all. It's nothing. Let me clean up ..."

She seemed less concerned with her injury than with his reaction to it. When she had gone he stared down at the pale carpet, looking at two small, dark red spots. Her whole hand had been covered in blood. How could that be nothing?

She came back in, holding up a clean, unblemished hand. "See? Nothing."

She let him look, but when he tried to touch she pulled her hand away. "I'm all right, Peter, honestly. Why don't you get yourself another glass?"

He did as she said. But when he came back he looked at her blouse and saw that the abstract pattern had altered. There were more red splotches on the white silk now, and they were larger.

"You're bleeding," he said, shocked. "Liz, what *is* it? What's wrong?"

She looked down and pulled the jacket closed, and fastened it, hiding the bloodstained blouse. He saw how blood sprang out on her fingertips as she used her hands. He saw a line of blood on her neck, seeping above her collar. Horrified, he saw that her feet were bleeding, too.

"I'm going to call a doctor," he said. "Or hospital ... who's your doctor?"

"Peter, sit down and don't be silly. You don't know anything about it."

Such was the force of habit—she was his mother, after all—that Peter sat down again. "What is it?" he asked, trying to sound calm. "Do you know what it means?"

"I'm not hurt," she said. "There's nothing wrong. No cuts or scratches. The blood ... it's just coming from my pores, like perspiration. There's no injury. I'm not in pain. I don't feel any weaker for the blood I've lost, and this has been happening all day. There's nothing a doctor could do."

Rivulets of blood were rolling down the smooth black leather of her shoes to be soaked up by the rough weave of the carpet.

"But it's not normal," said Peter. "Bleeding like that—there's something wrong! How do you know a doctor couldn't—"

"Hysterical bleeding," she said calmly. "Have you heard of that?"

He could not imagine anyone less hysterical than his mother. Even now, when anyone would be frightened, she was utterly rational. Her silk trousers stuck to her legs, dark and wet. "I've heard of hysterical symptoms," he said. "A woman who thought she was pregnant, who showed all the signs of pregnancy, even fooled the doctors, but . . . it was an imaginary pregnancy, an hysterical pregnancy, not real. Do you mean this is like that? Do you mean it's not real blood?"

"I feel very well," she said. "If I had lost as much blood as I appear to have lost, I can't believe I could feel this well. On the other hand, if it's not blood, what is it?" She opened her hand, and they both stared at the blood that pooled to fill her cupped palm. After a moment she looked about, finally poured the red liquid into a crystal ashtray. "It stains like real blood," she said. "I'm going to have to have these carpets done . . . I don't think I'll ever get it out of the mattress."

"How long? How long has this been going on?"

"I suppose it must have started in the night. The early morning, really. It was the bed's being wet which woke me . . ." A flicker of emotion, then. "It was a shock, I must admit. I have a strong stomach and the sight of blood, my own blood, has never really bothered me—I remember how much blood there was when you were born; when the midwife put you in my arms, you were simply covered in blood, every inch of you, and that didn't bother me at all—and yet, this morning, when I saw myself in so much blood . . . I had to think . . . it took me some time to realize that there was nothing wrong—nothing *else* wrong—with me, and that I felt fine." She shrugged. Blood began to seep from her cuffs, fat drops spattering the carpet.

"Just because you feel all right—look, you *must* see a doctor. No matter how you feel ... you can't go on like this, just bleeding forever."

"Yes, of course, I know that; I haven't lost my mind, Peter. And I haven't been alone—I've spoken to someone about it, to a nurse. She agrees with me. I'll see a doctor if I have to, if it doesn't stop naturally. But I'm sure it will stop ... If it's still happening in the morning, I promise you I'll phone my doctor."

"Morning!" Peter leaned forward, distressed, almost spilling his drink. "You don't mean you're going to wait until tomorrow?"

"It's too late to phone anyone now."

"But you can't go on bleeding like this all night! Doctors have answering services—there'd be someone on call. What's the nearest hospital?"

"Peter, do calm down, please. I have been taking care of myself for years. This is not an emergency. I do have some knowledge of what doctors can and cannot do, and I am not going to go and sit in some hospital casualty ward for hours when I can be comfortable here at home. If I must see a doctor, I would like it to be my own doctor, someone who at least knows me. I can wait. It's not going to get any worse in the next few hours." She raised her glass to her lips and drank while red from her fingers rolled down the side of the glass.

"That's crazy," said Peter. "You don't know it's not going to get worse—you don't know anything about it. You're not a doctor; you can't know. If something should happen—anything could happen. I won't let you stay here on your own all night."

"I've already thought of that, and I'm not going to be on my own. I've asked Jean to come round just as soon as she gets the old lady settled for the night."

"Who?"

"Jean Emery. She's a registered nurse. She looks after the old dear next door. Has done for the last few months. We've gotten to be quite good friends, and she often pops in for a cup of tea or a drink and a chat. In fact"—here Liz released a small, triumphant smile—"in fact, I've already seen her. She's seen *me*. Everything's under control. She agrees that there's no need for me to rush off to a doctor. She doesn't think there's anything a dcotor could do. She's trained, Peter. She'll know if I need help, if anything starts to go wrong. She'll know what to do. She's agreed to stay the night. So you see, there's nothing for you to worry about."

Peter drank the rest of his gin and tonic and went to pour himself another. "I want to meet this woman before I leave you. I'd like to talk to her."

"Well, of course. Nothing could be easier. Would you pour me another drink, too, darling?"

They had little enough to say to each other at the best of times. Now it was impossible. Her illness, or injury, made everything else sink into insignificance. Peter wished he could call a doctor and hand the problem over to someone else. Frightened and ill at ease, he drank too much. Liz left him after quarter of an hour to shower and change. She returned wearing a black jersey dress for a much larger woman. It covered most of her body, voluminously, but left her lower legs bare. He couldn't stop staring at them. When the first bright drops of blood appeared he felt guilty, as if the pressure of his gaze had done it. Every few minutes she wiped her hands on a dark cloth that she then tucked into the chair cushions, out of sight.

"Your face isn't bleeding," he said.

"No, not yet. But my scalp has started."

He shuddered, finished what was in his glass, and looked at his watch. Nearly eight o'clock. He thought of Anna, waiting in the restaurant. He was about to ask if he could use the telephone when the doorbell chimed.

Jean Emery wore a crisp uniform and cap, and the very sight of her made him feel better. She was probably his mother's age, but her black hair was well sprinkled with gray, and instead of Liz's elegance she had a kind of solidity, and an air of practical efficiency that Peter instinctively trusted. He looked from her clear hazel eyes to her humorous mouth and liked her still more. He reminded himself that he was drunk. With a belligerence he didn't feel he demanded, "You know what's happening to my mother?"

"You must be Peter," said the nurse calmly. "I'm glad to meet you at last; Liz has told me so much about you."

"But what about her? Is she going to be all right?"

The women exchanged glances.

"He's worried about me," said Liz.

"You didn't explain ... ?"

Liz wrinkled her nose ever so slightly, pursing her lips in distaste, and Peter, staring at her, was assailed by a memory more than fourteen years old. She'd had that same expression when he asked her where babies came from, and she had given him a vague and unsatisfactory answer.

Jean gave a sigh that was half a laugh. "How about a cup of tea, Peter? I could certainly use one."

"I'm drinking gin," he said.

"Perhaps you've had enough gin for now, eh?" She had a smile that stopped his anger. He nodded obediently.

"I'll put the kettle on," said Liz, and left them alone.

"Sit down, Peter, do. I've been run off my feet today." Jean settled herself on the couch.

"Look, I'm sorry if I seem a bit abrupt, but I'm very worried about my ... about Liz. She won't let me call a doctor."

"There's no need for a doctor."

"But she's bleeding!"

Jean nodded. "Yes, and I can see that's very worrying for you. Will you believe me when I tell you there's nothing to worry about? It's a change, and of course there are some risks; understandably, you're nervous. But you needn't be frightened. There is nothing wrong. Your mother is going to be fine."

"But what's ... what's happening?"

For just a moment Jean's steady gaze seemed to flicker, and Peter intuited reluctance to speak about female secrets to a man. "She's my *mother*," he said fiercely.

"Yes, of course, of course. That's why ... Your mother is a very special woman, I don't know if you appreciate that, Peter."

He nodded impatiently. "Just tell me what's wrong."

"Nothing is wrong. That's what I want you to understand. This is a normal . . . Have you heard of what they call the 'change of life'?"

Peter frowned. "Yes, of course. It means when women . . . when women can't . . . when women stop . . . at a certain age . . ." He felt hot and uncomfortable.

"Yes, I think you understand. You needn't spell it out."

"But I thought that was when women *stopped* bleeding!" he blurted.

Jean smiled. "You weren't wrong. But people aren't all exactly alike. It takes different women in different ways, the change of life."

Liz came back into the room then, bearing a tray. "Here we are," she said.

Peter looked at his watch. He was sure he was blushing. He had blundered in where he was not wanted, and he knew he wouldn't be able to question Jean further. Maybe it would be all right; she was, after all, a nurse, and Liz seemed comfortable with her. Nagging away at him was the awareness that even if he left now he would be almost an hour late to meet Anna.

"I can't stay," he said. "I'm supposed to meet someone for dinner."

"Of course, I didn't mean to delay you," Liz said. "Run along. Really, Peter, you needn't worry about me."

He looked at the blood pooling at her feet, and then he looked at Jean. "Are you *sure* . . . ?"

"Quite sure," said Jean.

"And you'll stay with her?"

"I will."

"And call a doctor if there's anything . . ."

"Oh, Peter—"

"You have my word. Now run along. Come back in the morning, and see how different everything will be then."

"I will," said Peter. "I will be back in the morning. But if anything happens tonight, if anything changes or you're worried at all, please call me. It doesn't matter what time it is. Will you do that?"

"Everything is going to be all right," said the nurse. "I'll let you know as soon as there's anything to know."

He was afraid that Anna would not be there, but she was in the Malaysian restaurant, eating. She looked up from her satay, unperturbed, as he rushed in.

"I went ahead and ordered, I didn't think you'd mind. You can start eating some of mine and then order whatever else you like."

"I'm sorry I'm late, but—"

"Oh, that's all right. I know how parents can be."

"It's not that—there was something wrong—I mean, something really odd, she was bleeding, you see, and it wouldn't stop." He knocked over the chair in his first attempt to sit down. "Sorry. Anyway, I tried to get her to phone a doctor, but she wouldn't, kept insisting she was fine, but of course I couldn't leave her, I didn't know—"

"Peter, have you been drinking?"

"A couple of gins. Well, maybe three or four. It was a shock. I mean, well, if you'd seen her, and all that blood . . ." He gestured helplessly.

"Blood? Your mother? Bleeding? What happened?"

"Oh, she wasn't hurt, it wasn't like that, but it had been going on all day. She said when she woke up the bed was soaked, but she didn't feel weak, there wasn't any pain, and her friend Jean, she's the nurse, when she came in she obviously wasn't bothered at all. Explained it to me, calmed me down. Perfectly natural, change of life, she said. Well, of course I'd heard of that, and I guess my mother is getting to that sort of age, but I never imagined it could come on like that, with so much blood. I thought it was only when women, you know, stopped."

Anna gazed at him sympathetically. "Heavier bleeding than normal," she murmured. "Yes, I think I've read about that. There can be all sorts of different symptoms, I believe. Was your mother very upset?"

"Her! No, not at all. It was me who got upset. She kept telling me she felt fine and it didn't hurt and it was nothing to worry about, but I couldn't believe it." Relief flowed through him, stronger than alcohol. It was all right. Anna's acceptance convinced him this was something women had to suffer but could cope with, and there was nothing he, as a man, either could or should do.

He was able to eat and enjoy his dinner, and afterward they went to Anna's flat. Her flatmate was there with her bloke, and they invited Peter and Anna to watch a new video with them. It was just some low-budget slasher movie, and normally he would have found it as great a laugh as the others did, but now the sight of all that fake gore reminded him unpleasantly of his mother. He shifted uneasily on the couch. How much blood could someone lose and still survive? He excused himself—"No, no, don't stop it on my account"—and went to the toilet. At the sink, watching clear water stream over his hands he recalled the redness flowing from his mother.

All at once he couldn't remember if he had left Anna's number with Jean Emery or only his own. He could call—but it was nearly midnight. He thought of his mother's icy annoyance if he should wake her. How many times over the years had he evoked her disapproval by being obtuse, by misunderstanding, by demanding attention she found it a bore to provide? He was a grown-up now, their lives were separate. That was how she wanted it. She hadn't asked for his help, and there was nothing he could do for her.

When he opened the bathroom door Anna was standing there in her dressing gown, smiling at him. "Who cares how the stupid video ends. Let's go to bed."

Yet even in bed with his love, happy and exhausted, he could not relax enough to sleep. Jean had told him to come back in the morning, but what was happening now? How much blood could a person lose and still survive?

"Peter?"

"Yes?"

"Are you worrying about your mother still?"

Love for her, gratitude for her empathy, coursed through him like a lesser orgasm. He rolled over and kissed her. "You're a mind reader."

"Hardly."

"You do think she's all right? I mean that it's normal and . . ."

"Peter, I'm not a doctor. I did a first-aid course last year, but that hardly qualifies me to make a diagnosis, especially sight unseen. If the bleeding was very heavy it could be a problem. But how heavy . . . I mean, I don't suppose she told you how often she had to change her—"

"Oh, she didn't have to say, I could see. Her clothes were soaked, absolutely soaked, in half an hour. Every time she touched anything, the slightest pressure, like handing me a glass, the blood would pour out of her. It poured out of her hands, it ran down her legs and arms, it was everywhere, she was bleeding from every pore, except on her face."

While he was speaking, Anna had sat up and switched on the bedside lamp. "You *are* awake."

"What's the matter?"

"What's the matter? You're telling me your mother had blood streaming out of her, that she was bleeding all over her body—"

"But you said it was normal."

"Normal!"

"Well, that it could be; you said . . ." he trailed off, unable to remember exactly what she had said and realizing that it didn't matter because he had obviously misunderstood.

"There is no way that somebody bleeding from every pore, somebody soaked in blood, could be normal. Think about it."

"But Jean said . . . and my mother . . . I thought it was the change of life. Even you said some bleeding could be normal."

"Some bleeding. Normal bleeding. Not like that."

Peter hunched his shoulders, feeling resentful. What the hell was normal bleeding? If he bled, he knew he was injured. But women bled every month, and that was supposed to be normal, unless they bled too heavily, or on the wrong days, or when they were pregnant, at which point it became a cause for concern. How was he supposed to interpret such female mysteries? Women said one thing and then, using the same words, they said another. *They* knew what they meant, and the men who couldn't understand were the ones at fault. He wanted to wash his hands of the whole messy female business.

"Peter, get up. Get dressed." She was already up, pulling on the dark sweater and skirt she had worn earlier. "We've got to go over there."

"They don't want me. They sent me away."

"You can't leave your mother alone at a time like this."

"She's with a nurse," he said sullenly.

"A nurse who says it's normal."

They made eye contact at last, and the frail structure of his childish resentment collapsed. Of course he would go if Liz needed him, even if she couldn't admit her need. Despite the emotional distance between them there was also an unbreakable bond. She would always be his mother.

Anna phoned for a cab, and then he tried to call his mother. There was no reply.

"Maybe they've gone. Maybe the nurse took your mother to the hospital," Anna suggested.

Or maybe Jean was so busy attempting to stanch the flow of blood that she simply couldn't be bothered with the telephone. Horrific, chaotic, incomprehensible images, as from some particularly nasty video, crowded his brain. His heart raced and he broke out in a sweat. He should never have left. He should be there now. Liz had no one else. Jean was only a stranger.

Seeing his distress, Anna hugged him tightly. "There, there. It'll be all right."

All the way to Holland Park in the cab—a much swifter journey at this hour of the night than it would have been in heavier traffic—he clung to Anna's warm, strong hand, trying to control the fits of shivering that rocked his body. Her words, even when they lapsed into the almost meaningless baby talk of pure reassurance, were his life-line to sanity. It would be all right because Anna said it would.

There was no reply when he rang the bell, and he froze in helpless panic.

"You said you had a key," Anna reminded him.

"Oh, yes, of course . . ."

She took it from his trembling fingers and let them into the house.

The front room was empty. The blood on the carpet looked even more horrible now that it had dried. There were sounds from the back of the house. Anna put her arm around Peter and walked him through.

Jean was in the bedroom, but not Liz. He thought for a horrible moment that he glimpsed his mother's body, wet, collapsed, and impossibly shrunken, lying in a heap of bloodstained clothes at the foot of the bed, but before he could investigate his attention was caught by what lay on the bed: a tiny baby, newborn by the look of it, all red, as if covered in a glistening second skin of blood.

"You're just in time," said Jean. She was beaming. Her once-fresh uniform was a bloody mess. "I was going to give you a ring—it all happened a bit quicker than I thought, but I guess you sensed that, eh? Nothing like the bond between parent and child, I always say."

The baby opened its mouth and began to squall.

"Hush, hush, Lizzie," said Jean. "Hush, now, Peter's home." She lifted the baby and held it out toward Peter. "Congratulations," she said. "You have a lovely daughter."

THE CROOKED MAN

CHARLES BEAUMONT

~~~~~~~~~~~~~~~~~~~~~~~~~~

> "The girl's hands caressed his arms and the touch
> became suddenly repugnant to him. Unnatural.
> Terribly unnatural."

----

*The tale behind Charles Beaumont's "The Crooked Man"
makes for a little slice of magazine publishing history. And
though it, too, like "Ravissante," is considered by cogno-
scenti a "famous" tale, the reason lies less in the variety of
admiring interpretive analyses and more in the conformist
social climate of its time, the Eisenhower years.*

*Back then was the heyday of men's magazine fiction
(and men's magazines, in general), probably having
something to do with the market created by huge popula-
tions of guys—soldiers in two wars, WW II and the Ko-
rean—trained by circumstance to equate reading and
leisure. It was, as well, the formative era for* Playboy,
*which, in August 1955, was where "The Crooked Man"
appeared. (Actually bought the previous year for publication by a different, competing manly periodical, it is
claimed, at any rate, that their case of cold feet caused*

the rights to be returned to Beaumont, who then offered it to Playboy.*)*

However, by the time it ran, either genuine rumors of its subversive content or an exceedingly canny p.r. sense— or perhaps a little of both—had created an opportunity for the Playboy *editors (with Ray Russell listed second on the masthead at the time, just under founder-philosopher Hugh Hefner) to pat themselves on the back for their fearlessness, explaining to readers in a note that a special editorial meeting had first had to be convened to discuss the matter.*

Irate letters did follow the publication of "The Crooked Man" and were duly printed. But since they seemed willfully to have all missed the point of Beaumont's satire, seeing prejudice where, in fact, the opposite was true, the "controversy" quickly subsided, and author and magazine both went on to other things. In Charles Beaumont's case, however, this meant a brilliant writing career (for magazines, films, and television) cut short by tragic illness. Only twenty-five when he wrote the story you're about to read, he died in 1967, aged thirty-eight.

"Professing themselves to be wise, they became fools ... who changed the truth of God into a lie ... for even their women did change the natural use into that which is against nature: and likewise also the men, leaving the natural use of the woman, burned in their lust one toward another; men with men working that which is unseemly ..."

—St. Paul: Romans, I

He slipped into a corner booth away from the dancing men, where it was quietest, where the odors of musk and frangipani hung less heavy on the air. A slender lamp glowed softly in the booth. He turned it down: down to where only the club's blue overheads filtered through the beaded curtain, diffusing, blurring the image thrown back by the mirrored walls of his light, thin-boned handsomeness.

"Yes sir?" The barboy stepped through the beads and stood smiling. Clad in gold-sequined trunks, his greased muscles seemed to roll in independent motion, like fat snakes beneath his naked skin.

"Whiskey," Jesse said. He caught the insouciant grin, the broad white-tooth crescent that formed on the young man's face. Jesse looked away, tried to control the flow of blood to his cheeks.

"Yes sir," the barboy said, running his thick tanned fingers over his solar plexus, tapping the fingers, making them hop in a sinuous dance. He hesitated, still smiling, this time questioningly, hopefully, a smile deep drenched in admiration and desire. The Finger Dance, the accepted symbol, stopped: the pudgy brown digits curled into angry fists. "Right away, sir."

Jesse watched him turn; before the beads had tinkled together he watched the handsome athlete make his way imperiously through the crowd, shaking off the tentative hands of single men at the tables, ignoring the many desire symbols directed toward him.

That shouldn't have happened. Now the fellow's feelings were hurt. It hurt enough, he would start thinking, wondering—and that would ruin everything. No. It must be put right.

Jesse thought of Mina, of the beautiful Mina— It was such a rotten chance. It *had* to go right!

"Your whiskey, sir," the young man said. His face looked like a dog's face, large, sad; his lips were a pouting bloat of line.

Jesse reached into his pocket for some change. He started to say something, something nice.

"It's been paid for," the barboy said. He scowled and laid a card on the table and left.

The card carried the name E. J. Two Hobart, embossed, in lavender ink. Jesse heard the curtains tinkle.

"Well, hello. I hope you don't mind my barging in like this, but—you didn't seem to be with anyone ..."

The man was small, chubby, bald; his face had a dirty growth of beard and he looked out of tiny eyes encased in bulging contacts. He was bare to the waist. His white hairless chest drooped and turned in folds at the stomach. Softly, more subtly than the barboy had done, he put his porky stubs of fingers into a suggestive rhythm.

Jesse smiled. "Thanks for the drink," he said. "But I really am expecting someone."

"Oh?" the man said. "Someone—special?"

"Pretty special," Jesse said smoothly, now that the words had become automatic. "He's my fiancée."

"I see." The man frowned momentarily and then brightened. "Well, I thought to myself, I said: E. J., a beauty like that couldn't very well be unattached. But— well, it was certainly worth a try. Sorry."

"Perfectly all right," Jesse said. The predatory little eyes were rolling, the fingers dancing in one last-ditch attempt. "Good evening, Mr. Hobart."

Bluey veins showed under the whiteness of the man's nearly female mammae. Jesse felt slightly amused this time: it was the other kind, the intent ones, the humorless ones like—like the barboy—that repulsed him, turned him ill, made him want to take a knife and carve unspeakable ugliness into his own smooth ascetic face.

The man turned and waddled away crabwise. The club was becoming more crowded. It was getting later and heads full of liquor shook away the inhibitions of the earlier hours. Jesse tried not to watch, but he had long ago given up trying to rid himself of his fascination. So he watched the men together. The pair over in the far corner, pressed close together, dancing with their bodies, never moving their feet, swaying in slow lissome movements to the music, their tongues twisting in the air, jerking, like pink snakes, contracting to points and curling invitingly, barely making touch, then snapping back. The Tongue Dance ... The couple seated by the bar. One a Beast, the other a Hunter, the Beast old, his cheeks caked hard and cracking with powder and liniments, the perfume rising from his body like steam; the Hunter, young but unhandsome, the fury evident in his eyes, the hurt anger at having to make do with a Beast— from time to time he would look around, wetting his lips in shame. . . . And those two just coming in, dressed in Mother's uniforms, tanned, mustached, proud of their station. . . .

Jesse held the beads apart. *Mina must come soon.* He wanted to run from this place, out into the air, into the darkness and silence.

No. He just wanted Mina. To see her, touch her, listen to the music of her voice. . . .

Two women came in, arm in arm, Beast and Hunter, drunk. They were stopped at the door. Angrily, shrilly, told to leave. The manager swept by Jesse's booth, muttering about them, asking why they should want to come dirtying up The Phallus with their presence when they had their own section, their own clubs—

Jesse pulled his head back inside. He'd gotten used to the light by now, so he closed his eyes against his multiplied image. The disorganized sounds of love got louder, the singsong syrup of voices: deep, throaty, baritone, falsetto. It was crowded now. The Orgies would begin before long and the couples would pair off for the cubicles. He hated the place. But close to Orgy-time you didn't get noticed here—and where else was there to go? Outside, where every inch of pavement was patrolled electronically, every word of conversation, every movement recorded, catalogued, filed?

Damn Knudson! Damn the little man! Thanks to him, to the Senator, Jesse was now a criminal. Before, it wasn't so bad—not this bad, anyway. You were laughed at and shunned and fired from your job, sometimes kids lobbed stones at you, but at least you weren't hunted. Now—it was a crime. A sickness.

He remembered when Knudson had taken over. It had been one of the little man's first telecasts; in fact, it was the platform that got him the majority vote:

"Vice is on the upswing in our city. In the dark corners of every Unit perversion blossoms like an evil flower. Our children are exposed to its stink, and they wonder—*our children wonder*—why nothing is done to put a halt to this disgrace. We have ignored it long enough! The time has come for *action*, not mere words. The perverts who infest our land must be flushed out, eliminated *completely*, as a threat not only to public morals but to society at large. These sick people must be cured and made normal. The disease that throws men and women together in this dreadful abnormal relationship and leads to acts of retrogression—retrogression that will, unless it is stopped and stopped fast, push us inevitably back to the status of animals—this is to be considered as any other disease. It must be conquered as heart trouble, cancer, polio, schizophrenia, paranoia, all other diseases have been conquered. . . ."

The Women's Senator had taken Knudson's lead and issued a similar pronunciamento and then the bill became a law and the law was carried out.

Jesse sipped at the whiskey, remembering the Hunts. How the frenzied mobs had gone through the city at first, chanting, yelling, bearing placards with slogans: WIPE OUT THE HETEROS! KILL THE QUEERS! MAKE OUR CITY CLEAN AGAIN! And how they'd lost interest finally after the passion had worn down and the novelty had ended. But they had killed many and they had sent many more to the hospitals. . . .

He remembered the nights of running and hiding, choked dry breath glued in his throat, heart rattling loose. He had been lucky. He didn't look like a hetero. They said you could tell one just by watching him walk—Jesse walked correctly. He fooled them. He was lucky.

And he was a criminal. He, Jesse Four Martin, no different from the rest, tube-born and machine-nursed, raised in the Character Schools like everyone else—was terribly different from the rest.

It had happened—his awful suspicions had crystallized—on his first formal date. The man had been a Rocketeer, the best high quality, even out of the Hunter class. Mother had arranged it carefully. There was the dance. And then the ride in the space-sled. The big man had put an arm about Jesse and—Jesse knew. He knew for certain and it made him very angry and very sad.

He remembered the days that came after the knowledge: bad days, days fallen upon evil, black desires, deep-cored frustrations. He had tried to find a friend at the Crooked Clubs that flourished then, but it was no use. There was a sensationalism, a bravura to these people, that he could not love. The sight of men and women together, too, shocked the parts of him he could not change, and repulsed him. Then the vice squads had come and closed up the clubs and the heteros were forced underground and he never sought them out again or saw them. He was alone.

The beads tinkled.

"Jesse—" He looked up quickly, afraid. It was Mina. She wore a loose man's shirt, an old hat that hid her golden hair: her face was shadowed by the turned-up collar. Through the shirt the rise and fall of her breasts could be faintly detected. She smiled once, nervously.

Jesse looked out the curtain. Without speaking, he put his hands about her soft thin shoulders and held her like this for a long minute.

"Mina—" She looked away. He pulled her chin forward and ran a finger along her lips. Then he pressed her body to his, tightly, touching her neck, her back, kissing her forehead, her eyes, kissing her mouth. They sat down.

They sought for words. The curtains parted.

"Beer," Jesse said, winking at the barboy, who tried to come closer, to see the one loved by this thin handsome man.

"Yes sir."

The barboy looked at Mina very hard, but she had turned and he could see only the back. Jesse held his breath. The barboy smiled contemptuously then, a smile that said: You're insane—I was hired for my beauty. See my chest, look—a pectoral vision. My arms, strong; my lips—come, were there ever such sensuous ones? And you turn me down for this bag of bones. . . .

Jesse winked again, shrugged suggestively, and danced his fingers: *Tomorrow, my friend, I'm stuck tonight. Can't help it. Tomorrow.*

The barboy grinned and left. In a few moments he returned with the beer. "On the house," he said, for Mina's benefit. She turned only when Jesse said, softly:

"It's all right. He's gone now."

Jesse looked at her. Then he reached over and took

off the hat. Blond hair rushed out and over the rough shirt.

She grabbed for the hat. "We mustn't," she said. "Please—what if somebody should come in?"

"No one will come in. I told you that."

"But what if? I don't know—I don't like it here. That man at the door—he almost recognized me."

"But he didn't."

"Almost though. And then what?"

"Forget it. Mina, for God's sake. Let's not quarrel."

She calmed. "I'm sorry, Jesse. It's only that—this place makes me feel—"

"—what?"

"Dirty." She said it defiantly.

"You don't really believe that, do you?"

"No. I don't know. I just want to be alone with you."

Jesse took out a cigarette and started to use the lighter. Then he cursed and threw the vulgarly shaped object under the table and crushed the cigarette. "You know that's impossible," he said. The idea of separate Units for homes had disappeared, to be replaced by giant dormitories. There were no more parks, no country lanes. There was no place to hide at all now, thanks to Senator Knudson, to the little bald crest of this new sociological wave. "This is all we have," Jesse said, throwing a sardonic look around the booth, with its carved symbols and framed pictures of entertainment stars—all naked and leering.

They were silent for a time, hands interlocked on the tabletop. Then the girl began to cry. "I—I can't go on like this," she said.

"I know. It's hard. But what else can we do?" Jesse tried to keep the hopelessness out of his voice.

"Maybe," the girl said, "we ought to go underground with the rest."

"And hide there, like rats?" Jesse said.

"We're hiding here," Mina said, "like rats."

"Besides, Parner is getting ready to crack down. I know, Mina—I work at Centraldome, after all. In a little while there won't be any underground."

"I love you," the girl said, leaning forward, parting

her lips for a kiss. "Jesse, I do." She closed her eyes. "Oh, why won't they leave us alone? Why? Just because we're que—"

"Mina! I've told you—don't ever use that word. It isn't true! *We're* not the queers. You've got to believe that. Years ago it was *normal* for men and women to love each other: they married and had children together; that's the way it was. Don't you remember anything of what I've told you?"

The girl sobbed. "Of course I do. I do. But, darling, that was a long time ago."

"Not so long! Where I work—listen to me—they have books. You know, I told you about books? I've read them, Mina. I learned what the words meant from other books. It's only been since the use of artificial insemination—not even five hundred years ago."

"Yes, dear," the girl said. "I'm sure, dear."

"Mina, stop that! We are not the unnatural ones, no matter what they say. I don't know exactly how it happened—maybe, maybe as women gradually became equal to men in every way—or maybe solely because of the way we're born—I don't know. But the point is, darling, the whole world was like us, once. Even now, look at the animals—"

"Jesse! Don't you dare talk as if we're like those horrid little dogs and cats and things!"

Jesse sighed. He had tried so often to tell her, show her. But he knew, actually, what she thought. That she felt she was exactly what the authorities told her she was—God, maybe that's how they all thought, all the Crooked People, all the "unnormal" ones. . . .

The girl's hands caressed his arms and the touch became suddenly repugnant to him. Unnatural. Terribly unnatural.

Jesse shook his head. Forget it, he thought. Never mind. She's a woman and you love her and there's nothing wrong nothing wrong nothing wrong in that . . . or am I the insane person of old days who was insane because he was so sure he wasn't insane because—

"Disgusting!"

It was the fat little man, the smiling masher, E. J. Two Hobart. But he wasn't smiling now.

Jesse got up quickly and stepped in front of Mina. "What do you want? I thought I told you—"

The man pulled a metal disk from his trunks. "Vice squad, friend," he said. "Better sit down." The disk was pointed at Jesse's belly.

The man's arm went out the curtain and two other men came in, holding disks.

"I've been watching you quite a while, mister," the man said. "Quite a while."

"Look," Jesse said, "I don't know what you're talking about. I work at Centraldome and I'm seeing Miss Smith here on some business."

"We know all about that kind of business," the man said.

"All right—I'll tell you the truth. I forced her to come here. I—"

"Mister—didn't you hear me? I said I've been watching you. All evening. Let's go."

One man took Mina's arm, roughly; the other two began to propel Jesse out through the club. Heads turned. Tangled bodies moved embarrassedly.

"It's all right," the little fat man said, his white skin glistening with perspiration. "It's all right, folks. Go on back to whatever you were doing." He grinned and tightened his grasp on Jesse's arm.

Mina didn't struggle. There was something in her eyes—it took Jesse a long time to recognize it. Then he knew. He knew what she had come to tell him tonight: that even if they hadn't been caught—she would have submitted to the Cure voluntarily. No more worries then, no more guilt. No more meeting at midnight dives, feeling shame, feeling dirt. . . .

Mina didn't meet Jesse's look as they took her out into the street.

"You'll be okay," the fat man was saying. He opened the wagon's doors. "They've got it down pat now—couple days in the ward, one short session with the doctors; take out a few glands, make a few injections, attach a few wires to your head, turn on a machine: presto! You'll be surprised."

The fat officer leaned close. His sausage fingers danced wildly near Jesse's face.

"It'll make a new man of you," he said.

Then they closed the doors and locked them.

ON THE LAKE OF LAST WISHES

CLAUDIA O'KEEFE

"There was a great deal of sorrow in his passion,
a great deal of love in his anger."

*Imagine the swirling snowstorm in a tiny souvenir globe,
a placid but potentially volatile landscape that only you
control. Yet what if suddenly you found yourself lost inside that scene and not quite in charge anymore? It's an
unsettling notion, certainly, and one that doubtless could
be used to great effect.*

Though not here.

*Averse to giving away any element of this memorable
story, I merely wanted to hint at those generative forces
at work in it. What Claudia O'Keefe has done, however,
is imagine the imaginary world of someone with extremely powerful reasons for longing to be elsewhere.*

That night, Wilona woke from real life, and found herself by the side of the same lake as the night before.
Though the bank on which she lay was hard clay, cool

and as damp as the night around her, a duvet sewn of magnolia leaves had been laid out beneath her, filled with moss. Under her head was a celadon-green pillow made of cloth softer than any lamb suede she had ever felt. A single magnolia blossom drifted down from the branches over her head and brushed her throat, as it tumbled noiselessly onto the duvet. She sat up.

She was alert now. Waiting.

She stood. The lake's incandescent surface was the tranquil dark silver of a black pearl. It reflected perfectly the reeds and rushes surrounding it. For a moment she worried about her appearance and considered walking down to the shore to check herself in the water. Just as she had the night before, however, she knew without a doubt that there was no need to be afraid. She was beautiful. She looked better, much, much better than she did in real life.

Her hair would be long, fine and straight, but fluid. A russet-gold. Her face would be long, the bones underneath strong and curved as if made by someone who carved violins from expensive wood. Every line would be softened by the quietest of shadows and her skin would match the color found on the palest Siamese cat, creamy with a faint tan. The complexion would be unmarred.

She was dressed in a fine mail, the chinks made from rose alabaster carved into the shapes of leaves and fitted one over another. It did not feel heavy. She was strong. In her grasp was a book of poems and stories written in another place, by a no longer childish but not yet fully adult hand. Her hand.

Her wait was short. Out of the cloudless sky flew a magnificent black swan, circling over the water. Its wingspan was more than twenty feet across, its eyes and legs the same silver-black as the lake. So dark were the bird's feathers they were barely distinguishable from the night until it dipped below the level of the reeds and landed with a graceful splash. Its breastbone as it cut the water left behind gentle ripples, like the raised ornamentation on the back of a woman's hand mirror.

The swan drifted back and forth on the lake, eyeing

her warily but with interest. Whether it was shyness or reluctance or fear, she couldn't say, but it had done this last night for what she figured to be nearly an hour. Then it had taken off again and stroked toward the horizon long before dawn was due.

Tonight, however, she grew impatient. Instead of holding still, she moved quietly to the water's edge. The swan noticed at once and stopped in the center of the lake.

She didn't understand. Every time so far, every detail had been under her control, everything ordered and predictable and eerily peaceful, just the way she wanted it. Why wouldn't the swan come near?

Though she wore short gray boots more exquisite than any she could ever hope to own for real, she didn't care. She stepped into the water and began to wade toward the swan. It surprised her then, suddenly swimming toward her.

Wilona backed out of the lake and up the bank, almost returning to the magnolia tree.

Gliding, the swan reached the shore. Sweeping itself onto dry land with a single beat of his wings, he was bird no more. Rather, he was a young man, as she'd known he must be; a year or two older at the most than she was. He was built sparely, with refined, supple arms and chest and neck. His black hair ruffled in the breeze like feathers blown against their grain.

He bowed his head slightly as he walked up the bank, lowered gaze watching algae give way to bare clay and then low moss. Shame seemed an indelible part of his expression. She didn't understand it. It wasn't what she had expected.

She went to the duvet and sat down on it, thinking he would follow.

He shook his head. "You don't want me to," she felt, not heard, him tell her.

"Yes, I do," she said aloud and stood up again to fetch him.

But when she tried to embrace him, he no longer had arms. They had become wings again. Her encounter with his human form was so brief, she had time to touch his hair only once, running fingers along soft locks as razor-edged as feathers, before her arms encircled a swan's neck, and the bird nipped her on the shoulder to make her stop.

Wilona opened her eyes and stared at the tray positioned over her hospital bed, vials of drugs lined up against its near edge, waiting for injection into her IV. She still clutched her journal, but its cover was grimy and discolored from holding it with feverish hands. She could feel that her panties were wet. She'd come in her sleep. The nurses would know she'd had a wet dream, but say nothing. The nurses knew everything about her.

Wilona fell into a fitful lethargy after writing only a few lines of the dream into her book. Woke to write a few more, then became only semiconscious once again. The third time she dredged herself out of the fever, her parents were perched on the edges of their chairs at her bedside, her father looking angry as he usually did, not angry at her, just angry, and her mother surreptitiously inventorying the increasing sarcomas covering her daughter's hands and arms, using their size and number as an indicator of the amount of time left.

"Those hard-hearted legislative bastards may not have any feelings," her father started, "... or guts ..." then digressed, "Don't any of them have daughters? Doesn't one damn politician in this country have children anymore?" Though he didn't notice it, he punctuated nearly every word by stabbing himself in the back of his hand with his mahogany pen. The short blue marks made an inappropriate counterpoint to his expensive manicure.

Wilona looked from her father's to her mother's hands. The more widespread the sarcomas on Wilona's hands became, the more obsessively her father had begun caring for his own hands. Her mother, however, no longer painted her nails or cared for her cuticles, or even put lotion on her hands. Her mother's were penance and a statement of self-consciousness and the desperate state she had been put in by her daughter's illness. They were also meant to try to ease the horrible contrast between the diseased and the healthy.

Wilona hated how much their hands told her, but she knew both of her parents loved her. She smiled at them.

"I swear," her father said, "if I could take just a few of those condescending idiots and—"

"How are you today, honey?" her mother interrupted. "Are you still recovering from your trip?" Her voice caught after "recovering," as the censor in her head must have told her what an awful choice of phrasing that had been. "Do you need me to talk to the doctor?"

About morphine, was what she meant.

". . . but the rest of the state is behind you, Willie sweetie. Look what started pouring in today!" Her father hefted two huge canvas sacks, with scuff marks all over them. From the post office, and stuffed with letters, padded envelopes, and boxes.

She thought of the stories regularly carried in the tabloids, about sick people whose lives were spared by letter-writing campaigns from concerned readers, as if the human body was a television show you could save from cancellation.

The pressure in her head was so severe it was frustrating trying to listen to him. She felt like parts of her brain were being forced up against the inside of her forehead, which was exactly what her rapidly growing lymphomas were doing. Just enduring the pain made her want to hyperventilate, as if she were putting forth some great physical effort, running the hundred-yard hurdles, over and over again, endlessly without a break. Under such a regime even the best athlete would break down, cramping and moaning. But she couldn't breathe deeply or quickly at all. The tumor had already damaged her lungs, she needed to take oxygen periodically.

Even lifting her gaze to meet her parents' depleted her as well. She kept trying to do it, kept trying and trying. She couldn't believe something so simple as moving her eyes was such a big deal.

So she continued to stare at their hands. After a while it became completely impossible to concentrate on her father's voice anyway, and she closed her eyes.

"Do you want me to talk to the doctor?" her mother asked again, sounding very close to Wilona's right ear.

"No, Mom," she said. She didn't like to talk anymore. Her words were slurred because of the tumors. It scared her mother too much.

Hoping her smile followed her into unconsciousness, she let herself drift away.

The swan circled and circled overhead. Monotonously. Calmly. Conserving energy. Gliding. Beating his wings only when it was necessary to stay aloft.

He was stalling. He was afraid to come down.

But she had called him here, so eventually he had to come down.

When he did, he landed at the end of the lake farthest from her, so far away she didn't even hear his wings ruffling the surface. He swam aimlessly about a tiny inlet, acting as if she weren't there. Every once in a while, however, the swan's head and neck would loop gracefully around, on the pretense that the bird wanted to preen his feathers. But she knew he watched her.

Wilona decided to walk around to his shore. For some reason, her mail felt heavier that night, the air lukewarm instead of cool. Her surroundings weren't as invigorating as they had been during her previous visits. Her stride grew short, then shorter, until finally, no matter how much she pushed, she couldn't prod her legs beyond a listless walk. It took her most of the night to round the lake.

He never left, though. He never moved to an inlet farther on. It was almost dawn when she crouched by the water's edge on a bench made of taupe-colored pebbles the size of peas, and watched him swimming idly, twenty feet away. For several minutes she studied him, while scooping up water and listening to it sift through her fingers, dribble back into the lake.

"Why are you ashamed to come to me?" she asked finally.

He didn't answer, but flew toward her onto the shore, transforming into the same young man as before. He walked past her, up a low hill covered knee-deep in poppies.

Turning, he beckoned to her, then disappeared over the crest of the hill.

She followed and came soon to a peach tree, alone on the landscape. Its long, narrow leaves were so dark a green that the logic of this world suggested they used the darkness the way other trees used sunlight. The tree was filled with ripe fruit. He plucked one and handed it to her. Its skin was velvety black. She cupped a hand over it, then hesitated and let go.

Sensing her fear, he urged it on her again.

"It's beautiful," she said, "but ..."

Reaching for it, he stared at her with a serious expression and then took the first bite himself. His throat quivered slightly as he swallowed, reminding her of the swan. The fruit inside the black skin was a rich rose-orange.

He offered the peach to her again, holding it with the tips of his fingers so that when she took it, there would be little chance of physical contact between them. Once more she wrapped her hand around it.

"It's beautiful," she said. Then she darted around his outstretched arm and kissed the juice left on his lips. "But it's not what I want."

Startled, he shied back, dropping the peach.

"What's wrong?" she asked.

"You can't let me touch you," a soft, clear voice circled her thoughts. "I'll kill you."

"Why would I be afraid of that now? Do you think I'm afraid?"

"I'm not talking about fear. You've called Death's child," the tones grew shaky. "I'm his son."

His transformation into bird did not go smoothly. His face was still human as he lifted above the tree, his breast more skin than feather.

She couldn't tell if he had made himself completely swan before he disappeared. She picked up the peach. The exposed flesh was covered in hard, little nodules of dried mud, which she carefully brushed away. Raising the fruit to her lips, she tasted his taste again, hot and sweet, juice too startling and potent to drink, like tea made from rich mead instead of water.

*   *   *

Coming to, she saw a nurse by her bedside with a needle stuck into her IV. They'd begun morphine. Her body and mind relaxed into a deeper uselessness. The new drug wouldn't get rid of the pain, so much as deny her access to it. To her, the drug was making her smaller in a sense, making her ... *less,* as she was able to feel less.

"Have you been practicing your lucid dreaming?" a male voice asked.

"I'm sorry, what?" It was her therapist sitting in a chair on the opposite side of the bed.

"Hi," he said.

"Hi."

"Have you tried it, yet?" he asked with sincere interest. For the first time she noticed his hair was black. Was he the source for her dream swan? She wasn't sure, she didn't want to discount it, but he seemed too old at twenty-eight and, she thought ruefully, definitely too heavy to fly.

"The dreaming?" she asked.

"Yeah. I was wondering if you'd tried it and if it was helping."

"No," she told him.

She couldn't say if he believed that. He sat patiently waiting for her to begin, for her to give him a topic to latch on to. She couldn't start and right then that determined the subject for this session. They were going to talk about anger, about her getting the disease, and about living out the rage it had engendered no matter the amount of time she had left to do it.

Her mother was back the next morning, babbling under pressure. No doubt she'd received a bad report from the doctor before she'd stepped in.

"Daddy and I were thinking," she said. "About your journal. You write so well, and I can tell from looking at the book that you've just about used up all the pages. Would you like us to do something special with it, um, when you're done with it?"

Though Wilona hated to show how possessive she felt

about it, she clutched the book closer to her under the sheets.

"Perhaps take it to a publisher?" her mother asked.

Thankfully, their conversation was interrupted. Out in the hallway, they heard a fight going on with someone in a wheelchair. Wilona figured it to be around six-thirty in the morning, the time they got the more ambulatory up and moving toward their various therapeutic destinations.

"Let me walk, dammit," shouted a male voice emptied of most emotions other than resentment.

Robber soles and rubber wheels squeaked sharply, sounding like a tussle on a basketball court.

"Why can't you just let me push you?" Another man's voice. "Survivors know better than to waste their strength on the trivial stuff. They save it up, to use for what's really important."

"I've been putting my strength in a goddamned Keogh account for the last two days. I'm tired of being in beds and wheelchairs and loungers. Now, please! Let me walk."

Several seconds of nothing but background hospital noise. Wilona's nurse moved on to the patient in the next bed. A horrendous sigh came from outside.

"Okay, Bryce, that's what you want, that's what we'll do. Come on, get up." Stifled grunting. A wheelchair sent banging into the wall just to the left of Wilona's open door. Uncoordinated feet shuffling forward in vinyl-soled slippers. "But if you get dizzy and puke up your entire intestinal tract like the last time, I am *not* taking the heat."

"That's what I love about you, Harold. You're just a demon for responsibility." This said by the tall male patient finally being helped past her door on foot by an orderly. Bryce, the hospital worker had called him. He looked both younger and older than Wilona estimated him to be, about twenty-four. Younger because he was big-boned and meant to carry a lot of weight, which he wasn't now. And older because the pain lines and the uneven complexion of disease were already settling into his face, the skin graying around his lips and eyes.

Bryce must have begun exhibiting the full symptoms only recently. He still looked pretty much okay. His hair, cut in big, blunt shocks, flopped down over his face, but it was still shiny and thick. It wasn't drained of life yet, being a healthy dark brown. While he'd clearly lost weight, he still had an athlete's shoulders, and his calves, visible below the hospital gown, made her think of a pole vaulter she'd had a crush on in her sophomore year.

Just then, Bryce turned his attention away from the orderly, a gesture of defiance, and glanced into Wilona's room. Since she was closest to the door, she was the first person he saw. Only his eyes registered his sudden discomfort at the sight she presented. Then he recognized her. The intensity in his eyes said he was adamant about that recognition, though he couldn't place it.

Ten feet from now, he'd figure out who she was. He'd remember her face from the news. The young woman who'd testified before state and federal health agencies for more money to educate teens on the dangers of careless sex. The girl who wanted politicians to spend more money for shelters and hospices. The girl who some critics said used her condition's gruesome appearance as a terrorist tactic.

His last expression as he passed her door was fright, very personal and deep. He'd seen times to come in her. She turned her face sharply away.

Don't look at me, she thought. *Please.*

Wilona's duvet was turning brown and brittle. Before, the magnolia's foliage had always stayed green, eternally new, but now the leaves were drying. They took on scalpel edges and sharp points like the disposable prickers used to draw drops of blood for typing. Dozens of them stuck her in the arms when she rolled over and sat up. From inside the duvet, the moss padding wheezed dust with each movement.

The dampness was gone, the night's cool, too. Heat had shrunken the lake and evaporated the midnight-blue clouds that often lingered near the sunset horizon. The reeds and rushes smelled brackish. The air was fever dry. For hours, she sat near motionless on the duvet, wishing she would wake up. What good was this place now, when the swan wouldn't come to her, and the disease was taking it over? She'd never known that dying magnolia blossoms felt exactly like pieces of old, popped balloons, rubbery and tired.

Every once in a while, she thought she detected movement far away in the sky, a familiar silhouette. But each time it was only her imagination, or a shimmer in the rapidly heating atmosphere.

She heard someone bawling and choking and coughing up. It woke her up.

It was her.

I'm suffocating.

She could feel them, her lungs heavy and sodden as steaming cardboard inside her chest. Ever since the doctor had listed the side effects she could expect from the tumors, Wilona had lived with a constant, justified panic of not getting enough air. The struggle between what her involuntary reflexes wanted and what her body could still deliver was a losing one.

Crying out hoarsely for the nurse, she raked at her chest and fumbled for the call button. A hand she couldn't see pulled hers away from the controls. She scratched and wrestled for them. Desperation gave her the edge to wrest the call switch back, then press the button again and again.

Until she felt the oxygen tube being shoved up her nostril. The chill rush of oxygen streamed through her nasal passages and down her windpipe.

"Shh, Wilona," said the graveyard duty nurse, "we've got the oxygen going. The doctor will be here in a minute, sweetie. So you try not to fight so much, okay?"

She tried to quiet herself, to be good and please the nurse, but the panic wouldn't go away, and she realized she no longer had control of her emotions. They weren't even valid emotions anymore, it seemed, but noises her messed-up brain was using to scare her.

When the doctor came in, he pronounced her to have pneumocytosis, which "we were prepared for, Wilona."

Trying to reassure. "We haven't been caught off guard. We know how to deal with it."

Stupid things, she thought. *They all say such stupid things.*

She spent a restless, terrified day, trying to breathe better and clear her badly blurred vision by blinking again and again.

She did survive this first battle with pneumonia. Antibiotics worked for the time being. Her vision improved a little, but it was closing down, the peripheral portion gone and the bouts of bleariness becoming longer. Her headaches reached a point where she'd black out periodically from the pain.

During the sleepless times, she missed her world by the lake, but even when she could sleep, she didn't go there. Every time she felt herself lapsing she told herself she'd wake up there, but it never happened. It wasn't that she didn't dream any longer. She dreamed. Of all the things she should be doing but was too lazy to work on anymore. She began to wonder if the part of her mind that would normally allow her access to the lake was already destroyed, dead before her.

For hours she stared at her IV. *This thing will never leave my arm, for as long as I live,* she thought. It drove her crazy, kind of. Made her want to rip at the needle. In fact, she dared herself to, worked herself up to the idea during the more delirious moments, and would have done it a couple of times if she hadn't felt so drained, so beyond will.

During her next visit from the staff psychotherapist, she told him about her urge to do it. She tuned out his response, though, and put herself on automatic for his questions.

What must it be like for the therapist to be here? she wondered instead. *What a weird concept, therapy for the dying. Social science's version of last rites,* she thought, *a fundamental anathema, and sort of an extravagance of resources, too.*

She may not have listened, but the therapist must have spoken to someone. When she was feeling only a little bit better, they made a special exception and wheeled her out to the atrium one morning. A registered nurse had to sit nearby to monitor her alone.

Wilona had been trying to catch up on her stories about the dreams ever since the pneumonia. She'd put off chronicling that last dream by the dying lake for days. Always, she'd been an overachiever. Her parents had been proud of that fact, and she'd been proud of it. There had never been a time when she didn't have about ten projects going at once.

"You feel anger, don't you?" the therapist had asked her once or twice. "Toward the disease. Anger about what it's doing to you."

He never asked if Wilona had anger toward herself. Or what she really had. Guilt.

Guilt because she no longer worked at anything really. She had allowed college and her projects to fall away. She felt like a loser.

Today, though, she determined to accomplish something, even if all that meant was a couple of paragraphs about the last dream. If all she did was to explain why she'd needed to make up the world by the lake.

She tried convincing herself that sitting out among the ficus and camelias and ferns, basking in the sunlight coming through the greenhouse windows, gave her the energy she needed to work. She took up her mechanical pencil and arduously aligned its tip with the first blank line on a page she could barely make out.

Seconds later her finger muscles cramped and she lost her grip on the pencil. Two sentences were evidently beyond her. The pencil rolled and dropped to the floor.

"Here, let me," said a male voice she knew. The pencil was picked up and laid next to her hand splayed on the wheelchair's tray.

Bryce.

"Doesn't look broken," he said, picked it up again, clicked some fresh lead into the tip, then laid it down.

Wilona didn't move to retrieve it. All her concentration was placed in keeping her hand from jerking spastically in front of him.

He still looked good. Relatively. Of course, it had only

been about two and a half weeks since she'd seen him outside her door, but she suspected he'd be the type to stay almost handsome until close to the end.

"You know, if you want, you could dictate to me," he said. She caught him discreetly reading over her shoulder.

"No." With her good hand, she softly closed the book. She was terrified of what he might have read. "Thank you, though."

"What is it?" he asked. "What you're writing, I mean."

"Personal."

He nodded. He'd been standing when he'd retrieved the pencil for her, crouching beside her chair while he talked, with his hair smelling incongruently of Physoderm, instead of shampoo or, worse, too many days of restless sleep. Now he sagged to the white-tiled floor and sat cross-legged next to her.

"What do you write about?" he said, persisting. "Do you write about being afraid? Maybe letters to people that'll, you know, live on? Apologizing? Wishing them well? Or just what you're feeling from day to day?"

"Dreams," she said.

He glanced up, very intent. His eyes suddenly had too much concern in them, even for someone sensitized to this issue.

"What type of dreams?"

Her response was bitter, but she was proud of the honesty. She'd never been so forthright. She wasn't ashamed of the bitterness.

"Things I don't ever get to have," she told him.

Bryce flinched. He looked down at his knees. In a few minutes he got up and moved to another part of the atrium without having said another word.

She was puzzled and hurt by the reaction. It destroyed her confidence in publicly admitting her bitterness, just as swiftly as she'd mustered it up.

The sky was purple-white with lightning, striking again and again, split seconds apart. It was coming her way. Thunder cracked so loudly, it felt as if she were shut up in a room with it, as if it bounced off the ceiling of her world by the lake. Rain refused to fall, though, and the clouds looked thin and empty. Not even a breeze came up to brush the final leaves off the magnolia, or spread the piles of them beneath it tumbling along the shore.

Wilona sat against the tree's trunk, idly tearing the duvet apart tiny piece by tiny piece. The duvet had represented so much to her when this place had still been alive. Now it only made her angry. Each leaf was surprisingly tough, stiff like water-ruined leather after it's dried. Almost impossible to rip.

She knew she should get away from the tree. Besides herself, it was the only object of any height for the lightning to strike. But this was her world and she understood the lightning intimately. She couldn't escape it. The disease had finally broken into her night kingdom. This was a dream, after all. Not reality, but an analog of it. The lightning was going to hit her no matter where she went. She knew exactly what it would feel like.

Like sharpened thorns in her blood, the pain pricking new wounds deep inside her where neither she nor the doctors could get to them; excruciating tears in muscle and artery and bone. Such agony could drive her mind into that surreal place where mad people lived, never precisely awake, nor living the temporary terrors the healthy dreamed while asleep.

So when she pictured herself running over the sullen landscape, the barren hills, hunting for shelter, crouching uselessly in shallow ravines, it seemed more reasonable to simply sit and wait.

The swan dove at her from behind, surprising her from a direction he'd never chosen before. His wings raked her face as he flew around the tree, one claw ripping out a strand of her hair. Had it been intentional? His feathers smelled of ozone.

He stalled out his flight prior to reaching the shore, and landed as a man with his back facing her. He was furious. He was frustrated.

Knocked flat by his pass, Wilona hadn't yet gotten to her feet when he spun about.

"Who do you think you are to keep calling me here?

You know I don't want you to." His words burned in her mind's ear.

"This is my world. *I'm* in control here. And I want you to give me what no one else will or can," she said.

"Release from your pain," he said accusingly. "You want me to take it away by taking away your life."

"I want you to touch me."

"And kill you." Nearly hissing.

"I'm already about to die. Why do I have to keep saying it? I'm about to die. I'm *ready* to die!"

"But if I touch you here, you die that much quicker."

"So?"

"It's a choice."

"And I'm making it."

Suddenly her cheek stung. It had taken this long for the slap from his feathers to register. ". . . I wasn't asking you to kill me."

I can't say it. She couldn't. But she wanted to.

She had to.

"I was asking you to make love to me."

He looked at her in silent incredulity.

"So I wouldn't have died without knowing what real love felt like," she explained.

"When I was a little girl I'd go to church," she went on, "waiting to hear God's voice, looking at the stained glass and expecting to hear God whisper in my ear, desperately wishing he would speak up. He wouldn't have had to say much, just call my name. But you know he doesn't speak to people. Not really. You know it in your heart, but don't want to admit it to yourself. You think, how powerful is this God anyway? How real is he if he can't even whisper, I love you, Wilona, in the warm, golden voice you imagine him having.

"That's the way it was with the man who gave me this. I kept thinking the act would make us *lovers,* that this special intimacy was waiting for me, because that's what the movies say happens. But I knew it wasn't really special, not with him or anyone else before. I kept telling myself over and over it could be that way if I only believed. But I never heard the words, *I love you, Wilona.* I never even felt them, *I love you, Wilona.* Never.

"That's why I called you here. I thought you could show me how love was supposed to feel. Even if there's nothing after I die, I wanted to know there was something real about love when I was alive."

He didn't move. Not a muscle in his face moved.

She felt horrible. Rejected. She didn't bother to apologize as she turned away. He could probably tell from the stunned regret she showed that she was sorry. She walked toward the tree, to sit on the other side and forget the lake until she finally woke up.

Three steps later, a ticklish breeze lifted the hair behind her ear. Turning for a last look, she was startled when her face met his hand, which he cupped delicately about her cheek.

His eyes narrowed with mistrust, not of her, she thought, not of her, but of what he did, and he took her down roughly to the bank's powdery dust, dust so fine it puffed and rippled out around her head like silk.

There was a great deal of sorrow in his passion, a great deal of love in his anger. He made love as if this were the only pleasure he would be allowed again, and she realized that in that they were too alike.

Afterward Wilona lay very still next to him in their world, one hand resting on her breast, feeling her speeding pulse tapping against her fingers at a dozen places just below her skin. It felt like rain pattering inside herself. As it slowed, the storm above finally broke. Droplets stippled the dust on their faces, and cooled their feverish bodies.

She woke weeping silently. Of all the ways she had expected to feel, she'd never thought she would cry. But she was awake for only the briefest of moments, just enough time to taste a tear on her lips.

"Your hair is russet-gold," he murmured. "The bones beneath your face are curved and strong, as if sculpted by one who makes the finest violins ... each line softened by the quietest of shadows."

AGAIN

RAMSEY CAMPBELL

"All at once he was stumbling wildly toward the hall, for he was terrified that she would unbolt the bedroom and let out the thing in the bed. But when he threw open the kitchen door, what confronted him was far worse."

Ramsey Campbell, one of the most important figures in contemporary horror writing, began making his mark at a young age, selling his first story to legendary Arkham House editor August Derleth when he was only sixteen. That was three decades ago, and—clichés come in very handy at moments like this—he's been going strong ever since, still in his native Liverpool, still producing vivid, unsettling fiction that manages to be at once organic and yet cerebral.

Critic and writer Douglas Winter, an early champion of Campbell in the States, has noted how the author of such works as The Hungry Moon *and* Ancient Images *succeeds in bending "the traditional English ghost story, with its settings of upper-class elegance and sentimentalized wildernesses, to the modern urban landscape of the middle and lower classes." This thoughtful observation is exactly applicable to the scene that is set and the charac-*

ters who appear in "Again." But be aware, brave reader, that even Ramsey Campbell himself considers the tale at hand, the story of an impulsive and much-regretted daylight detour, to be perhaps just a bit too "odd."
He should know.

_____

Before long Bryant tired of the Wirral Way. He'd come to the nature trail because he'd exhausted the Liverpool parks, only to find that nature was too relentless for him. No doubt the trail would mean more to a botanist, but to Bryant it looked exactly like what it was: an overgrown railway divested of its line. Sometimes it led beneath bridges hollow as whistles, and then it seemed to trap him between the banks for miles. When it rose to ground level it was only to show him fields too lush for comfort, hedges, trees, green so unrelieved that its shades blurred into a single oppressive mass.

He wasn't sure what eventually made the miniature valley intolerable. Children went hooting like derailed trains across his path, huge dogs came snuffling out of the undergrowth to leap on him and smear his face, but the worst annoyances were the flies, brought out all at once by the late June day, the first hot day of the year. They blotched his vision like eye strain, their incessant buzzing seemed to muffle all his senses. When he heard lorries somewhere above him he scrambled up the first break he could find in the brambles, without waiting for the next official exit from the trail.

By the time he realized that the path led nowhere in particular, he had already crossed three fields. It seemed best to go on, even though the sound he'd taken for lorries proved, now that he was in the open, to be distant tractors. He didn't think he could find his way back even if he wanted to. Surely he would reach a road eventually.

Once he'd trudged around several more fields he wasn't so sure. He felt sticky, hemmed in by buzzing and green—a fly in a fly trap. There was nothing else beneath the unrelenting cloudless sky except a bungalow, three fields, and a copse away to his left. Perhaps he could get a drink there while asking the way to the road.

The bungalow was difficult to reach. Once he had to retrace his journey around three sides of a field, when he'd approached close enough to see that the garden which surrounded the house looked at least as overgrown as the railway had been.

Nevertheless someone was standing in front of the bungalow, knee-deep in grass—a woman with white shoulders, standing quite still. He hurried round the maze of fences and hedges, looking for his way to her. He'd come quite close before he saw how old and pale she was. She was supporting herself with one hand on a disused bird-table, and for a moment he thought the shoulders of her ankle-length caftan were white with droppings, as the table was. He shook his head vigorously, to clear it of the heat, and saw at once that it was long white hair that trailed raggedly over her shoulders, for it stirred a little as she beckoned to him.

At least, he assumed she was beckoning. When he reached her, after he'd lifted the gate clear of the weedy path, she was still flapping her hands, but now to brush away flies, which seemed even fonder of her than they had been of him. Her eyes looked glazed and empty; for a moment he was tempted to sneak away. Then they gazed at him, and they were so pleading that he had to go to her, to see what was wrong.

She must have been pretty when she was younger. Now her long arms and heart-shaped face were bony, the skin withered tight on them, but she might still be attractive if her complexion weren't so gray. Perhaps the heat was affecting her—she was clutching the bird-table as though she would fall if she relaxed her grip—but then why didn't she go in the house? Then he realized that must be why she needed him, for she was pointing shakily with her free hand at the bungalow. Her nails were very long. "Can you get in?" she said.

Her voice was disconcerting: little more than a breath, hardly there at all. No doubt that was also the fault of the heat. "I'll try," he said, and she made for the house at once, past a tangle of roses and a rockery so overgrown it looked like a distant mountain in a jungle.

She had to stop breathlessly before she reached the

bungalow. He carried on, since she was pointing feebly
at the open kitchen window. As he passed her he found
she was doused in perfume, so heavily that even in the
open it was cloying. Surely she was in her seventies? He
felt shocked, though he knew that was narrow-minded.
Perhaps it was the perfume that attracted the flies to her.

The kitchen window was too high for him to reach
unaided. Presumably she felt it was safe to leave open
while she was away from the house. He went round the
far side of the bungalow to the open garage, where a
dusty car was baking amid the stink of hot metal and
oil. There he found a toolbox, which he dragged round
to the window.

When he stood the rectangular box on end and lev-
ered himself up, he wasn't sure he could squeeze
through. He unhooked the transom and managed to
wriggle his shoulders through the opening. He thrust
himself forward, the unhooked bar bumping along his
spine, until his hips wedged in the frame. He was stuck
in midair, above a grayish kitchen that smelled stale,
dangling like the string of plastic onions on the far wall.
He was unable to drag himself forward or back.

All at once her hands grabbed his thighs, thrusting up
toward his buttocks. She must have clambered on the
toolbox. No doubt she was anxious to get him into the
house, but her sudden desperate strength made him uneasy, not least because he felt almost assaulted. Nevertheless she'd given him the chance to squirm his hips,
and he was through. He lowered himself awkwardly,
head first, clinging to the window frame while he swung
his feet down before letting himself drop.

He made for the door at once. Though the kitchen
was almost bare, it smelled worse than stale. In the sink
a couple of plates protruded from water the color of
lard, where several dead flies were floating. Flies crawled
over smeary milk bottles on the windowsill or bumbled
at the window, as eager to find the way out as he was.
He thought he'd found it, but the door was mortise-
locked, with a broken key that was jammed in the hole.

He tried to turn the key, until he was sure it was no
use. Not only was its stem snapped close to the lock, the

key was wedged in the mechanism. He hurried out of the kitchen to the front door, which was in the wall at right angles to the jammed door. The front door was mortise-locked as well.

As he returned to the kitchen window he bumped into the refrigerator. It mustn't have been quite shut, for it swung wide open—not that it mattered, since the refrigerator was empty except for a torpid fly. She must have gone out to buy provisions—presumably her shopping was somewhere in the undergrowth. "Can you tell me where the key is?" he said patiently.

She was clinging to the outer sill, and seemed to be trying to save her breath. From the movements of her lips he gathered she was saying "Look around."

There was nothing in the kitchen cupboards except a few cans of baked beans and meat, their labels peeling. He went back to the front hall, which was cramped, hot, almost airless. Even here he wasn't free of the buzzing of flies, though he couldn't see them. Opposite the front door was a cupboard hiding mops and brushes senile with dust. He opened the fourth door of the hall, into the living room.

The long room smelled as if it hadn't been opened for months, and looked like a parody of middle-class taste. Silver-plated cannon challenged each other across the length of the pebble-dashed mantelpiece, on either side of which were portraits of the royal family. Here was a cabinet full of dolls of all nations, here was a bookcase of *Reader's Digest* Condensed Books. A personalized bullfight poster was pinned to one wall, a ten-gallon hat to another. With so much in it, it seemed odd that the room felt disused.

He began to search, trying to ignore the noise of flies—it was somewhere farther into the house, and sounded disconcertingly like someone groaning. The key wasn't on the obese purple suite or down the sides of the cushions; it wasn't on the small table piled with copies of *Contact,* which for a moment, giggling, he took to be a sexual contact magazine. The key wasn't under the bright green rug, nor on any of the shelves. The dolls gazed unhelpfully at him.

He was holding his breath, both because the unpleasant smell he'd associated with the kitchen seemed even stronger in here and because every one of his movements stirred up dust. The entire room was pale with it; no wonder the dolls' eyelashes were so thick. She must no longer have the energy to clean the house. Now he had finished searching, and it looked as if he would have to venture deeper into the house, where the flies seemed to be so abundant. He was at the far door when he glanced back. Was that the key beneath the pile of magazines?

He had only begun to tug the metal object free when he saw it was a pen, but the magazines were already toppling. As they spilled over the floor, some of them opened at photographs: people tied up tortuously, a plump woman wearing a suspender belt and flourishing a whip.

He suppressed his outrage before it could take hold of him. So much for first impressions! After all, the old lady must have been young once. Really, that thought was rather patronizing too—and then he saw it was more than that. One issue of the magazine was no more than a few months old.

He was shrugging to himself, trying to pretend that it didn't matter to him, when a movement made him glance up at the window. The old lady was staring in at him. He leapt away from the table as if she'd caught him stealing, and hurried to the window, displaying his empty hands. Perhaps she hadn't had time to see him at the magazines—it must have taken her a while to struggle through the undergrowth around the house—for she only pointed at the far door and said "Look in there."

Just now he felt uneasy about visiting the bedrooms, however absurd that was. Perhaps he could open the window outside which she was standing, and lift her up—but the window was locked, and no doubt the key was with the one he was searching for. Suppose he didn't find them? Suppose he couldn't get out of the kitchen window? Then she would have to pass the tools up to him, and he would open the house that way. He made himself go to the far door while he was feeling confident.

At least he would be away from her gaze, wouldn't have to wonder what she was thinking about him.

Unlike the rest he had seen of the bungalow, the hall beyond the door was dark. He could see the glimmer of three doors and several framed photographs lined up along the walls. The sound of flies was louder, though they didn't seem to be in the hall itself. Now that he was closer they sounded even more like someone groaning feebly, and the rotten smell was stronger too. He held his breath and hoped that he would have to search only the nearest room.

When he shoved its door open, he was relieved to find it was the bathroom—but the state of it was less of a relief. Bath and washbowl were bleached with dust; spiders had caught flies between the taps. Did she wash herself in the kitchen? But then how long had the stagnant water been there? He was searching among the jars of ointments and lotions on the window ledge, all of which were swollen with a fur of talcum powder; he shuddered when it squeaked beneath his fingers. There was no sign of a key.

He hurried out, but halted in the doorway. Opening the door had lightened the hall, so that he could see the photographs. They were wedding photographs, all seven of them. Though the bridegrooms were different—here an airman with a thin mustache, there a portly man who could have been a tycoon or a chef—the bride was the same in every one. It was the woman who owned the house, growing older as the photographs progressed, until in the most recent, where she was holding on to a man with a large nose and a fierce beard, she looked almost as old as she was now.

Bryant found himself smirking uneasily, as if at a joke he didn't quite see but which he felt he should. He glanced quickly at the two remaining doors. One was heavily bolted on the outside—the one beyond which he could hear the intermittent sound like groaning. He chose the other door at once.

It led to the old lady's bedroom. He felt acutely embarrassed even before he saw the brief transparent night-

dress on the double bed. Nevertheless he had to brave
the room, for the dressing table was a tangle of bracelets
and necklaces, the perfect place to lose keys; the mirror
doubled the confusion. Yet as soon as he saw the photographs that were leaning against the mirror, some instinct made him look elsewhere first.

There wasn't much to delay him. He peered under the
bed, lifting both sides of the counterpane to be sure. It
wasn't until he saw how gray his fingers had become
that he realized the bed was thick with dust. Despite the
indentation in the middle of the bed, he could only assume that she slept in the bolted room.

He hurried to the dressing table and began to sort
through the jewelry, but as soon as he saw the photographs his fingers grew shaky and awkward. It wasn't
simply that the photographs were so sexually explicit—
it was that in all of them she was very little younger, if at
all, than she was now. Apparently she and her bearded
husband both liked to be tied up, and that was only the
mildest of their practices. Where was her husband now?
Had his predecessors found her too much for them? Bryant had finished searching through the jewelry by now,
but he couldn't look away from the photographs, though
he found them appalling. He was still staring morbidly
when she peered in at him, through the window that was
reflected in the mirror.

This time he was sure she knew what he was looking
at. More, he was sure he'd been meant to find the photographs. That must be why she'd hurried round the outside of the house to watch. Was she regaining her
strength? Certainly she must have had to struggle
through a good deal of undergrowth to reach the window in time.

He made for the door without looking at her, and
prayed that the key would be in the one remaining
room, so that he could get out of the house. He strode
across the hall and tugged at the rusty bolt, trying to
open the door before his fears grew worse. His struggle
with the bolt set off the sound like groaning within the
room, but that was no reason for him to expect a torture
chamber. Nevertheless, when the bolt slammed all at

once out of the socket and the door swung inward, he staggered back into the hall.

The room didn't contain much: just a bed and the worst of the smell. It was the only room where the curtains were drawn, so that he had to strain his eyes to see that someone was lying on the bed, covered from head to foot with a blanket. A spoon protruded from an open can of meat beside the bed. Apart from a chair and a fitted wardrobe, there was nothing else to see—except that, as far as Bryant could make out in the dusty dimness, the shape on the bed was moving feebly.

All at once he was no longer sure that the groaning had been the sound of flies. Even so, if the old lady had been watching him he might never have been able to step forward. But she couldn't see him, and he had to know. Though he couldn't help tiptoeing, he forced himself to go to the head of the bed.

He wasn't sure if he could lift the blanket, until he looked in the can of meat. At least it seemed to explain the smell, for the can must have been opened months ago. Rather than think about that—indeed, to give himself no time to think—he snatched the blanket away from the head of the figure at once.

Perhaps the groaning had been the sound of flies after all, for they came swarming out, off the body of the bearded man. He had clearly been dead for at least as long as the meat had been opened. Bryant thought sickly that if the sheet had really been moving, it must have been the flies. But there was something worse than that: the scratches on the shoulders of the corpse, the teeth marks on its neck—for although there was no way of being sure, he had an appalled suspicion that the marks were quite new.

He was stumbling away from the bed—he felt he was drowning in the air that was thick with dust and flies—when the sound recommenced. For a moment he had the thought, so grotesque he was afraid he might both laugh wildly and be sick, that flies were swarming in the corpse's beard. But the sound was groaning after all, for the bearded head was lolling feebly back and forth on the pillow, the tongue was twitching about the grayish lips, the blind eyes were rolling. As the lower half of the body began to jerk weakly but rhythmically, the long-nailed hands tried to reach for whoever was in the room.

Somehow Bryant was outside the door and shoving the bolt home with both hands. His teeth were grinding from the effort to keep his mouth closed, for he didn't know if he was going to vomit or scream. He reeled along the hall, so dizzy he was almost incapable, into the living room. He was terrified of seeing her at the window, on her way to cut off his escape. He felt so weak he wasn't sure of reaching the kitchen window before she did.

Although he couldn't focus on the living room, as if it weren't really there, it seemed to take him minutes to cross. He'd stumbled at last into the front hall when he realized that he needed something on which to stand to reach the transom. He seized the small table, hurling the last of the contact magazines to the floor, and staggered toward the kitchen with it, almost wedging it in the doorway. As he struggled with it, he was almost paralyzed by the fear that she would be waiting at the kitchen window.

She wasn't there. She must still be on her way around the outside of the house. As he dropped the table beneath the window, Bryant saw the broken key in the mortise lock. Had someone else—perhaps the bearded man—broken it while trying to escape? It didn't matter, he mustn't start thinking of escapes that had failed. But it looked as if he would have to, for he could see at once that he couldn't reach the transom.

He tried once, desperately, to be sure. The table was too low, the narrow sill was too high. Though he could wedge one foot on the sill, the angle was wrong for him to squeeze his shoulders through the window. He would certainly be stuck when she came to find him. Perhaps if he dragged a chair through from the living room—but he had only just stepped down, almost falling to his knees, when he heard her opening the front door with the key she had had all the time.

His fury at being trapped was so intense that it nearly

blotted out his panic. She had only wanted to trick him into the house. By God, he'd fight her for the key if he had to, especially now that she was relocking the front door. All at once he was stumbling wildly toward the hall, for he was terrified that she would unbolt the bedroom and let out the thing in the bed. But when he threw open the kitchen door, what confronted him was far worse.

She stood in the living-room doorway, waiting for him. Her caftan lay crumpled on the hall floor. She was naked, and at last he could see how gray and shriveled she was—just like the bearded man. She was no longer troubling to brush off the flies, a couple of which were crawling in and out of her mouth. At last, too late, he realized that her perfume had not been attracting the flies at all. It had been meant to conceal the smell that was attracting them—the smell of death.

She flung the key behind her, a new move in her game. He would have died rather than try to retrieve it, for then he would have had to touch her. He backed into the kitchen, looking frantically for something he could use to smash the window. Perhaps he was incapable of seeing it, for his mind seemed paralyzed by the sight of her. Now she was moving as fast as he was, coming after him with her long arms outstretched, her gray breasts flapping. She was licking her lips as best she could, relishing his terror. Of course, that was why she'd made him go through the entire house. He knew that her energy came from her hunger for him.

It was a fly—the only one in the kitchen that hadn't alighted on her—which drew his gaze to the empty bottles on the windowsill. He'd known all the time they were there, but panic was dulling his mind. He grabbed the nearest bottle, though his sweat and the slime of milk made it almost too slippery to hold. At least it felt reassuringly solid, if anything could be reassuring now. He swung it with all his force at the center of the window. But it was the bottle which broke.

He could hear himself screaming—he didn't know if it was with rage or terror—as he rushed toward her, brandishing the remains of the bottle to keep her away until he reached the door. Her smile, distorted but glee-ful, had robbed him of the last traces of restraint, and there was only the instinct to survive. But her smile wid-ened as she saw the jagged glass—indeed, her smile looked quite capable of collapsing her face. She lurched straight into his path, her arms wide.

He closed his eyes and stabbed. Though her skin was tougher than he'd expected, he felt it puncture drily, again and again. She was thrusting herself onto the glass, panting and squealing like a pig. He was slashing desper-ately now, for the smell was growing worse.

All at once she fell, rattling on the linoleum. For a moment he was terrified that she would seize his legs and drag him down on her. He fled, kicking out blindly, before he dared open his eyes. The key—where was the key? He hadn't seen where she had thrown it. He was almost weeping as he dodged about the living room, for he could hear her moving feebly in the kitchen. But there was the key, almost concealed down the side of a chair.

As he reached the front door he had a last terrible thought. Suppose this key broke too? Suppose that was part of her game? He forced himself to insert it carefully, though his fingers were shaking so badly he could hardly keep hold of it at all. It wouldn't turn. It would—he had been trying to turn it the wrong way. One easy turn, and the door swung open. He was so insanely grateful that he almost neglected to lock it behind him.

He flung the key as far as he could and stood in the overgrown garden, retching for breath. He'd forgotten that there were such things as trees, flowers, fields, the open sky. Yet just now the scent of flowers was sick-ening, and he couldn't bear the sound of flies. He had to get away from the bungalow and then from the coun-tryside—but there wasn't a road in sight, and the only path he knew led back toward the Wirral Way. He wasn't concerned about returning to the nature trail, but the route back would lead him past the kitchen window. It took him a long time to move, and then it was because he was more afraid to linger near the house.

When he reached the window, he tried to run while tiptoeing. If only he dared turn his face away! He was almost past before he heard a scrabbling beyond the window. The remains of her hands appeared on the sill, and then her head lolled into view. Her eyes gleamed brightly as the shards of glass that protruded from her face. She gazed up at him, smiling raggedly and pleading. As he backed away, floundering through the undergrowth, he saw that she was mouthing jerkily. "Again," she said.

KIN TO LOVE

T. H. WHITE

"They say that pity is akin to love. So is its opposite. Ferocity is even closer kin."

The lasting reputation of Terence Hanbury White rests entirely on the appeal of his drolly rehashed Arthurian epic, The Once and Future King. *However, also very much in the fantasy way of things is his tale of the lake-locked Lilliputian colony,* Mistress Masham's Repose; *it, too, has had its passionate devotees over the years. But White's other writing, which includes such short stories as the unforgettably outrageous monster tale "The Troll," is little known.*

Yet "Kin to Love" happens to be a tightly controlled work of sympathetic art that perfectly embodies the theme of Shudder Again. *It's also a story that makes it hard, once you've absorbed its chilling exposition of human causality, to push away for long any of its dangerous images, or isolated, refractory moments: now burrowed into your psyche, I'm afraid they plan to stay there.*

The defense talked about epilepsy, moral responsibility, and whether he understood the nature and quality of his act. Is anybody responsible for anything? You can only go by common sense.

He was a handsome boy of twenty-one, a Rudolph Valentino to look at. He did not follow the conventions which are expected to go with masculine beauty in fiction. He was not a gigolo, or vain, or self-satisfied, and did not trade on his good looks. He thought his personal appearance effeminate, in fact, and spent part of his time trying to alter it. He used solid brilliantine, in the effort to flatten the natural wave of his fair hair. He did exercises for two hours every day with an elastic chest-expander. He avoided his eyes in mirrors, being reluctant to look at himself. He was fascinated by guns and daggers, which he associated with virility. He was desperately, ashamedly, confusedly sexual.

He was undependable about money, and had been on probation for theft. They called him a delinquent.

His name was Edward Norvic, an orphan. His few friends called him Rudy, which he hated. Although he had yellow hair, he had long, black eyelashes which fanned his cheeks. In shape and figure he looked like Donatello's statue of the adolescent David, or was it Perseus? He was sometimes pursued by middle-aged scoutmasters or shifty clergymen, and had more than once succumbed to them, to his grief, although his nature was fiercely heterosexual. About this, as about money, he was not reliable. He deplored his weakness. He chased females persistently, not confidently, unaware of his attractions, so that his uncertainty made him unsuccessful and furtive in following the pursuit.

If he was a Valentino at all, he was a secretive, lonely, introverted specimen of the type, who brooded about sex and despised it and dreaded his lusts.

The Norvics who had adopted him—an elderly couple—had been kind and nonconformist, giving him love and punishment, so that the two were mixed in his mind. This was the trouble. Their love for the good part of him was fused with repression for what they thought the bad part. If they had been unpleasant and loveless people, he could have felt contempt for their standards and could have defied their sanctions. But they loved him, and he loved them, so he accepted their standards while failing to live up to them. His sexual rigor, which might have taken and given so much pleasure, was contorted by morals foreign to his nature—morals which he accepted because they came with affection. He was affectionate himself. He was not clever or artistic or well educated. His levels were more or less those of Garth in the strip cartoons of the *Daily Mirror*. He was neither strong nor weak, though he thought himself weak. He did not see that he failed his commandments because they were too high for him. All he knew was that he failed them. So he was driven to do it secretly. He had been given a conscience. He was prim.

None of these facts was of importance to the judge at the trial, because they were not covered by the McNaughton Rules. The nearest cliché for the legal mind turned out to be that he was "a moral defective."

On the day of the murder, Norvic rode his racing-type pedal cycle to the woods near Fullerton in the afternoon. It was his half-day holiday.

He was armed with a spring knife or stiletto, expensively bought from a friend in the merchant navy who had got it in Naples, and with an out-of-date Holland revolver which had belonged to a police officer in India thirty years before. It had three rounds of modern ammunition in its six chambers. The weapons were his fetish.

He did not go to the woods with a conscious purpose. Or rather, he had two separate purposes, and was not fully aware of either of them. Even this is not quite accurate. His official purpose was to pass the time and for exercise, woodcraft, or a long walk during which he would probably imagine himself a commando leader, or a parachutist, or perhaps some sort of gangster or federal agent—in any case, an armed and athletic person without inhibitions. His unconscious hope, which is perhaps the main hope of most people aged twenty-one, most of the time, was to meet, examine, meditate upon, and if possible accost females. These he wished to violate, not fondle. At the trial, they argued about knowing the difference between right and wrong. The point which everybody missed was that it was this knowledge which made him homicidal. The ferocity of his sex was due to believing too much in right and wrong. He thought it was wrong to fondle women, so he had to rape them. He was a plugged volcano which could only erupt by violence. He had accepted, but could not observe, the standards of the class which had adopted him.

He had had five women in his life, three of them minors, with clumsy, ungentle, uncomprehending, selfish acquisition, followed by shame. But it had been with their consent. He had thrillingly beaten one of them with a willow stick.

He was kind to animals. His cruelty was associated with sex. Apart from this, he was not particularly good and not particularly bad—a confused, unattractive youth, with abnormal but fairly common instincts, which he had not selected for himself—an explosive mixture well tamped by taboos which made them more explosive—a stupid and ordinary mind of little charm or promise—a lout. But he had never murdered anybody before, and he might never have murdered anybody again. On the whole, he was not unlike his fellow men. His more repellent features were the lies, willfulness, and despotic selfishness common to children of six years old. His mental age was not much higher.

It was a sparkling day in the early summer, the tree leaves virgin green, with their egg-shaped sun specks dancing on the rather shabby undergrowth of woods which were too close to a successful watering place—too much frequented by lovers, trippers, and the litter-makers of holiday resorts. It was a "beauty spot."

He locked his bicycle and left it in a ditch beside a rustic stile. He sauntered and imagined among verdant trees, striving confusedly with all the sinful lusts of the flesh. His imaginations, like Boswell's at the same age, were of the seraglio. Most people are like Boswell, only they don't say so.

Mrs. Evans, the district nurse, was a middle-aged or elderly Welsh widow with a faint mustache. She was shaped like a beer barrel with bow legs, or perhaps like a Queen Anne bureau—a short, stout, warm-hearted body of tireless good hope and not much intelligence, who bicycled through sun or rain or snow or thunder, year in and year out, from confinement to confinement, in a personal aura of kindness and help. Like many fat people, she had small feet on which she could move at British Legion whist-drives-and-dances with wonderful lightness and grace. Like many ugly or at least homely women, she was feminine and modest and dainty in her person. She had knickknacks in her small, cozy, clean parlor—china ornaments bearing the arms of Bournemouth or Margate, and earthenware porringers in brown and green and biscuit color with admonitions written on them, such as Tak' Anither Drap o'Tay, or Set Ye Down And Bide A Wee.

She used to adore her husband, who had been devoted to her, but they had been childless. When the husband died, seven years before, he had left her the cottage in which she lived alone—in which she sustained herself with a nice chop or a cheering cup of Camp Coffee or some Ovaltine and sugar biscuits, sleeping sound and living decently, warmed at evening by the merry gas fire after the drag of her daily round, companied by a Persian cat.

She was afraid of what she anxiously called Doggies, though she tried to be polite to them. The ones who detected this weakness treated her with contempt and animosity, as if she were a postman, while the ones who liked her tried to jump up—an approach which she believed to be menacing.

She had an amethyst brooch in the shape of a lucky spider.

Mrs. Evans was wheeling her battered cycle through the woodland path on a shortcut to Fairbourne, where she had a case of paralysis, an old-age pensioner. There was nothing she could do for the old man except see that he was kept clean and comfortable, visiting him once a week. They were cronies. He called her Matty.

She was thinking about various subjects, none of which were connected with physical passion. They were whether she would have a poached egg or a tin of baked herrings for her tea, whether her sister in Aberystwyth could be persuaded to come to Fullerton for her annual holiday, whether she had better stop at the doctor's to get more morphia for Mrs. Norton, whether the sea was really blue or how blue on the Isle of Capree, and if you could get fresh butter there, why as was commonly said it should be assumed that the earth went around the sun when it obviously did not move, whether she had remembered to leave the back window open for the cat, and what a pity it was that the bluebells were all broken or pulled up by the trippers who visited Fairbourne-Church-in-the-Woods.

When she heard the man walking behind her, she was not disturbed.

There were lovers all over the place hereabouts, and her heart warmed to them. Why not, poor things? They were young and spring was still in the air. She knew the quotation about a young man's fancy and one of her favorite statements was It Is Love that Makes the World Go Round. Such had been her experience with Mr. Evans. She plodded on sturdily with her bicycle, rolling slightly on the bandy legs.

But the footsteps continued, not getting nearer or farther. She looked over her shoulder.

Except for dogs—and this was only due to the repulsion of a cat lover—Mrs. Evans had never been afraid of anything outside herself. She was a qualified nurse for whom spurting arteries and hideous diseases and the butchery of surgeons held no terrors. She could cope with fits and hysterics and drunks and even lunatics, for she had once worked in a private asylum for four months. But this time it was not outside herself—it was not a "patient." It was personal to herself, to her femininity, to the delicacy of her womanhood. Young people are surprised to learn, and unwilling to believe, that even plump, elderly, and uncomely women may still think of themselves as female. It is difficult and rather ludicrous to realize that the fat old things we meet may have remained what they always were inside—may have remained modest virgins, or tender dreamers, or teasing flirts whose airy graces have been betrayed only by the Judas of the body.

Mrs. Evans began to run, thrusting her bicycle through the long grass beside the path, which was too thick for cycling.

Edward Norvic began to run too.

If she had gone on walking, he would have walked as well. But, by the act of flight, she had taken on the role of a quarry, which forced him to be the hunter. He had been "setting" her before. Shooting dogs—pointers for instance—will stand rigid for ages, setting a cat, but when the cat runs they have to run too. While she walked, she had been a stout district nurse. When she ran, she was a woman, the pursued. She had made herself his prey, and that made him the captor. She had lost her individuality and become a sex. The very way she ran, the actual action of her haunches and slope of her shoulders in the dowdy uniform reminded him of every Eve since Adam, jerking the arrow of his loins. He had to run, as if they were tied together. He had to capture her, to pounce, to seize, embrace, subdue. He had no intention of killing her. He had to lay her for the burning mastery.

Mrs. Evans began to scream when he caught her. This was worse. This made him feel that she expected to be killed.

So he had to kill her.

They say that pity is akin to love. So is its opposite. Ferocity is even closer kin.

The condemned cell in that particular prison was separated from the main block. It stood in the yard by itself, a mean little building of two rooms and a narrow corridor. The prisoners spent exactly twenty-four hours in it, being brought at eight o'clock on one morning and hanged at eight o'clock the next. Convicts called it the Topping Shed.

The smaller or living room was about sixteen feet square—the flimsy, institutional walls being of one brick thickness. Most of the north wall was taken up by a large window of frosted glass with bars and wire netting. There were two doors. One door was the entry from the

yard. The other door—the exit—would open only once
for every prisoner. Doomfully shut, foreboded, dodged
by the eye, it dominated the shoddy, unloved chamber
with a looming, belly-sinking blank. It was what you
turned your mind away from.

And yet this room was in a way loved, when in use.
When not in use, it was a bare, scrubbed cube, main-
tained by the Office of Works, with a floor of unstained
boards. But for the customer, it was furnished. It was
even furnished with a kind of rueful affection—an apolo-
getic kindness, a wish to comfort. The governor himself
would send across his own armchair. There were two
stiff chairs for the warders of the death watch. There
was a table for draughts or backgammon or games of
cards. On the board floor there was a pathetic little drug-
get. The bed had clean sheets and blankets, as neat as
a hospital. Indeed, it was the waiting room for a lethal
hospitality.

The warders who sat in the deadly room with Norvic
were genuinely kind men, not like the thuggish jailers
or policemen of fiction. They had fine-drawn, friendly,
smiling faces, paternal and ministering, like helpful
nurses giving individual attention and support in a kind
nursing home.

One of them always sat with his chair-back masking
the door.

They talked their best.

Behind the door was a narrow, tiled corridor, like the
approach to a public lavatory, scarcely a pace wide.
Across this corridor, not along it, only a yard away, was
the door to the other room. This was bigger, like a
squash court or a gymnasium without apparatus. It was
much higher than the cell and solidly built—the cell
being, in fact, a kind of lean-to erected against its outer
wall. There was no furniture whatever, except for two
fixtures. One was a cast-iron girder padded with gray
felt in the middle, from which there hung three ropes.
The middle rope was leather-lined at the noose, which
ran through a metal eye and was temporarily held open
with pack thread. The other two ropes were without
nooses. The second fixture was the trapdoor underneath

the girder. It was ten or twelve feet square and consisted of two wooden flaps hinged at the outer edges, just like the double doors of a barn laid flat instead of upright. On each flap was a ring bolt. To each ring there was a stout cord. When not in use, these cords were neatly curled in circles—maritime-looking, shipshape, and Bristol fashion. At present they were stretched at right angles to the hinges. They were for lifting the flaps again, after use. In the middle of the trap, a white circle was drawn in chalk, where the prisoner was to stand. On either side of it, crossing the trap at right angles, there was a loose safety board, like the planks which plasterers and housepainters use. These were for the hangman and the two prison officers to stand on, when the time came, steadying themselves by holding the two spare ropes. The only other feature in the void, still, echoing gymnasium was the lever which released the trap. It stood from the floor like a lever in a railway signal box, only smaller, or like the high hand brake of an old-fashioned car.

Such was the Topping Shed: a living room and a dying room was all it had.

The prison governor was a miniature Santa Claus, without the whiskers. Pink-cheeked and twinkling, five and a half feet high, looking healthier and younger than his nearly sixty years, he loved the country prison. It was not as a prison that he loved it, but as a place which he had made better—a place which his optimism and kindness had improved to the very limit allowed by reasonable deterrence. The hideousness of man was responsible for the hideousness of jails, but the governor had put his faith in man and done his best for both of them. The gardens were looked after by volunteer labor among the convicts, and lovingly looked after. With a strange and touching sort of pride they had trimmed the name of the prison in clipped letters along the box borders of the paths. The Victorian façades had all sorts of creepers and potted plants and geraniums and vegetable fancies. The sills of the barred windows were color-washed to cheer them up. The old-fashioned cells were neat, centrally heated, with good mattresses and blan-

kets, a chamberpot and three library books each week.
For those who behaved themselves—which was nearly
all of them—there was a recreation room for an hour
and a half every evening, with a dart board and a radio.
Nor were they segregated all day. In the summer they
might be breaking stones in the yard, in the winter chop-
ping kindling wood in a big shed—but in company, and
not in strict silence. The water of the shower baths was
really hot, the cooking plainly good on excellent Aga
cookers. In the prison church there was not one bar or
bolt or handcuff. For many years a local scallywag had
habitually broken a shop window every Christmas Eve,
proceeding at once to the police station under his own
power, to give himself up. He did it for his winter holiday, and for the turkey dinner on Christmas Day.

Through this home—for it was a home, with a sort of
family feeling and esprit de corps of its own—the
sprightly, Dickensian governor moved with proprietor-
ship, rubbing his soft hands together and being kind. He
was not weak or cranky, and nobody took advantage of
him. At a certain line, he could be as firm as rock.

He was married to a pippin who was as apple-cheeked
as he was himself, with a grown-up family. He was
ashamed of being the overlord among men whose liberty
had been taken from them. When he conducted visitors
over the prison, he made nervous, propitiatory little
jokes about the dungeons and torture chambers and Madame Tussaud's. He was fond of Gilbert and Sullivan
operas. If he and his wife had been birds, they would
have been budgerigars, twittering merrily in a clean cage.

He had never had an execution before.

At two minutes to eight, the governor, the chaplain,
the doctor, the hangman, and two warders opened the
outer door of the living room.

The death watch stood up. Edward Norvic stood up.
It would take ninety seconds.

The governor patted Edward Norvic, pressing his arm
with warmth and tenderness and encouragement. He had
seen to it that he was "given something" before his
breakfast. The chaplain began to read. The hangman

pinioned the prisoner. The paling warders sustained themselves in military fashion, assuming faces of wood.

Edward Norvic found that there were no bones in his legs; instead, soda water. He was shaking tremendously, but not with fear. He observed himself from outside, independently shaking. They slipped the bag over his head.

The door was opened.

The door to the other room, to the operating room, was open already. Through it they wheeled or led or hustled or companied the cooperating patient, docile to his fatal operation.

Quickly on the trapdoor, so that his despairing blindfold, nuzzling the new room avidly for a last lookful of life, might not through linen see one detail. Quickly the ready noose over his hooded dumbness, and the straps around his legs for walking never more to be needed. Quickly the governor's signal and the heave on the standing lever.

The trap fell open with a sickening thud, unmasking the whitewashed walls of the pit, twelve feet square and deep. If the neck broke, if the rope twanged, both sounds were swallowed by the thundering, bouncing trap. The already stretched cord did not creak. It swayed and revolved. Nothing was to be seen of Edward Norvic.

The first thing was to get everybody out of the place. Such were the instructions. The governor began to shepherd them through the door, pushing them in the small of the back, saying, "Out, out!" They hurried, jostling in the narrow doorway. They glanced, each one, but only the flash of a glance, into the white Hell which had opened under them as they passed it. The rope thrilled and swung.

In the fresh air, with dry mouths and the blood drained from their temples, they dispersed or split into groups. The chaplain went to his office. The governor walked up and down with the doctor. The hangman paired with the chief warder. The others stood about at hand. Cigarettes were lighted, a necessary relaxation of rules. They tried with painful levity to think of dirty stories. They had to keep it up for thirty minutes.

The dirty stories, in the clear sunlight of the high-walled, empty yard, were better than speculation. They were better than wondering why, if hanging is supposed to be so instantaneous an exit, the now priapic corpse should need a half hour on the gallows—better than wondering why, even at the postmortem, the doctor's first duty might be to make a small incision and cut the spinal cord. It was better than wondering why an ill-topped man might sometimes snore, and hearts, though hanged, beat on.

When the alloted time was over and the pit had been revisited—the governor and the doctor climbing down first—when life had been pronounced extinct and the subsequent machinery set in motion—when nothing knowable was left of the mind of Edward Norvic, the governor went back to his own house.

There, in the kitchen, as he had hoped and known she would be, was his wife in her dressing gown, making coffee. She put her soft arms around his neck. He held her tight. He conducted her upstairs, silently, urgently, pleading.

The Father Christmas face, in the act of orgasm, bore much the same expression of agony and congestion as the dead boy's profile wore, cooling in the mortuary.

SAME TIME, SAME PLACE

MERVYN PEAKE

"For eight days we met thus, and parted thus, and
with every meeting we knew more firmly than ever
that whatever the difficulties that would result,
whatever the forces against us, yet it was now that
we must marry, now, while the magic was upon us."

*There is logic, Mervyn Peake would have us see, in this
splendidly dreadful narrative of a young man's first (and
last) love affair. But since it is the sort of logic most
often encountered once our conscious minds have been
smothered in sleep, it demands only that we accept it exactly as it presents itself—no questions asked, no prying
behind the curtain. Too close a search to pin it down,
and all that will be revealed is its essential evanescence,
fading away like the Cheshire cat's grin.*

*Peake, ever the master fantasist, understands the special
quality of inevitability that dream logic bestows upon a
story—and isn't falling in love, anyway, a state of being with
all the normal rules suspended and a peculiar logic all its
own? "Same Time, Same Place" shares some notes of hor-*

ridness, I think, with the slightly later "Ravissante" (it's like Aickman compressed and speeded up) and also with an earlier tale by Robert Bloch, the title of which, "The Unspeakable Betrothal," might apply equally well here.

That night, I hated father. He smelt of cabbage. There was cigarette ash all over his trousers. His untidy mustache was yellower and viler than ever with nicotine, and he took no notice of me. He simply sat there in his ugly armchair, his eyes half closed, brooding on the Lord knows what. I hated him. I hated his mustache. I even hated the smoke that drifted from his mouth and hung in the stale air above his head.

And when my mother came through the door and asked me whether I had seen her spectacles, I hated her too. I hated the clothes she wore; tasteless and fussy. I hated them deeply. I hated something I had never noticed before; it was the way the heels of her shoes were worn away on their outside edges—not badly, but appreciably. It looked mean to me, slatternly, and horribly human. I hated her for being human—like father.

She began to nag me about her glasses and the threadbare condition of the elbows of my jacket, and suddenly I threw my book down. The room was unbearable. I felt suffocated. I suddenly realized that I must get away. I had lived with these two people for nearly twenty-three years. I had been born in the room immediately overhead. Was this the life for a young man? To spend his evenings watching the smoke drift out of his father's mouth and stain that decrepit old mustache, year after year—to watch the worn away edges of my mother's heels—the dark brown furniture and the familiar stains on the chocolate-colored carpet? I would go away; I would shake off the dark, smug mortality of the place. I would forgo my birthright. What of my father's business into which I would step at his death? What of it? To hell with it.

I began to make my way to the door but at the third step I caught my foot in a ruck of the chocolate-colored carpet and in reaching out my hand for support, I sent a pink vase flying.

Suddenly I felt very small and very angry. I saw my mother's mouth opening and it reminded me of the front door and the front door reminded me of my urge to escape—to where? To where?

I did not wait to find an answer to my own question, but, hardly knowing what I was doing, ran from the house.

The accumulated boredom of the last twenty-three years was at my back and it seemed that I was propelled through the garden gate from its pressure against my shoulder blades.

The road was wet with rain, black and shiny like oilskin. The reflection of the street lamps wallowed like yellow jellyfish. A bus was approaching—a bus to Piccadilly, a bus to the never-never land—a bus to death or glory.

I found neither. I found something which haunts me still.

The great bus swayed as it sped. The black street gleamed. Through the window a hundred faces fluttered by as though the leaves of a dark book were being flicked over. And I sat there, with a sixpenny ticket in my hand. What was I doing! Where was I going?

To the center of the world, I told myself. To Piccadilly Circus, where anything might happen. What did I *want* to happen?

I wanted life to happen! I wanted adventure; but already I was afraid. I wanted to find a beautiful woman. Bending my elbow I felt for the swelling of my biceps. There wasn't much to feel. "Oh, hell," I said to myself. "Oh, damnable hell: this is *awful.*"

I stared out of the window, and there before me was the Circus. The lights were like a challenge. When the bus had curved its way from Regent Street and into Shaftesbury Avenue, I alighted. Here was the jungle all about me and I was lonely. The wild beasts prowled around me. The wolf packs surged and shuffled. Where was I to go? How wonderful it would have been to have known of some apartment, dimly lighted; of a door that opened to the secret knock, three short ones and one long one—where a strawberry blonde was waiting—or perhaps, better still, some wise old lady with a cup of tea, an old lady, august and hallowed, and whose heels were not worn down on their outside edges.

But I knew nowhere to go either for glamour or sympathy. Nowhere except The Corner House.

I made my way there. It was less congested than usual. I had only to queue for a few minutes before being allowed into the great eating palace on the first floor. Oh, the marble and the gold of it all! The waiters coming and going, the band in the distance—how different all this was from an hour ago, when I stared at my father's mustache.

For some while I could find no table and it was only when moving down the third of the long corridors between tables that I saw an old man leaving a table for two. The lady who had been sitting opposite him remained where she was. Had she left, I would have had no tale to tell. Unsuspectingly I took the place of the old man and in reaching for the menu lifted my head and found myself gazing into the midnight pools of her eyes.

My hand hung poised over the menu. I could not move for the head in front of me was magnificent. It was big and pale and indescribably proud—and what I would now call a greedy look seemed to me then to be an expression of rich assurance; of majestic beauty.

I knew at once that it was not the strawberry blonde of my callow fancy that I desired for glamour's sake, nor the comfort of the tea-tray lady—but this glorious creature before me who combined the mystery and exoticism of the former with the latter's mellow wisdom.

Was this not love at first sight? Why else should my heart have hammered like a foundry? Why should my hand have trembled above the menu? Why should my mouth have gone dry?

Words were quite impossible. It was clear to me that she knew everything that was going on in my breast and in my brain. The look of love which flooded from her eyes all but unhinged me. Taking my hand in hers she returned it to my side of the table where it lay like a dead thing on a plate. Then she passed me the menu. It meant nothing to me. The hors d'oeuvres and the sweets were all mixed together in a dance of letters.

What I told the waiter when he came, I cannot remember, nor what he brought me. I know that I could not eat it. For an hour we sat there. We spoke with our eyes, with the pulse and stress of our excited breathing—and toward the end of this, our first meeting, with the tips of our fingers that in touching each other in the shadow of the teapot seemed to speak a language richer, subtler, and more vibrant than words.

At last we were asked to go—and as I rose I spoke for the first time. "Tomorrow?" I whispered. "Tomorrow?" She nodded her magnificent head slowly. "Same place? Same time?" She nodded again.

I waited for her to rise, but with a gentle yet authoritative gesture she signaled me away.

It seemed strange, but I knew I must go. I turned at the door and saw her sitting there, very still, very upright. Then I descended to the street and made my way to Shaftesbury Avenue, my head in a whirl of stars, my legs weak and trembling, my heart on fire.

I had not decided to return home, but found nevertheless that I was on my way back—back to the chocolate-colored carpet, to my father in the ugly armchair—to my mother with her worn shoe heels.

When at last I turned the key it was near midnight. My mother had been crying. My father was angry. There were words, threats, and entreaties on all sides. At last I got to bed.

The next day seemed endless but at long last my excited fretting found some relief in action. Soon after tea I boarded the west-bound bus. It was already dark but I was far too early when I arrived at the Circus.

I wandered restlessly here and there, adjusting my tie at shop windows and filing my nails for the hundredth time.

At last, when waking from a day dream as I sat for

the fifth time in Leicester Square, I glanced at my watch and found I was three minutes late for our tryst.

I ran all the way panting with anxiety but when I arrived at the table on the first floor I found my fear was baseless. She was there, more regal than ever, a monument of womanhood. Her large, pale face relaxed into an expression of such deep pleasure at the sight of me that I almost shouted for joy.

I will not speak of the tenderness of that evening. It was magic. It is enough to say that we determined that our destinies were inextricably joined.

When the time came for us to go I was surprised to find that the procedure of the previous night was once more expected of me. I could in no way make out the reason for it. Again I left her sitting alone at the table by the marble pillar. Again I vanished into the night alone, with those intoxicating words still on my lips. "To-morrow . . . tomorrow . . . same time . . . same place . . ."

The certainty of my love for her and hers for me was quite intoxicating. I slept little that night and my restlessness on the following day was an agony both for me and my parents.

Before I left that night for our third meeting, I crept into my mother's bedroom and opening her jewel box I chose a ring from among her few trinkets. God knows it was not worthy to sit upon my loved one's finger, but it would symbolize our love.

Again she was waiting for me although on this occasion I arrived a full quarter of an hour before our appointed time. It was as though, when we were together, we were hidden in a veil of love—as though we were alone. We heard nothing else but the sound of our voices, we saw nothing else but one another's eyes.

She put the ring upon her finger as soon as I had given it to her. Her hand that was holding mine tightened its grip. I was surprised at its power. My whole body trembled. I moved my foot beneath the table to touch hers. I could find it nowhere.

When once more the dreaded moment arrived, I left her sitting upright, the strong and tender smile of her farewell remaining in my mind like some fantastic sunrise.

For eight days we met thus, and parted thus, and with every meeting we knew more firmly than ever that whatever the difficulties that would result, whatever the forces against us, yet it was now that we must marry, now, while the magic was upon us.

On the eighth evening it was all decided. She knew that for my part it must be a secret wedding. My parents would never countenance so rapid an arrangement. She understood perfectly. For her part she wished a few of her friends to be present at the ceremony.

"I have a few colleagues," she had said. I did not know what she meant, but her instructions as to where we should meet on the following afternoon put the remark out of my mind.

There was a registry office in Cambridge Circus, she told me, on the first floor of a certain building. I was to be there at four o'clock. She would arrange everything.

"Ah, my love," she had murmured, shaking her large head slowly from side to side, "how can I wait until then?" And with a smile unutterably bewitching, she gestured for me to go, for the great memorial hall was all but empty.

For the eighth time I left her there. I knew that women must have their secrets and must be in no way thwarted in regard to them, and so, once again I swallowed the question that I so longed to put to her. Why, oh, why had I always to leave her there—and why, when I arrived to meet her, was she always there to meet me?

On the following day, after a careful search, I found a gold ring in a box in my father's dressing table. Soon after three, having brushed my hair until it shone like sealskin, I set forth with a flower in my buttonhole and a suitcase of belongings. It was a beautiful day with no wind and a clear sky.

The bus fled on like a fabulous beast, bearing me with it to a magic land.

But alas, as we approached Mayfair we were held up

more than once for long stretches of time. I began to get restless. By the time the bus had reached Shaftesbury Avenue I had but three minutes in which to reach the office.

It seemed strange that when the sunlight shone in sympathy with my marriage, the traffic should choose to frustrate me. I was on the top of the bus and, having been given a very clear description of the building, was able, as we rounded at last in Cambridge Circus, to recognize it at once. When we came alongside my destination the traffic was held up again and I was offered the perfect opportunity of disembarking immediately beneath the building.

My suitcase was at my feet and as I stopped to pick it up I glanced at the windows on the first floor—for it was in one of those rooms that I was so soon to become a husband.

I was exactly on a level with the windows in question and commanded an unbroken view of the interior of the first-floor room. It could not have been more than a dozen feet away from where I sat.

I remember that our bus was hooting away, but there was no movement in the traffic ahead. The hooting came to me as through a dream for I had become lost in another world.

My hand was clenched upon the handle of the suitcase. Through my eyes and into my brain an image was pouring. The image of the first-floor room.

I knew at once that it was in that particular room that I was expected. I cannot tell you why, for during those first few moments I had not seen her.

To the right of the stage (for I had the sensation of being in a theater) was a table loaded with flowers. Behind the flowers sat a small pin-striped registrar. There were four others in the room, three of whom kept walking to and fro. The fourth, an enormous bearded lady, sat on a chair by the window. As I stared, one of the men bent over to speak to her. He had the longest neck on earth. His starched collar was the length of a walking stick, and his small bony head protruded from its extremity like the skull of a bird. The other two gentlemen who kept crossing and recrossing were very difficult. One was bald. His face and cranium were blue with the most intricate tattooing. His teeth were gold and they shone like fire in his mouth. The other was a well-dressed young man, and seemed normal enough until as he came for a moment closer to the window I saw that instead of a hand, the cloven hoof of a goat protruded from the left sleeve.

And then suddenly it all happened. A door of their room must have opened for all at once all the heads in the room were turned in one direction and a moment later a something in white trotted like a dog across the room.

But it was no dog. It was vertical as it ran. I thought at first that it was a mechanical doll, so close was it to the floor. I could not observe its face, but I was amazed to see the long train of satin that was being dragged along the carpet behind it.

It stopped when it reached the flower-laden table and there was a good deal of smiling and bowing and then the man with the longest neck in the world placed a high stool in front of the table and, with the help of the young man with the goat foot, lifted the white thing so that it stood upon the high stool. The long satin dress was carefully draped over the stool so that it reached to the floor on every side. It seemed as though a tall dignified woman was standing at the civic altar.

And still I had not seen its face, although I knew what it would be like. A sense of nausea overwhelmed me and I sank back on the seat, hiding my face in my hands.

I cannot remember when the bus began to move. I know that I went on and on and on and that finally I was told that I had reached the terminus. There was nothing for it but to board another bus of the same number and make the return journey. A strange sense of relief had by now begun to blunt the edge of my disappointment. That this bus would take me to the door of the house where I was born gave me a twinge of homesick pleasure. But stronger was my sense of fear. I prayed that there would be no reason for the bus to be held up again in Cambridge Circus.

I had taken one of the downstairs seats for I had no wish to be on an eye level with someone I had deserted. I had no sense of having wronged her but she had been deserted nevertheless.

When at last the bus approached the Circus, I peered into the half darkness. A street lamp stood immediately below the registry office. I saw at once that there was no light in the office and as the bus moved past I turned my eyes to the group beneath the street lamp. My heart went cold in my breast.

Standing there, ossified as it were into a malignant mass—standing there as though they never intended to move until justice was done—were the five. It was only for a second that I saw them but every lamp-lit head is for ever with me—the long-necked man with his bird skull head, his eyes glinting like chips of glass; to his right the small bald man, his tattooed scalp thrust forward, the lamplight gloating on the blue markings. To the left of the long-necked man stood the youth, his elegant body relaxed, but a snarl on his face that I still sweat to remember. His hands were in his pockets but I could see the shape of the hoof through the cloth. A little ahead of these three stood the bearded woman, a bulk of evil—and in the shadow that she cast before her I saw in that last fraction of a second, as the bus rolled me past, a big whitish head, very close to the ground.

In the dusk it appeared to be suspended above the curb like a pale balloon with a red mouth painted upon it—a mouth that, taking a single diabolical curve, was more like the mouth of a wild beast than a woman.

Long after I had left the group behind me—set as it were for ever under the lamp, like something made of wax, like something monstrous, long after I had left it I yet saw it all. It filled the bus. They filled my brain. They fill it still.

When at last I arrived home I fell weeping upon my bed. My father and mother had no idea what it was all about but they did not ask me. They never asked me.

That evening, after supper, I sat there, I remember, six years ago in my own chair on the chocolate-colored carpet. I remember how I stared with love at the ash on my father's waistcoat, at his stained mustache, at my mother's worn away shoe heels. I stared at it all and I loved it all. I needed it all.

Since then I have never left the house. I know what is best for me.

THE MODEL

ROBERT BLOCH

"She moved close, too close, close enough so that
I could feel the heat pouring off her in waves. Heat,
and perfume, and a kind of vibration that echoed
in her husky voice. 'I need a child,' she said."

*It was Robert Bloch's 1959 novel of the same name that
inspired the Alfred Hitchcock masterpiece* Psycho. *And
judging from the American female public's lessened standards of personal hygiene—for some years, anyway, after
the film's original release—it's clear that any blend of horror and sex in which Bloch's had a hand will be of the
high-impact variety.*

*Obvious, too, is Bloch's lifelong fascination with the
aberrant, whether it be the blood lust of Jack the Ripper,
a character he's turned to numerous times, or whether
it's the malign intentions of a large assortment of other
unnatural creatures, ranging from (never quite) straight-
forward vampires to purveyors of (nearly always) ines-
capable satanic pacts. E. F. Bleiler, genre scholar
extraordinaire, gets it just right when he speaks approv-
ingly of Bloch's "personal, brash black humor" along
with his "opulence of imagination." Both of these descriptions allow us to see that Bloch's accomplishment—like*

that of so many of his peers—is achieved not just by his leaping out and screeching "Boo!" when one is least expecting it but by a more complex play of iconoclastic leanings, bizarre conceits, and dark wit. Add to these an intuitive grasp of how to make us suspect every mild-mannered motel clerk of homicidal tendencies and you have a career that's spanned over half a century of popularity.

"The Model," while not ultimately a subtle story, is nonetheless a genuinely surprising one—and could just as easily (apologies to Naomi Wolf) have been titled "The Beauty Myth."

———————

Before I begin this story, I must tell you that I don't believe a word of it.

If I did, I'd be just as crazy as the man who told it to me, and he's in the asylum.

There are times, though, when I wonder. But that's something you'll have to decide for yourself.

About the man in the asylum—let's call him George Milbank. Age thirty-two, according to the records, but he looked older; balding, running to fat, with a reedy voice and a facial tic that made me a little uptight watching him. But he didn't act or sound like a weirdo.

"And I'm not," he said, as we sat there in his room on the afternoon of my visit. "That's why Dr. Stern wanted you to see me, isn't it?"

"What do you mean?" I was playing it cool.

"Doc told me who you were, and I know the kind of stuff you write. If you're looking for material—"

"I didn't say that."

"Don't worry, I'm glad to talk to you. I've been wanting to talk to someone for a long time. Someone who'll do more than just put down what I say in a case history and file it away. They've got me filed away now and they're never going to let me out of here, but somebody should know the truth. I don't care if you write it up as a story, just so you don't make me out bananas. Because I'm going to tell it like it is, so help me God. If there *is* a God. That's what worries me—I mean, what kind of a God would create someone like Vilma?"

That's when I became conscious of his facial tic, and it disturbed me. He noticed my reaction and shook his head. "Don't take my word for it," he said. "Just look at the women in the magazine ads. High-fashion models, you know the type? Tall, thin, all arms and legs, with no bust. And those high cheekbones, the big eyes, the face frozen in that snotty don't-touch-me look.

"I guess that's what got to me. Just as it was supposed to. I took Vilma's look as a challenge." His face twitched again.

"You don't like women, do you?" I said.

"You're putting me on." For the first and only time he grinned. "Man, you're talking to one of the biggest womanizers in the business!" Then the grin faded. "At least I was, until I met Vilma.

"It all came together on a cruise ship—the *Morland*, one of those big new Scandinavian jobs built for the Caribbean package tours. Nine ports in two weeks, conducted shore trips to all the exotic native clipjoints.

"But I was aboard for business, not pleasure. McKay-Phipps, the ad agency I worked for, pitched Apex Camera a campaign featuring full-page color spreads in the fashion magazines. You know the setup—big, arty shots of a model posed against tropical resort backgrounds with just a few lines of snob-appeal copy below. *She travels in style. Her outfit—a Countess D'Or original. Her camera—an Apex.* That kind of crud, right?

"OK, it was their money and who the hell am I to say how they throw it around? Besides, it wasn't even one of my accounts. But Ben Sanders, the exec who handled it, went down the tube with a heart attack just three days before sailing, and I got nailed for the assignment.

"I didn't know diddly about the high-fashion rag business or cameras either, but no problem. The D'Or people sent along Pat Grigsby, their top design consultant, to take charge of the wardrobe end. And I had Smitty Lane handling the actual shooting. He's one of the best in the business, and he got everything lined up before we left—worked out a complete schedule of what shots we'd take and where, checked out times and locations, wired ahead for clearances and firmed up the arrangements. All I had to do was come along for the ride and see that everyone showed up at the right place at the right time.

"So on the face of it I was home free. Or away from home free. There are worse things than two weeks on a West Indies cruise in February with all expenses paid. The ship was brand-new, with a dozen top-deck staterooms, and they'd booked one for each of us. None of those converted broom-closet cabins, and if we wanted we could have our meals served in and skip the first-sitting hassle in the dining room.

"But you don't give a damn about my vacation, and neither did I. Because it turned out to be a real downer.

"Like I said, the *Morland* hit nine ports in two weeks, and we were scheduled to do our thing in every one of them. Smitty wanted to shoot with natural light, so that meant we had to be on location and ready for action by 11 A.M. Since most of the spots he'd picked out were resorts halfway across the various islands, we had to haul out of the sack before seven, grab a fast continental breakfast, and drag all the wardrobe and equipment onto a chartered bus by eight. You ever ride a 1959 VW mini-bus over a stretch of rough back country road in steam-bath temperatures and humidity? It's the original bad trip.

"Then there was the business of setting up. Smitty was good but a real nitpicker, you know? And by the time Pat Grigsby was satisfied with the looks of the outfits and the way they lined up in the viewfinder and we got all those extra-protection shots, it was generally two o'clock. We had our pics but no lunch. So off we'd go, laughing and scratching, in the VW that had been baking in the sun all day, and if we boarded the ship again by four-thirty we were just in time for Afternoon Bingo.

"About the rest of the cruise, I've got good news and bad news.

"First the bad news. Smitty didn't play Afternoon Bingo. He played the bar—morning, afternoon, and night. And Pat Grigsby was butch. She must have made her move with Vilma early on and gotten thanks-but-no-thanks, because by the third day out the two of them weren't speaking except in the line of duty. So that left Vilma and me.

"This was the good news.

"I've already told you what those high-fashion models look like, and I guess I made it sound like a grunt from a male chauvinist pig, but that's because of what I know now. At the time, Vilma Loring was something else. One thing about models—they know how to dress, how to move, what to do with makeup and perfume. What it adds up to is poise. Poise, and what they used to call femininity. And Vilma was all female.

"Maybe Women's Lib is a good thing, but those intellectual types, psychology majors with the stringy hair and the blue jeans, always turned me off.

"Vilma turned me on just looking at her. And I looked at her a lot. The way she handled herself when we were shooting—a real pro. While the rest of us were frying and dying under the noon sun, she stayed calm, cool, and collected. No sweat, not a hair out of place, never any complaints. The lady had it.

"She had it, and I wanted it. That's why I made the scene with her as often as I could, which wasn't very much on the days we were in port. She always sacked out after we got back from a location and I couldn't get her to eat with me; she liked to have meals in the stateroom so she wouldn't have to bother with clothes and makeup. Naturally that was my cue to go into the my-stateroom-or-yours routine, but she wasn't buying it. So during our working schedule I had to settle for evenings.

"You know the kind of fun and games they have on shipboard. Second-run movies for the old ladies with blue hair, dancing on a dime-size floor to the music of a combo that would make Lawrence Welk turn in his baton. And the floor shows—tap dancers, magic acts, overage vocalists direct from a two-year engagement at Caesars Palace—in the men's room.

"So we did a lot of time together just walking the deck. With me suggesting my room for a nightcap and she giving me that it's-so-lovely-out-here-why-don't-we-look-at-the-dolphins routine.

"I got the message, but I wasn't about to scrub the mission. And on the days we spent at sea I stayed in there. I used to call Vilma every morning after breakfast and when she wasn't resting or doing her nails I lucked out. She was definitely the quiet type and dummied up whenever I asked a personal question, but she was a good listener. As long as I didn't pressure her she stayed happy, I picked up my cue from that and played the waiting game.

"She didn't want to swim? OK, so we sat in deck chairs and watched the action at the pool. No shuffle-board or deck tennis because the sun was bad for her complexion? Right on, we'd hit the lounge for the cock-tail hour, even though she didn't drink. I kept a low profile, but as time went on I had to admit it was getting to me.

"Maybe it was the cruise itself that wore me down. The atmosphere, with everybody making out. Not just the couples, married or otherwise; there was plenty going for singles, too. Secretaries and schoolteachers who'd saved up for the annual orgy, getting it all to-gether with used-car salesmen and post-graduate beach bums. Divorcées with silicone implants and new dye jobs were balling the gray-sideburn types who checked out Dow Jones every morning before they went ashore. By the second week, even the little old ladies with the blue hair had paired off with the young stewards who'd hired on for stud duty. The final leg, two days at sea from Puerto Rico to Miami, was like something out of a porno flick, with everybody getting it on. Everybody but me, sitting there watching with a newspaper over my lap.

"That's when I had a little Dear Abby talk with my-self. Here I was, wasting my time with an entry who wouldn't dance, wouldn't drink, wouldn't even have din-ner with me. She wasn't playing it cool, she was playing it frigid.

"OK, she was maybe the most beautiful broad I've ever laid eyes on, but you can't look forever when you're not allowed to touch. She had this deep, husky voice that

seemed to come from her chest instead of her throat, but
she never used it for anything but small talk. She had a
way of staring at you without blinking, but you want
someone to look *at* you, not through you. She moved
and walked like a dream, but there comes a time when
you have to wake up.

"By the time I woke up it was our last night out and
too late. But not too late to hit the bar. There was the
usual ship's party and I'd made a date to take Vilma to
the floor show. I didn't cancel it—I just stood her up.

"Maybe I was a slow learner or a sore loser. I didn't
give a damn which it was, I'd just had it up to here. No
more climbing the walls; I was going to tie one on, and
I did.

"I went up aft to a little deck bar away from the
action, and got to work. Everybody was making the
party scene so I was the only customer. The bartender
wanted to talk but I turned him off. I wasn't in the mood
for conversation; I had too much to think about. Such
as, what the hell had come over me these past two
weeks? Running after a phony teaser like some goddam
kid with the hots—it made no sense. Not after the first
drink, or the second. By the time I ordered the third,
which was a double, I was ready to go with Vilma and
hit her right in the mouth.

"But I didn't have to. Because she was there. Standing
next to me, with that way-out tropical moon shining
through the light blue evening gown and shimmering
over her hair.

"She gave me a big smile. 'I've been looking for you
everywhere,' she said. 'We've got to talk.'

"I told her to forget it, we had nothing to discuss. She
just stood there looking at me, and now the moonlight
was sparkling in her eyes. I told her to get lost, I never
wanted to see her again. And she put her hand on my
arm and said, 'You're in love with me, aren't you?'

"I didn't answer. I couldn't answer, because it all came
together and it was true. I *was* in love with Vilma. That's
why I wanted to hit her, to grab hold of her and tear
that dress right off and—

"Vilma took my hand. 'Let's go to my room,' she said.

"Now there's a switch for you. Two weeks in the deep-freeze and now this. On the last night, too—we'd be docking in a few hours and I still had to pack and be ready to leave the ship early next morning.

"But it didn't matter. What mattered is that we went right to her stateroom and locked the door and it was all ready and waiting. The lights were low, the bed was turned down, and the champagne was chilling in the ice bucket.

"Vilma poured me a glass, but none for herself. 'Go ahead,' she said. 'I don't mind.'

"But I did, and I told her so. There was something about the setup that didn't make sense. If this was what she wanted, why wait until the last minute?

"She gave me a look I've never forgotten. 'Because I had to be sure first.'

"I took a big gulp of my drink. It hit me hard on top of what I'd already had, and I was all through playing games. 'Sure of what?' I said. 'What's the matter, you think I can't get it up?'

"Vilma's expression didn't change. 'You don't understand. I had to get to know you and decide if you were suitable.'

"I put down my empty glass. 'To go to bed with?'

"Vilma shook her head. 'To be the father of my child.'

"I stared at her. 'Now wait a minute—'

"She gave me that look again. 'I have waited. For two weeks I've been waiting, watching you and making up my mind. You seem to be healthy, and there's no reason why our offspring wouldn't be genetically sound.'

"I could feel that last drink but I knew I wasn't stoned. I'd heard her loud and clear. 'You can stop right there,' I told her. 'I'm not into marriage, or supporting a kid.'

"She shrugged. 'I'm not asking you to marry me, and I don't need any financial help. If I conceive tonight, you won't even know about it. Tomorrow we go our separate ways—I promise you'll never even have to see me again.'

"She moved close, too close, close enough so that I could feel the heat pouring off her in waves. Heat, and perfume, and a kind of vibration that echoed in her husky voice. 'I need a child,' she said.

"All kinds of thoughts flashed through my head. She was high on acid, she was on a freak sex-trip, some kind of a nut case. 'Look,' I said. 'I don't even know you, not really—'

"She laughed then, and her laugh was husky too. 'What does it matter? You want me.'

"I wanted her, all right. The thoughts blurred together, blended with the alcohol and the anger, and the only thing left was wanting her. Wanting this big beautiful blond babe, wanting her heat, her need.

"I reached for her and she stepped back, turning her head when I tried to kiss her. 'Get undressed first,' she said. 'Oh, hurry—please—'

"I hurried. Maybe she'd slipped something into my drink, because I had trouble unbuttoning my shirt and in the end I ripped it off, along with everything else. But whatever she'd given me I was turned on, turned on like I've never been before.

"I hit the bed, lying on my back, and everything froze; I couldn't move, my arms and legs felt numb because all the sensation was centered in one place. I was ready, so ready I couldn't turn off if I tried.

"I know because I kept watching her, and there was no change when she lifted her arms to her neck and removed her head.

"She put her head down on the table and the long blond hair hung over the side and the glassy blue eyes went dead in the rubbery face. But I couldn't stir, I was still turned on, and all I remember is thinking to myself, Without a head how can she see?

"Then the dress fell and there was my answer, moving toward me. Bending over me on the bed, with her tiny breasts almost directly above my face so that I could see the hard tips budding. Budding and opening until the eyes peered out—the *real* eyes, green and glittering deep within the nipples.

"And she bent closer; I watched her belly rise and fall, felt the warm, panting breath from her navel. The last thing I saw was what lay below—the pink-lipped, bearded mouth, opening to engulf me. I screamed once, and then I passed out.

"Do you understand now? Vilma had told me the truth, or part of the truth. She was a high-fashion model, all right—but a model for *what*?

"Who made her, and how many more did they make? How many hundreds or thousands are there, all over the world? Models—you ever notice how they all seem to look alike? They could be sisters, and maybe they are. A family, a race from somewhere outside, swarming across the world, breeding with men when the need is upon them, breeding in their own special way. The way she bred with me—"

I ran out then, when he lost control and started to scream. The attendants went in and I guess they quieted him down, because by the time I got to Dr. Stern's office down the hall I couldn't hear him anymore.

"Well?" Stern said. "What do you make of it?"

I shook my head. "You're the doctor. Suppose you tell me."

"There isn't much. This Vilma—Vilma Loring, she called herself—really existed. She was a working professional model for about two years, registered with a New York agency, living in a leased apartment on Central Park South. Lots of people remember seeing her, talking to her—"

"You're using the past tense," I said.

Stern nodded. "That's because she disappeared. She must have left her stateroom, left the ship as soon as it docked that night in Miami. No one's managed to locate her since, though God knows they've tried, in view of what happened."

"Just what *did* happen?"

"You heard the story."

"But he's crazy—isn't he?"

"Greatly disturbed. That's why they brought him here after they found him the next morning, lying there on the bed in a pool of blood." Stern shrugged. "You see, that's the one thing nobody can explain. To this day, we don't know what became of his genitals."

SILVER CIRCUS

A. E. COPPARD

"Gone wife, gone friend; there were no more journeys now."

*With his born-storyteller's spell-casting talents, English writer
A. E. Coppard was for several decades a much-anthologized
writer. But though he wrote many sorts of tales—whimsical,
moral, allegorical, fantastical, macabre—his work ultimately
can be classified as belonging to no particular genre; sadly,
that may now be why he is rarely seen in collections devoted
to any of them. He himself termed his output of over one
hundred short stories "modern folk tales"; today, however,
a fair portion deserve instead the description "timeless."*

*"Silver Circus" is one of those. And, as you will see,
its very palpable shudders are grounded in nothing more
singular, more grotesque than what human nature has to
offer in the way of horror when it puts its cruelly imaginative energies to the task.*

I

Hans Siebenhaar, a street porter, is basking on his stool
in a fine street of Vienna, for anybody to hire for any

sort of job. He is a huge man with a bulbous hairless face that somehow recalls a sponge, and this sponge is surmounted by a flat peaked hat encircled by a white band bearing these words in red: *Wiener Dienstmann*. His voice, which we shall hear later on, is a vast terrifying voice that seems to tear a rent in Space itself. At fifty years of age Hans is a conspicuous man. But a street porter! Not a profitable way of life, yet it must serve, and must continue to serve. It is a hot July morn, tropical; there are many noises, but no one speaks. The fruit-stall women are silent and hidden; they have pinned newspapers around the edges of their big red umbrellas. It is stifling, languorous; one thinks of lilac, of cool sea, of white balloons; the populace tears off its hat, fans itself desperately, sips ice in the cafés, and still perspires. The very street sounds are injurious to the mind. The drivers of carts wear only their breeches, their bodies are brown as a Polynesian's and lovely to behold.

Just such a day it was as the day twelve months gone when Mitzi Siebenhaar, his second wife, had run away with that Julius Damjancsics. Yes, please very much, she had left him. Hans took off his hat. After contemplating its interior as though it were a coffer of extraordinary mystery, he sighed huskily into it. How was it possible to understand such an accident? Smoothing his brown bald skull with the other hand, he collected so much sweat upon his hairy freckled fingers that as he shook them the drops simply splashed upon the pavement. Young Mitzi! It was her youth. Ah, God bless, she had the pull of him there, a whole fifteen years, fifteen years younger; youth as well as beauty, beauty as well as youth. At thirty-five she was as lovely as a girl, fitful and furious just like a girl, so he was only able to keep her for one little year; that is to say, keep her faithful, to himself. One little year! That is not long, but for a man of fifty it is so difficult, yes; but then Julius Damjancsics was just as old. And she had gone off with him! What could she see in Julius Damjancsics? How was it possible to understand such an accident? They had all been friends together, and Julius could play the mandolin, but Hans could pound him into dust. What could she see in

Julius Damjancsics? He could crush him in one fist, like a gherkin. If he had caught them—but that was difficult too. Belgrade he had gone to, for Julius Damjancsics was a Serbian, and Buda-Pesth he had gone to, for Mitzi was Hungarian, but this Julius was a wandering fellow and very deceitful. So. Well, it was pitiful to think of in such hot weather, there was nothing to be done, he had come back to Vienna. And now here he was brooding, here he was groaning; pitiful to think of. At last he said to himself: "Let us wipe our tears and forget that Christ died. *Gloria Patri et Filio et Spiritu Sancto,*" he murmured, for he was a good Catholic man, as Father Adolf of Stefans Dom could testify.

"Porter!" cried a voice.

Hans looked up quickly and put on his hat.

"Sir," said he.

A big man, with a big important foreign face and fat and flourishing appearance and shiny black boots with gray cloth tops stood as it were examining the porter. Although the boots were fastened with what appeared to be pearl buttons, they were rather uncared for, but to offset this a large gold watch chain was lavishly displayed, with jeweled tiepin and studs. The man's fists were in his trousers pockets; he twirled a long, thin cigar between his rich red lips. Immense and significant, he might have been a Turk or a Tartar, but he was neither; he was the boss of a Rumanian Circus.

"Come with me, I want you," and the huge Hans followed the circus man to a *Biergarten,* where another man was waiting who might have been a Tartar or a Turk. He called him Peter, he was certainly his brother, and Peter called him Franz. All three sat down and drank together.

"Tell me, Hans Siebenhaar," said Franz, "you are a strong man?"

"Yes, I am a strong man, that is so."

"You have a good voice?"

"Please—" Hans paused. "I am no singer, not much."

"Ah! No, no, no. You have a strong voice to speak, to shout, you can make great sounds with your voice?"

"Oh, ay," Hans agreed. "I have a strong voice, that

is so, very strong. I can make a noise." And there and then he accorded them a succession of hearty bellows in testimony. There was only one other occupant of the *Biergarten*, a man with an Emperor Franz-Josef sort of face and white whiskers like the wings of an easy chair, who sat smoking a china pipe under an acacia tree. And he seemed to be deaf, for he did not take the slightest notice of the appalling outcry. Two waiters rushed with alarm into the garden, but Franz waved them away.

"Good," said Franz reflectively. "Listen now." And sitting there between the brothers Hans heard them propound to him a scheme that smote him with amazement and bereft him of sympathy; it filled him indeed with any and every emotion but that of satisfaction. They wanted him, in brief, to become a tiger.

"No." Hans was indignant, and he was contemptuous. "I do not understand, but I do not do this."

Not at once, they cried, not today. No, no. Plenty of time, a week's time in fact. And they would instruct him in the art of impersonating a tiger, they would rehearse him, and for a single performance, one night only, they would give him two hundred Austrian shillings. Peter the Turk decided it was far too much money. Franz the Tartar invoked his God.

There is more in this, thought Hans, than strokes my ear; I have to beware of something. Aloud he inquired: "Two hundred shillings?"

"Two hundred," said Peter.

"Shillings," echoed Franz, scratching the table with a wooden toothpick.

"And, please very much, I am to do?"

They told him what he was to do. He was to be sewn up in the skin of a tiger; he was to enact the part of a tiger in their menagerie; he was to receive two hundred shillings. Very, very simple for a strong man. Hans Siebenhaar was to be sewn up in the tiger's hide for two hundred shillings; he was to prance and fight and hideously roar in the best way he knew so that the hearts of the audience be rocked within them and fly into their throats—and the two hundred shillings were his. It was his voice, it was because of his great bellowing tigerish voice that they had come to him. Such a voice was worth some riches to them, and so they were going to pay two hundred shillings for his services.

"Two hundred shillings?" murmured Hans.

"Two hundred," said Peter, and Franz said, "Two hundred."

It is not, thought Hans, to be sneezed at, but there is more in this than strokes my hearing; I must be wary.

"Why do you not have," he asked them, "a real tiger?"

"But we had!" they both cried.

"And now he is dead," said Peter.

"A real proper tiger," Franz declared.

"But now he is dead," repeated his brother. "Ah, he had paws like a hassock."

"And the ferocity!"

"Beautiful," said Peter. "He died of grief."

"No, no, no," objected Franz. "I would not say that of this tiger."

"But yes," affirmed Peter. "Of grief. He loved me, and lately I married again."

"The heart was broken, yes, perhaps," Franz admitted.

"His voice died away like a little whistle." There was sorrow in Peter's eyes. "No fury."

"Two hundred shillings," said Franz.

"Brrr-o-o-o-owh!" Hans suddenly roared, and skipping up he began capering and pawing madly about the garden. "Ookah, pookah, boddle, oddle, moddle, miowh!" he roared.

The deaf old gentleman with the Franz-Josef whiskers gently laid his china pipe on the table before him; he neither observed nor heeded Hans, he only put his fingers into his mouth and extracted his false teeth. These he calmly examined, as though they were a foreign substance he had never noticed before and was wondering how it came to be there. Hans began crashing over the tables and chairs; waiters rushed into the garden and, flinging themselves upon the perspiring maniac, rolled him over into a corner.

"That is good," cried Franz, "very good!"

"Absolutely," Peter said, "absolutely!"

Three waiters clung to Hans Siebenhaar with the clear intention of throttling him.

"Enough!" shouted Franz. "Let him go," and with his powerful hands he dragged two of the waiters from the prostrate body of Hans as you would draw two pins from a pincushion, and likewise did Peter do with the other waiter.

"It is all right," said Franz, and Peter said it was quite all right. They gave the waiters a few coins and soothed them. In the meantime Hans had resumed his seat, and the deaf old gentleman was replacing his teeth.

To Hans the brothers said, "Listen," and Hans listened. Their circus menagerie was now on view in the Prater, and at the festival next week they had contemplated to stage a novel performance, nothing less than a combat between a lion and a tiger—ah, good business!— but just at this critical moment what does their tiger do?

"It dies," suggested Hans.

"Dies," agreed Franz. "It dies. So now!"

"Yes, now?" Hans said, and nodded.

"You must be our tiger, that is the simple fact of the business. You have the voice of a tiger, and the character. You will get the two hundred shillings. Hooray! It is like lapping honey, yes."

"But what is this?" cried Hans. "To fight a lion!"

"Pooh," Peter said. "It is more friendly and harmless than any kitten."

"No," said Hans. "No."

"Yes," said Franz. "Yes. It is, it is but a caterpillar, I tell you."

"No!" shouted Hans.

"It has no teeth."

"Not I," cried the intended victim.

"It has been in our family for a hundred years."

"Never," declared Hans with absolute finality, and he got up as if to go. But the brothers seized each an arm and held him down in his chair.

"Have no fear, Mr. Siebenhaar; it will love you. Two hundred and fifty shillings!"

"No, I will not—ha!"

"Mr. Siebenhaar, we can guarantee you. Three hundred shillings," said Peter.

"And fifty," added Franz.

"Three hundred and fifty!" repeated Hans. "So? But what? I cannot fight a lion. No, no. I am not a woman. I have my courage, but what is three hundred and fifty shillings for my life's blood and bones?" In short, a lion was not the kind of thing Mr. Siebenhaar was in the habit of fighting.

"Ach! Your blood and bones will be as safe as they are in your trousers. You will not have to fight this lion—"

"No, I will not—ha!"

"—you have only to play with it. This lion does not fight, Mr. Siebenhaar; it will not, it cannot."

"Why so?"

"It is too meek; it is like a lamb in a meadow that cries baa. You have only to prance about before it and roar and roar, to make a noise and a fuss. It will cringe before you. Have no fear of him. A show, you understand, make a show."

"I understand a show," said Hans, "but, please very much, permit me, I will not make a spectacle of my blood and bones."

"So help me Heaven!" shouted Franz, exasperated, "do you think we want your bones?"

"Not a knuckle!" cried Hans.

Peter intervened. "You misunderstand us, Mr. Siebenhaar; we desire only entertainment, we do not want a massacre."

"You do not want a massacre!"

"A massacre is very well in its way, perhaps, in its time and place," Peter continued, "but a massacre is one thing, and this is another."

"Thank you," said Hans, "it is very clear, that is very good."

And Franz and Peter intimated that they were simple men of business whose only care it was to bring joy and jollity into the life of the Viennese populace; that the fury of the lion was a figment, its courage a mockery, its power a profanation of all men's cherished fears. It there was one animal in the world more deserving the kindness and pity of mankind, more subservient, more mercifully disposed than any other, Franz assured him, it was a lion. And if there was one lion among all lions more responsive to the symptoms of affection, added Peter, it was this identical lion. Was three hundred and fifty shillings nothing to him?

"No," Hans conceded.

"Is it a bunch of beans?"

"No, no."

"Three hundred and fifty shillings is three hundred and fifty shillings, is it not?" Peter questioned him; and Hans replied, "For what is past, yes; but for what is yet to come, no. The future—pardon, gentleman, does not lie in our behinds."

"Three hundred and fifty shillings is three hundred and fifty shillings, it is not a bunch of beans," said Franz severely. They had men in their employ who implored him on their knees to be honorably permitted to enact the part of this tiger, but they had not the physique, they had not the voice, and, if Mr. Siebenhaar would pardon him, they had not the artist's delicate touch. One thing he, Franz, was certain of: he knew an artist when he saw one, hence this three hundred and fifty shillings.

At the end of it Hans once more determined to wipe his tears and forget that Christ died. In effect, he agreed to be sewn up on such and such a date in the tiger's hide and to make a manifestation with Messrs. Franz and Peter's ingenuous lion, on the solemnest possible undertaking that no harm should befall his own blood and bones.

"Thunder and lightning! What could harm you?"

"Good."

And after parting from Hans, and when they were well out of hearing, Mr. Franz said: "Ha, ha!" and Mr. Peter said: "Ho, ho!"

II

Hans Siebenhaar had several rehearsals before the eventful day. Submitting himself to be sewn up in the tiger's skin, he dashed his paws upon the floor, pranced, gnashed, snarled, whirled his mechanical tail, and delivered himself of a gamut of howls eminently tigerish. Perfectly satisfactory.

"Where," Hans would ask, "do you keep this old lion?"

"Yes," the brothers always replied, "he is not well, he is sleeping; you see him next time."

And thus it happened that Hans did not see his adversary until they met in the cage of battle. The morning of that day was dull and Hans too was dull, for on awakening he felt so strange, so very unwell, that he greatly feared he would have to send Franz word that he could not come to perform his tiger; but as the day wore on and brightened, Hans, sitting on his stool in the sunny street, brightened with it, and while thinking of the three hundred and fifty shillings his sickness left him. A nice sum of money that! And what would he do with it? Ah, please very much, what would he not have done if Mitzi, the shameless one, had not forsaken him! They might have gone again, as they had gone of old, on one of those excursions to the Wiener Wald. He liked excursions, they were beautiful. With their happy companions they could climb the mountains, prowl in the forest for raspberries and mushrooms, and at noon they would sit under the chestnuts in the *Biergarten* at the Hunter's Meadow and lap the rich soup and gulp lager and talk of love and wealth and food and childhood. That was life, that was wonderful. Then they would all go and loaf in the grass and Mitzi would throw off her frock and lie half naked, browning her sleek shining body, while Julius Damjancsics thrummed his mandolin and they all murmured songs. Ah, such music! She loved it. She had a dimple behind each shoulder, a rare thing, very beautiful. In the cool of the evening there would be dancing, and they would be at Dreimarkstein in time to see the fireworks go up from the Prater—he liked fireworks, lovely. Or to the trotting races, they might go and win some more money, for when luck was on you the fancy could never deceive; beautiful horses, he loved horses. Or to the baths at Gänsehaufel—the things one could do with a little money! But there was no longer any

Mitzi, she had gone with Julius Damjancsics. Gone wife, gone friend; there were no more journeys now. But a man with three hundred and fifty shillings need never lack companions, there was a lot of friendship in three hundred and fifty shillings. But that Mitzi—she was very beautiful, that little Mitzi.

So the day wore on and the evening came and the Prater began to sparkle with the lights of its many booths and cafés, to throb with its music, for youth was gallant and gay and there was love and money in the world. It was the hour at last. Hans had been sewn up in the tiger's skin. Now he crouched in a corner of a shuttered cage, alone, trembling in darkness, seeing no one and seen of none. There was a door in the side of his cage that led into a large empty lighted cage, and beyond that was another like his own in which walked a lion. At a certain moment the doors of the end cages would be opened and he would have to go into that central cage and face the other beast. But no, he could not, he was limp with fear. To the stricken man came the excited voices of the people coming in to witness his calamity, and the harsh tones of the trumpeting band playing in pandemonium outside on the platform, where there was a large poster of a combat between a tiger and a lion. Hans recalled that the lion's teeth were buried in the tiger's belly amid the gushing blood, and it seemed that his very heart violently cried, "No! No! Let me out!"

Beating upon the walls of his cage he gasped, "In Christ's name, let me out!" but nobody heeded, no one replied, and although he tore at his tiger skin, his paws were too cumbersome for him to free himself. He was in a trap, he knew now he had been trapped. For an eternal anguishing time the clamor went on, then that dreadful side door which led into the central cage slid quietly open. Hans saw that this cage was yet empty, the lion's door was still closed, he was to be the first to enter. But he averted his eyes, he lay in the corner of his trap and would not budge from it. Almighty Heaven! was he going to sacrifice himself for a few pitiful pieces of silver that he had never seen and never would see?

He was not fit to do it, he was an old man, even his wife, Mitzi, had left him for another man—did they not know that! And all day long he had been unwell, sick as a dog. As he lay in his corner, refusing to budge and sweating most intensely, a sharp iron spear came through the bars and pricked him savagely in the behind. With a yell he leaped up, trying to snatch the spear. He would use it, it would save him—but he could not grasp it with his giant paws. Then came bars of red-hot iron searing him, and more spears; he was driven screaming into the central cage. The door closed behind him and he was left alone behind those terrible bars with a vast audience gazing at him. Then, ah then, in a frenzy, an epilepsy of fear, he dashed himself so violently against the bars that the crowd was spellbound. The band played riotously on, drowning his human cries. The outer side door slid open, there was silence in that other cage, but he dared not turn to meet whatever was there; he crouched half swooning, until he caught sight of a face in the audience that he knew. Wonder of God! It was Mitzi, herself! Oh, but there was something to fight for now and he turned resolutely. As he did so, there was a titter in the audience that surged into general laughter—the lion had come into the cage. Truly, it was a cadaverous lion. Without the least display of ferocity or fear it stepped quietly into that cage and fixed its strong eyes upon the eyes of its enemy. Not a leap did it make, not a roar did it give, it padded forward quietly, and the tiger retreated before it. Thus they circled and circled round the cage. Would that mocking laughter never stop?

God! Hans could bear it no longer, he turned and faced the lion, in appearance bold, though trembling in his soul. The lion paused too.

"*Pater noster qui es in cœlis,*" Hans gasped involuntarily.

To his unspeakable astonishment he heard the lion answer:

"*Et ne nos inducas in tentationem. Sed libera nos a malo.*"

In an incredible flash Hans realized that the lion also

was a spurious creature like himself; his fears vanished, he knew now the part he had to play, and he hurled himself upon the lion, howling:

"Brrr-o-o-owh! Ookah, pookah, boddle, oddle, moddle, miowh!"

Over they rolled, lion and tiger, together, and the onlookers shook with mirth.

"Not so rough, brother!" cried a voice from inside the lion, and the tones struck a strange echo in the mind of Hans Siebenhaar. They disengaged and stood up on all fours facing each other. From the moment's silence that ensued there issued a piercing cry of fear from a woman in the audience. Hans turned. The lion turned. It was Mitzi, shrieking: "Julius! Watch out!" Hans's throbbing mind caught at that fatal name, Julius. By all the gods, was it possible! Heaven and hell, he would tear the heart out of *that* lion! *Not so rough, brother!* Ha, ha, he knew it now, that voice! Ho, ho! and with a cruel leap he jumped with his heels savagely in the middle of the lion's back, the back of Julius Damjancsics, thief of Mitzi, the beloved of Hans, and down sank the lion with the tiger tearing at its throat as fearfully as any beast of the jungle. Ah, but how the people applauded; this was good in spite of the deception! They had paid to see a real lion and a real tiger contending, and they felt defrauded, insulted; but this was good, yes, it was very comical, good, good. When they noticed a man's hand appear outside the flapping paw of the tiger their joy was unbounded.

"Tear him!" they cried, as one cries to a hound with a fox. "Ha, ha, tear him!" And Hans's loosened hand ripped up the seam in the lion's neck, and his hand went searching within the rent for a throat to tear. At once the teeth of Julius ground themselves upon it; in a trice Hans's smallest finger was gone, severed. But Hans never uttered a cry, he gripped the throat with his wounded hand and crushed everlastingly upon it, moment after moment, until he knew that Julius Damjancsics was gone, and for ever, to hell or glory, whatever destiny had devised for him. The lion moved no more, it lay on its back with its hind legs crooked preposterously, its forelegs outspread like one crucified. The people hushed their laughter as Hans slunk trembling and sweating from that droll oaf wrapped in a lion's skin. He was afraid of it now and he crawled on all fours to the bars of the cage. The thing behind him was awfully still. The onlookers were still. They were strange, as strange as death. Mitzi was there, craning forward, her face as pale as snow. Hans caught hold of the cage bars and lifted himself to his feet. The onlookers could hear wild tormenting sobs bursting from the throat of the tiger as it hung ridiculously there. The door of Hans's first cage now slid open again, it was finished, he could go. But Hans did not go.

HONEYMOON

CLEMENT WOOD

"Hurrying through her preparations, she crept between the crinkly chill sheets. She lay breathless; a
sudden little shiver went through her. Pretty cold,
for May. . . ."

*Please remember that any story you've never read is a
new one. And Clement Wood's perfectly horrid "Honeymoon," a shocker too long unseen, should keep you gasping short little breaths after it ends just as surely as if it
had been written only yesterday. Even if we want to agree
that courtships are much different nowadays and to believe, besides, that young husbands and wives are better
acquainted with one another than in past eras—well, can
we be so certain?*

*Still, what Wood, a writer better known for his poetry
and musical interests, has come up with in the way of
conjugal rights should be enough to give divorce a good
name.*

Edith Cary rested herself on the couch, crossed a fine
pair of legs briskly, pulled out a black and white holder
and a carton of cheap cigarettes. "—None? Oh, I forgot

you didn't. . . . I will have a match; thanks. . . ." She
leaned back, squirming until the pillows were hollowed
properly; the smoke came out in a gray cone, flowering
at the base, then disintegrating palely. Her eyes narrowed invitingly. "Now, Doris, how does it feel? —Being
engaged! Come on—"

"Why . . . er . . . it's fine, Edie."

"All happened while I was away! Hmm. . . . I didn't
know Harvey—'Doctor Campbell,' I suppose I'll have to
call him now—I didn't dream he was giving you a rush."

"N-n-no. He wasn't exactly."

"Sly thing! I know it. . . . You were going around with
George Stickney . . . the Mu Gamma boys—and, of
course, that poor little ensign from Texas—when I went
South—"

"Y-yes, I was."

"Come on! You're as talky as a Chesapeake clam.
How does it feel?" She leaned forward, eyes taking in
the other girl's quiet comeliness. "—Live lover, is he?"
Her tones sinuated eagerly, intimately.

Doris Orr was worth her study. Stiff and palely beautiful as a girl on a Dutch pastel, she sat facing her friend.
The folds of her dress, a sheer thing of dull blue and
tan, were as moveless as marble; the full column of her
neck, the steady stateliness of her profile, unclouded
blue eyes below a low coil of dull yellow-gold hair—she
was almost a waxen flower, hued in blue and tan and
delicate pink, below a gray light. There was just the
faintest flicker of surprise in her eyes; the breath of a
crease appeared on her forehead, and disappeared at
once. "He's—he's nice. . . . Harvey is."

"Does he—does he . . . love you up, a lot? Don't mind
me, Doris—I'm an old married woman, remember. Ed
and I . . . before we were married—you know how it
is. . . . All engaged people do. It's great, isn't it?"

The summer shadow mottled the brow again, and was
gone again. "Y-yes. It's great, Edie." There was little
comprehension in the agreement.

"Don't come the baby with me! You know what I
mean—petting, a feel or so, and all. . . . You've been out
with boys a lot— No girl could be fussed to as many

hops as you have—here, and at Annapolis. . . . How far do you let him go?"

"I—I don't quite— You mean—"

"My Gawd! The girl can't be as innocent as she looks! Does he kiss you, Doris—hard?"

"He . . . kisses . . . me, Edie. That is, when we got engaged—"

"—Since?"

"N-n-no. I don't think he has."

The young wife's beady black eyes closed to an appraising slit. "Other men kiss you?"

"Oh, yes . . . on the cheek."

"On the lips? Hard?" The cross-examination was brisk, merciless.

"Of course not. I wouldn't let—"

"—Nor Harvey—beg pardon, Doctor Campbell?"

"I suppose he—will. . . ."

"I suppose so." She nodded her head profoundly several times. "That all the lovemaking you've had?"

"Why . . . er . . . yes."

"How do you girls grow up, and know so damned little? You aren't the first's told me. . . . From the time I was a kid, I know—most girls do—a lot, anyhow. It's natural. I suppose your old maid aunt told you not to let a man paw over you—"

"Yes, Aunt Ethel—"

"Oh, Lord! And—he doesn't make you?"

"Why, Edie!"

With a definitive gesture she laid down the half-smoked cigarette. "Would you mind telling me what you're getting married for?"

Blue and dull gold studied her with a tiny show of perturbation. "What do people get married for, Edie? It was about time . . . I'm twenty-four; I can't go to Hopkins parties and Annapolis hops forever, with kids half my age. . . . It was time."

"Yes," judicially.

"It was time for him, too. You know, old General Campbell's very anxious to have a boy—a grandson— that he can leave all he has to. Tom—Harvey's brother, the architect, you know—they have only one child, a girl; Elizabeth can't have any more . . . Marian's not married. . . . Ellen—Harvey's other sister, you remember, who married the man from Philadelphia, George What's-his-name—Scott, or Shott, or— Anyway, they had a boy, and it died; they've had two girls since. . . . Not a single grandson. He'll leave a whole lot more, the General will, to Harvey, if we had a boy. . . . Oh, yes, it was Short. . . . George Short. He'll leave a whole lot more—"

"I suppose Harvey explained it all to you?"

"Oh, yes. He and his mother." She nodded in placid relief.

"And that's why you're marrying?"

"Of course."

"You poor kid!" She stuck a second cigarette in with sudden vigor. "Give us another match. . . . Come over and sit by mother, that's a dear little Doris. . . . So your job's to have a boy, to take care of old General Campbell's wad! You don't mind?"

"Of course not! Why—"

"We've never had any. We've decided—Ed and I—we're not going to have any kids till we're good and ready. My figure's passable, now. . . . Not for little Edie!"

"But—is that—"

"Well?"

"—Right? I should think you'd be crazy to—"

"Exactly. I'd be crazy to have one—and me only twenty-six! Couple of years more—we'll settle down, and have a couple . . . maybe three. . . ."

"And you can—can—"

"Regulate it? You bet your sweet oxfords! No surprise parties in our family. Not till we're good and ready. . . . We had an awful scare last fall. . . . False alarm—"

"Oh."

"And you've grown up, without knowing— Hasn't anybody talked to you, Doris?"

"Mmm. . . . I know what you mean, now. . . . Harvey's going to give me a book to read. . . . You see, we want a lot of sons. The more boys we have, the more money he gets."

"I see."

"He's a doctor, you know. . . . He'll know all about it,

of course. His mother explained why they were so anxious for him to marry a good strong healthy girl—"

"And you're elected. You poor infant! He hasn't even kissed you—since the engagement.... Not once?"

"Not once."

"Thank God, it isn't my funeral! If Ed treated me like that, I'd find out who the blonde or brunette was, and spoil her good looks for her, good and plenty.... Of course, I'm glad ... because you are—"

A last patter of rice against the Pullman steps, a couple of disheveled slippers crudely thrown.... The train trembled, was off.... Triumphant agitated waving from the tall man on the top step, and the blossoming Doris beside him.... A wild cacophony from auto horns, as a last salvo to the joyful pair.... The train pulled out of the Baltimore shed, gathering momentum in silent power. Through the window the drab blocks of wooden apartment houses.... Stretches of freer country.... Trees, a still pool.... Cows, great heads down.... Blurred tiny human figures.... Soothing click of the heavy cars over the rail junctions.... They were off.

Young Doctor Campbell sat on the stateroom seat, facing his recently acquired wife. He was tall, his face a trifle thin; the eyes peered through heavy lenses in a blond composition frame; the thin lips were parted in a slight smile. The girl's face would have earned a possessory smile from any man. Except for a slight wash of unusual color, she was the same stiff beauty as always. The dark gray-blue traveling frock had the look of chiseled marble; her full face was stately and firm, her unclouded eyes were blue sky; not one stray wisp of hair broke the formal monotony of its dressing.

"Well," he exhaled genially. "May I smoke, in here?"

"Of course—"

"... Glad it's over with?"

"I suppose it is." There was a breath of coquetry in her look. This dried, when it awoke no response.

"Silly lot of foolishness people make over weddings, don't they?"

"Y-y-yes."

"Glad it's over with.... Good cigar—one of father's."

"Oh." There did not seem much else to say about it.

A seed that her friend Edith had planted had been working beneath the surface. Timidly the girl approached the subject. "You—you haven't ever gone with girls much, have you, Harvey? In college, I mean—or since."

"I should say not! I don't like 'em—" He blew out a passable ring, which was gone before it had quite assumed its shape. "Except you, of course. You're all right."

"I—I mean, there isn't anybody else . . . that you care for—" Her voice was low, although her gaze was level. "—That you care for now—"

"I should say not. What a notion!"

"I was just . . . wondering—"

"Not me. I just never liked 'em. I was too busy, in Johns Hopkins . . . then, medical. . . . Since then, too. Then Dad said it was time for me to get married. So— here we are."

"Oh."

After a little pause, they strolled forward for supper. The constraint gradually disappeared. She did not find him at all gallant—he regarded, for instance, the meal as something necessary to be started, conducted, and finished in a workmanlike manner. It was a pleasant relief to pass out of the sticky drizzle of sentimentality that Aunt Ethel had reveled in . . . other girls, too. He was matter-of-fact, Harvey. . . . She liked it.

Until the meal was over, it was the fare—their likes and dislikes—that they discussed. When they returned to the stateroom, there was a moment's embarrassment—the porter had made up the beds, without instructions. He knew newlyweds when he saw them! They mutually overlooked this, and sat down as best they might, and continued to talk. It was the details of the trip that were explained and exclaimed over, next; and then the prospects in his profession. There was a big opening in Baltimore, and an even finer one in Philadelphia, where his uncle lived. Of course, he was not really earning anything now; an intern hardly ever did. But with the five thousand a year his father had given them, to start on ... and when they had a son, they could expect more ... much more.

The prospect brightened him suddenly; her face borrowed the anticipatory pleasure.

"It's dark.... I suppose we might go to bed—pretty soon." His tone was casual; partly in defense—an undercurrent of bashful panic would not entirely down.

"I sup-p-pose so...." Her breath came more quickly; her breasts rose and fell without her will.

"There's one thing I ought to say," he began gravely. "I had always intended, as a mere matter of consideration to the woman I married, to—to start married life as easily as possible—"

"Yes—" She prompted his hesitancy.

"Say the first week or ten days—just to—to lie quietly beside her, you know ... sort of out of consideration—"

"—Yes."

"But, I don't know.... Unless it's necessary.... Dad's so anxious to have a grandson— You see how it is. So, unless you insist—"

She was suddenly breathless: she had shouldered the burden, and would not flinch now. "—No."

"That's better, I'm sure.... I'll go back to the smoker, then while you ... get ready.... Your bag's right under that seat; I saw it—"

As he retreated, a bit precipitately, she smiled at his consideration. He would not embarrass her, by opening the bag, full of its girl's nothings of lace and lingerie....

Hurrying through her preparations, she crept between the crinkly chill sheets. She lay breathless; a sudden little shiver went through her. Pretty cold, for May....

She began to realize that her haste had not been necessary: he did not come. The excitement mounted; she feared that it would keep her awake all night. Gradually the soft warmth of covers, the yielding comfort of the pillow, the purring rush of the train, made her drowse.

Suddenly her eyes spread wide. A click at the door—it opened. She pulled the sheet to her chin. He was back.

"All ready?" His tone was kindly. "I'll—I'll turn the light out, for a few minutes ... while I ..."

She lay in the darkness, watching the inscrutable

drawn shades. The train slowed for some village, stopped, commenced again.... She endeavored to reconstruct the scene outside in her imagination, to keep from thinking of things closer and more disquieting. Suddenly the light washed bright again. Her eyes were fascinated by his quiet lavender pajamas. She pretended not to see them; it did not seem quite proper....

"All ready?"

She smiled back faintly.

He turned, and fumbled under the seat. Then he came to the berth, holding a black something in his hand. He seated himself on the edge—she could see what he held now: it was his medical case, a small black satchel. It sprung open; there was the tingle of steel meeting steel, as his hands fumbled within. His brow corrugated, his expression was intense. At last he brought out a pair of shiny steel scissors. He examined it critically in the light. Her heart pounded unevenly, her breath choked.

The black bag was replaced on the floor. He came toward her, holding out the scissors like a weapon. "This won't hurt—" he began.

In speechless fascination her eyes, rounder and rounder, watched the menacing hands. Firmly he pulled back the covers; she shivered abruptly, and lay twitching. "—Just a membrane. Over in a minute. It won't hurt—"

With deft speed, almost too quick for her to sense his motions, he placed something white and folded beneath her. "It will bleed just a minute," he continued professionally. "There.... Just a little wider. Steady, now ... steady.... It won't hurt—"

A little sudden shriek. She bit her lips, to keep back any more. The room blurred and danced. It hadn't really hurt, much....

He was wiping off the scissors on a piece of gauze, and replacing them in the satchel. With soothing certainty he stanched the blood on a second piece.

"Good, clean job.... I think that's all right...."

The light was out again. She felt his stiff hand depress the edge of the bed.

There was a little quaver in her voice. "Won't you ... k-kiss me, Harvey?"

"Of course. . . . Afterward."

A few minutes later he kissed her good night. She felt the vast wall of him hunched up between her and the passage. His breathing grew regular, and roughened.

"Harvey—" She whispered it, suddenly afraid.

. . . Only the harsh regular breathing. . . .

Marriage! And this was it.

THE PARASITE

ARTHUR CONAN DOYLE

"And the most dreadful part of it all is my own loneliness. Here I sit in a commonplace English bow window, looking out upon a commonplace English street with its garish buses and its lounging policeman, and behind me there hangs a shadow which is out of all keeping with the age and place."

The preceding story was a long-forgotten tale by a little-known writer (or at least one unfamiliar to readers today). "The Parasite," however, is something different, a rarely seen work by a writer who is as famous right now as he has been for the past century and more—since 1888, to be exact, when "A Study in Scarlet" introduced to the ages the more-than-human and infinitely larger-than-life Sherlock Holmes.

Yet Sir Arthur Conan Doyle, trained as a medical man but preferring the career of author, did not stop at his tales of detection, though they proved, a bit to his dismay, to be his bread and butter. Writing energetically throughout his life, he produced historical and lost race novels, poems, and essays, as well as many macabre short stories treating themes of implacable cruelty, strange science, and supernatural horror.

As a signpost in Doyle's own personal development, "The Parasite," actually, is particularly interesting, dealing as it does with the uncertain territory of psychic phenomena. While the plot derives its tension from the anguish of the hapless narrator's diminishing skepticism as he is forced, most unpleasantly, to believe in powers he would otherwise have refused to credit, Doyle himself was soon to be a convert to spiritualist beliefs. At the time of the writing of "The Parasite," though, this was not yet the case, and here he was making sensationalistic use of unnatural abilities he then saw only as possessing the potential to introduce havoc into rational man's orderly existence.

Still, Doyle had been curious, at least, about spiritualist subjects since his university years, and in 1882—twelve years before this story was written—he and a friend, spurred on by reports issued by the Society of Psychical Research, had attempted to reproduce experiments proving the possibility of thought transference. They did not, of course, succeed. But subsequently he found himself increasingly fascinated by the claims of trance mediums, and after suffering the loss of his brother-in-law in the First World War, he became unshakably convinced that the mind could indeed receive messages from beyond the grave.

Thankfully, however, at the time he gave fictional birth to the sinister Miss Penclosa of "The Parasite," he had not yet arrived at such a stage of acceptance—otherwise, this already chilling tale of unrequited passion might have turned out even nastier.

I

March 24. The spring is fairly with us now. Outside my laboratory window the great chestnut tree is all covered with the big, glutinous, gummy buds, some of which have already begun to break into little green shuttlecocks. As you walk down the lanes you are conscious of the rich, silent forces of nature working all around you. The wet earth smells fruitful and luscious. Green shoots are peeping out everywhere. The twigs are stiff with their sap;

and the moist, heavy English air is laden with a faintly resinous perfume. Buds in the hedges, lambs beneath them—everywhere the work of reproduction going forward!

I can see it without, and I can feel it within. We also have our spring when the little arterioles dilate, the lymph flows in a brisker stream, the glands work harder, winnowing and straining. Every year nature readjusts the whole machine. I can feel the ferment in my blood at this very moment, and as the cool sunshine pours through my window I could dance about in it like a gnat. So I should, only that Charles Sadler would rush upstairs to know what was the matter. Besides, I must remember that I am Professor Gilroy. An old professor may afford to be natural, but when fortune has given one of the first chairs in the university to a man of four-and-thirty he must try and act the part consistently.

What a fellow Wilson is! If I could only throw the same enthusiasm into physiology that he does into psychology, I should become a Claude Bernard at the least. His whole life and soul and energy work to one end. He drops to sleep collating his results of the past day, and he wakes to plan his researches for the coming one. And yet, outside the narrow circle who follow his proceedings, he gets so little credit for it. Physiology is a recognized science. If I add even a brick to the edifice, everyone sees and applauds it. But Wilson is trying to dig the foundations for a science of the future. His work is underground and does not show. Yet he goes on uncomplainingly, corresponding with a hundred semimaniacs in the hope of finding one reliable witness, sifting a hundred lies on the chance of gaining one little speck of truth, collating old books, devouring new ones, experimenting, lecturing, trying to light up in others the fiery interest which is consuming him. I am filled with wonder and admiration when I think of him, and yet, when he asks me to associate myself with his researches, I am compelled to tell him that, in their present state, they offer little attraction to a man who is devoted to exact science. If he could show me something positive and objective, I might then be tempted to approach the question from its physiological side. So long as half his subjects are tainted with *charlatanerie* and the other half with hysteria we physiologists must content ourselves with the body and leave the mind to our descendants.

No doubt I am a materialist. Agatha says that I am a rank one. I tell her that is an excellent reason for shortening our engagement, since I am in such urgent need of her spirituality. And yet I may claim to be a curious example of the effect of education upon temperament, for by nature I am, unless I deceive myself, a highly psychic man. I was a nervous, sensitive boy, a dreamer, a somnambulist, full of impressions and intuitions. My black hair, my dark eyes, my thin, olive face, my tapering fingers, are all characteristic of my real temperament, and cause experts like Wilson to claim me as their own. But my brain is soaked with exact knowledge. I have trained myself to deal only with fact and with proof. Surmise and fancy have no place in my scheme of thought. Show me what I can see with my microscope, cut with my scalpel, weigh in my balance, and I will devote a lifetime to its investigation. But when you ask me to study feelings, impressions, suggestions, you ask me to do what is distasteful and even demoralizing. A departure from pure reason affects me like an evil smell or a musical discord.

Which is a very sufficient reason why I am a little loath to go to Professor Wilson's tonight. Still I feel that I could hardly get out of the invitation without positive rudeness; and now that Mrs. Marden and Agatha are going, of course I would not if I could. But I had rather meet them anywhere else. I know that Wilson would draw me into this nebulous semiscience of his if he could. In his enthusiasm he is perfectly impervious to hints or remonstrances. Nothing short of a positive quarrel will make him realize my aversion to the whole business. I have no doubt that he has some new mesmerist or clairvoyant or medium or trickster of some sort whom he is going to exhibit to us, for even his entertainments bear upon his hobby. Well, it will be a treat for Agatha, at any rate. She is interested in it, as woman usually is in whatever is vague and mystical and indefinite.

10:50 P.M. This diary-keeping of mine is, I fancy, the outcome of that scientific habit of mind about which I wrote this morning. I like to register impressions while they are fresh. Once a day at least I endeavor to define my own mental position. It is a useful piece of self-analysis, and has, I fancy, a steadying effect upon the character. Frankly, I must confess that my own needs what stiffening I can give it. I fear that, after all, much of my neurotic temperament survives, and that I am far from that cool, calm precision which characterizes Murdoch or Pratt-Haldane. Otherwise, why should the tomfoolery which I have witnessed this evening have set my nerves thrilling so that even now I am all unstrung? My only comfort is that neither Wilson nor Miss Penclosa nor even Agatha could have possibly known my weakness.

And what in the world was there to excite me? Nothing, or so little that it will seem ludicrous when I set it down.

The Mardens got to Wilson's before me. In fact, I was one of the last to arrive and found the room crowded. I had hardly time to say a word to Mrs. Marden and to Agatha, who was looking charming in white and pink, with glittering wheat-ears in her hair, when Wilson came twitching at my sleeve.

"You want something positive, Gilroy," said he, drawing me apart into a corner. "My dear fellow, I have a phenomenon—a phenomenon!"

I should have been more impressed had I not heard the same before. His sanguine spirit turns every firefly into a star.

"No possible question about the bona fides this time," said he, in answer, perhaps, to some little gleam of amusement in my eyes. "My wife has known her for many years. They both come from Trinidad, you know. Miss Penclosa has only been in England a month or two, and knows no one outside the university circle, but I assure you that the things she has told us suffice in themselves to establish clairvoyance upon an absolutely scientific basis. There is nothing like her, amateur or professional. Come and be introduced!"

I like none of these mystery mongers, but the amateur

least of all. With the paid performer you may pounce upon him and expose him the instant that you have seen through his trick. He is there to deceive you, and you are there to find him out. But what are you to do with the friend of your host's wife? Are you to turn on a light suddenly and expose her slapping a surreptitious banjo? Or are you to hurl cochineal over her evening frock when she steals round with her phosphorus bottle and her supernatural platitude? There would be a scene, and you would be looked upon as a brute. So you have your choice of being that or a dupe. I was in no very good humor as I followed Wilson to the lady.

Anyone less like my idea of a West Indian could not be imagined. She was a small, frail creature, well over forty, I should say, with a pale, peaky face, and hair of a very light shade of chestnut. Her presence was insignificant and her manner retiring. In any group of ten women she would have been the last whom one would have picked out. Her eyes were perhaps her most remarkable, and also, I am compelled to say, her least pleasant, feature. They were gray in color—gray with a shade of green—and their expression struck me as being decidedly furtive. I wonder if furtive is the word, or should I have said fierce? On second thoughts, feline would have expressed it better. A crutch leaning against the wall told me what was painfully evident when she rose: that one of her legs was crippled.

So I was introduced to Miss Penclosa, and it did not escape me that as my name was mentioned she glanced across at Agatha. Wilson had evidently been talking. And presently, no doubt, thought I, she will inform me by occult means that I am engaged to a young lady with wheat-ears in her hair. I wondered how much more Wilson had been telling her about me.

"Professor Gilroy is a terrible skeptic," said he; "I hope, Miss Penclosa, that you will be able to convert him."

She looked keenly up at me.

"Professor Gilroy is quite right to be skeptical if he has not seen anything convincing," said she. "I should have thought," she added, "that you would yourself have been an excellent subject."

"For what, may I ask?" said I.

"Well, for mesmerism, for example."

"My experience has been that mesmerists go for their subjects to those who are mentally unsound. All their results are vitiated, as it seems to me, by the fact that they are dealing with abnormal organisms."

"Which of these ladies would you say possessed a normal organism?" she asked. "I should like you to select the one who seems to you to have the best balanced mind. Should we say the girl in pink and white?—Miss Agatha Marden, I think the name is."

"Yes, I should attach weight to any results from her."

"I have never tried how far she is impressionable. Of course some people respond much more rapidly than others. May I ask how far your skepticism extends? I suppose that you admit the mesmeric sleep and the power of suggestion."

"I admit nothing, Miss Penclosa."

"Dear me, I thought science had got further than that. Of course I know nothing about the scientific side of it. I only know what I can do. You see the girl in red, for example, over near the Japanese jar. I shall will that she come across to us."

She bent forward as she spoke and dropped her fan upon the floor. The girl whisked round and came straight toward us, with an inquiring look upon her face, as if someone had called her.

"What do you think of that, Gilroy?" cried Wilson, in a kind of ecstasy.

I did not dare to tell him what I thought of it. To me it was the most barefaced, shameless piece of imposture that I had ever witnessed. The collusion and the signal had really been too obvious.

"Professor Gilroy is not satisfied," said she, glancing up at me with her strange little eyes. "My poor fan is to get the credit of that experiment. Well, we must try something else. Miss Marden, would you have any objection to my putting you off?"

"Oh, I should love it!" cried Agatha.

By this time all the company had gathered round us in a circle, the shirtfronted men, and the white-throated women, some awed, some critical, as though it were something between a religious ceremony and a conjurer's entertainment. A red velvet armchair had been pushed into the center, and Agatha lay back in it, a little flushed and trembling slightly from excitement. I could see it from the vibration of the wheat-ears. Miss Penclosa rose from her seat and stood over her, leaning upon her crutch.

And there was a change in the woman. She no longer seemed small or insignificant. Twenty years were gone from her age. Her eyes were shining, a tinge of color had come into her sallow cheeks, her whole figure had expanded. So I have seen a dull-eyed, listless lad change in an instant into briskness and life when given a task of which he felt himself master. She looked down at Agatha with an expression which I resented from the bottom of my soul—the expression with which a Roman empress might have looked at her kneeling slave. Then with a quick, commanding gesture she tossed up her arms and swept them slowly down in front of her.

I was watching Agatha narrowly. During three passes she seemed to be simply amused. At the fourth I observed a slight glazing of her eyes, accompanied by some dilation of her pupils. At the sixth there was a momentary rigor. At the seventh her lids began to droop. At the tenth her eyes were closed, and her breathing was slower and fuller than usual. I tried as I watched to preserve my scientific calm, but a foolish, causeless agitation convulsed me. I trust that I hid it, but I felt as a child feels in the dark. I could not have believed that I was still open to such weakness.

"She is in the trance," said Miss Penclosa.

"She is sleeping!" I cried.

"Wake her, then!"

I pulled her by the arm and shouted in her ear. She might have been dead for all the impression that I could make. Her body was there on the velvet chair. Her organs were acting—her heart, her lungs. But her soul! It had slipped from beyond our ken. Whither had it gone?

What power had dispossessed it? I was puzzled and disconcerted.

"So much for the mesmeric sleep," said Miss Penclosa. "As regards suggestion, whatever I may suggest Miss Marden will infallibly do, whether it be now or after she has awakened from her trance. Do you demand proof of it?"

"Certainly," said I.

"You shall have it." I saw a smile pass over her face, as though an amusing thought had struck her. She stooped and whispered earnestly into her subject's ear. Agatha, who had been so deaf to me, nodded her head as she listened.

"Awake!" cried Miss Penclosa, with a sharp tap of her crutch upon the floor. The eyes opened, the glazing cleared slowly away, and the soul looked out once more after its strange eclipse.

We went away early. Agatha was none the worse for her strange excursion, but I was nervous and unstrung, unable to listen to or answer the stream of comments which Wilson was pouring out for my benefit. As I bade her good night Miss Penclosa slipped a piece of paper into my hand.

"Pray forgive me," said she, "if I take means to overcome your skepticism. Open this note at ten o'clock tomorrow morning. It is a little private test."

I can't imagine what she means, but there is the note, and it shall be opened as she directs. My head is aching, and I have written enough for tonight. Tomorrow I dare say that what seems so inexplicable will take quite another complexion. I shall not surrender my convictions without a struggle.

March 25. I am amazed, confounded. It is clear that I must reconsider my opinion upon this matter. But first let me place on record what has occurred.

I had finished breakfast, and was looking over some diagrams with which my lecture is to be illustrated, when my housekeeper entered to tell me that Agatha was in my study and wished to see me immediately. I glanced at the clock and saw with surprise that it was only half-past nine.

When I entered the room, she was standing on the hearth rug facing me. Something in her pose chilled me and checked the words which were rising to my lips. Her veil was half down, but I could see that she was pale and that her expression was constrained.

"Austin," she said, "I have come to tell you that our engagement is at an end."

I staggered. I believe that I literally did stagger. I know that I found myself leaning against the bookcase for support.

"But—but—" I stammered. "This is very sudden, Agatha."

"Yes, Austin, I have come here to tell you that our engagement is at an end."

"But surely," I cried, "you will give me some reason! This is unlike you, Agatha. Tell me how I have been unfortunate enough to offend you."

"It is all over, Austin."

"But why? You must be under some delusion, Agatha. Perhaps you have been told some falsehood about me. Or you may have misunderstood something that I have said to you. Only let me know what it is, and a word may set it all right."

"We must consider it all at an end."

"But you left me last night without a hint at any disagreement. What could have occurred in the interval to change you so? It must have been something that happened last night. You have been thinking it over and you have disapproved of my conduct. Was it in mesmerism? Did you blame me for letting that woman exercise her power over you? You know that at the least sign I should have interfered."

"It is useless, Austin. All is over."

Her voice was cold and measured; her manner strangely formal and hard. It seemed to me that she was absolutely resolved not to be drawn into any argument or explanation. As for me, I was shaking with agitation, and I turned my face aside, so ashamed was I that she should see my want of control.

"You must know what this means to me!" I cried. "It is the blasting of all my hopes and the ruin of my life!

You surely will not inflict such a punishment upon me unheard. You will let me know what is the matter. Consider how impossible it would be for me, under any circumstances, to treat you so. For God's sake, Agatha, let me know what I have done!"

She walked past me without a word and opened the door.

"It is quite useless, Austin," said she. "You must consider our engagement at an end." An instant later she was gone, and before I could recover myself sufficiently to follow her, I heard the hall door close behind her.

I rushed into my room to change my coat, with the idea of hurrying round to Mrs. Marden's to learn from her what the cause of my misfortune might be. So shaken was I that I could hardly lace my boots. Never shall I forget those horrible ten minutes. I had just pulled on my overcoat when the clock upon the mantelpiece struck ten.

Ten! I associated the idea with Miss Penclosa's note. It was lying before me on the table, and I tore it open. It was scribbled in pencil in a peculiarly angular handwriting.

MY DEAR PROFESSOR GILROY [it said]: Pray excuse the personal nature of the test which I am giving you. Professor Wilson happened to mention the relations between you and my subject of this evening, and it struck me that nothing could be more convincing to you than if I were to suggest to Miss Marden that she should call upon you at half-past nine tomorrow morning and suspend your engagement for half an hour or so. Science is so exacting that it is difficult to give a satisfying test, but I am convinced that this at least will be an action which she would be most unlikely to do of her own free will. Forget anything that she may have said, as she has really nothing whatever to do with it, and will certainly not recollect anything about it. I write this note to shorten your anxiety, and to beg you to forgive me for the momentary unhappiness which my suggestion must have caused you.

Yours faithfully,

HELEN PENCLOSA.

Really, when I had read the note, I was too relieved to be angry. It was a liberty. Certainly it was a very great liberty indeed on the part of a lady whom I had only met once. But, after all, I had challenged her by my skepticism. It may have been, as she said, a little difficult to devise a test which would satisfy me.

And she had done that. There could be no question at all upon the point. For me hypnotic suggestion was finally established. It took its place from now onward as one of the facts of life. That Agatha, who of all women of my acquaintance has the best balanced mind, had been reduced to a condition of automatism appeared to be certain. A person at a distance had worked her as an engineer on the shore might guide a Brennan torpedo. A second soul had stepped in, as it were, had pushed her own aside, and had seized her nervous mechanism, saying: "I will work this for half an hour." And Agatha must have been unconscious as she came and as she returned. Could she make her way in safety through the streets in such a state? I put on my hat and hurried round to see if all was well with her.

Yes. She was at home. I was shown into the drawing room and found her sitting with a book upon her lap.

"You are an early visitor, Austin," said she, smiling.

"And you have been an even earlier one," I answered.

She looked puzzled. "What do you mean?" she asked.

"You have not been out today?"

"No, certainly not."

"Agatha," said I seriously, "would you mind telling me exactly what you have done this morning?"

She laughed at my earnestness.

"You've got on your professional look, Austin. See what comes of being engaged to a man of science. However, I will tell you, though I can't imagine what you want to know for. I got up at eight. I breakfasted at half-past. I came into this room at ten minutes past nine and began to read the *Memoirs of Mme. de Rémusat*. In a few minutes I did the French lady the bad compliment of dropping to sleep over her pages, and I did you, sir, the very flattering one of dreaming about you. It is only a few minutes since I woke up."

"And found yourself where you had been before?"

"Why, where else should I find myself?"

"Would you mind telling me, Agatha, what it was that you dreamed about me? It really is not mere curiosity on my part."

"I merely had a vague impression that you came into it. I cannot recall anything definite."

"If you have not been out today, Agatha, how is it that your shoes are dusty?"

A pained look came over her face.

"Really, Austin, I do not know what is the matter with you this morning. One would almost think that you doubted my word. If my boots are dusty, it must be, of course, that I have put on a pair which the maid had not cleaned."

It was perfectly evident that she knew nothing whatever about the matter, and I reflected that, after all, perhaps it was better that I should not enlighten her. It might frighten her, and could serve no good purpose that I could see. I said no more about it, therefore, and left shortly afterward to give my lecture.

But I am immensely impressed. My horizon of scientific possibilities has suddenly been enormously extended. I no longer wonder at Wilson's demonic energy and enthusiasm. Who would not work hard who had a vast virgin field ready to his hand? Why, I have known the novel shape of a nucleolus, or a trifling peculiarity of striped muscular fiber seen under a 300-diameter lens, fills me with exultation. How petty do such researches seem when compared with this one which strikes at the very roots of life and the nature of the soul! I had always looked upon spirit as a product of matter. The brain, I thought, secreted the mind, as the liver does the bile. But how can this be when I see mind working from a distance and playing upon matter as a musician might upon a violin? The body does not give rise to the soul, then, but is rather the rough instrument by which the spirit manifests itself. The windmill does not give rise to the wind, but only indicates it. It was opposed to my whole habit of thought, and yet it was undeniably possible and worthy of investigation.

And why should I not investigate it? I see that under yesterday's date I said, "If I could see something positive and objective, I might be tempted to approach it from the physiological aspect." Well, I have got my test. I shall be as good as my word. The investigation would, I am sure, be of immense interest. Some of my colleagues might look askance at it, for science is full of unreasoning prejudices, but if Wilson has the courage of his convictions, I can afford to have it also. I shall go to him tomorrow morning—to him and to Miss Penclosa. If she can show us so much, it is possible that she can show us more.

II

March 26. Wilson was, as I had anticipated, very exultant over my conversion, and Miss Penclosa was also demurely pleased at the result of her experiment. Strange what a silent, colorless creature she is save only when she exercises her power! Even talking about it gives her color and life. She seems to take a singular interest in me. I cannot help observing how her eyes follow me about the room.

We had the most interesting conversation about her own powers. It is just as well to put her views on record, though they cannot, of course, claim any scientific weight.

"You are on the very fringe of the subject," said she, when I had expressed wonder at the remarkable instance of suggestion which she had shown me. "I had no direct influence upon Miss Marden when she came round to you. I was not even thinking of her that morning. What I did was to set her mind as I might set the alarum of a clock so that at the hour named it would go off of its own accord. If six months instead of twelve hours had been suggested, it would have been the same."

"And if the suggestion had been to assassinate me?"

"She would most inevitably have done so."

"But this is a terrible power!" I cried.

"It is, as you say, a terrible power," she answered gravely, "and the more you know of it the more terrible will it seem to you."

"May I ask," said I, "what you meant when you said that this matter of suggestion is only at the fringe of it? What do you consider the essential?"

"I had rather not tell you."

I was surprised at the decision of her answer.

"You understand," said I, "that it is not out of curiosity I ask, but in the hope that I may find some scientific explanation for the facts with which you furnish me."

"Frankly, Professor Gilroy," said she, "I am not at all interested in science, nor do I care whether it can or cannot classify these powers."

"But I was hoping—"

"Ah, that is quite another thing. If you make it a personal matter," said she, with the pleasantest of smiles, "I shall be only too happy to tell you anything you wish to know. Let me see; what was it you asked me? Oh, about the further powers. Professor Wilson won't believe in them, but they are quite true all the same. For example, it is possible for an operator to gain complete command over his subject—presuming that the latter is a good one. Without any previous suggestion he may make him do whatever he likes."

"Without the subject's knowledge?"

"That depends. If the force were strongly exerted, he would know no more about it than Miss Marden did when she came round and frightened you so. Or, if the influence was less powerful, he might be conscious of what he was doing, but be quite unable to prevent himself from doing it."

"Would he have lost his own willpower, then?"

"It would be overridden by another stronger one."

"Have you ever exercised this power yourself?"

"Several times."

"Is your own will so strong, then?"

"Well, it does not entirely depend upon that. Many have strong wills which are not detachable from themselves. The thing is to have the gift of projecting it into another person and superseding his own. I find that the power varies with my own strength and health."

"Practically, you send your soul into another person's body."

"Well, you might put it that way."

"And what does your own body do?"

"It merely feels lethargic."

"Well, but is there no danger to your own health?" I asked.

"There might be a little. You have to be careful never to let your own consciousness absolutely go; otherwise, you might experience some difficulty in finding your way back again. You must always preserve the connection, as it were. I am afraid I express myself very badly, Professor Gilroy, but of course I don't know how to put these things in a scientific way. I am just giving you my own experiences and my own explanations."

Well, I read this over now at my leisure, and I marvel at myself! Is this Austin Gilroy, the man who has won his way to the front by his hard reasoning power and by his devotion to fact? Here I am gravely retailing the gossip of a woman who tells me how her soul may be projected from her body, and how, while she lies in a lethargy, she can control the actions of people at a distance. Do I accept it? Certainly not. She must prove and reprove before I yield a point. But if I am still a skeptic, I have at least ceased to be a scoffer. We are to have a sitting this evening, and she is to try if she can produce any mesmeric effect upon me. If she can, it will make an excellent starting point for our investigation. No one can accuse *me*, at any rate, of complicity. If she cannot, we must try and find some subject who will be like Cæsar's wife. Wilson is perfectly impervious.

10 P.M. I believe that I am on the threshold of an epoch-making investigation. To have the power of examining these phenomena from inside—to have an organism which will respond, and at the same time a brain which will appreciate and criticize—that is surely a unique advantage. I am quite sure that Wilson would give five years of his life to be as susceptible as I have proved myself to be.

There was no one present except Wilson and his wife. I was seated with my head leaning back, and Miss Penclosa, standing in front and a little to the left, used the same long, sweeping strokes as with Agatha. At each of them a warm current of air seemed to strike me, and to suffuse a thrill and glow all through me from head to foot. My eyes were fixed upon Miss Penclosa's face, but as I gazed the features seemed to blur and to fade away. I was conscious only of her own eyes looking down at me, gray, deep, inscrutable. Larger they grew and larger, until they changed suddenly into two mountain lakes toward which I seemed to be falling with horrible rapidity. I shuddered, and as I did so some deeper stratum of thought told me that the shudder represented the rigor which I had observed in Agatha. An instant later I struck the surface of the lakes, now joined into one, and down I went beneath the water with a fullness in my head and a buzzing in my ears. Down I went, down, down, and then with a swoop up again until I could see the light streaming brightly through the green water. I was almost at the surface when the word "Awake!" rang through my head, and, with a start, I found myself back in the armchair, with Miss Penclosa leaning on her crutch, and Wilson, his notebook in his hand, peeping over her shoulder. No heaviness or weariness was left behind. On the contrary, though it is only an hour or so since the experiment, I feel so wakeful that I am more inclined for my study than my bedroom. I see quite a vista of interesting experiments extending before us, and am all impatience to begin upon them.

March 27. A blank day, as Miss Penclosa goes with Wilson and his wife to the Suttons'. Have begun Binet and Ferré's *Animal Magnetism*. What strange, deep waters these are! Results, results, results—and the cause an absolute mystery. It is stimulating to the imagination, but I must be on my guard against that. Let us have no inferences nor deductions, and nothing but solid facts. I *know* that the mesmeric trance is true; I *know* that mesmeric suggestion is true; I *know* that I am myself sensitive to this force. That is my present position. I have a large new notebook which shall be devoted entirely to scientific detail.

Long talk with Agatha and Mrs. Marden in the evening about our marriage. We think that the summer vac. (the beginning of it) would be the best time for the wedding. Why should we delay? I grudge even those few months. Still, as Mrs. Marden says, there are a good many things to be arranged.

March 28. Mesmerized again by Miss Penclosa. Experience much the same as before, save that insensibility came on more quickly. See Notebook A for temperature of room, barometric pressure, pulse, and respiration as taken by Professor Wilson.

March 29. Mesmerized again. Details in Notebook A.

March 30. Sunday, and a blank day. I grudge any interruption of our experiments. At present they merely embrace the physical signs which go with slight, with complete, and with extreme insensibility. Afterward we hope to pass on to the phenomena of suggestion and of lucidity. Professors have demonstrated these things upon women at Nancy and at the Salpêtrière. It will be more convincing when a woman demonstrates it upon a professor, with a second professor as a witness. And that I should be the subject—I, the skeptic, the materialist! At least, I have shown that my devotion to science is greater than to my own personal consistency. The eating of our own words is the greatest sacrifice which truth ever requires of us.

My neighbor, Charles Sadler, the handsome young demonstrator of anatomy, came in this evening to return a volume of Virchow's *Archives* which I had lent him. I call him young, but, as a matter of fact, he is a year older than I am.

"I understand, Gilroy," said he, "that you are being experimented upon by Miss Penclosa.

"Well," he went on, when I had acknowledged it, "if I were you, I should not let it go any further. You will think me very impertinent, no doubt, but, nonetheless, I feel it to be my duty to advise you to have no more to do with her."

Of course I asked him why.

"I am so placed that I cannot enter into particulars as freely as I could wish," said he. "Miss Penclosa is the friend of my friend, and my position is a delicate one. I can only say this: that I have myself been the subject of some of the woman's experiments, and that they have left a most unpleasant impression upon my mind."

He could hardly expect me to be satisfied with that, and I tried hard to get something more definite out of him, but without success. Is it conceivable that he could be jealous at my having superseded him? Or is he one of those men of science who feel personally injured when facts run counter to their preconceived opinions? He cannot seriously suppose that because he has some vague grievance I am, therefore, to abandon a series of experiments which promise to be so fruitful of results. He appeared to be annoyed at the light way in which I treated his shadowy warnings, and we parted with some little coldness on both sides.

March 31. Mesmerized by Miss P.

April 1. Mesmerized by Miss P. (Notebook A.)

April 2. Mesmerized by Miss P. (Sphygmographic chart taken by Professor Wilson.)

April 3. It is possible that this course of mesmerism may be a little trying to the general constitution. Agatha says that I am thinner and darker under the eyes. I am conscious of a nervous irritability which I had not observed in myself before. The least noise, for example, makes me start, and the stupidity of a student causes me exasperation instead of amusement. Agatha wishes me to stop, but I tell her that every course of study is trying, and that one can never attain a result without paying some price for it. When she sees the sensation which my forthcoming paper on "The Relation Between Mind and Matter" may make, she will understand that it is worth a little nervous wear and tear. I should not be surprised if I got my F. R. S. over it.

Mesmerized again in the evening. The effect is produced more rapidly now, and the subjective visions are less marked. I keep full notes of each sitting. Wilson is leaving for town for a week or ten days, but we shall not interrupt the experiments, which depend for their value as much upon my sensations as on his observations.

April 4. I must be carefully on my guard. A complication has crept into our experiments which I had not reckoned upon. In my eagerness for scientific facts I have been foolishly blind to the human relations between Miss Penclosa and myself. I can write here what I would not breathe to a living soul. The unhappy woman appears to have formed an attachment for me.

I should not say such a thing, even in the privacy of my own intimate journal, if it had not come to such a pass that it is impossible to ignore it. For some time—that is, for the last week—there have been signs which I have brushed aside and refused to think of. Her brightness when I come, her dejection when I go, her eagerness that I should come often, the expression of her eyes, the tone of her voice—I tried to think that they meant nothing, and were, perhaps, only her ardent West Indian manner. But last night, as I awoke from the mesmeric sleep, I put out my hand, unconsciously, involuntarily, and clasped hers. When I came fully to myself, we were sitting with them locked, she looking up at me with an expectant smile. And the horrible thing was that I felt impelled to say what she expected me to say. What a false wretch I should have been! How I should have loathed myself today had I yielded to the temptation of that moment! But, thank God, I was strong enough to spring up and hurry from the room. I was rude, I fear, but I could not, no, I *could* not, trust myself another moment. I, a gentleman, a man of honor, engaged to one of the sweetest girls in England—and yet in a moment of reasonless passion I nearly professed love for this woman whom I hardly know. She is far older than myself and a cripple. It is monstrous, odious; and yet the impulse was so strong that had I stayed another minute in her presence, I should have committed myself. What was it? I have to teach others the workings of our organism, and what do I know of it myself? Was it the sudden upcropping of some lower stratum in my nature—a brutal primitive instinct suddenly asserting itself? I could almost believe the tales of obsession by evil spirits, so overmastering was the feeling.

Well, the incident places me in a most unfortunate position. On the one hand, I am very loath to abandon a series of experiments which have already gone so far, and which promise such brilliant results. On the other, if this unhappy woman has conceived a passion for me— But surely even now I must have made some hideous mistake. She, with her age and her deformity! It is impossible. And then she knew about Agatha. She understood how I was placed. She only smiled out of amusement, perhaps, when in my dazed state I seized her hand. It was my half-mesmerized brain which gave it a meaning, and sprang with such bestial swiftness to meet it. I wish I could persuade myself that it was indeed so. On the whole, perhaps, my wisest plan would be to postpone our other experiments until Wilson's return. I have written a note to Miss Penclosa, therefore, making no allusion to last night, but saying that a press of work would cause me to interrupt our sittings for a few days. She has answered, formally enough, to say that if I should change my mind I should find her at home at the usual hour.

10 P.M. Well, well, what a thing of straw I am! I am coming to know myself better of late, and the more I know the lower I fall in my own estimation. Surely I was not always so weak as this. At four o'clock I should have smiled had anyone told me that I should go to Miss Penclosa's tonight, and yet, at eight, I was at Wilson's door as usual. I don't know how it occurred. The influence of habit, I suppose. Perhaps there is a mesmeric craze as there is an opium craze, and I am a victim to it. I only know that as I worked in my study I became more and more uneasy. I fidgeted. I worried. I could not concentrate my mind upon the papers in front of me. And then, at last, almost before I knew what I was doing, I seized my hat and hurried round to keep my usual appointment.

We had an interesting evening. Mrs. Wilson was present during most of the time, which prevented the embarrassment which one at least of us must have felt. Miss

Penclosa's manner was quite the same as usual, and she expressed no surprise at my having come in spite of my note. There was nothing in her bearing to show that yesterday's incident had made any impression upon her, and so I am inclined to hope that I overrated it.

April 6 (evening). No, no, no, I did not overrate it. I can no longer attempt to conceal from myself that this woman has conceived a passion for me. It is monstrous, but it is true. Again, tonight, I awoke from the mesmeric trance to find my hand in hers, and to suffer that odious feeling which urges me to throw away my honor, my career, everything, for the sake of this creature who, as I can plainly see when I am away from her influence, possesses no single charm upon earth. But when I am near her, I do not feel this. She rouses something in me, something evil, something I had rather not think of. She paralyzes my better nature, too, at the moment when she stimulates my worse. Decidedly it is not good for me to be near her.

Last night was worse than before. Instead of flying I actually sat for some time with my hands in hers talking over the most intimate subjects with her. We spoke of Agatha, among other things. What could I have been dreaming of? Miss Penclosa said that she was conventional, and I agreed with her. She spoke once or twice in a disparaging way of her, and I did not protest. What a creature I have been!

Weak as I have proved myself to be, I am still strong enough to bring this sort of thing to an end. It shall not happen again. I have sense enough to fly when I cannot fight. From this Sunday night onward I shall never sit with Miss Penclosa again. Never! Let the experiments go, let the research come to an end; anything is better than facing this monstrous temptation which drags me so low. I have said nothing to Miss Penclosa, but I shall simply stay away. She can tell the reason without any words of mine.

April 7. Have stayed away as I said. It is a pity to ruin such an interesting investigation, but it would be a greater pity still to ruin my life, and I *know* that I cannot trust myself with that woman.

11 P.M. God help me! What is the matter with me? Am I going mad? Let me try and be calm and reason with myself. First of all I shall set down exactly what occurred.

It was nearly eight when I wrote the lines with which this day begins. Feeling strangely restless and uneasy, I left my rooms and walked round to spend the evening with Agatha and her mother. They both remarked that I was pale and haggard. About nine Professor Pratt-Haldane came in, and we played a game of whist. I tried hard to concentrate my attention upon the cards, but the feeling of restlessness grew and grew until I found it impossible to struggle against it. I simply *could* not sit still at the table. At last, in the very middle of a hand, I threw my cards down, and with some sort of an incoherent apology about having an appointment, I rushed from the room. As if in a dream I have a vague recollection of tearing through the hall, snatching my hat from the stand, and slamming the door behind me. As in a dream, too, I have the impression of the double line of gas lamps, and my bespattered boots tell me that I must have run down the middle of the road. It was all misty and strange and unnatural. I came to Wilson's house; I saw Mrs. Wilson and I saw Miss Penclosa. I hardly recall what we talked about, but I do remember that Miss P. shook the head of her crutch at me in a playful way, and accused me of being late and of losing interest in our experiments. There was no mesmerism, but I stayed some time and have only just returned.

My brain is quite clear again now, and I can think over what has occurred. It is absurd to suppose that it is merely weakness and force of habit. I tried to explain it in that way the other night, but it will no longer suffice. It is something much deeper and more terrible than that. Why, when I was at the Mardens' whist table, I was dragged away as if the noose of a rope had been cast round me. I can no longer disguise it from myself. The woman has her grip upon me. I am in her clutch. But I must keep my head and reason it out and see what is best to be done.

But what a blind fool I have been! In my enthusiasm over my research I have walked straight into the pit, although it lay gaping before me. Did she not herself warn me? Did she not tell me, as I can read in my own journal, that when she has acquired power over a subject she can make him do her will? And she has acquired that power over me. I am for the moment at the beck and call of this creature with the crutch. I must come when she wills it. I must do as she wills. Worst of all, I must feel as she wills. I loathe her and fear her, yet, while I am under the spell, she can doubtless make me love her.

There is some consolation in the thought, then, that those odious impulses for which I have blamed myself do not really come from me at all. They are all transferred from her, little as I could have guessed it at the time. I feel cleaner and lighter for the thought.

April 8. Yes, now, in broad daylight, writing coolly and with time for reflection, I am compelled to confirm everything which I wrote in my journal last night. I am in a horrible position, but, above all, I must not lose my head. I must pit my intellect against her powers. After all, I am no silly puppet, to dance at the end of a string. I have energy, brains, courage. For all her devil's tricks I may beat her yet. May! I *must*, or what is to become of me?

Let me try to reason it out! This woman, by her own explanation, can dominate my nervous organism. She can project herself into my body and take command of it. She has a parasite soul; yes, she is a parasite, a monstrous parasite. She creeps into my frame as the hermit crab does into the whelk's shell. I am powerless. What can I do? I am dealing with forces of which I know nothing. And I can tell no one of my trouble. They would set me down as a madman. Certainly, if it got noised abroad, the university would say that they had no need of a devil-ridden professor. And Agatha! No, no, I must face it alone.

III

I read over my notes of what the woman said when she spoke about her powers. There is one point which fills me with dismay. She implies that when the influence is slight the subject knows what he is doing, but cannot control himself, whereas when it is strongly exerted he is absolutely unconscious. Now, I have always known what I did, though less so last night than on the previous occasions. That seems to mean that she has never yet exerted her full powers upon me. Was ever a man so placed before?

Yes, perhaps there was, and very near me, too. Charles Sadler must know something of this! His vague words of warning take a meaning now. Oh, if I had only listened to him then, before I helped by these repeated sittings to forge the links of the chain which binds me! But I will see him today. I will apologize to him for having treated his warning so lightly. I will see if he can advise me.

4 P.M. No, he cannot. I have talked with him, and he showed such surprise at the first words in which I tried to express my unspeakable secret that I went no further. As far as I can gather (by hints and inferences rather than by any statement), his own experience was limited to some words or looks such as I have myself endured. His abandonment of Miss Penclosa is in itself a sign that he was never really in her toils. Oh, if he only knew his escape! He has to thank his phlegmatic Saxon temperament for it. I am black and Celtic, and this hag's clutch is deep in my nerves. Shall I ever get it out? Shall I ever be the same man that I was just one short fortnight ago?

Let me consider what I had better do. I cannot leave the university in the middle of the term. If I were free, my course would be obvious. I should start at once and travel in Persia. But would she allow me to start? And could her influence not reach me in Persia, and bring me back to within touch of her crutch? I can only find out the limits of this hellish power by my own bitter experience. I will fight and fight and fight—and what can I do more?

I know very well that about eight o'clock tonight that craving for her society, that irresistible restlessness, will come upon me. How shall I overcome it? What shall I do? I must make it impossible for me to leave the room. I shall lock the door and throw the key out of the window. But, then, what am I to do in the morning? Never mind about the morning. I must at all costs break this chain which holds me.

April 9. Victory! I have done splendidly! At seven o'clock last night I took a hasty dinner, and then locked myself up in my bedroom and dropped the key into the garden. I chose a cheery novel, and lay in bed for three hours trying to read it, but really in a horrible state of trepidation, expecting every instant that I should become conscious of the impulse. Nothing of the sort occurred, however, and I awoke this morning with the feeling that a black nightmare had been lifted off me. Perhaps the creature realized what I had done, and understood that it was useless to try to influence me. At any rate, I have beaten her once, and if I can do it once, I can do it again.

It was most awkward about the key in the morning. Luckily, there was an undergardener below, and I asked him to throw it up. No doubt he thought I had just dropped it. I will have doors and windows screwed up and six stout men to hold me down in my bed before I will surrender myself to be hag-ridden in this way.

I had a note from Mrs. Marden this afternoon asking me to go round and see her. I intended to do so in any case, but had not expected to find bad news waiting for me. It seems that the Armstrongs, from whom Agatha has expectations, are due home from Adelaide in the *Aurora*, and that they have written to Mrs. Marden and her to meet them in town. They will probably be away for a month or six weeks, and as the *Aurora* is due on Wednesday, they must go at once—tomorrow, if they are ready in time. My consolation is that when we meet again there will be no more parting between Agatha and me.

"I want you to do one thing, Agatha," said I, when we were alone together. "If you should happen to meet Miss Penclosa, either in town or here, you must promise me never again to allow her to mesmerize you."

Agatha opened her eyes.

"Why, it was only the other day that you were saying how interesting it all was, and how determined you were to finish your experiments."

"I know, but I have changed my mind since then."

"And you won't have it anymore?"

"No."

"I am so glad, Austin. You can't think how pale and worn you have been lately. It was really our principal objection to going to London now that we did not wish to leave you when you were so pulled down. And your manner has been so strange occasionally—especially that night when you left poor Professor Pratt-Haldane to play dummy. I am convinced that these experiments are very bad for your nerves."

"I think so, too, dear."

"And for Miss Penclosa's nerves as well. You have heard that she is ill?"

"No."

"Mrs. Wilson told us so last night. She described it as a nervous fever. Professor Wilson is coming back this week, and of course Mrs. Wilson is very anxious that Miss Penclosa should be well again then, for he has quite a program of experiments which he is anxious to carry out."

I was glad to have Agatha's promise, for it was enough that this woman should have one of us in her clutch. On the other hand, I was disturbed to hear about Miss Penclosa's illness. It rather discounts the victory which I appeared to win last night. I remember that she said that loss of health interfered with her power. That may be why I was able to hold my own so easily. Well, well, I must take the same precautions tonight and see what comes of it. I am childishly frightened when I think of her.

April 10. All went very well last night. I was amused at the gardener's face when I had again to hail him this morning and to ask him to throw up my key. I shall get a name among the servants if this sort of thing goes on. But the great point is that I stayed in my room without the slightest inclination to leave it. I do believe that I am shaking myself clear of this incredible bond—or is it only that the woman's power is in abeyance until she recovers her strength? I can but pray for the best.

The Mardens left this morning, and the brightness

seems to have gone out of the spring sunshine. And yet
it is very beautiful also as it gleams on the green chestnuts opposite my windows, and gives a touch of gaiety
to the heavy, lichen-mottled walls of the old colleges.
How sweet and gentle and soothing is Nature! Who
would think that there lurked in her also such vile forces,
such odious possibilities! For of course I understand that
this dreadful thing which has sprung out at me is neither
supernatural nor even preternatural. No, it is a natural
force which this woman can use and society is ignorant
of. The mere fact that it ebbs with her strength shows
how entirely it is subject to physical laws. If I had time,
I might probe it to the bottom and lay my hands upon
its antidote. But you cannot tame the tiger when you
are beneath his claws. You can but try to writhe away
from him. Ah, when I look in the glass and see my own
dark eyes and clear-cut Spanish face, I long for a vitriol
splash or a bout of the smallpox. One or the other might
have saved me from this calamity.

I am inclined to think that I may have trouble tonight.
There are two things which make me fear so. One is
that I met Mrs. Wilson in the street, and that she tells
me that Miss Penclosa is better, though still weak. I find
myself wishing in my heart that the illness had been her
last. The other is that Professor Wilson comes back in a
day or two, and his presence would act as a constraint
upon her. I should not fear our interviews if a third
person were present. For both these reasons I have a
presentiment of trouble tonight, and I shall take the
same precautions as before.

April 10. No, thank God, all went well last night. I
really could not face the gardener again. I locked my
door and thrust the key underneath it, so that I had to
ask the maid to let me out in the morning. But the precaution was really not needed, for I never had any inclination to go out at all. Three evenings in succession at
home! I am surely near the end of my troubles, for Wilson will be home again either today or tomorrow. Shall
I tell him of what I have gone through or not? I am
convinced that I should not have the slightest sympathy
from him. He would look upon me as an interesting

case, and read a paper about me at the next meeting of the Psychical Society, in which he would gravely discuss the possibility of my being a deliberate liar, and weigh it against the chances of my being in an early stage of lunacy. No, I shall get no comfort out of Wilson.

I am feeling wonderfully fit and well. I don't think I ever lectured with greater spirit. Oh, if I could only get this shadow off my life, how happy I should be! Young, fairly wealthy, in the front rank of my profession, engaged to a beautiful and charming girl—have I not everything which a man could ask for? Only one thing to trouble me, but what a thing it is!

Midnight. I shall go mad. Yes, that will be the end of it. I shall go mad. I am not far from it now. My head throbs as I rest it on my hot hand. I am quivering all over like a scared horse. Oh, what a night I have had! And yet I have some cause to be satisfied also.

At the risk of becoming the laughingstock of my own servant, I again slipped my key under the door, imprisoning myself for the night. Then, finding it too early to go to bed, I lay down with my clothes on and began to read one of Dumas's novels. Suddenly I was gripped—gripped and dragged from the couch. It is only thus that I can describe the overpowering nature of the force which pounced upon me. I clawed at the coverlet. I clung to the woodwork. I believe that I screamed out in my frenzy. It was all useless, hopeless. I *must* go. There was no way out of it. It was only at the outset that I resisted. The force soon became too overmastering for that. I thank goodness that there were no watchers there to interfere with me. I could not have answered for myself if there had been. And besides the determination to get out, there came to me, also, the keenest and coolest judgment in choosing my means. I lit a candle and endeavored, kneeling in front of the door, to pull the key through with the feather end of a quill pen. It was just too short and pushed it farther away. Then with quiet persistence I got a paper knife out of one of the drawers, and with that I managed to draw the key back. I opened the door, stepped into my study, took a photograph of myself from the bureau, wrote something across it, placed it in the inside pocket of my coat, and then started off for Wilson's.

It was all wonderfully clear, and yet disassociated from the rest of my life, as the incidents of even the most vivid dream might be. A peculiar double consciousness possessed me. There was the predominant alien will, which was bent upon drawing me to the side of its owner, and there was the feebler protesting personality, which I recognized as being myself, tugging feebly at the overmastering impulse as a led terrier might at its chain. I can remember recognizing these two conflicting forces, but I recall nothing of my walk, nor of how I was admitted to the house.

Very vivid, however, is my recollection of how I met Miss Penclosa. She was reclining on the sofa in the little boudoir in which our experiments had usually been carried out. Her head was rested on her hand, and a tiger-skin rug had been partly drawn over her. She looked up expectantly as I entered, and as the lamplight fell upon her face, I could see that she was very pale and thin, with dark hollows under her eyes. She smiled at me, and pointed to a stool beside her. It was with her left hand that she pointed, and I, running eagerly forward, seized it—I loathe myself as I think of it—and pressed it passionately to my lips. Then, seating myself upon the stool, and still retaining her hand, I gave her the photograph which I had brought with me, and talked and talked and talked—of my love for her, of my grief over her illness, of my joy at her recovery, of the misery it was to me to be absent a single evening from her side. She lay quietly looking down at me with imperious eyes and her provocative smile. Once I remember that she passed her hand over my hair as one caresses a dog; and it gave me pleasure—the caress. I thrilled under it. I was her slave, body and soul, and for the moment I rejoiced in my slavery.

And then came the blessed change. Never tell me that there is not a Providence! I was on the brink of perdition. My feet were on the edge. Was it a coincidence that at that very instant help should come? No, no, no; there is a Providence, and its hand has drawn me back. There is something in the universe stronger than this devil woman with her tricks. Ah, what a balm to my heart it is to think so!

As I looked up at her I was conscious of a change in her. Her face, which had been pale before, was now ghastly. Her eyes were dull, and the lids drooped heavily over them. Above all, the look of serene confidence had gone from her features. Her mouth had weakened. Her forehead had puckered. She was frightened and undecided. And as I watched the change my own spirit fluttered and struggled, trying hard to tear itself from the grip which held it—a grip which, from moment to moment, grew less secure.

"Austin," she whispered, "I have tried to do too much. I was not strong enough. I have not recovered yet from my illness. But I could not live longer without seeing you. You won't leave me, Austin? This is only a passing weakness. If you will only give me five minutes, I shall be myself again. Give me the small decanter from the table in the window."

But I had regained my soul. With her waning strength the influence had cleared away from me and left me free. And I was aggressive—bitterly, fiercely aggressive. For once at least I could make this woman understand what my real feelings toward her were. My soul was filled with a hatred as bestial as the love against which it was a reaction. It was the savage, murderous passion of the revolted serf. I could have taken the crutch from her side and beaten her face in with it. She threw her hands up, as if to avoid a blow, and cowered away from me into the corner of the settee.

"The brandy!" she gasped. "The brandy!"

I took the decanter and poured it over the roots of a palm in the window. Then I snatched the photograph from her hand and tore it into a hundred pieces.

"You vile woman," I said, "if I did my duty to society, you would never leave this room alive!"

"I love you, Austin; I love you!" she wailed.

"Yes," I cried, "and Charles Sadler before. And how many others before that?"

"Charles Sadler!" she gasped. "He has spoken to you?

So, Charles Sadler, Charles Sadler!" Her voice came through her white lips like a snake's hiss.

"Yes, I know you, and others shall know you, too. You shameless creature! You knew how I stood. And yet you used your vile power to bring me to your side. You may, perhaps, do so again, but at least you will remember that you have heard me say that I love Miss Marden from the bottom of my soul, and that I loathe you, abhor you! The very sight of you and the sound of your voice fill me with horror and disgust. The thought of you is repulsive. That is how I feel toward you, and if it pleases you by your tricks to draw me again to your side as you have done tonight, you will at least, I should think, have little satisfaction in trying to make a lover out of a man who has told you his real opinion of you. You may put what words you will into my mouth, but you cannot help remembering—"

I stopped, for the woman's head had fallen back, and she had fainted. She could not bear to hear what I had to say to her! What a glow of satisfaction it gives me to think that, come what may, in the future she can never misunderstand my true feelings toward her. But what will occur in the future? What will she do next? I dare not think of it. Oh, if only I could hope that she will leave me alone! But when I think of what I said to her— Never mind; I have been stronger than she for once.

April 11. I hardly slept last night, and found myself in the morning so unstrung and feverish that I was compelled to ask Pratt-Haldane to do my lecture for me. It is the first that I have ever missed. I rose at midday, but my head is aching, my hands quivering, and my nerves in a pitiable state.

Who should come round this evening but Wilson. He has just come back from London, where he has lectured, read papers, convened meetings, exposed a medium, conducted a series of experiments on thought transference, entertained Professor Richet of Paris, spent hours gazing into a crystal, and obtained some evidence as to the passage of matter through matter. All this he poured into my ears in a single gust.

"But you!" he cried at last. "You are not looking well.

And Miss Penclosa is quite prostrated today. How about the experiments?"

"I have abandoned them."

"Tut, tut! Why?"

"The subject seems to me to be a dangerous one."

Out came his big brown notebook.

"This is of great interest," said he. "What are your grounds for saying that it is a dangerous one? Please give your facts in chronological order, with approximate dates and names of reliable witnesses with their permanent addresses."

"First of all," I asked, "would you tell me whether you have collected any cases where the mesmerist has gained a command over the subject and has used it for evil purposes?"

"Dozens!" he cried exultantly. "Crime by suggestion—"

"I don't mean suggestion. I mean where a sudden impulse comes from a person at a distance—an uncontrollable impulse."

"Obsession!" he shrieked, in an ecstasy of delight. "It is the rarest condition. We have eight cases, five well attested. You don't mean to say—" His exultation made him hardly articulate.

"No, I don't," said I. "Good evening! You will excuse me, but I am not very well tonight." And so at last I got rid of him, still brandishing his pencil and his notebook. My troubles may be bad to bear, but at least it is better to hug them to myself than to have myself exhibited by Wilson, like a freak at a fair. He has lost sight of human beings. Everything to him is a case and a phenomenon. I will die before I speak to him again upon the matter.

April 12. Yesterday was a blessed day of quiet, and I enjoyed an uneventful night. Wilson's presence is a great consolation. What can the woman do now? Surely, when she has heard me say what I have said, she will conceive the same disgust for me which I have for her. She could not, no, she *could* not, desire to have a lover who had insulted her so. No, I believe I am free from her love—but how about her hate? Might she not use these powers of hers for revenge? Tut! why should I frighten myself over shadows? She will forget about me, and I shall forget about her, and all will be well.

April 13. My nerves have quite recovered their tone. I really believe that I have conquered the creature. But I must confess to living in some suspense. She is well again, for I hear that she was driving with Mrs. Wilson in the High Street in the afternoon.

April 14. I do wish I could get away from the place altogether. I shall fly to Agatha's side the very day that the term closes. I suppose it is pitiably weak of me, but this woman gets upon my nerves most terribly. I have seen her again, and I have spoken with her.

It was just after lunch, and I was smoking a cigarette in my study, when I heard the step of my servant Murray in the passage. I was languidly conscious that a second step was audible behind, and had hardly troubled myself to speculate who it might be, when suddenly a slight noise brought me out of my chair with my skin creeping with apprehension. I had never particularly observed before what sort of sound the tapping of a crutch was, but my quivering nerves told me that I heard it now in the sharp wooden clack which alternated with the muffled thud of the footfall. Another instant and my servant had shown her in.

I did not attempt the usual conventions of society, nor did she. I simply stood with the smoldering cigarette in my hand, and gazed at her. She in her turn looked silently at me, and at her look I remember how in these very pages I had tried to define the expression of her eyes, whether they were furtive or fierce. Today they were fierce—coldly and inexorably so.

"Well," said she at last, "are you still of the same mind as when I saw you last?"

"I have always been of the same mind."

"Let us understand each other, Professor Gilroy," said she slowly. "I am not a very safe person to trifle with, as you should realize by now. It was you who asked me to enter into a series of experiments with you, it was you who won my affections, it was you who professed your love for me, it was you who brought me your own photograph with words of affection upon it, and, finally, it was you who on the very same evening thought fit to insult me most outrageously, addressing me as no man has ever dared to speak to me yet. Tell me that those words came from you in a moment of passion and I am prepared to forget and to forgive them. You did not mean what you said, Austin? You do not really hate me?"

I might have pitied this deformed woman—such a longing for love broke suddenly through the menace of her eyes. But then I thought of what I had gone through, and my heart set like flint.

"If ever you heard me speak of love," said I, "you know very well that it was your voice which spoke, and not mine. The only words of truth which I have ever been able to say to you are those which you heard when last we met."

"I know. Someone has set you against me. It was he!" She tapped with her crutch upon the floor. "Well, you know very well that I could bring you this instant crouching like a spaniel to my feet. You will not find me again in my hour of weakness, when you can insult me with impunity. Have a care what you are doing, Professor Gilroy. You stand in a terrible position. You have not yet realized the hold which I have upon you."

I shrugged my shoulders and turned away.

"Well," said she, after a pause, "if you despise my love, I must see what can be done with fear. You smile, but the day will come when you will come screaming to me for pardon. Yes, you will grovel on the ground before me, proud as you are, and you will curse the day that ever you turned me from your best friend into your most bitter enemy. Have a care, Professor Gilroy!" I saw a white hand shaking in the air, and a face which was scarcely human, so convulsed was it with passion. An instant later she was gone, and I heard the quick hobble and tap receding down the passage.

But she has left a weight upon my heart. Vague presentiments of coming misfortune lie heavy upon me. I try in vain to persuade myself that these are only words of empty anger. I can remember those relentless eyes too clearly to think so. What shall I do—ah, what shall I do? I am no longer master of my own soul. At any moment this loathsome parasite may creep into me, and then—I must tell someone my hideous secret—I must tell it or go mad. If I had someone to sympathize and advise! Wilson is out of the question. Charles Sadler would understand me only so far as his own experience carries him. Pratt-Haldane! He is a well-balanced man, a man of great common sense and resource. I will go to him. I will tell him everything. God grant that he may be able to advise me!

IV

6:45 P.M. No, it is useless. There is no human help for me; I must fight this out single-handed. Two courses lie before me. I might become this woman's lover. Or I must endure such persecutions as she can inflict upon me. Even if none come, I shall live in a hell of apprehension. But she may torture me, she may drive me mad, she may kill me: I will never, never, never give in. What can she inflict which would be worse than the loss of Agatha, and the knowledge that I am a perjured liar, and have forfeited the name of gentleman?

Pratt-Haldane was most amiable, and listened with all politeness to my story. But when I looked at his heavyset features, his slow eyes, and the ponderous study furniture which surrounded him, I could hardly tell him what I had come to say. It was all so substantial, so material. And, besides, what would I myself have said a short month ago if one of my colleagues had come to me with a story of demonic possession? Perhaps I should have been less patient than he was. As it was, he took notes of my statement, asked me how much tea I drank, how many hours I slept, whether I had been overworking much, had I had sudden pains in the head, evil dreams, singing in the ears, flashes before the eyes—all questions which pointed to his belief that brain congestion was at the bottom of my trouble. Finally he dismissed me with a great many platitudes about open-air exercise, and avoidance of nervous excitement. His prescription, which was for chloral and bromide, I rolled up and threw into the gutter.

No, I can look for no help from any human being. If I consult any more, they may put their heads together and I may find myself in an asylum. I can but grip my courage with both hands, and pray that an honest man may not be abandoned.

April 15. It is the sweetest spring within the memory of man. So green, so mild, so beautiful! Ah, what a contrast between nature without and my own soul so torn with doubt and terror! It has been an uneventful day, but I know that I am on the edge of an abyss. I know it, and yet I go on with the routine of my life. The one bright spot is that Agatha is happy and well and out of all danger. If this creature had a hand on each of us, what might she not do?

April 16. The woman is ingenious in her torments. She knows how fond I am of my work, and how highly my lectures are thought of. So it is from that point that she now attacks me. It will end, I can see, in my losing my professorship, but I will fight to the finish. She shall not drive me out of it without a struggle.

I was not conscious of any change during my lecture this morning save that for a minute or two I had a dizziness and swimminess which rapidly passed away. On the contrary, I congratulated myself upon having made my subject (the functions of the red corpuscles) both interesting and clear. I was surprised, therefore, when a student came into my laboratory immediately after the lecture, and complained of being puzzled by the discrepancy between my statements and those in the textbooks. He showed me his notebook, in which I was reported as having in one portion of the lecture championed the most outrageous and unscientific heresies. Of course I denied it, and declared that he had misunderstood me, but on comparing his notes with those of his companions, it became clear that he was right, and that I really had made some most preposterous statements. Of course I shall explain it away as being the result of a moment of aberration, but I feel only too sure that it will be the first of a series. It is but a month now to the end of the session, and I pray that I may be able to hold out until then.

April 26. Ten days have elapsed since I have had the heart to make any entry in my journal. Why should I record my own humiliation and degradation? I had vowed never to open it again. And yet the force of habit is strong, and here I find myself taking up once more the record of my own dreadful experiences—in much the same spirit in which a suicide has been known to take notes of the effects of the poison which killed him.

Well, the crash which I had foreseen has come—and that no further back than yesterday. The university authorities have taken my lectureship from me. It has been done in the most delicate way, purporting to be a temporary measure to relieve me from the effects of overwork, and to give me the opportunity of recovering my health. Nonetheless, it has been done, and I am no longer Professor Gilroy. The laboratory is still in my charge, but I have little doubt that that also will soon go.

The fact is that my lectures had become the laughing-stock of the university. My class was crowded with students who came to see and hear what the eccentric professor would do or say next. I cannot go into the detail of my humiliation. Oh, that devilish woman! There is no depth of buffoonery and imbecility to which she has not forced me. I would begin my lecture clearly and well, but always with the sense of coming eclipse. Then as I felt the influence I would struggle against it, striving with clenched hands and beads of sweat upon my brow to get the better of it, while the students, hearing my incoherent words and watching my contortions, would roar with laughter at the antics of their professor. And then, when she had once fairly mastered me, out would come the most outrageous things—silly jokes, sentiments as though I were proposing a toast, snatches of ballads, personal abuse even against some member of my class. And then in a moment my brain would clear again, and my lecture would proceed decorously to the end. No wonder that my conduct has been the talk of the colleges. No wonder that the University Senate has been compelled to take official notice of such a scandal. Oh, that devilish woman!

And the most dreadful part of it all is my own loneliness. Here I sit in a commonplace English bow window, looking out upon a commonplace English street with its garish buses and its lounging policeman, and behind me there hangs a shadow which is out of all keeping with the age and place. In the home of knowledge I am weighed down and tortured by a power of which science knows nothing. No magistrate would listen to me. No paper would discuss my case. No doctor would believe my symptoms. My own most intimate friends would only look upon it as a sign of brain derangement. I am out of all touch with my kind. Oh, that devilish woman! Let her have a care! She may push me too far. When the law cannot help a man, he may make a law for himself.

She met me in the High Street yesterday evening and spoke to me. It was as well for her, perhaps, that it was not between the hedges of a lonely country road. She asked me with her cold smile whether I had been chastened yet. I did not deign to answer her. "We must try another turn of the screw," said she. Have a care, my lady, have a care! I had her at my mercy once. Perhaps another chance may come.

April 28. The suspension of my lectureship has had the effect also of taking away her means of annoying me, and so I have enjoyed two blessed days of peace. After all, there is no reason to despair. Sympathy pours in to me from all sides, and everyone agrees that it is my devotion to science and the arduous nature of my researches which have shaken my nervous system. I have had the kindest message from the council advising me to travel abroad, and expressing the confident hope that I may be able to resume all my duties by the beginning of the summer term. Nothing could be more flattering than their allusions to my career and to my services to the university. It is only in misfortune that one can test one's own popularity. This creature may weary of tormenting me, and then all may yet be well. May God grant it!

April 29. Our sleepy little town has had a small sensation. The only knowledge of crime which we ever have is when a rowdy undergraduate breaks a few lamps or comes to blows with a policeman. Last night, however, there was an attempt made to break into the branch of the Bank of England, and we are all in a flutter in consequence.

Parkenson, the manager, is an intimate friend of mine, and I found him very much excited when I walked round there after breakfast. Had the thieves broken into the counting house, they would still have had the safes to reckon with, so that the defense was considerably stronger than the attack. Indeed, the latter does not appear to have ever been very formidable. Two of the lower windows have marks as if a chisel or some such instrument had been pushed under them to force them open. The police should have a good clue, for the woodwork had been done with green paint only the day before, and from the smears it is evident that some of it has found its way on to the criminal's hands or clothes.

4:30 P.M. Ah, that accursed woman! That thrice accursed woman! Never mind! She shall not beat me! No, she shall not! But, oh, the she-devil! She has taken my professorship. Now she would take my honor. Is there nothing I can do against her, nothing save— Ah, but, hard pushed as I am, I cannot bring myself to think of that!

It was about an hour ago that I went into my bedroom, and was brushing my hair before the glass, when suddenly my eyes lit upon something which left me so sick and cold that I sat down upon the edge of the bed and began to cry. It is many a long year since I shed tears, but all my nerve was gone, and I could but sob and sob in impotent grief and anger. There was my house jacket, the coat I usually wear after dinner, hanging on its peg by the wardrobe, with the right sleeve thickly crusted from wrist to elbow with daubs of green paint.

So this was what she meant by another turn of the screw! She had made a public imbecile of me. Now she would brand me as a criminal. This time she has failed. But how about the next? I dare not think of it—and of

Agatha and my poor old mother! I wish that I were dead!

Yes, this is the other turn of the screw. And this is also what she meant, no doubt, when she said that I had not realized yet the power she has over me. I look back at my account of my conversation with her, and I see how she declared that with a slight exertion of her will her subject would be conscious, and with a stronger one unconscious. Last night I was unconscious. I could have sworn that I slept soundly in my bed without so much as a dream. And yet those stains tell me that I dressed, made my way out, attempted to open the bank windows, and returned. Was I observed? Is it possible that some one saw me do it and followed me home? Ah, what a hell my life has become! I have no peace, no rest. But my patience is nearing its end.

10 P.M. I have cleaned my coat with turpentine. I do not think that anyone could have seen me. It was with my screwdriver that I made the marks. I found it all crusted with paint, and I have cleaned it. My head aches as if it would burst, and I have taken five grains of antipyrine. If it were not for Agatha, I should have taken fifty and had an end of it.

May 3. Three quiet days. This hell fiend is like a cat with a mouse. She lets me loose only to pounce upon me again. I am never so frightened as when everything is still. My physical state is deplorable—perpetual hiccough and ptosis of the left eyelid.

I have heard from the Mardens that they will be back the day after tomorrow. I do not know whether I am glad or sorry. They were safe in London. Once here they may be drawn into the miserable network in which I am myself struggling. And I must tell them of it. I cannot marry Agatha so long as I know that I am not responsible for my own actions. Yes, I must tell them, even if it brings everything to an end between us.

Tonight is the university ball, and I must go. God knows I never felt less in the humor for festivity, but I must not have it said that I am unfit to appear in public. If I am seen there, and have speech with some of the elders of the university it will go a long way toward showing them that it would be unjust to take my chair away from me.

11:30 P.M. I have been to the ball. Charles Sadler and I went together, but I have come away before him. I shall wait up for him, however, for, indeed, I fear to go to sleep these nights. He is a cheery, practical fellow, and a chat with him will steady my nerves. On the whole, the evening was a great success. I talked to everyone who has influence, and I think that I made them realize that my chair is not vacant quite yet. The creature was at the ball—unable to dance, of course, but sitting with Mrs. Wilson. Again and again her eyes rested upon me. They were almost the last things I saw before I left the room. Once, as I sat sideways to her, I watched her, and saw that her gaze was following someone else. It was Sadler, who was dancing at the time with the second Miss Thurston. To judge by her expression, it is well for him that he is not in her grip as I am. He does not know the escape he has had. I think I hear his step in the street now, and I will go down and let him in. If he will—

May 4. Why did I break off in this way last night? I never went downstairs, after all—at least, I have no recollection of doing so. But, on the other hand, I cannot remember going to bed. One of my hands is greatly swollen this morning, and yet I have no remembrance of injuring it yesterday. Otherwise, I am feeling all the better for last night's festivity. But I cannot understand how it is that I did not meet Charles Sadler when I so fully intended to do so. Is it possible— My God, it is only too probable! Has she been leading me some devil's dance again? I will go down to Sadler and ask him.

Midday. The thing has come to a crisis. My life is not worth living. But, if I am to die, then she shall come also. I will not leave her behind, to drive some other man mad as she has me. No, I have come to the limit of my endurance. She has made me as desperate and dangerous a man as walks the earth. God knows I have never had the heart to hurt a fly, and yet, if I had my hands now upon that woman, she should never leave this room alive. I shall see her this very day, and she shall learn what she has to expect from me.

I went to Sadler and found him, to my surprise, in bed. As I entered he sat up and turned a face toward me which sickened me as I looked at it.

"Why, Sadler, what has happened?" I cried, but my heart turned cold as I said it.

"Gilroy," he answered, mumbling with his swollen lips, "I have for some weeks been under the impression that you are a madman. Now I know it, and that you are a dangerous one as well. If it were not that I am unwilling to make a scandal in the college, you would now be in the hands of the police."

"Do you mean—" I cried.

"I mean that as I opened the door last night you rushed out upon me, struck me with both your fists in the face, knocked me down, kicked me furiously in the side, and left me lying almost unconscious in the street. Look at your own hand bearing witness against you."

Yes, there it was, puffed up, with spongelike knuckles, as after some terrific blow. What could I do? Though he put me down as a madman, I must tell him all. I sat by his bed and went over all my troubles from the beginning. I poured them out with quivering hands and burning words which might have carried conviction to the most skeptical. "She hates you and she hates me!" I cried. "She revenged herself last night on both of us at once. She saw me leave the ball, and she must have seen you also. She knew how long it would take to reach home. Then she had but to use her wicked will. Ah, your bruised face is a small thing beside my bruised soul!"

He was struck by my story. That was evident. "Yes, yes, she watched me out of the room," he muttered. "She is capable of it. But is it possible that she has really reduced you to this? What do you intend to do?"

"To stop it!" I cried. "I am perfectly desperate; I shall give her fair warning today, and the next time will be the last."

"Do nothing rash," said he.

"Rash!" I cried. "The only rash thing is that I should postpone it another hour." With that I rushed to my room, and here I am on the eve of what may be the great crisis of my life. I shall start at once. I have gained one thing today, for I have made one man, at least, realize the truth of this monstrous experience of mine. And, if the worst should happen, this diary remains as a proof of the goad that has driven me.

Evening. When I came to Wilson's, I was shown up, and found that he was sitting with Miss Penclosa. For half an hour I had to endure his fussy talk about his recent research into the exact nature of the spiritualistic rap, while the creature and I sat in silence looking across the room at each other. I read a sinister amusement in her eyes, and she must have seen hatred and menace in mine. I had almost despaired of having speech with her when he was called from the room, and we were left for a few moments together.

"Well, Professor Gilroy—or is it Mr. Gilroy?" said she, with that bitter smile of hers. "How is your friend Mr. Charles Sadler after the ball?"

"You fiend!" I cried. "You have come to the end of your tricks now. I will have no more of them. Listen to what I say." I strode across and shook her roughly by the shoulder. "As sure as there is a God in heaven, I swear that if you try another of your deviltries upon me I will have your life for it. Come what may, I will have your life. I have come to the end of what a man can endure."

"Accounts are not quite settled between us," said she, with a passion that equaled my own. "I can love, and I can hate. You had your choice. You chose to spurn the first; now you must test the other. It will take a little more to break your spirit, I see, but broken it shall be. Miss Marden comes back tomorrow, as I understand."

"What has that to do with you?" I cried. "It is a pollution that you should dare even to think of her. If I thought that you would harm her—"

She was frightened, I could see, though she tried to brazen it out. She read the black thought in my mind, and cowered away from me.

"She is fortunate in having such a champion," said she. "He actually dares to threaten a lonely woman. I must really congratulate Miss Marden upon her protector."

The words were bitter, but the voice and manner were more acid still.

"There is no use talking," said I. "I only came here to tell you—and to tell you most solemnly—that your next outrage upon me will be your last." With that, as I heard Wilson's step upon the stair, I walked from the room. Ay, she may look venomous and deadly, but, for all that, she is beginning to see now that she has as much to fear from me as I can have from her. Murder! It has an ugly sound. But you don't talk of murdering a snake or of murdering a tiger. Let her have a care now.

May 5. I met Agatha and her mother at the station at eleven o'clock. She is looking so bright, so happy, so beautiful. And she was so overjoyed to see me. What have I done to deserve such love? I went back home with them, and we lunched together. All the troubles seem in a moment to have been shredded back from my life. She tells me that I am looking pale and worried and ill. The dear child puts it down to my loneliness and the perfunctory attentions of a housekeeper. I pray that she may never know the truth! May the shadow, if shadow there must be, lie ever black across my life and leave hers in the sunshine. I have just come back from them, feeling a new man. With her by my side I think that I could show a bold face to anything which life might send.

5 P.M. Now, let me try to be accurate. Let me try to say exactly how it occurred. It is fresh in my mind, and I can set it down correctly, though it is not likely that the time will ever come when I shall forget the doings of today.

I had returned from the Mardens' after lunch, and was cutting some microscopic sections in my freezing microtone, when in an instant I lost consciousness in the sudden hateful fashion which has become only too familiar to me of late.

When my senses came back to me I was sitting in a small chamber, very different from the one in which I had been working. It was cozy and bright, with chintz-covered settees, colored hangings, and a thousand pretty little trifles upon the wall. A small ornamental clock ticked in front of me, and the hands pointed to half-past three. It was all quite familiar to me, and yet I stared about for a moment in a half-dazed way until my eyes fell upon a cabinet photograph of myself upon the top of the piano. On the other side stood one of Mrs. Marden. Then, of course, I remembered where I was. It was Agatha's boudoir.

But how came I there, and what did I want? A horrible sinking came to my heart. Had I been sent here on some devilish errand? Had that errand already been done? Surely it must; otherwise, why should I be allowed to come back to consciousness? Oh, the agony of that moment! What had I done? I sprang to my feet in my despair, and as I did so a small glass bottle fell from my knees on to the carpet.

It was unbroken, and I picked it up. Outside was written "Sulphuric Acid. Fort." When I drew the round glass stopper, a thick fume rose slowly up, and a pungent, choking smell pervaded the room. I recognized it as one which I kept for chemical testing in my chambers. But why had I brought a bottle of vitriol into Agatha's chamber? Was it not this thick, reeking liquid with which jealous women had been known to mar the beauty of their rivals? My heart stood still as I held the bottle to the light. Thank God, it was full! No mischief had been done as yet. But had Agatha come in a minute sooner, was it not certain that the hellish parasite within me would have dashed the stuff into her— Ah, it will not bear to be thought of! But it must have been for that. Why else should I have brought it? At the thought of what I might have done my worn nerves broke down, and I sat shivering and twitching, the pitiable wreck of a man.

It was the sound of Agatha's voice and the rustle of her dress which restored me. I looked up, and saw her blue eyes, so full of tenderness and pity, gazing down at me.

"We must take you away to the country, Austin," she said. "You want rest and quiet. You look wretchedly ill."

"Oh, it is nothing!" said I, trying to smile. "It was only a momentary weakness. I am all right again now."

"I am so sorry to keep you waiting. Poor boy, you must have been here quite half an hour! The vicar was in the drawing room, and as I knew that you did not care for him, I thought it better that Jane should show you up here. I thought the man would never go!"

"Thank God he stayed! Thank God he stayed!" I cried hysterically.

"Why, what is the matter with you, Austin?" she asked, holding my arm as I staggered up from the chair. "Why are you glad that the vicar stayed? And what is this little bottle in your hand?"

"Nothing," I cried, thrusting it into my pocket. "But I must go. I have something important to do."

"How stern you look, Austin! I have never seen your face like that. You are angry?"

"Yes, I am angry."

"But not with me?"

"No, no, my darling! You would not understand."

"But you have not told me why you came."

"I came to ask you whether you would always love me—no matter what I did, or what shadow might fall on my name. Would you believe in me and trust me however black appearances might be against me?"

"You know that I would, Austin."

"Yes, I know that you would. What I do I shall do for you. I am driven to it. There is no other way out, my darling!" I kissed her and rushed from the room.

The time for indecision was at an end. As long as the creature threatened my own prospects and my honor there might be a question as to what I should do. But now, when Agatha—my innocent Agatha—was endangered, my duty lay before me like a turnpike road. I had no weapon, but I never paused for that. What weapon should I need, when I felt every muscle quivering with the strength of a frenzied man? I ran through the streets, so set upon what I had to do that I was only dimly conscious of the faces of friends whom I met—dimly conscious also that Professor Wilson met me, running with equal precipitance in the opposite direction. Breathless but resolute I reached the house and rang the bell. A white-cheeked maid opened the door, and turned whiter yet when she saw the face that looked in at her.

"Show me up at once to Miss Penclosa," I demanded.

"Sir," she gasped, "Miss Penclosa died this afternoon at half-past three!"

Notes on the Authors

Nancy A. Collins (American, 1959–), who burst upon the scene with the post-punk vampire novel *Sunglasses After Dark* (1989), is the author also of *Tempter* (1990) and *In the Blood* (1992). She has won the Horror Writers of America Bram Stoker Award for Best First Novel and the British Fantasy Society's Icarus Award. Her short fiction is represented in numerous recent collections, including *The Best of Pulphouse* and *Hotter Blood,* and she is the current writer for DC Comics' *Swamp Thing* series.

Thomas Ligotti (American, 1953–) is the author of two highly acclaimed collections, *Songs of a Dead Dreamer* (1989) and *Grimscribe: His Lives and Works* (1991). Drawn, he says, to the tradition of horror that reveals "the outrageously strange and terrible as integral to existence," he has suggested to an interviewer that his own writings might be termed "confrontational escapism." He is currently preparing a third group of stories, *Noctuary,* for publication.

Ray Bradbury (American, 1920–) is the premier American writer of fantasy in the second half of the twentieth century. From his early appearances in *Weird Tales* (macabre stories later collected in *Dark Carnival,* a 1947

Arkham House edition highly coveted by collectors) through such recent efforts as *A Graveyard for Lunatics* (1991), a phantasmagorical Hollywood murder mystery, he has been a prolific and influential imaginative force. Often alternating, sometimes blending, whimsy and shocks to amazing effect—who can forget, after all, one's first reading of *The Martian Chronicles* (1950)?—Bradbury has kept on producing fiction of such continuing readability as to stand well outside any limits imposed by changing literary fashion. Among his many other books are *The October Country* (1955), *Something Wicked This Way Comes* (1962), and *Long After Midnight* (1976). And such films as *It Came From Outer Space*, *The Beast From 20,000 Fathoms*, *Farenheit 451*, and *The Illustrated Man* have been made from his original stories.

Elizabeth Jane Howard (British, 1923–) trained as an actress but left the theater in 1947, soon establishing a new career as a reviewer, editor, and fiction writer. In 1950 she was awarded the John Llewellyn Rhys Memorial Prize for her first novel, *The Beautiful Visit*, a book dedicated to her friend Robert Aickman with whom she was then collaborating on *We Are for the Dark* (1951). Her other works include the stunning tour de force of marital breakdown, *The Long View* (1956), and *Getting It Right* (1982), which was made into a film starring Sir John Gielgud. Currently she is publishing in installments the historical novel sequence *The Cazalet Chronicle*.

Ray Russell's (American, 1924–) books include *The Case Against Satan* (1962), a novel of a priest's struggle to reclaim a possessed young girl from demonic forces predating *The Exorcist* by nearly a decade; *Unholy Trinity* (1964); and *Incubus* (1976). He has been the author of numerous screenplays, among them the 1963 Ray Milland vehicle, *The Man With the X-Ray Eyes* (directed by Roger Corman), a film admiringly described by Stephen King as "one of the most interesting and offbeat little horror movies ever made." Also, in his role as executive editor at *Playboy* Russell produced, but took no official credit for, two important collections, *The Playboy Book of Science Fiction and Fantasy* (1966) and *The Playboy Book of Horror and the Supernatural* (1967).

David Kuehls (American, 1960–) began his creative relationship with the auteur of *The Birds* when he took on the task of producing the program notes for a college Hitchcock festival. He has since lunched with George Romero and conducted interviews with Clive Barker, Dan Simmons, Fred Saberhagen, and Rex Miller, among others. Currently he is a literary associate for *Fangoria*.

Arthur Machen's (British, 1863–1947) name often gives people trouble, but the easiest way to get the pronunciation right is to remember that it rhymes with "bracken." Born in Wales, he moved to London at the age of twenty where he began the energetic literary career that would occupy the rest of his long life. However, prolific as he was, much of the writing he did to sustain himself was featured in forgotten periodicals and has never been collected. Yet the survival of his visionary genre work has always been assured and he is rightly seen as a continuing major influence in the field to this day. Among his many books are the collections *The Three Impostors* (1895), *The House of Souls* (1906), *Ornaments in Jade* (1924), and *The Children of the Pool and Other Stories* (1936); the autobiographical novel *The Hill of Dreams* (1907); and the patriotic popular success *The Angel of Mons: The Bowmen, and Other Legends of the War* (1915).

May Sinclair (British, 1865–1946), according to the distinguished authority on supernatural fiction, E. F. Bleiler, is an underrated writer in the field. The fiction for which she is best known, however, is mainstream, and such novels as *Mary Olivier* (1919), its heroine a young woman growing up in a repressive Victorian household, are still being read today. A feminist, a follower of Freud, and an admirer of Shaw, Wells, and Joyce, Sinclair often experimented with subjective prose technique. Two of her collections, *Uncanny Stories*

(1923) and *The Intercessor, and Other Stories* (1931), contain numerous startling and quietly grim tales of love's failures and the wayward consequences of desire.

Harlan Ellison (American, 1934–), like Stephen King, is a Romantic and an Enthusiast, full of billboard-sized passions and gripes and the desire always to share direct printouts from Synapse Central. This has led to a prolific career of award-winning stories (nearly a thousand of them), books, and scripts, and a lifetime of proffering his opinions, which lay, kicking and screaming for reaction, atop most of his prose. Depending on one's mood, it can be a pretty irresistible combination. Among his best-known titles are *Ellison Wonderland* (1962), the 1969 novella *A Boy and His Dog, Spider Kiss* (originally *Rockabilly*, 1961), *Deathbird Stories* (1975), *Strange Wine* (1978), *Angry Candy* (1988), and *Mefisto in Onyx* (1993). Nor should one omit *The Glass Teat*, a 1970 collection of "essays of opinion on television," which Spiro Agnew reportedly tried to have suppressed. And wearing yet another of his creative hats, Ellison has also been much acclaimed for his editorship of the complacency-shattering *Dangerous Visions* anthologies (1967 and 1972), which ushered in the new era of risk-taking, crossover genre fiction.

J. G. Ballard (British, 1930–) was born in Shanghai, the son of a businessman, and spent the war years following Pearl Harbor with his family in a civilian internment camp. Memories of this transformative experience are vividly seen in the novel *Empire of the Sun* (1984), undoubtedly his best-known work because of the film made from it by Steven Spielberg in 1987. Considered by many "the grand master of modern British science fiction" (although he may also be seen as a richly imaginative, consistently daring surrealist writer whose oeuvre transcends genre labels), Ballard launched his career in the late 1950s with stories in Michael Moorcock's *New Worlds SF* and other new-fiction magazines. His actual first novel, *The Wind From Nowhere* (1962), he has disowned, preferring to cite *The Drowned World* (also

1962) as his debut work. Other books include *The Atrocity Exhibition* (1970), *The Unlimited Dream Company* (1979), *The Day of Creation* (1987), and *The Kindness of Women* (1991).

Sarah Smith (American, 1947–), descended from Revolutionary War soldiers on both sides of the conflict, lives again in her native New England after a peripatetic childhood. "I started writing at eleven," she says, "ghost stories and *Twilight Zone* horror stuff." Using a Fulbright for study at London's Slade Film School, she continued on to graduate school at Harvard, creating her own specialization in fiction-and-film. While employed as a computer consultant in the late 1980s, she joined the Cambridge Speculative Fiction Workshop and began once more to write short stories. In addition to her novel *The Vanished Child* (1992), she is the author of *King of Space,* an interactive hypertext fiction, to which there will soon be a sequel, *The Bunraku Stars.* She is also a contributor to *Future Boston,* an sf history of the city from 1990–2100 (1993).

Robert Aickman (British, 1914–81) once likened ghost stories to poetry; certainly, when his own fiction is taken as an exemplar, the comparison holds. The grandson of Richard Marsh (author of the still-readable, if campily entertaining, fin de siècle horror classic *The Beetle*), Aickman actually preferred the term "strange stories" to describe his output. And it is apt, for ambiguity lies at the heart of the effects he creates. In any Aickman story, one finds characters who, though never quite certain exactly what has just transpired, recognize only too well that they have been irrevocably transformed by it— if they only knew what *it* was. His collections, all of them absolutely worth seeking out, are *Dark Entries* (1964), *Powers of Darkness* (1966), *Sub Rosa* (1968), *Cold Hand in Mine* (1975), *Tales of Love and Death* (1977), and *Painted Devils* (1979).

Lisa Tuttle (American, 1952–) moved to Britain in 1980 after a career as a journalist in her native Texas and now lives on the remote west coast of Scotland. Her books include the novels *Familiar Spirit* (1983), *Windhaven*, with George R. R. Martin (1987), *Gabriel* (1987), *Lost Futures* (1992), along with the short-story collections *A Nest of Nightmares* (1986), *A Spaceship Built of Stone* (1987), and *Memories of the Body* (1992). In 1974 she won the John W. Campbell Award for best new science fiction writer. Her recent anthology, *Skin of the Soul* (1991), featured original contemporary horror writing by women, and her unusual oral history, *Heroines: Women Inspired by Women* (1988, U.K. only), is worth seeking out.

Charles Beaumont (American, 1929–67), according to *The Penguin Encyclopedia of Horror and the Supernatural,* was "one of the few authors in the genre who found more horror in his life than in his writing." However, despite his early death from a hideously degenerative illness that moved quickly through his body when he should have been in his prime, Beaumont's legacy is an impressive one. His stories, which ranged from the hard-boiled to the gently fantastic, from the dystopian to the merely disillusioned, are collected in *The Hunger* (1957), *Shadow Play* (1957), *Night Ride* (1960), *The Magic Man* (1965), and others. Among his screen credits are *Queen of Outer Space* (1958), *The Haunted Palace* (1963), *Masque of the Red Death* (1964), and *The Seven Faces of Dr. Lao* (1964).

Claudia O'Keefe (American, 1958–) numbers among her nonwriting jobs stints as a civilian shepherdess for the Air Force and as a keno girl at a Lake Tahoe casino. Her first novel, *Black Snow Days,* appeared as an Ace "Special" in 1990; it was the last manuscript acquired by the late science fiction editor Terry Carr for this prestigious line of debut titles. She has had stories in *Pulphouse, Aboriginal SF,* and *Midnight Zoo,* and currently is completing two novels, *Gawkers* and *Carnal Angels. Ghosttide,* an anthology of horror, dark fantasy, and suspense edited by O'Keefe, was published in 1992.

Ramsey Campbell (British, 1946–) has repeatedly received warm praise from his peers, including Stephen King and Clive Barker—it was the latter, in fact, who contributed the foreword to Campbell's brilliantly titled Scream Press collection *Scared Stiff: Tales of Sex and Death* (1987). His own stories are compiled in the volumes *The Inhabitants of the Lake and Others Less Welcome* (1964), *Demons by Daylight* (1973), *Cold Print* (1985), *Dark Feasts* (1987), and others. He has also edited several collections, notably *Superhorror* (1976) and *The Gruesome Book* (1982). His novels include *The Doll Who Ate His Mother* (1976), *The Face That Must Die* (1979), *The Nameless* (1981), *Incarnate* (1983), and *The Hungry Moon* (1986). Winner of both the British and World Fantasy Awards, he is currently overseeing publication of what he terms the "bumper anthology" of his first thirty years, *Alone With the Horrors* (1993).

T. H. White (British, 1906–64) continued to revise and add to his magnum opus, *The Sword in the Stone*, so that what had begun as a trilogy in the late 1930s wound up as a quintet by the time of his death. The books comprising it are *The Sword in the Stone* (1938), *The Queen of Air and Darkness* (also known as *The Witch in the Wood*, 1939), *The Ill-Made Knight* (1940), *The Candle in the Wind* (1958), and *The Book of Merlyn* (released posthumously, 1977). Shot through with intentional anachronisms, which act as sort of prop and scenery "dustmops" while also making approachable human beings out of heretofore mythic figures, *The Sword in the Stone*, though still highly readable, nonetheless remains quaint. This is because it cannot help but reflect the mores of its own actual time—England between the wars—which if not quite so remote to audiences today as King Arthur's Britain is hourly more distant. In addition to *Mistress Masham's Repose* (1946), White's other works include *Earth Stopped, or Mr. Marx's Sporting Tour* (1934), *The Elephant and the Kangaroo* (1947), *The Goshawk*, a book on falconry (1951), and *The Book of Beasts*, an annotated translation of a twelfth-century Latin bestiary (1954).

Mervyn Peake (British, 1911–68), whose great fantasy epic is the *Gormenghast* trilogy, has often been compared to Dickens, with admirers pointing to the grand scale of Peake's canvas and his rich cast of (often grotesque) characters whose fates enmesh us. Still, there is no arguing that *David Copperfield,* say, is far less of an acquired taste. The three volumes are *Titus Groan* (1946), *Gormenghast* (1950), and *Titus Alone* (1959), and this last, written as Peake's final illness was overtaking him, actually received a sort of "restorative" revision in 1970, when Langdon Jones, a Peake devotee, reedited it as he believed the author would have wished. Peake was also a poet, a stage designer, and an illustrator. (While his rendering of *Alice in Wonderland* will never replace Tenniel's, it has definite period charm.)

Robert Bloch (American, 1917–) developed his interest in horror, he has often told interviewers, after the delicious experience of being frightened as a boy by the 1926 Lon Chaney vehicle *Phantom of the Opera.* This experience, it seems, caused him to wet his pants at the theater, returning home to sleep with the lights on for the next three years. Soon, however, he began avidly reading the now legendary pulp magazine *Weird Tales* to which he later became an important contributor. As a young man he corresponded with H. P. Lovecraft and even, in homage, appropriated some elements of the influential older writer's Cthulhu Mythos for his own early tales. Bloch's output has been large, and he has repeatedly demonstrated his versatility by garnering awards in horror, mystery, science fiction, and fantasy. Although he has frequently written for television (episodes of *Star Trek* and *Alfred Hitchcock Presents,* among others) and for movies (including *Straitjacket,* 1964; *Torture Garden,* 1967; *Asylum,* 1972) it is worth noting that Bloch's own novel sequel, *Psycho 2* (1982), was not, in fact, the story filmed as the 1983 release of the same name. Other novels include *The Scarf* (1947), *Firebug* (1961), *American Gothic* (1974), and *Night of the Ripper* (1984); among his collections are *The Opener of the Way* (1945), *Blood Runs Cold* (1961), *Yours Truly, Jack the Ripper* (1962),

The Skull of the Marquis de Sade (1965), and *Cold Chills* (1977). More recently he has edited the collection *Psycho-Paths* (1991) and published the novels *Firebug* (1988), *Lori* (1990), and *The Jekyll Legacy* (1990).

A. E. Coppard (British, 1878–1957) had almost no formal education, but persisting in his auto-didactic efforts while supporting his family as an accountant in an Oxford engineering firm, he was able to meet and draw support from such younger aspiring writers as Robert Graves and Aldous Huxley. He published his first book, the collection *Adam and Eve and Pinch Me,* in 1921, two years after quitting his job in favor of a full-time writing career. Happily, it enjoyed an immediate success, and in the decades that followed he kept up a steady stream of stort-story volumes. In 1946 August Derleth at Arkham House selected what he deemed Coppard's best fantasy and ghost tales to appear in the compilation *Fearful Pleasures.* Among Coppard's other titles are *Clorinda Walks in Heaven* (1922), *Silver Circus* (1928), *Ninepenny Flute* (1937), and *The Dark-Eyed Lady* (1947).

Clement Wood (American, 1888–1950) was born, raised, and educated in the South but left to take his law degree at Yale in 1911. He returned home, soon succeeding Hugo Black, later a Supreme Court justice, as chief presiding magistrate of the Central Recorder's Court in Birmingham, Alabama. But he was removed for "lack of judicial temperament" when he insisted on jailing the state's lieutenant governor for contempt of court. After this definite career setback, he bought (he told friends) a one-way ticket to New York: there he briefly worked for Upton Sinclair as his secretary and then began to teach writing at New York University. He published widely (under his own name and pseudonymously) as a poet, lyricist, journalist, critic, short-story writer, novelist, and biographer; he also edited numerous anthologies, quiz and game books, reference books, and texts. His novels include *Mountain* (1920), *Folly* (1925), and *The Shadow From the Bogue* (1927).

Arthur Conan Doyle (British, 1859–1930) is one of the most popular authors ever to win the attention of the reading public and it is all owing to his invention of a single character, Sherlock Holmes, who has not been off the world's stage since his relatively inauspicious debut in 1888. But in addition to the much-loved cases found in the Holmesian canon (collected in such volumes as *The Adventures of Sherlock Holmes,* 1891, and *The Memoirs of Sherlock Holmes,* 1894), Doyle continually pursued other literary interests, including the writing of a considerable body of weird fiction. Among his titles, the contents of which fall into the horror, fantasy, and supernatural genres, are *Dreamland and Ghostland* (1886), *The Captain of the Polestar and Other Tales* (1890), *Round the Fire Stories* (1908), *The Last Galley: Impressions and Tales* (1911), and *The Maracot Deep* (1929). (The last named also contains two stories that are considered science fiction.) *The Edge of the Unknown* (1930), a work of nonfiction, was the last of his books to appear before his death; in it one finds accounts of his own spiritualist encounters and psychic experiences.

ROC

JOURNEY TO FANTASTICAL REALMS

☐ **KNIGHTS OF THE BLOOD created by Katherine Kurtz and Scott MacMillan.** A Los Angeles policeman is out to solve an unsolved mystery—that would pitch him straight into the dark and terrifying world of the vampire. (452569—$4.99)

☐ **KNIGHTS OF THE BLOOD: *At Sword's Point* by Katherine Kurtz and Scott MacMillan.** A generation of Nazi vampires has evolved with a centuries-old agenda hell-bent on world domination, and the only way LAPD Detective John Drummond can save himself is to grab a sword and commit bloody murder. (454073—$4.99)

☐ **A SONG FOR ARBONNE by Guy Gavriel Kay.** "This panoramic, absorbing novel beautifully creates an alternate version of the medieval world.... Kay creates a vivid world of love and music, magic, and death."—*Publishers Weekly* (453328—$5.99)

☐ **THE BROKEN GODDESS by Hans Bemmann.** A young man's search for a myth brought to life takes him back in time to realms where talking beasts and magical powers are all too real. Can he ever turn back? (453484—$9.00)

☐ **CURSE OF THE MISTWRAITH *The Wars of Light and Shadow* by Janny Wurts.** A bold fantasy epic of half-brothers who are heirs to powers of light and shadow.
(453069—$22.00)

☐ **VOYAGE OF THE FOX RIDER by Dennis L. McKiernan.** Mage Amar and a Pysk embark on a quest to find the vanished Farrix, a quest that will see them roving the world aboard the fabled ship of Aravan the Elf. (452844—$15.00)

*Prices slightly higher in Canada

Buy them at your local bookstore or use this convenient coupon for ordering.

PENGUIN USA
P.O. Box 999 — Dept. #17109
Bergenfield, New Jersey 07621

Please send me the books I have checked above.
I am enclosing $_____ (please add $2.00 to cover postage and handling). Send check or money order (no cash or C.O.D.'s) or charge by Mastercard or VISA (with a $15.00 minimum). Prices and numbers are subject to change without notice.

Card #_____ Exp. Date _____
Signature_____
Name_____
Address_____
City _____ State _____ Zip Code _____

For faster service when ordering by credit card call **1-800-253-6476**

Allow a minimum of 4-6 weeks for delivery. This offer is subject to change without notice.

If you and/or a friend would like to receive the *ROC Advance*, a bimonthly newsletter featuring all the newest and hottest ROC books and authors, on a complimentary basis, please fill out this form and return it to:

ROC Books/Penguin USA
375 Hudson Street
New York, NY 10014

Your Address
Name _____
Street _____ Apt. # _____
City _____ State _____ Zip _____

Friend's Address
Name _____
Street _____ Apt. # _____
City _____ State _____ Zip _____